Adventures with the Master

By

Gary Edward Gedall

Published by

From Words to Worlds,

Lausanne, Switzerland

www.fromwordstoworlds.com

ISBN: 2-940535-10-1
ISBN 13: 978-2-940535-10-1

By the same Author

About the Author

Gary Edward Gedall is a state registered psychologist, psychotherapist, trained in Ericksonian hypnosis and EMDR.

He has ordinary and master's degrees in Psychology from the Universities of Geneva and Lausanne and an Honours Degree in Management Sciences from Aston University in the UK.

He has lived as an associate member of the Findhorn Spiritual Community, has been a regular visitor to the Osho meditation centre in Puna, India. And as part of his continuing quest into alternative beliefs and healing practices, he completed the three-year practical training, given by the Foundation for Shamanic Studies in 2012.

He is now, (2014 – 2016), studying for a DAS, (Diploma of Advanced Studies), as a therapist using horses.

His hobbies are; writing, western riding and spoiling his children. Quora writer of the year 2015

He is currently living and working in Lausanne, Switzerland.

Disclaimer:

The characters and events related in my books are a synthesis of all that I have seen and done, the people that I have met and their stories. Hence, there are events and people that have echoes with real people and real events, however no character is taken purely from any one person and is in no way intended to depict any person, living or dead.

Table of Contents

Acknowledgements

First and foremost, I'd must thank my wife, Mona, who has invited and supported me in many of the adventures; (shamanism, western riding, EMDR, etc.), that have served as important elements in my life and in the creation of this book.

Then to Kyra, my daughter, who insisted that I entertain her, on a weekly basis, with a new chapter, while participating in outdoor exercising.

To J.J. who asked me to create a hypnotic induction for him, which became the first chapter of the book.

And finally to Rohan, who is a constant inspiration in my life.

The Sickly Child

He was a sickly child, or so his parents treated him. During both the winter and summer months, he was not allowed out without his hat on and all four flaps down. He was not allowed to fight with the boys, nor was he allowed to climb up the mountainside for fear that he would slip and hurt himself. Every cough or sniffle was treated like a potential fatal disease, and he was kept in the house until all signs of sickness had passed.

His parents were convinced of this approach after having failed to react to his older brother's first signs of sickness and then having to watch him wither away and die, with them incapable of saving him.

Of course they had him exercise; under their ever-watchful eyes, he could run and jump and play games with the other children, only not run or jump or play in a dangerous way.

And so the years passed; the young man was well aware of his fragility, and appreciated his parents' diligence in their care of his well-being.

All was fine until he came to the end of his school time; as the family had little wealth, the only options open to the young man were to go and work in the barley fields, to join the army, or to enter the local monastery and train to become a monk.

Working in the fields was a physically tough job. Just planting the *qingke* would be more than the boy could cope with, never mind all the rest, and with the short growing season, he would be working almost nonstop.

As for the army; that was, of course, totally out of the question.

So the only possibility left was that of the monastery. A major problem, however, was that the life and discipline of a young novice monk was not without hardship and, from the point of view of his protective parents, not without danger. The only solution was to beg an audience with the "Young Master" (the name given to the now head of the monastery by his own master, due to the fact that he was the youngest monk ever to reach that level).

The parents sent a message to the monastery, pleading for a meeting with the Master to explain the situation. The message was received and a young monk was dispatched to the house to listen to what the parents wished to discuss.

They were a little put out that they were expected to talk to this young monk and not directly to the Master himself, but he reassured them that he was there simply to listen to their desires and to find out a little more about their son, so that the Master would not have to waste his time asking relatively unimportant questions and they could then discuss the important issue directly without introduction.

The spring was here but was passing quite quickly; the fields were being prepared to be sown for the barley crops, and young men were already joining the village workforce. Others were leaving to begin their training for the army. Those that had offered themselves up to become monks had already been accepted to enter the monastery. Only the sickly child had not yet been summoned to meet the "Young Master," and he was the only one who could decide on who could enter. Already, every morning, waiting for the message to arrive had become a type of slow torture, to be summonsed to their interview; "their interview" because it was also the parents who were waiting to speak to the venerable master so as to explain exactly why their son had to be accepted to become a monk, but due to his fragility that he would need to be given a special program, so as not to strain his sickly body too much.

The days passed and the family became increasingly stressed, for the period of choosing was all the same limited. The army recruits had now left, and the fields were advancing with the necessary preparations. Even though the novice monks were still with their families, all was arranged for their training, and each had been assigned to a master who would oversee the first part of his initiation. The parents of the other boys were beginning to gossip and point at them from little huddles, in corners, in the marketplace, in the square. But worse, much worse than that, was the knowledge that quite soon the head of the monastery would be leaving to pass the hotter summer months in his mountain cabin, in retreat, with only one privileged young monk in attendance.

If he should leave before accepting the boy into the order, they would have no option but to send him into the fields, to work his poor fragile body, from morning till night under the blazing sun, with the high chance of his being caught in one of the many heavy summer rain showers.

They tried on several occasions to inquire as to the likely moment of the interview, but each time they had to accept the same response: the Master is aware of your demand and will send for you in due course.

The days continued to pass, the neighbours to gossip, and the sun to climb, higher and higher in the heavens at midday.

"He's going to go up the mountain; he's going to leave our son to die working in the fields," groaned the mother. "Go again and demand to see the Master."

"But I went only yesterday. If I keep going every day, we might vex them, and then all would be lost."

"If he leaves for the mountain, all will be lost anyway. At least they will be reminded how important it is that we see him."

"I'm sure that they all are very clear how important it is for us. I have been almost once every two days."

"Maybe you should go every day, then." Fortunately for everyone, at that moment there was a knock at the door. The young man in priests' robes smiled at the older man who opened the door.

"The Young Master will expect you at six tomorrow morning. Please do not be late, he will not wait. *Kale shoo*."

"Thank you, and goodbye to you, too." They both bowed; the older man smiled, the younger man did not.

At a quarter to six, all three members of the family were waiting expectantly outside the monastery gates.

At six o'clock, a gong was struck and the gate opened. A young monk dressed as a master opened the gate. He was bald or his head was clean shaven, as were many of that order, and not very tall (who was?); his back was straight and his pale green eyes were piercing.

It was only when he started to speak and they heard the whistle behind his words that they realised that he was, in fact, much, much older than he seemed. That his skin, although still tightly covering his face and neck, was a mass of deeply etched lines, and his hands had so many brown patches on them, it was hard to find the white skin underneath.

"Master," the father cried, placing his palms together in front of his heart and bowing slightly, "thank you for agreeing to see us. We have waited impatiently for this day."

"Patience is an important virtue." He then stopped, turned around, went through the gate, and closed it gently. The family looked at each other, not understanding. Several seconds later the gate opened and the monk reappeared. He looked gently but firmly at the father, gave a slight bow, and said, "Good morning."

They were still mystified, until suddenly the mother screamed at the father, "The scarf, you fool, have you forgotten all your manners?" The father quickly searched in his pocket and pulled out the *jáldar* that he had prepared to offer to the Master. The Master took it gracefully and smiled as he wrapped it gently around the other man's neck.

"Good," he nodded. "And now," he said, turning to the son, "you see these packs?" He gestured towards a pile of objects just inside the gate. "You will bring them with us."

"But he cannot carry all those bags; he is much too fragile for that. That is why we needed to speak to you," the mother sobbed.

"That is too bad. You see, I have been very busy these last few weeks; many, many things to do and to prepare before my departure to my summer lodging. I just couldn't make time to see you before. And now, as you can see, I am at the point of leaving."

"But Master, please." Now it was the turn of the father to plead. "It is very important that we speak to you, to explain about our son, that although he is not the strongest of young men, he is totally committed to becoming a monk."

"Then all is well; he can begin training tomorrow. You will be here at five o'clock and begin cleaning the dormitories."

"But no, please, your excellence, he is not like the others. He hasn't the strength at this time."

"That shouldn't stop him entering the monastery. If he is that committed"—the parents looked relieved—"he can apply again next year."

"But that would mean that he would have to spend a year working in the fields."

"A year in the fields would help him to find his strength."
"Please, Master." The young man spoke for the first time. "Please listen to what we have to say."

"You wish to enter the monastery this year?"

"Yes, Master."

"You wish to explain to me about your limitations?"

"I must."

"Then walk with me awhile. When all that we need to share we have shared, you can release yourself of your burdens and return here. Someone else will then take your place, and I will continue my journey with another."

"But he cannot possibly carry all those things, and up a hill."

"Mother, it seems that it is the only way. We will talk awhile, then I will leave the space for someone stronger and he can finish the journey with the Master. *Kali shu.*"

"*Kali pai*, my son." The father turned, protecting his wife with his arm across her shoulders, to leave his only remaining son. Somewhere he knew that he would never see his sickly, fragile boy ever again; somehow he was totally right.

※ ※ ※

It took quite some minutes for the young man to charge himself with the assorted bags, pots, and utensils. It might have taken less time if he hadn't slowed himself down worrying just how he was going to manage to carry all these things for even the few hundred metres that it would take to explain to the Master exactly just how fragile he was.

At last they were underway.

"Master," began the young man.

"Listen to the birdsong. It is so wonderful, first thing in the morning, as the world is waking up, to walk slowly and quietly, so as to bathe in the early morning sounds and smells."

The young man was much too afraid of the venerable old man to ignore this clear demand for silence, and as they were truly not walking very fast, and the road was still relatively flat, and the bags and stuff were not quite as heavy as all that, he chose to accept that he would have to walk a little further than planned. He would just have to have a late breakfast with his parents when he got back.

The path started to ascend and the young man started again to worry about how long they would have to stay in silence. Every metre walking up the mountain would have to be covered again going down.

"Master," the young man tried again.

"My son, you look stressed, but there is nothing to be stressed about. We are having a little early morning stroll. Have you ever been up this mountain before?"

"A little bit. A few summers ago, some of the boys decided to play a trick on our parents, to go and hide in a cave that one of them said he knew of up the mountain. So we started to climb up, but we couldn't find it, so we carried on climbing, looking for it, but in the end we had to give up and go back down, as it was starting to get dark."

"And what were the reactions of the parents?"

"Well some of them didn't seem to mind at all; the boys often would go off during the day and not get back till it got dark." "And your parents?"

"They...they were very upset. They had already noticed that I was missing some time before and had started looking for me. My mother was really very upset. She started crying when she saw me. She kept asking if I was all right, if I was hurt, if I was injured in any way."

"And how did you feel?"

"I felt very guilty for having worried them so. I was not allowed to climb up the mountain."

"But you knew before you started to climb that you were not allowed to do so?"

"I didn't want the other boys to laugh at me anymore, so I told myself that it would be all right and that nothing bad would happen."

"And did something bad happen?"

"My parents were very worried."

"Yes, you had already told me that." And they carried on in silence for a while.

"You see that ridge, sticking out, way up there?" He pointed his staff at a point quite some ways up the mountain.

"Yes, Master."

"That is the end of this path." The young man shook his head.

"That is a place I could never reach."

The Master rubbed his bald dome. "A sickly, fragile boy could never climb so high. It would take a strong, devoted disciple."

"Master, should I go down the mountain now so that one can come and take my place?"

"But we have not yet had our little talk, have we? You are to explain to me why you are so invested in becoming a monk, but why it is that you are not capable of fulfilling the duties of one, and with all that, why I should agree to you entering the monastery having this special program." He stopped for a second, but then continued. "You haven't changed your mind, have you?"

"No, no, Master, I just thought...you know, when you said about needing to have a strong, devoted disciple to accompany you to the end of this path, that maybe you wanted me to find you one."

"Of course, of course, but it is not quite the moment for you to return to the village. You see, it is already time to take a pause and to heat some Po Cha."

At least that was something he did know how to do. His mother had kept him with her so much during his young life that cooking and making butter tea were everyday habits for him.

The Master had two skins with him; one contained water, the other was filled with *chaku*. He only had to boil some water and add it to the concentrated tea, then add some salt and butter, and drink it hot.

The Master sat idly watching the clouds as the young man made the tea. When the tea was served, the old man put his hand in a sack he was carrying and pulled out two round balls.

"You might like this with your tea." He handed over a sweet barley cake in exchange for the cup of steaming liquid. He took the sweet cake, poured himself a bowl of Po Cha, and sat down to taste the snack. It was the best barley cake he had ever tasted; here, at least, there were benefits for being in close contact with the head of the monastery.

They ate and drank in silence, as merited a good cup of Po Cha and a Zanba cake; one had to respect a moment like that. "Good?"

"Very good, Master."

"They make us good Zanba."

"Yes, very good Zanba." And with that, they set off again. The young man was a little at a loss just how to start the conversation with the venerable Master. He had to admit that he was a little afraid and very much in awe of this spiritually powerful man.

"Young man."

"Yes, Master?"

"Look at your feet." The boy stopped walking and stared at his feet. "No, keep walking, but notice your feet. Watch each step; feel how it is every time that you raise one foot, notice how the weight changes in your body. The foot on the ground is full, the foot in the air is empty." The boy stumbled, almost fell down. "Be careful, when we stop our bodies from following their automatic sequences, something as terribly complex as walking becomes chaotic. No, I did not say to stop what you are doing. Again; concentrate on the walking. Notice also your breath, how your body breathes. No, do not bend so forward, you will break your back. You can watch your feet by just leaning slightly forward. Keep the lower back slightly rounded, it will balance the weight of the bags and relax the belly. You must also allow yourself to be aware of the weight of your body and the bags AND the breathing. Never, ever forget the breath; breath is life. When you stop breathing you are dead. If you only breathe half, then you are half dead, many people live their whole lives being half dead. As we ascend the mountain, you will need to relax and open your body to breathe more. There is less oxygen, and while one is going up, the body does not always have time to accommodate itself to this change." As he was trying to watch his feet, notice his breathing, and listen to and understand all that was being told to and explained to him, there was still a little critical part of his brain that was shouting, *But I don't need to know all this! I'm not going up the mountain. I can't go all*

11

the way up, it's just not possible. I'm going to explain to him about my fragility and return home to the village to await his return. I will need to speak soon or I will be too late to eat lunch with my parents. And what about the after-lunch sleep that I must take?

"Master, can I speak with you about—"

"Quiet now, this is important. I know that you have important things to discuss, I have not forgotten. I understand that to reach the end of this path is an impossible thing for you to be doing. Fear not, young one, I will not force you to go beyond what is not possible for you. I will allow you to leave the path well before you arrive at a point beyond your true capacities and capabilities. But now, look at your feet!"

As he was partly reassured, and because, honestly, he had little choice, he resumed the exercise, focusing on the raising and lowering of each foot in turn. He noticed his breath, how the chest and belly, when relaxed, created a wave of in-breathe and then out-breathe—slow, rhythmic, graceful, like the tops of the barley spikes in early autumn when the breeze is light and playful. He became aware of his muscles, working in groups of left and right, swaying up and left, then down and right, his breath leading or following (sometimes it seemed one way, sometimes the opposite), his body as a beautiful series of linked energy circles.

"Stop."

"What?"

"It is time to eat. I am an old man; I cannot walk far without stopping often, so now we must eat. Make more tea and prepare the *tsampa*." Again they rested in silence while the meal was prepared and consumed.

12

"I suppose that you no longer have the habit of a sleep after having eaten."

"But yes, I always have a sleep after lunch."

"Young children and old men..." He was a little vexed to be grouped together with "young children," but to have eaten well and to have the space to then have his afternoon nap was more than he had expected. Things were not quite that bad for the moment. After the sleep, he would insist that they have the discussion, and he would be home well before nightfall.

Something tapped him on the shoulder. "Get up already! Even I, an old man, don't need to sleep the whole afternoon through. Get up!" He was not used to being woken up in this fashion, and his first reaction was one of anger. But remembering where he was and who he was with forced him to contain his reaction, tidy his sleeping roll, arrange the cooking and foodstuffs, all the while fuming quietly to himself about the unfairness of life and how people can be so rude and unfair.

They had been walking for some time before the old man turned to him and said, "This anger that you are feeling, how is it for you?"

"What do you mean?"

"What is your body experiencing at this moment?"

"I'm feeling anger."

"Idiot! Are you so stupid that you cannot tell the difference between your mind, your emotions, and your body?"

"I didn't understand." The anger was now increasing, but he made a big effort to stay polite in front of the old monk.

"I asked you what you were feeling in your BODY, understand? The physical sensation in your body of the anger."

13

"I'm just feeling very angry."

"And your stupidity, it is not helping my mood, either. Now, we will try again. Focus on your body, you know, that mass of flesh and bones that you have dragged against your emotional will up to here. That which you connected to before when you focused on your walking and the breath. Move the emotional element into the bags; you can take it back later, if you should need it. The mental dimension can shut up for now; it will surely come back at another time. Now! Focus on your body, feel what is happening in your lower back, in your chest, in your neck, along the line of your shoulders, at the root of your skull."

Something strange happened when he began to invoke various parts of the body; the focus of the anger, being negative thoughts and feelings, began to change, and he started to move his attention towards the parts referred to.

"The bottom of my back is a little tense, but I feel something more around the front."

"Good, good, continue."

"My chest area feels a little...closed. My throat, my throat, I feel a little like I'm going to be sick, to vomit."

"Those are the words and emotions that you have half swallowed, like a chunk of poisoned meat. You want and need to cough them up and spit them out, but not now, for this is a moment of awareness, not of action. To release a portion of the anger now would be more comfortable, but it is the built-up tension that allows you to notice what is happening inside of you. Continue."

"I feel something in my shoulders that I have difficulty describing, but what I feel is that I want to hit someone or something."

"Very good, very good. Now another step, a little more difficult. Allow yourself to connect to other moments when you have had such sensations, such a desire to punch and to hurt."

"No, no, not ever. I don't like to hurt. Hurting is bad, wrong. I'm not like that."

"No, of course you're not. You could never have those feelings, those impulses, they are impossible for you."

"That's right, impossible for me."

"Totally impossible." Why did he keep repeating it? What was he trying to say, to express, to get him to understand? After a moment the penny dropped.

"You are making fun of me!"

"Does that make you angry?"

"Yes."

"Even want to hit me?"

He knew that he was being goaded, but the feeling was getting the better of him. And even if it was so unacceptable to express it, and to an elder—even more so to a monk, and not at all to this Master—he just wanted to let himself go and say, "Yes, yes, I do feel anger towards you, and I could feel a desire to punch you."

The reply shocked him. "Good, very good. You see, it is not at all impossible for you to feel anger, even angry enough to feel the desire to punch someone."

"But this is not a good thing!"

"This is a great thing; you are in contact with your real emotions. The body does not lie, and through a correct connection with it, we can know what we honestly feel."

"But anger and violence cannot be good things to feel."

"To go beyond anger is a wonderful work to undertake, and can bring beautiful peace and harmony to the body and spirit. To deny anger that is real and exists is not only dishonest, but also dangerous and destructive for body and soul."

He listened closely to the wise words of the Master, and carried on walking awhile.

"Feeling anger is okay?"

"We are human beings, every emotional experience and expression is there for something useful. Anger is here to show us when something really upsets us. What is the most appropriate reaction to this signal depends very much on what the situation is and how many choices we might have on how to react. Many animals have very few choices: flight, fight, feign death, or fade into the background. As children we also have limited choices, depending on our family and social systems, but as adults we can work towards having more and more choices. Anger can trigger violence, conflict, and destruction, both for the person receiving the violence and he who expresses it. However, anger can also initiate creativity, enterprise, and initiative; the energy moves towards growth and new life. Of course, anger eventually can turn towards compassion; we see beyond the act or words that hurt us, into the heart and soul of the other, and we appreciate that they are only expressing their own pain and suffering. Then we can only pity them, and do our utmost to help them to heal themselves."

"But first we have to become aware of and admit that we are angry?"

"Exactly."

"But just being angry doesn't change anything."

"Becoming aware of our anger is only the first half of the first step: knowing why we are feeling angry. This is, of course, due to someone or some event in the present, but most often when we feel really angry it is almost always also due to the reawakening and remembering of other similar situations or events of the past that have never been successfully resolved. When I forced you to wake up just now, which negative events in the past where reactivated?"

"I'm always being told what to do in my life. I never have the right to choose. Go to bed now, get up now, go outside and play, don't go outside and play, wear this, wear that, don't wear this, don't wear that. Morning till night, every move I make, everything I eat, drink, do, think, everything!"

"And you are someone who has no anger in him?"

"Maybe, really, I only have anger in me."

"That I really, really doubt. And more than that, you can do many things well,"

"Like what?"

"Like make tea. You see, I am but a fragile old man, and I must stop quite often and take rests and drink tea. So I am very lucky to have someone with me that is so good at making tea."

He didn't really know what motivated him to be so disrespectful, but before he could stop himself, he responded, "Only if you have some more Zanba to exchange for it."

The Master stopped and turned towards the young man, who realised, too late, that he had allowed himself to go much too far with the Master. The old man looked sternly at him for many seconds, than broke into a wide grin. "Why, of course I have. Hurry, heat the water."

The break was over and they were back walking along the path. They walked for a while in silence before the Master turned to the boy.

"I have not forgotten that you are here to explain to me exactly why you wish to become a monk, why you are so fragile, and why I should accept you into the order even if you cannot fulfil the duties of a novice monk. So, in order that I can understand all this, tell me about yourself, your family, your life."

"But my parents told the other monk all about us."

"Yes, yes, I know, but now I'd like to hear the way you tell the story."

And so the young man began to tell the old monk the story of his life. A story that began even before he was born, with the short, sad life of his older brother. And of how, from the very moment that he was born, he was coddled, cocooned, and over-cared for. In this version of the story, the anxiety and overprotection by the parents had suddenly begun to be expressed in terms of limitation, almost suffocation.

"Wait, this is not what I was told, this is all wrong."

"What is wrong?"

"You have always respected the wishes of your parents, you have appreciated their concerns for you, you have never expressed any question of their choices for your protection and your wellbeing. Being so sickly and fragile, you have always agreed that you needed to be kept safe from the many dangers that the world threatened you with."

"Maybe I did. Maybe I thought that I was weak and sickly and fragile, but now I know that it isn't true. I am not a weak, fragile boy, I do not need to be so protected, I can be strong, I can face the world. I...I...I...I can make it to the very top of this mountain."

"You really, really believe that you can?"

"Yes, Master, I believe that I can."

The Master gently nodded his head several times. "You know, I believe you can. Yes, I believe you can. Look up, what do you see?"

"The path, it continues."

"But to the right?"

"Another path that leads to a little cabin."

"Yes, my young disciple, we have arrived. Go on ahead and start the tea."

Somewhere he knew that he would never see that sickly, fragile boy ever again; somehow he was totally right.

No Space for Reflection

It was very late when the disciple opened his eyes. The sun was high and the air already heating up. Every muscle ached in his young body; never before had he forced his body so hard or for so long. His heart seemed to be beating very fast, and his breathing was speeded up. He also had a bit of a headache, which was quite unusual for him and made him feel quite irritable.

What a fool I have been to let myself be tricked by that Master. I do not have the health or the strength to do these things. It was a total folly to have climbed so high, and carrying all those bags as well. Today I will explain to him that he was mistaken and that I cannot stay up here with him. He expects too much of me. I have done much, much more than I was supposed to do, I have come all the way up the mountain. My parents will be beside themselves with worry and concern.

"Good afternoon, young man, do you plan to sleep all the day?" His cheerful attitude irritated him even more.

"Master, we must talk." He was not at all accustomed to speaking to his elders like that, but his mood was really not at its best.

"Yes, yes, of course we must, but I am making some more *chaku*. Of course, that should be the task of another." The meaning of that statement was clear enough. "Having enough *chaku* to make my teas is a very important job. Being an old man and very set in my ways, four bowls of tea per day is a dependence that I have built up over many years." And with that, he turned and left to watch the boiling pot.

The concentrated beverage was made from a block of solid tea from the province of Pemagul, which had to be boiled for several hours to absorb enough flavour so as to still give the strong Po Cha taste when mixed with salt and yak butter, after being diluted in boiling water.

Muttering to himself about the unfairness of the world, he got up from the mat on the floor. He got up much too quickly; his head started to swim, and he had to crouch down again for fear that he might fall. He had never been this high up the mountains, and even if he was accustomed to the air, much too thin for most of the other planet dwellers, ascending nearly a thousand metres in the course of less than twenty-four hours was much too much for his system to integrate; headaches and nausea are the usual unfortunate side effects.

He stayed down for quite some moments before he heard his nemesis calling out for him.

"I have made you a bowl of Po Cha. It is only good if drunk hot. I have made it a little stronger than usual. It will help with the nausea."

He dragged himself slowly and carefully from the floor. He had felt fine coming up the mountain, even ecstatic at the end. True, he didn't remember much after arriving at the cabin; he vaguely remembered dropping the bags to the floor, and after that he must have just unrolled his mat and dropped into a deep, deep sleep. The increasing headache had arrived with his regaining consciousness in the morning.

The late morning air was cool and stimulating. Further down on the plateau it would be already warm, but here, much higher up, the sun had yet to warm the air.

"Breathe slower and deeper, it will help to compensate for the thinness of this air, high up."

"Doesn't it affect you?"

"It used to, but one soon gets used to it, and after a few summers up here the body learns how to cope."

"Well, I'm not going to stay long enough for that, not even one time."

"Of course, you are always free to go, at any time. Of the prisons that bind us, the most are in our minds."

"And what is that meant to mean?"

"Nothing, just the ramblings of an old man."

"Master, you may be old, but you do not ramble."

"Even when you block yourself from me because you feel the need to return from whence you came, you can allow yourself to be correct with me. That deserves a reward. Here, take your bowl of tea and one of my Zanba cakes, *tsampa*, that you can eat at home."

Breathing slowly and deeply had helped a little, so he took the bowl and the barley cake and settled down to a late sort of breakfast.

"I cannot stay up here."

"So you have expressed."

"I am not the strong disciple that you need to look after you during your retreat."

"You certainly have a weak mind."

"More a weak body, Master."

"No, your body is not so weak, physical strength is but a miniscule part of the whole. It is your will that is weak; you are emotionally crippled and mentally handicapped, that is why you feel weak. Your energetic body is small and miserable; you have no contact with your chi. You have been possessed by a demon; that demon lives on your physical, mental, and emotional energies. He feeds off your life force, leaving you weak and apathetic. That demon is your parents' trauma and your own beliefs."

"I don't understand what it is that you are talking about."

"I know, I know, but for working in the fields one does not need to know too much of these things."

"Working in the fields! But I came up all this way with you, I carried your bags, and I prepared food and drink. I have done everything that has been asked of me. It's not fair, it's really not fair."

"Yes, my child, it really is not fair. Just when you are offered the opportunity of a lifetime, you find yourself incapable to stretch out and take it. To have grown up with so many restrictions and limitations, to be but a fraction of the man that you are capable of being, and now, to have to renounce all that, to close the door yourself, to the prison of your life, that really is so unfair."

"I don't know what you are talking about."

23

"Again, I can feel the anger mounting within you. If you cannot understand that which I am talking about, then something within you is blocking me. When you try to push a heavy object over a rough surface, the resistance creates heat. The same thing occurs when information tries to traverse the pathways of your mind. Thoughts, beliefs, and emotions can create resistance, that resistance creates heat, and that heat becomes irritation and eventually anger."

"If I am not understanding what you are saying, that is irritating. There is no need to talk of resistance."

"As you wish. How are you feeling now?"

"Better." It was true, and there was no denying it. "Much better." The strong tea and sweet cakes had helped, but just sitting down and allowing his body to adjust was the main factor. Having spent all his life at a quite high altitude, even playing and running like the other children, he was already adapted to the thinner mountain air. Ascending hundreds of metres in less than a day had gone far beyond what his body could cope with short term, and even stationary, asleep, his body had had difficulty functioning correctly. Now, breathing slowly and deeply, which, even though irritated by the discussion, he had succeeded to continue to do, was feeding his system enough oxygen to operate without discomfort.

"You wish to play a little game with me?"

"What game?"

"I believe that it is called 'arm wrestling.' Of course, if you are still feeling too weak to compete against an old man..."

"I don't understand."

"You really must be a very stupid young man."

"You want to arm wrestle with me?"

"Yes, if you feel that you are not still feeling too weak."

"If you want." They moved to either side of a big flat rock and knelt down. The younger man continued to move quite slowly, but the nausea had ceased to be a problem. "You really want to do this?"

"Why not?" The old man settled himself on the floor and placed his left elbow on the rock, his left hand, relaxed, close to his face, waiting for the younger man to position himself.

"Why the left hand, Master?"

"Why, because I am left-handed, of course. Do you think that I would risk losing against you? I am still the champion left-hander of the temple." The young man doubtfully placed his elbow close to that of the older man and offered his own left hand to be grasped by the Master. Before he could close his grip on the skinny, small claw, the Master closed his hand on the disciple's and, in the same movement, twisted it towards himself and forced the surprised man's hand down, hard, onto the rock.

"Oww! That wasn't fair," he complained, "I wasn't ready."

"Well, you will be next time."

"And I'm not left-handed."

"Neither am I," he smiled, getting up, taking his tea and slowly sitting back down on a rock.

"I don't understand anything," he muttered, refilling his own tea and going to sit down again. "Sorry." He placed his tea on the floor and went to refill the Master's bowl.

"You will, you will." And they finished their breakfast in silence.

25

The morning was spent cleaning the little hut, carefully emptying the bag, and putting everything away in its right place. The Master was very particular about where each item was placed or stored, and due to the fact that the disciple was still acclimatising himself to the higher altitude, this took quite a long time.

Eventually everything was to the Master's satisfaction and they stopped to eat a well-earned lunch. After the bowls were washed and put away, the Master proposed that they go for a little walk to help digest their meal.

After some minutes of walking, old man turned back to his student. "You are still angry."

"Yes, I am." He stopped and thought for a moment. "And one of the reasons that I am angry is that you seem to think that you always know what I am feeling."

"And why shouldn't I?" The answer took the young man aback, as he had expected the Master to respond to his slightly aggressive affirmation of being angry, not to his criticism of knowing his feelings.

"It's not normal to be able to know what someone else is feeling."

"Oh, quite the opposite, it is totally normal to know what others are feeling. It is not normal not to."

"How can it be normal?"

"How else am I to know how to be with you if I don't know how you're feeling?"

"What do you mean?"

"If I didn't know you, and I couldn't trust that you wouldn't attack me if you were angry or felt I was a danger to you, or that you wanted something I had, I would have to keep you always at a safe distance."

"But you know that isn't true."

"How do I know?"

"Well...well...well, I'd tell you, of course." Here he was sure, he had won this little argument.

"And if you couldn't talk?"

"But of course I can talk, we all can talk."

"The animals, can they talk? And our long-ago ancestors, do you think they could talk?"

"Why not?"

"Because babies cannot talk when they are born, not even months after. A horse can stand on its legs almost immediately after it arrives on this earth and within hours it can walk. One can see the progress of evolution of each being by watching the individual changes of each infant. The human child takes many years to fully develop; hence, the human species has taken many tens of thousands of years to evolve; to learn to stand, to walk, and to talk. Human beings must have lived for many, many generations before learning how to speak. We are physically weak creatures; we survive by living in communities. To live together one needs to be able to communicate, to understand, to read the other."

"But it's just not possible to do that."

"Not for most people."

"That is what I was saying." They came to a grassy knoll, where they stopped to sit.

"For two reasons: firstly, because they've forgotten how, and secondly, because they don't want to remember how."

"What do you mean, they've forgotten and they don't want to remember?"

"There once was a village, much like most others, where the children would have their homework diaries completed by the teachers, with remarks on their performance."

"Their school marks?"

"Yes, their academic notes and other points—behaviour, attitude, and other general information."

"But that is quite usual."

"Absolutely. And from that information, the parents were able to know whether to praise or scold their offspring, whether they should worry about their schooling or not."

"So?"

"So, some of the children decided that they didn't want their parents knowing about what was happening at school; that the teachers had all the competences and authority necessary to resolve whatever problems, academic or behavioural, that the students might have. That way, the parents wouldn't have to worry or complain about their child's school activities, and home life would therefore be more peaceful and harmonious."

"So what happened?"

"The heads of the schools all met and the leaders of the demand presented their arguments in front of this committee. The heads listened attentively to the idea of suppressing all reports to the parents and leaving the teachers to deal, not hassled by the unhappy parents. Unhappy about some aspect of the student's schooling, which, since it was the teacher that informed the parents, he would already know about. More than that, it was, just

28

the same, the teacher that would be responsible for finding the most appropriate solution. The involvement of the parents only created disharmony in the home and unnecessary disruption for the teacher."

"And did the committee agree with the students?"

"What do you think of their argument?"

"The way you say it, it sounds very reasonable." For someone who had just finished his own schooling, the idea sounded totally reasonable.

"And so did the school heads; from then on, all reports to the parents were suppressed."

"And then what?"

"What do you mean?"

"What happened after that?"

"Nothing happened after that."

"But didn't that create problems?"

"Maybe."

"What is the point of this story?"

"The point of the story?"

"Why have you told me this story?"

"Isn't it obvious?"

"If it was obvious, I wouldn't be asking."

"Hmm, you might have a point there." The disciple, not knowing the Master well, had no idea if the Master was becoming senile, was confused, was creating confusion as a teaching technique, or was just playing with him. Whatever was the response, he wasn't enjoying the exchange; it was both upsetting and tiring.

"Please, why did you tell me this story?"

"Do you think it a good story?"

"I think that maybe it is time to return to my parents. Even working in the fields cannot be as bad as this."

"Are you sure about that?" Of course he wasn't, and it was quite a silly threat if one really thought about it.

"Please can you tell me the point of the story."

"What were we talking about before?"

"That talking was something that people didn't do very long ago." "Good, you were listening and you can remember, very good. But before that, what was the subject?"

"That you could tell what I was feeling?" Here he sounded much more doubtful.

"Exactly." The disciple then waited for the Master to continue, to explain, to clarify. He didn't.

"The story about the school has something to do with your being able to read what I am feeling?"

"Something to do with your not being able to know what I am feeling." This student was intrigued.

"Because the children didn't want the parents to know, they stopped showing them their reports and the parents were also relieved of the responsibility of knowing what was happening at school, so they were all better off."

"Continue."

"Are you sort of saying that before, we were all able to read each other's feelings, but then we stopped wanting to, so now we can't?"

"I have a question for you. If at some time, one of the students wanted to show his report to his parents, do you think that he still could?"

"Sure."

"And that his parents would still be capable of reading it?"

"I don't see why not."

"So, do you think that we cannot read each other or that we have just stopped doing it?"

"Wait a minute, there is something wrong here. I don't quite understand what, but there is something not right."

"Very good."

"What are trying to do? You are trying to do something with my head, I can feel it."

"Yes, yes, I am."

"What are you trying to do?"

"I'm trying to open it up."

"Open it up?"

"Don't be so worried. By open it up, I mean to get you to start to think. What you have somehow noticed is that I had linked the story with your ability to read my feelings, without expressly doing so."

"And it was that that was making me feel bad?"

"Was it?"

"So, what you are saying is that before, we could read each other's feelings, then we stopped because we didn't want other people to read them, but we could read them again if we wanted to?"

"Does that make sense?"

"No. If we didn't want people to read our feelings, that wouldn't stop us reading their feelings."

"Continue."

"So we must also have chosen to stop reading them. The parents, the parents must also have decided to stop reading the teachers' reports. They preferred not to know what was happening so they wouldn't have to deal with it. But wouldn't there be times when the teacher, or even the student, would want the parents to know something?"

"Then they could, of course, in that instance choose to communicate something. That is where talking comes in."

"And I could learn to read your feelings?"

"You could learn to read everybody's feelings. Even more than that, there are other things that we can read."

"Like what?"

"Some people can read people's bodies; they can tell what hurts, and where, and sometimes how to heal them. Others can connect to the thoughts of others, and can sometimes know what they will say or do next."

"My parents sometimes do that."

"Then there are those that can enter into the dreams of others, or their memories, or maybe other things than that."

"What can I do?"

"How should I know?"

"Don't you know?"

"You seem disappointed."

"I thought that you would show me how to read other people." "Why would you want to be able to do that?"

"Well...well...well, it would be a good thing."

"It would give you power over the others. It would compensate for always feeling weak, incapable, inferior." The disciple stopped for a moment before answering.

"It is not a good reason for learning to do that."

"Well done, you are already advancing well. Maybe we should experiment to see exactly what you are capable of before we start to judge how appropriately you can do it."

"You will teach me?"

"I cannot teach you."

"Oh."

"I can only help you to open the window to you consciousness. When the window is open, what you can or choose to see, that is for you to find out."

"Really? You will show me how to read people?"

"No. Please learn to listen. I will help you to open yourself to the other. After that, it is up to you."

"Thank you, thank you! When do we start?"

"If you are sitting comfortably, now we begin."

"What am I to do?"

"First listen, then follow, then experience, then integrate, then practice, then be."

"Okay, I'm listening."

"Look up, look to the skies, look at the clouds. Allow your creativity and your imagination to create images, pictures, stories; floating, changing, metamorphosing, growing, shrinking, sailing, melting, joining things. All sorts of things: people, animals, houses, objects, mountains, rivers.

"Allow your body to breathe; fully and deeply, softly and slowly. Your breath is a wave that flows up through your body, out, out into the infinite ocean of the universe; meeting, merging, mixing, capturing the eternal life energy, only to return, re-entering your personal, inner world, descending back, down to the shores of your solid, physical being. And once there, to release its rich abundance of force, so to be absorbed and nourish the very person that you are.

"Take all the time you need. You have all the time in the universe, all the time of the past, present, and future. Now I will rest here, next to you, and you will continue your journey, accompanied by the gentle sounds of nature as you release your mind from its old shackles of reason and logic."

And with that final instruction, the old man settled himself comfortably onto the soft grass, now well warmed by the afternoon sun, and fell deeply, deeply asleep.

The time did pass and, if truth be told, after a certain length of time, the disciple succumbed to the soft grasses and warm sunshine, and he too slept.

"So this is how you follow my instructions?" He woke up to find himself being gently prodded by the Master's staff.

"I am sorry, Master, it won't happen again."

"And how can you be sure of that?"

"Well, I will do my best not to fall asleep again while watching the clouds."

"But you cannot be sure, to be certain to never, ever, ever fall asleep while meditating."

"No."

"So you should not promise things that are not within your power to control."

"Well, I'm sorry, is that okay?" There was a certain irritation in the young man's voice.

"Did you ever speak to your parents in this way?"

"No, I"—suddenly he bowed his head and dropped his voice—"I am truly sorry, Master. I will do all that is in my power to never fall asleep while looking at clouds again."

The old man shook his head and tapped him heavily on the shoulder with the stick. "You still have so much to learn, so far to go."

"Ow! What did you do that for? I was correct and polite and humble."

"And that is why I hit you with my stick."

"I don't understand."

"Good, then we agree that you still have much to learn. Come, let us return, I am hungry for my dinner." And with that, he turned and headed back towards the house.

Dinner was finished and they were sitting round the fire drinking a last cup of Po Cha.

"Master?"

"Yes, Dhargey?"

"What was I supposed to have experienced this afternoon?"

"Other than falling asleep?" The younger man did not respond to this latest attack. "It is a first step towards seeing."

"But we have done that before; lying down on the grass, looking at the clouds, imagining what they could be."

"So, was it the same for you as those other times?" He took a moment to answer.

"No, no, it was different."

"How was it different?"

"Before, I was always sure that I was here, lying on the ground, and the clouds were up there, away, up in the sky...separate from me."

"And this afternoon?"

"This afternoon...this afternoon, I was not separate. I wasn't part of the clouds, but I wasn't on the ground, either."

"And the other times, how much control did you have over them?"

"Control? One cannot control the clouds."

"This afternoon?"

"Of course I...but yes, now I remember, it was later on. I did, I did, I could start to shape them, to move them. Yes, I was able to control the clouds. Will I learn to be able to control the weather?"

"That is another discipline altogether, something that is not important for you to learn."

"But I could learn?"

"Better first learn to control yourself. Now go and wash up, it is time for prayers and sleep."

The next day they rose quite early, breakfasted, and set off. The disciple carried only that which was necessary to make tea, which confused him as they walked further and further up the mountain, this time in total silence. *He must surely turn back soon, or we will pass the whole day without eating. My parents have always insisted that I eat very regularly. Maybe he is so lost in his thoughts he has not realised how far or for how long we have been walking.*

"I am quite aware of the time."

"I didn't say anything."

"You started to walk even slower than usual, and you looked back down the path several times—hence, you were wondering when we would be turning back."

"Master."

"Yes?"

"Sometimes I find you very irritating."

"You would speak like that to your parents?"

"Not before, but maybe now."

"Good, there is progress after all."

"But are we not going to descend soon?"

"No, I wish to bring you somewhere, so that I might show you something. Unfortunately, you are still walking so very slowly that I fear not to arrive before nightfall."

"But I need to eat."

"We all need to eat; it is a basic animal need. What we do not need is to eat every four hours; that is the need of a baby. You are not still a baby, are you?"

"No, but my parents—"

"Are not here. I am an old man; I need, more than you, to look after my health. What I can cope with, you can surely cope with. Here, I have gathered some leaves while walking, we can chew on these. It will alleviate your feeling of hunger."

"But my hunger is not just a feeling, it is real. I need to eat, my stomach is starting to rumble."

"Your body is like a baby. When it screams that it wants something, it makes a lot of noise. Distract it, and most of the time it will forget what it was asking for and focus on something else. If it cannot be distracted, or if it comes back all the time to the first demand, then it is a real need and we should look to fulfilling that need."

"But Master, I am hungry."

"Your body has a habit of eating at this time. Here, chew this. If your body really needs food at this time, it will express that in many other ways. If not, then it is only your body reminding you that you are not following you usual habits."

He took the leaves and started to chew them; they had a sweet, minty flavour, although the texture was quite hard and chewy.

"Focus on the flavours and on the moving of your feet, which are, I will remind you, much, much too slow." And so he did; his attention alternating between the pleasant taste sensations and the comfortable, flowing movement of his body. It was only then that he realised that he had already acclimatised himself to the higher and higher altitudes. Climbing even further up today, he was experiencing nothing of the breathing problems of the day before.

"At last." They arrived at a plateau, and the disciple was most surprised to find a flowing river, fed from some melting glacier somewhere much higher up the mountain. In front of them was an impressive rock pool of at least eight feet across, the water tumbling in from a waterfall some ten feet above. It was a very beautiful and impressive sight.

"It is beautiful."

"Is that how you talk about your dinner?"

"What are you talking about?"

"Dinner."

"Dinner?"

"Yes, you said that you were hungry."

"But what is there to eat?"

"That is your whole problem; you cannot allow yourself to see beyond that which is on the surface." He entered into the pool.

38

"Come here." The disciple dropped his bags and also entered the pool. "Look down here, what do you see?"

"I see my reflection."

"And what do you imagine is in here?"

"Rocks?"

"Reflections and projections; that is all that exists for you. Your own reflection, or the projection of what you believe to be true. That is what blocks you from seeing into the souls of those around you."

"But it is impossible to see what is in the water; the sun is directly above us. It is science, I think. If it is sunny, you can see out of a window from the inside, but if you are outside, you can only see your reflection. And if you cannot see what is inside the house, you can only guess what is inside; that is logical." He seemed very pleased with his argument.

"And what if it was really important to know, to know what was happening inside the house?"

"I would go into the house and have a look."

"Oh, would you?"

"Yes, yes, I would."

"And if it was really important to know what was happening at the bottom of this pool?"

"I would...put my head under the water."

"Well?" The disciple took a breath and plunged his head under the water. Several seconds later he surfaced in great excitement.

"There are fish in the water! Here, so high in the mountain, there are fish."

"Yes, they come up here to spawn. It must have been a process of hundreds if not thousands of years for them to have gotten the habit to swim so far upstream, but here they are and here we are, and we have nothing for lunch."

"You eat fish?"

"You tell me." The disciple looked confused. "Okay, look into my eyes and think about killing things." The old man shook his head slightly, then nodded to show that he was ready. The young man concentrated his focus on the old man's eyes, breathed deeply in and out, then gave a cry of shock and horror, slipped back, and splashed full length into the flowing waters.

"What the...?"

"What did you see?" The old man seemed very concerned.

"There was a troop of riders, dressed in black and red, then I saw a flash of sunlight on a metal object, and then blood spurting out from something, and felt an awful feeling of fear."

"Oh." Now it was his turn to look uncomfortable. "Yes, very good. Go and catch some fish, we will cook some fish for our lunch." And with that, he turned and walked away, taking his story with him, leaving the young man to wonder as to exactly what he had connected to, and just how one could catch fish without neither a hook nor a net.

"You are not very good at this, are you?" He had recovered his poise and his sense of humour.

"How am I to catch fish without a net or a rod and hook?"

"Like a bear." He lowered himself into the clear waters. "First, find a spot out of the sunlight, so that your reflection is less troublesome. I thought you would have realised that already. Then we lean forward and lower our arms into the water. We should be able to see if there is something moving in the water. We then take a breath and gently allow the head to enter the aquatic world. That is how we stop seeing our own reflection and see into the reality below. Now we can see clearly if there is a fish close. When it comes easily in range, scoop and bat with the hand. The fish will be propelled towards the shore, and lunch will be served."

It took him quite some time to master the technique, but the Master seemed happy to relax on the bank, playing with his knife and some pieces of wood, while patiently waiting for the fish to arrive, which eventually materialised as two quite plump specimens. Quite soon the fire was ablaze, and the first fish was turning on the wooden spit that the Master had fashioned while waiting.

"Your lunch, Master."

"Come, split this one in two and we can eat it together."

"But no, I cannot do that, it is your fish. I will wait until mine is cooked. It is not right to take half your meal."

"Do you think that my act would be an act of self-sacrifice?"

"Why, yes."

"You have so much to learn. Here, eat and I will explain." He split the fish in two and offered a half to the disciple, who hesitatingly took it. "This is an act of enlightened self-interest. It takes quite a while for the fish to cook; it also takes quite a while to eat a whole fish. While you are waiting to eat, half of my fish is getting cold. Then your fish will be ready. I will have to wait, watching you eat, knowing that when you get to the second half, it too will be cold. By sharing my fish with you, we eat at the same time, and both portions will be hot and fresh. In fact, one could even read my act as purely motivated by self-interest."

"But we both benefit."

"The best of all possible worlds."

"Especially if we finish off with a hot bowl of butter tea."

"You see, you are not totally incapable of learning."

The night was beginning to fall by the time they arrived back at the house. He quickly started the fire, and was surprised to see the Master appear with food that he himself had not carried up the mountain.

"Do you think that I can pass weeks and weeks here with the few provisions that a weak youth felt able to carry? The other monks take turns coming up here and bringing me the food and supplies I need. Come, cook me something."

The meal was cooked, eaten, and cleared up.

"Master, please, what was it that I touched, before, while at the lake?"

"Come, Dhargey, put some more wood on the fire. I will tell you of the line of red and black. Not only that, but in the next few weeks I will tell you much of my journey, of my life."

"Master, you really don't have to. I am sorry, it was disrespectful to have even asked you that."

"No, Dhargey, it is important that I share this with you. When you have heard all, then you will understand. The story is not all easy to hear, but I will tell you what you need to know.

"The story begins during my seventh year..."

The Line of Red and Black

It was morning, the sun had already risen, and I was sitting eating breakfast with my parents.

"Why do we have storms?" I asked my father.

"It's just the weather, dear," replied my mother. She was preparing the *tsampa*. They liked it with cheese, but I would eat it just mixed with the tea.

"But why does the weather sometimes be nice and sometimes be not nice?"

"Because life is like that," my father replied, shaking his head in a tired way. Last year's storms had come, literally, out of a clear blue sky and had all but devastated that year's crop. My parents, like most of the people of the village, were quite traumatised by the violent rain, the fear of which kept everyone a little stressed. We were now coming to the moment of harvest, the day when everyone could start to live normally again, but we hadn't quite got there yet. People had become very nervous those days; it seemed that there was a real threat of storms.

"Jangbu, here, eat your breakfast. These are not things that a boy of seven should be worrying his little head about." She ruffled my hair as she placed the bowl in front of me. "You are too young to have such worries and concerns." She then turned to my father. "Children should be protected from the ugly side of life. They are too pure and too fragile."

My father put aside his salty tea and smiled at us both. "Yes, children should be protected from life's ugly sides. When you have finished breakfast, you go and play in the fields, and leave all the worries to your parents."

And that is just what I did.

The day was peaceful and warm; I liked to pass the time in the fields, away from all the noise and activity of the village. The other boys and girls of my age seemed to like all the work and bustle and commotion—many already had their own jobs and responsibilities—but my parents were happy to leave me, lost in the fields, lost in my dreams.

The thunder seemed to be coming from far off; I opened my eyes and looked to the heavens. I expected to see the heavy grey clouds amassing overhead, but I saw nothing, only a clear blue sky. I looked further off; yes, to the west, I could see the threat coming, the ominous black clouds, streaked with fiery red lightning bolts. Not that far off, but then again, not close enough to create the deep, rumbling thunder I had heard.

Sitting up, I realised that I couldn't hear it anymore. I lay down again and there it was. The sound was being transmitted through the ground, but what was it? Moments later, the explanation emerged from the tops of the barley, into my field of vision: a line of horsemen dressed in armour of red and black appeared.

I watched as the line of red and black rode quietly towards the village. It was a quiet that I would remember for the rest of my life. That quiet and the noise and screams that followed...

I didn't know what to do. Should I run towards the village to seek the safety and protection of my parents, or should I run away from the terror that I could hear from there? In my uncertainty, I took the other track—I froze.

Suddenly, bursting into the field, I could see first my mother, then my father, rushing towards me. I was quite far towards the other end of the field. I had made a little protection with some pieces of wood that I could hide under if I wanted to; they knew exactly where it was.

Even from that distance, I could hear their heavy breathing; they must have been running very fast to have escaped the mounted demons. It was then that I could also hear the panting of the horse. He was big and black, as was the rider who was pushing him hard to catch up to my parents.

As he caught up to my father, he reached over to the side and pulled out a short spear. He hardly had to throw it at all; the speed at which he was riding meant that he only had to direct it towards my father's back to impale him totally. I watched in horror and fascination as the metal point appeared, out of nowhere, exploding out of his chest and into the air.

My father's momentum kept him moving for a few more strides, as if the spear was dragging him further forward.

My mother was ignorant of all this; she was only aware of running away from the badness and coming to try and save me. I suppose that she must have heard the stamp of the hooves as the horse and rider gained on her, but she gave no sign of it.

As he had already used his spear on my father, he detached his axe to kill my mother. He passed her on her left side, the axe in his right hand.

Time slowed down.
The sun was still shining.
The sky was still blue.
The galloping horse flew in the air.
The blade of the axe reflected the sun.
The rider's moustache danced around his open mouth.
His teeth were tightly clenched.
His eyes were bright and shiny.
His arm arced gracefully.
Then descended like an eagle attacking a snow pigeon.
The blade sparkled and shone.
It sliced her neck in one clean blow.
The head seemed to be carried for a second on the flat of the blade.
Like a dish being served in a feast.
The body carried on running.
Blood spurting out of the neck.
The head was propelled from the blade.
The empty, bloodied body crumpled and fell.
The head flew in my direction.

46

The horse and rider continued towards me.

The fear mounted.

I curled myself under the wooden roof.

I looked up through the wooden slats.

I could see the enormous horse towering over me.

I made myself as small as possible.

I closed my eyes.

I waited for death.

And I waited, and I waited, and I waited.

I don't know how much time passed, but after waiting and waiting for death and nothing happening, I finally decided to move. My little body was also starting to hurt after lying still and tense for so long.

I opened my eyes and saw that the sky had already become quite dark; the rain could not be long coming. I crawled out from my little wooden box and fixed my eyes in the direction of the village. I did not want to see the remains of what had just happened in the field.

I managed to get to the end of the field without looking directly at the bodies of either of my parents. I had thought to go back to the village, with the idea that maybe there I could find someone to help me, but as I approached, I quickly realised that there was little hope of finding any help there. There was little chance of finding anyone alive.

They had set everything on fire before leaving, maybe to force everyone out of the houses, maybe just to leave nothing behind them, but just the same, everything was aflame. If there was no one alive and if there was nowhere to find any food, there was no sense in staying; but, as I had nowhere else to go, I just stood and watched the burning village.

The storm came, the rain that was the terror of my village, but it was too late. It could do no more harm to them; maybe it could even have saved them if it had come a little before.

Here I am, standing, the village is burning, the rain is pouring, and I have nowhere to go.

The rain creates rivers of tears on the streets of my burning village, but I am cold; I am cold in my body, I am cold in my heart.

The rain passes and I am still standing there; time is passing, the day is ending. I am feeling so, so tired. I need to sleep; I need to find a place to sleep. There is only one place that I know where I might feel safe enough to sleep, so I return to the field.

I notice the bodies of my parents out of the corner of my eye, but I manage not to look at them. The head must be somewhere over there, so I look hard the other way, hoping not to fall over it by accident.

My little wooden cave is not too wet; the wooden slats are quite close together, and the barley crop has also protected it a little. I curl up in a little ball of frozen exhaustion, hoping that by falling asleep I can wake up tomorrow, with the birds singing, my mother cooking *tsampa*, and all this but an awful, awful, awful nightmare.

The morning was bright and sunny, the birds sang, and the day was as beautiful as any that I'd ever lived. I crawled out of my box and started to look around me, until I thought I saw some-thing—then I remembered.

I turned in the opposite direction and started to run. I ran, and I ran, and I ran.

It wasn't fear that drove me; it must have been all the energy blocked and bottled up from the horrors of the day before.

It was some time before I slowed down. For a child of my age, a long time has no value other than the feeling that I had been running for hours and hours; there are no other points of reference.

What I did begin to notice was that I was both hungry and thirsty. There was a river that ran almost straight through our village on one side, and the mountain rose on the other, which meant that if I turned my back to the mountain, sooner or later I would find the river. That was what my father had told me many times in the past, when we had been out walking, and now my growing thirst easily reminded me of his words.

Seeing my father walking with me suddenly changed into seeing him running, running towards me, running away from the black horse, running away from the short, sharp spear; falling, falling, falling.

I fell.

I don't remember how long I slept
I don't remember getting up
I don't remember walking to the river.

I am in the river.
I am laughing and playing.
I have drunk the fresh, sparkling water.
I wash the berry juice from my sticky hands.

I am happy.
I am carefree.
Time is passing.
I am living with the river.
The river has become my best friend.

Time has no meaning.
Time is something from the past.
Time is a box of old and painful memories.
Time has no more interest for me, I live without it.

There is no pain
There are no thoughts
There is no yesterday or tomorrow
There is only this moment, there is only now.

There is a man
He wears a robe
He has come to sit with me
He asks me questions about myself
He asks me questions but I have no answers.

He wants me to go with him
He wants me to leave my river
He wants me to go down the mountain
He wants me to re-join the world of people.

He says that he is a monk
He says that the monks will look after me

He says that the monks will find me new parents
He says the monks and the parents will heal my wounds.

The monk sits with me and speaks to me of such wonderful
things The monk sits with me and tells of the sun, the moon
and stars The monk sits with me and sings me beautiful songs
The monk sits with me and I sleep in his arms

I love my river, she soothes me with her flowing
songs I love my river, she washes my scars and
wounds I love my river, she rocks me in her silver
arms I love my river, she asks me no questions.

The monk wants me to re-join the world of people.
The monk wants me to go down the mountain
The monk wants me to leave my river
The monk wants me to go with him

I will re-join the world of people.
I will go down the mountain I
will leave my river
I will go with him

A n d
S o
W e
G o .

Hunger Is good Sauce

It was still early morning when the Young Master prodded the disciple awake.

"Get up and make me some tea, you lazy good-for-nothing."

The tone was quite aggressive, and the young man, roughly awakened, reacted by covering his head and crying out, "Go away, I'm still sleeping! Make your own tea, it's too early."w

The old man prodded him again. "Get up and make my tea."

This time the younger man pulled the covers down from his head, opened his eyes, and cried out, "Oh, it's you! I thought it was a dream."

"It will become a nightmare if I don't get my tea soon."

"Yes, Master, of course, Master, many apologies, Master."

"Shut up and make the tea," he responded, in not an unfriendly way, as he walked out to take the morning air. The disciple quickly got up and hurried himself to heat the water to prepare the morning tea.

"What do you wish to eat with your tea?" he asked his Master as he brought out the steaming bowl.

"We will eat nothing for the moment; the tea will suffice for now." This was not the response that he was expecting. At least a bowl of *tsampa* would have been something. But as the Master ordered, they sat silently and drank their morning Po Cha.

"Come." He cleared the tea bowls and went to get the travelling bags. "No, we will not need those."

"Not even to make tea?"

"Not even to make tea."

"It will be a short walk, then?"

"The walk will end when it will be finished." These types of cryptic responses he would have to come to accept if he was to pass much time with the Master. He closed the door of the hut and followed the old man onto the path to continue to advance up the mountain.

The way became steeper and more difficult. It was odd to think that only two days ago, a weak, sickly, fragile boy had protested that he could not walk far—and yet, now, the same person, transformed into a strong, devoted disciple, began this steep climb without even a second thought.

"My son, watch the rising sun. Feel the life energy that it offers us every day of our lives."

"Yes, Master, it is truly magnificent."

"It is praiseworthy, no?"

"Yes, Master."

"So, raise your arms in praise of the sun. No, not like that, get your arms higher, up. Hands, cup them slightly, now more to the front, elbows just slightly bent. Yes, yes, that's good. Now keep them there and carry on walking."

"Master, how long must I keep my hands like this?"

"Does the sun ask every two minutes, how long should I keep shining?"

"But it is easier for the sun."

"Oh, now I have a disciple that passes his time chatting with the sun. Maybe I should be his disciple?"

"But Master, it is tiring to walk and to keep one's arms up so." "This I know, for you are not the only student to have praised the sun."

"So you know how tiring it is."

"Yes, I certainly do. I was a little younger than you are now." "Younger, Master? But one is not allowed—"

"I was a little younger than you. Keep up, walk a little faster. I am a weak old man, you should be able to walk much faster than me." "But, Master—"

"So, I was a little younger than you are now. My Master, who they called the 'Old Master,' had found out that I had entered the kitchens at night. I did not sleep well in those times, and I had partaken of a little midnight snack. Unfortunately, the snack that I had chosen to enjoy was the special Zanba cakes, especially made for him."

"Was he very angry?"

"I suppose that he must have been."

"You didn't know?"

"The Old Master was very advanced on his path, it was difficult to know what he thought or felt."

"So what happened?"

"He took me out into the courtyard and asked me if I had enjoyed the cakes. I admitted freely that I had. He then asked me what was the main thing that made the barley grow, which we could in no way control. Well, I thought about it for a moment. The ground; well, that was a little everywhere, so that couldn't count. Water; well, even if it didn't rain there were some reserves, so we could control it a bit. The sun! Yes, the sun. I turned to my master, quite pleased with myself, and replied, "The sun." Yes, he agreed, I should thank the sun for making the barley grow, from which the Zanba cakes were made. So I raised my hands to the sun. 'Good,' he said, 'now stay like that till I tell you to move, and remember, next time you think to eat my cakes, you will have to thank the sun again in my place.'"

"How long did you have to stay like that?"

"Long enough to realise that it wasn't worth it to steal any more of his Zanba cakes," replied the Master with a little smile.

"Master?"

"Yes?"

"Just how long must I walk in this fashion?"

"Do you think that you might ever be tempted to steal my Zanba cakes?"

"Surely not, Master."

"Then it must be almost time to finish this exercise."

"What more do I need to do?"

"You need to be aware of just how far you have walked with your arms raised to the sky."

The disciple turned back to discover that he had walked a great distance since the Master had instructed him to raise his arms. "Now, you can lower them."

They continued for a while in silence.

"Master?"

"Yes?"

"Is the story that you told me last night your own story?"

"Yes...why?"

"I just wondered."

"What did you wonder, Dhargey?"

"Well, if you were so traumatised as a child, how did you succeed to become a Master?"

"Many of the experiences and initiations that helped me become a Master were offered to me as a way to overcome my childhood traumas."

"Will you tell me about these experiences and initiations?"

"Yes, I will."

"When?"

"When it will do you the most good and amuse me the most."

They carried on for another half hour or so before he broke the silence again.

"Master?"

"Yes?"

"Will we be travelling far today?"

"You surely cannot be tired already."

"No, not at all, not at all. Although I must admit that I am surprising myself with my own capacity."

"That is because we are no longer poisoning your mind with the sick thoughts about your being weak."

"I was just thinking, we have no tea, nor do we even have a pot or a firebox."

"And just what was your little mind thinking, about our lack of pot or fire?"

"Well, even if you collected some leaves or if we caught more fish, we couldn't make any tea or cook the fish."

"A very finely reasoned reflection. And what, then, is your conclusion?"

"That either we turn back very soon or else we might miss lunch completely."

"With a mind as sharp as yours, you could make a great scholar."

"And you are making fun of me again." The old man smiled and hunched his shoulders.

"I have to find ways to amuse myself. When one gets to my age, one takes what one can."

"But you haven't answered my question."

"Did you ask one?"

"Well, sort of. Are we going to turn back now or not?"

"Quick, look here. You see these berries? They are quite rare. They only grow on this part of the mountain."

"They don't look very special."

"They are, so be careful with them. I want you to pick six of the reddest ones that you find. Be careful, don't crush them, and then put them carefully in your sack."

"What am I to do with them?"

"Put them carefully into you sack."

"I heard you say that, but what will I do afterwards with them?"

"I would have thought that to be totally obvious. Later, you will take them back out of the sack."

"I could have worked that out for myself."

"Maybe next time you will." And with that, he turned away from his disciple and continued on his path towards the summit of the hill.

Dhargey, muttering to himself, followed the Master some feet behind. He became lost in a series of thoughts and memories linked to the unfairness of the Master's actions and incomprehensibility of his thinking and communicating.

"It must be time for tea."

"You told me not to bring any," he replied in irritated manner.

"Quite right. We cannot have tea because, as you correctly have reminded me, I told you not to bring any. However, whether or not we have the means to make and drink tea, that in no way changes the awareness that about now is the time I have the habit to stop for tea."

"So what is the point of mentioning it if we cannot have it?"

"That is a question well worth answering." The disciple, who to some degree had been intentionally provoking the Master, was a little taken aback by this particularly reasonable response. "But first, as it is time to stop to relax and take a drink, I suggest that we cross this path here and—yes, there it is—we stop there by the side of that little stream."

The stream was quite small, and as the mountain fell away from them further down, the water then flowed down the other side. It was only having come so close that made it visible at all.

"Come sit. Here, I have brought two bowls. The water here is quite wonderful; cold, refreshing, and tasty."

"Tasty?"

"Come, sit here, the grass is soft, taste." He took the bowl from the old man and scooped some water up in it. "Wait, don't drink it like that, like simple water. First, sit, make yourself comfortable. Good. Now, imagine that you have been offered a bowl of the finest barley wine, very rare, very special. Good. Now, slowly, carefully, consciously, tip the bowl up and drizzle a small quantity of this exceptional liquid into your mouth. Good. But don't swallow; hold it in your mouth, let it voyage around your tongue, circle the inside of your mouth, explore between your teeth."

The effect was hypnotic; his focus totally on his mouth and his reactions to the water, swirling, seeping, swimming through his senses.

"Taste, touch, take your time, and when it is just the right moment, then swallow. Now wait, savour and inscribe in your soul this experience. Okay, now take another sip. Good. Enter deeper and deeper into the experience."

The world had slowed and shrunk, there was only his mouth, and the water. The liquid became a drug; the more he took, the more he wanted. Soon the bowl was empty. He got up to refill it.

"Enough!"

"Enough?"

"Enough, the experience is complete."

"But, I—"

"Enough. I have promised to explain to you the purpose of mentioning that it is time for tea, even if there is no possibility of having any. How much time has passed since you first sat down here?"

"I don't know."

"A lot of time, an hour or so, or just of few minutes?"

"I suppose it wasn't that long."

"But did it seem long while you were experiencing?"

"Yes, it seemed very long."

"And why did it seem so long?"

"Because I was enjoying it." There was an edge of irritation in his voice.

"Good, I am pleased that you find pleasure in your studies."

"These are studies?"

"You are here to learn, you learn through experiences; hence, these are your studies."

"Will I be tested on these studies?" There was now a tinge of concern in his voice.

"Certainly."

"When? How?"

"How should I know? This is not a regular school; we get tested as life tests us."

"As life tests us?"

"Of course."

"Oh." They were again climbing the mountainside. "So, about the tea break?"

"Time is a very easy and difficult thing to measure. On the one hand, it is easy to know when a day has passed. Even midday is not difficult to calculate. If one has the proper apparatus, sundials and hourglasses, it is possible to measure hours, even minutes and seconds. From there, watching the positions of the sun and the moon, counting the days, months, and years, is far from difficult. In fact, for hundreds of years man has been able to calculate and hence to some degree to control time. However, we humans are not mechanical devices; we can pass many hours without noticing that the time is passing, when we are taken with something. Time can seem to stand still when we are bored or waiting for something important. Time can be very condensed when the experience is strong enough. In moments of high intensity or traumatic experiences, then time seems to slow down, each moment becomes separated from its neighbour and we notice many, many details that otherwise would be impossible. You yourself experienced how meditation can warp our experiences to time. So, all in all, time is not at all fixed for the human being, it is variable and subjective. Without structure or important events time becomes nothing more than a stream of small happenings. Stop and watch a stream. How do you count the water that passes, that has passed? How do you differentiate that water? What makes one bowl of water different, more important, of more value, than the others? Without structure and separation our lives are just rivers of time, passing before, in front of, and then behind us. Time for tea is just my little way of structuring my day, which I wanted to share with you this morning."

"And what will be the next stopping moment, lunchtime?" Maybe it was lack of food, but the young disciple seemed to be lacking a certain respect for aged Master this day.

"Exactly. You have clearly understood my point." There was no sign that he had noticed any of the sarcasm with which the last remark was heavily laced.

They carried on in silence.

"Lunchtime," announced the Master, not even an ounce of sarcasm in his voice.

"Lunchtime?" The question was closer to an exclamation of anger; the feelings of injustice and abuse were clearly expressed through the short phrase.

"Yes," responded the Master equably, "it is time to stop for lunch."

"But we have nothing to eat for lunch!"

"You haven't lost them, have you?" Now it was his turn to sound a little irritated.

"Lost what? I didn't bring anything to eat. What are you talking about?"

"That which you have carefully placed into your sack, which, if I am not mistaken, I pointed out, you would, at some point, be taking out again."

"The berries? The six berries? That is what you plan for lunch?"

"You don't have to eat them all." The anger was rising again. This day had been nothing but irritation after irritation, but now it was just plain mockery.

"I haven't come here just for you to make fun of me. Here." He thrust his hand into his sack, grabbing the berries, then held them out towards the old man. "You want some lunch, you can have mine. I'm going back the house to get some proper food."

"You will not!" Suddenly the Master seemed twice as tall and half his age. "You will not go anywhere!" he roared. "You will sit down and do as I say. That, or you return to the village and go work in the fields."

"At least if I am working in the fields I can go home for lunch. My mother would be pleased to know that I am eating correctly."

"Fine, off you go, then. When you pass by the monastery, if you would have the goodness, please ask them to send up another monk to accompany me." And with that, he turned away from the young man to concentrate on the six small, red spheres, gently rolling round in the palm of his hand.

"Just like that, after all you've put me through, you would let me leave?"

"I have no power to hold you, Dhargey. You are now a man; you must make your own decisions."

"But don't you even care if I stay or if I leave?"

"Of course I care, I care very much. You are my disciple, I am your Master, our journey should be long and fruitful. If you leave now, you would be throwing away a most wonderful opportunity."

"So why would you let me go like that?"

"As I have said, I cannot keep you against your will. But also, I do not know everything. Maybe your path is not with me, maybe your path will lead you to working in the fields."

"I could never work in the fields."

"That, only time will tell. Stay or leave, maybe just the same, you will finish your journey working in the fields."

"Not if I choose to stay and become a monk."

"Never be too sure of anything, my son. Are you ready to dine with me?"

"On six berries?"

"Maybe only five." And the old man's face broke out into the sunniest of smiles. "Remember how it was with the water this morning?" They had sat themselves down and the Master had passed him one of the berries.

"Yes, I remember clearly the experience of this morning."

"Take the berry into your mouth, but be very careful, you must not crush it. Roll it around with your tongue; touch it delicately with your teeth. The skin is very fine, it is easy to break, so be very careful as you move the berry. Good, good. Now slide it towards the back of your mouth."

Suddenly, his face contorted slightly, his eyes opened wide, and then he swallowed.

"I, I'm sorry, Master."

"Not to worry, we still have five left. Here, take another." He leaned across and offered him another berry.

All passed well until Dhargey was instructed to play with the berry with his lips; a slight error and the berry slipped out of his mouth and onto the dirty ground. He quickly bent down to retrieve it, but was stopped by the Master.

"Here, we do not need to eat off the ground, we are not animals. Here, take this one." The second berry was the last one to be lost; however, the third berry was not the last that he needed to take from the Master. While rolling it between his teeth and tongue, he applied too much pressure and the fragile fruit burst. The juice was intensely bittersweet.

"Aggh."

"I did warn you not to break into it."

"But it's horrible. Why have chosen these berries and not others?"

"When you succeed in the exercise, then you will understand. We will try again."

After several minutes of rolling the fruit all round his mouth, from the very tips of his lips to the back of his tongue, he was instructed to relax on a rock that supported his back and his neck.

"Allow yourself to melt into the rock, all the time keeping your new awareness on the small fruit that is exploring your mouth. Now it is time to acquaint yourself with it, to really get to know it. Feel its shape; it's not really totally round, is it?"

He noticed the small indentation of the point where the fruit joins the stem.

"Notice its weight, its texture, how rough, how smooth. How it feels as it passes from tongue to teeth, the roof and the floor of your mouth, how it feels on your lips and on each side of your cheeks."

He could feel the now familiar feeling of drifting off into an altered state. He was now somehow also his mouth, not having a mouth but being his mouth. Every sensation had become bigger, clearer, total. And the berry, the berry had become an enormous presence in his being; he could sense it, picture it, touch it, as if he was inside his own mouth, pushing it, not with his tongue, teeth, lips, and cheeks, but as if he were inside, pushing an object bigger than himself, pushing with his whole body.

He wasn't aware if the Master was still talking or not; it didn't matter anymore, his own experience was all-consuming.

Slowly, slowly, he was becoming aware of a change in the surface of the berry. It was becoming softer; the firm, tight skin was becoming more elastic, less tight He applied some pressure to the surface and it gave to his force. At the same time, he began to notice the smell, taste, and body sensation that came from when or where, he knew not.

His first reference was a type of tingling; was it his tongue, his lips, the roof of his mouth, or his whole body? He knew already the intense bittersweet taste of the juice, but now it was that yet so much more. He could see, feel, hear, smell, and taste the two opposing elements.

Bitter; dark, green-red, night, heavy, slow, rough, base and
Sweet; bright, red-yellow, day, light, fast, smooth, acute

The two opposing camps, individual and unique, but now not only, for the two groups began to move, to flow into each other, creating complex creations of competing and completing components.

He sang and danced and swam and drank the liquid magic, until finally it began to fade and so to die. After, he more than likely slept, for it was late in the afternoon when he finally came to.

"Was it worth not going home for lunch?"

"Master, what happened?"

"I told you that the berries were special, but you first had to allow your body to clean itself out of the heavy food that we eat; then, you needed to learn how to create the contact with the energy of the fruit. After that, well, you know the rest. Come, it is getting dark and we have quite a walk back home. Then we will eat and I will tell you some more of my story."

The Moving Memory Mudra

The monk brought me to his village and placed me with an old couple. Well, to my seven-year-old eyes, they were old; they were in their thirties, but were worn from work and from sorrow. The work, we all know of, but the sorrow was due to the fact that they were childless. To be childless is neither a crime nor a sin, but it is an excuse for much gossip and reflection from other members of the community.

They had tried many times. She had gone on pilgrimages to holy temples and relics, she had spent days praying, walking around the temples and prostrating herself to statues of Buddha and other deities. For days, she would wake up every morning at five o'clock, get up and take a walk, and then do prostrations for an hour to purify herself and prepare her womb for a baby to enter. She had gone to sacred caves, placed a strand of her hair on a sacred tree, and prayed for a baby to come, to choose her, to choose them as a couple.

For you see, to bring a baby into the world is a sacred act. The intermediate being, the unborn baby, has karma to work through with the help of its parents, who then can also advance on their own life paths. The parents and the baby and the intermediate being who will become that baby are drawn together by the circumstances of their previous lives and the experiences they need to have in the future. Not only do we pass our heritage to our children culturally and genetically, but spiritually as well. Not to have a baby means that you limit your own evolution and cannot help another soul, either—but you probably know all this anyway.

The monk explained to them that I was sick and needed a very special looking after. They took me in with all their heart and their soul. This strange child that hardly spoke, never showed any emotion, good or bad, happiness or sadness, they welcomed as an intermediate being, not yet of this earth, he who will come after.

I was not at all easy as a child. I would scream in the night, I would dream those awful dreams of silver points piercing through my father's flesh, of the swishing of the blade that severed my mother's head like a stuffed blue sheep's head prepared for a feast. In the day I would often sit and stare at the distance, lost to this world, with my back to the wall and facing the doorway, just in case someone dangerous would enter. Then there were the times when something—a rolling ball, the reflected sun, a storm, a fire, blood— would send me off to my world of horrors; when I would freeze into total silence and immobility.

I took the longest time to start to trust anyone. First, Amala, my new mother, who would hold me in her plump arms, rocking me back to sleep, night after night after night. Then Jampa, my new father, who would stop whatever he was doing to seek me out at any time during the day, if I was in crisis. He would gently pick me up, carry me back to the house, sit down on his favourite chair—outside in the summer, inside during the winter—and hold me on his knees and wait.

His solid, patient presence would slowly penetrate through into my world of panic and loss. His quiet, hard body became one with my little wooden box shelter. And finally it came to be that, even lost in my nightmare flashbacks, I began to learn that by returning to my miniscule hut, I would feel safe. I could curl myself into a ball of battered emotions and release myself into a sleep—a sleep which was, in itself, a means of escape.

I could fall asleep, knowing that I could then awaken, far, far away from the reddened ground and blackened homes.

Kunchen, the monk, would often take me with him, on walks or into the monastery. I loved the sights and smells and sounds of the prayer meetings, and I would lose myself in a better, softer, safer world, whenever he would bring me to this magical, sacred sanctuary.

It took much longer for the adults and the children to gain my trust; they found me very strange and not friendly. But, as with many things in life, that changed and grew with time, and eventually I settled in as an accepted member of the community.

What weren't changing were my nightmares and flashbacks.

Kunchen had already started to teach me meditation, in the hope that by relaxing my mind, body, and emotions, a natural healing process could set to work to mend my broken spirit.

One of the techniques that he taught me was based on breathing alternately through one nostril and then the other. This, he informed me, was called Anuloma Viloma. To do this, I had to take up the Padmasana or lotus position, fold my two middle fingers on my right hand to form the Pranav Mudra, and then alternately press one side of my nose with the two outside fingers or with my thumb. This meant that sometimes I breathed through my left nostril and sometimes I breathed through the right one.

Kunchen explained to me that the breath is connected with life energy, and by learning to regulate the breath, we purify and open natural channels for energy to move freely so that the soul can heal itself.

I really hated these exercises for quite a long time. It seems that most of us have one nostril that is more open than the other, and that we breathe more with that one than the other. The other one is much less used and so is less efficient.

When I started the pranayama exercises, every time I was supposed to breathe in with my right nostril, I felt that I was suffocating, that I was going to faint and then die. Kunchen, although very loving and caring of me, could also be very strict. He would never let me stop until I had completed the exercise as he insisted that I do.

Over time, my right nostril became as efficient as my left one, and I finally began to feel the benefits of the exercise. I began to feel calmer, more relaxed, and more in control. When I was outside and something started to drag me back to that awful day, I would concentrate on my alternate breathing and it would calm me. After some time, the flashbacks ceased altogether; my calming technique had become totally automatic. However, each time that would happen, I would have to cut off from what I was doing, and that was very disturbing for me and those around me.

71

One day Kunchen came to me in the morning. He seemed very excited.

"Come, Jangbu, he is here."

"Who is here?"

"The one I have told you about, the healer of the soul."

It was true, Kunchen had spoken sometimes about a mysterious healer, an old monk, who had built a special prayer wheel and, using certain types of meditation, could help people heal themselves of their bad experiences.

What I did not know was that Kunchen had sent out a request for him to come to the monastery to try and cure me.

Kunchen raced us both to the great gates, just in time to see the old monk, driving a yak cart, enter in front of us.

"Can we help you with your equipment?"

"You can, but the boy must not see anything until all is prepared." So I was sent away to wait until I was called. I wandered into the temple and absentmindedly spun a prayer wheel until they sent for me.

The room was quite small but very well lit. The sun streamed through the small window, directly illuminating the large prayer wheel which was, for the moment, hidden under a heavy grey cloth.

"Come and sit down, boy." He pointed to a chair directly underneath the window. As I never sat with my back to an open door or window, I made to drag the chair to the wall.

"Don't move the chair!" he screamed at me, as if I was about to break his favourite bowl.

"What?"

"Don't move the chair. It is positioned at an exact distance from the wheel."

"Can't you just move the wheel, then?" I might have sounded rude, but sitting on the chair as it was placed was not going to happen.

"The wheel has been positioned in a very specific place; it is to do with the entry of the light from the sun. It is also because of that that this chamber has been chosen."

"I don't care about the sun or anything else. I'm not going to sit on that chair unless I can move it against the wall." I was starting to panic. I stopped for a moment to calm myself down with the breathing, but it did no good. I couldn't sit there with my undefended back towards the open window.

Kunchen came to my rescue.

"Jangbu cannot sit where his back is not protected."

"Then go and protect his back, so we can start our work. The sun will not wait all day, and without the sun I cannot work."

"If I stand behind you and protect your back, will that be okay?"

"I don't know, we could try. Here, stand there behind the chair," I placed him behind the chair, facing me, and turned back towards the wheel. I then sat down on the chair. I could feel his presence; he was close enough to touch me. I felt safe.

"Okay, it's fine for me."

"But not for me. You are blocking the sun from lighting the wheel. Here, sit down, that will do." He dragged another chair towards us and Kunchen sat down behind me. I wasn't sure that that would do for me, but he sat down with his legs circling my chair, touched my back gently with his hands, and again I felt in security.

"Can we begin?"

"I am ready."

"Good. Kunchen informs me that you are familiar with the Anuloma pranayama exercise."

"Yes."

"Good, then you will begin."

"How many repetitions should I do?"

"Until I feel that you are ready to continue. You may begin." I was not used to doing this while sitting on a chair, but I managed to take up the Padmasana posture just the same. I folded my two middle fingers on my right hand and began pressing my right nostril with my right thumb, all the time breathing in through my left nostril. I had learnt that this was the most comfortable way for me to start the exercise.

Even with my eyes closed, I knew that he was moving around the room and then walking behind me. I started to tense up. Kunchen must have noticed the change in my posture and guessed what was happening, as he gently placed both of his hands on the level of my shoulder blades, to comfort me and remind me that he was, literally, guarding my back.

I started to relax again, then I noticed that it had suddenly gone dark. Even with my eyes closed; even when concentrating on counting the seconds for the in-breath, the non-breath, the out-breath, and the waiting-breath, and how many times for each side; even while meditating on the flow of energy within my body, I still noticed that it had become dark in the room.

I stopped the exercise and opened my eyes.

"I have not told you to stop yet or to open your eyes." He was standing between me and the wheel. There was just one thick strip of sunlight that lit his chin and mouth. It was if he was speaking from behind a mask.

"Sorry." And with that, I returned to the breathing exercise.

"Enough, you may open your eyes and sit normally." I did as I was asked. There was another man in the room, a young monk that I had seen in and around the monastery. He was standing to one side of the room.

The old man moved out of the way of the prayer wheel. It was quite big, the thickness was about three times the size of my head, and it was as high as I was tall. It was all black with white inscriptions. Around the upper and lower rims were a number of prayers, but other than that there was nothing on it except one single design almost on line with my eyes. It was a hand, and on the tips of the two fingers visible there were red markings.

"You know, of course, the Pranav Mudra; you have been using it just now." It was exactly that, the two middle fingers bent into the palm and the two end fingers straight up, with the red colour on the fingertips.

He walked up to a point beside my head. He looked at the position of my eyes and the tilt of my head. "Bring it down two points." The monk, who had clearly been explained the mechanism, pushed a lever down twice. With each press, the wheel descended a little bit. The old man looked again at me.

"Look directly at the red fingertips," he said, which I did. "Down one more notch." The monk did as he was asked and the wheel dropped a little more. "Good."

He walked again towards the wheel. "When I start to move the wheel, you will follow the fingertips with your eyes. You will not move your head at all. When I stop moving it, you will take a deep breath. You may let your eyes close; you may let your head droop. Is this clear?"

"Yes, Master."

"Good. Now we need to talk a little of your past."

I could already feel the panic starting to rise. "Must we?"

"I see that you are already starting to connect with some feelings; that is good. I will explain what we will do and what is going to happen. We are going to find the most significant moment of your trauma. You will return to that moment, you will see it, you will feel it in your body. You will connect with all the sights, sounds, smells, thoughts, and feelings that are linked to that moment. I will move the wheel, and you will follow the fingers with your eyes, not with your head. You will notice what is happening with your thoughts and your feelings, but you will say nothing for the moment. I will stop the wheel, and you will take a deep breath. You may let your eyes close; you may let your head droop. Then I will ask you if there is anything that you wish to express. When you have expressed that which you need to express, then we will begin again."

"How long will we continue for?"

"Until it is done." There seemed to be nothing more to be said.

"Is this all clear for you?"

"Yes, Master."

"Then we will begin. First, and very importantly, if you should start to feel very unwell, you are to close your eyes and restart the

76

pranayama immediately. That will calm you down." This I knew and trusted.

"Now." His voice seemed to change; it became slower, richer, dreamy. "Now, I want you to let yourself drift back to that day, to the worst day of your young life."

"Do I have to?" Again I was panicking. I couldn't, shouldn't, mustn't; it was more than I could deal with. Again I felt the soft, strong, comforting hands of Kunchen protecting my back. He would now be with me; I wouldn't be quite so alone.

"What is the very, very worst moment that you experienced?" I thought back.

"My father was pierced with a spear, then my mother's head was chopped off and it flew towards me, and then the horse— that great big, black horse—might have crushed me, and the rider, with his thick black moustache, might find and kill me."

"And yet, for you, none of these are the very worst moment that you experienced." How did he know? By what magic could he see that there was something even worse?

"What was that moment, that moment when you held your hands balled up so tight, like you are doing now?" I hadn't noticed, but I was clenching my fists so tightly that they were beginning to hurt.

"Come, come, your body has given you away. You must not hide it anymore. Tell us, tell us, Jangbu, when did you stop feeling?" It was no good, he had ripped the protective cover off my memory. It was there again, as I was.

"It was when I had got to the village. I hoped that there would be some people left, left alive. There were many dead, mostly the men. I didn't see any women or children, they must have run away or been taken by the riders. It was then that I realised there was nobody to help me, to look after me, to save or protect me. I was alone, alone, alone..." My voice trailed off.

"Well done. Now keep that moment, that image, in front of you and follow the fingers with your eyes." I really didn't want to; I just wanted to curl up somewhere and go to sleep on my father's lap, and then the badness would fade away. But then again, I knew that I couldn't, that here I was and this was my opportunity to deal with this horror, once and for all. Kunchen had done well his job of convincing me that this monk could help where no other could. Well, we were all here, and now was the time to do this.

I followed the finger. I didn't seem to be thinking or feeling anything. It wasn't easy to follow, it went very quickly. First in one direction, until I could only see the hand with the eye on the same side, as it half disappeared around the side of the prayer wheel, then back, quickly towards the other side, again half disappearing around that side, where I could only follow it with the other eye. Like a game of passing the stick from one hand to the other, as quickly as possible, without thinking but without letting it drop from one hand until it was firmly in the grasp of the other.

"Move your eyes, not your head!" I had let the movement attract my head as well. We continued for a few more moments until he stopped the wheel. Suddenly the room was in total darkness. The other monk must have dropped a cover over the window, blocking out the rest of the light.

"A deep breath and then release." I breathed in deeply, held it for a few seconds, and then slowly let the air out, and some of my tension with it.

I cannot move. The village is on fire. Maybe he will come back and finish me off; then he would have killed the whole family this day. It seems that my legs are blocked, fixed to the ground, unable and unwilling to move. To move where, to do what? There is no one else but me, nowhere to go, nothing to do. Please, please come back, do it quick, like you did with them. They did not see you coming; they did not see you take out your spear or your axe; they did not see you prepare for their deaths. And then, in just the shortest instant it was done, it was over, this life had ended for them. All the hardship and sorrow and misery were transformed in an instant, their karma washed clean with their innocent blood. Well, here I am, standing, waiting, waiting for you to deliver me to death. I have nothing left to live for, you have seen to that. Now, please, I only ask for you to release me from this life. Then I can go and seek them out, if no more in this life, then in lives to come.

And I wait, and I wait and I wait, but he doesn't come, and I am forced to accept life and the empty loneliness that awaits me.

"Are you ready?" I raise my head to look at him, the light returns. "Do you have anything that you wish to share?"

"I wanted to die. I wanted him to come back and kill me, too." We waited in silence for a moment.

"You are a very brave boy. Keep being brave and carry on." With that, he moved out of the narrow beam of light, relighting the hand, the fingers that I was to follow, but only with my eyes, not with my head.

I continued to focus on the moving fingertips, the to-ing and fro-ing. I found it strangely soothing, even though I was still in the clutches of that awful moment.

"Stop, breathe, release." I re-plunged into my history.

Here I am, lost, alone, cold, and wretched. There is nothing to do, but doing nothing is no longer an option. He is not coming; I will not die this day. I have to move, I have to move away from this place, I need to look for and find a place of safety.

I run back to my wooden shelter. I avoid looking towards the bodies of my parents; I avoid the spot where my mother's head might have rolled. I crawl back into my little box, it is warm, it is safe. I fall asleep on the lap of my father, his soft, strong hand stroking my hair. I am safe.

I recount the experience to the old monk. "Can I go now?" "No, we have just begun. Connect again to the negative thoughts and feelings, and continue."

Again and again, my eyes followed the moving fingers.

Again I was standing on the edge of the village, this time fascinated by the flames, as if I'd never seen them before, how wonderful, how beautiful. I didn't want to leave, I had nowhere else to go, but I knew that I had to.

I left the village. Walking back towards the field, I could see the end of the pole sticking up, almost straight into the air. I walked over to the corpse of my dead father, knelt down, and kissed him on the back of the head.

I went to the body of my mother. I could not look directly at her headless trunk, but I found one of her hands. I held it gently in my own, then I kissed it softly, laid it back on the broken barley stalks, and walked off.

I walked through village until I found our house; it was burning like the others. I walked into the flaming building, looking for something. Here, lying on the ground, was a doll made for me when I was a baby. I wrapped it up in a cloth and found a shawl; I took them to my mother's body. I folded the baby in her arms, keeping my eyes closed so as not to see that there was no head, then I covered it all in the shawl. Then I could finally look at her and tell her goodbye.

I stood in the village, then turned and found myself in our village. I was alone, no one would play with me, I was too strange for the children to approach and I was too frightened of them to make the first step. I held out my hand and a girl came and took it. She pulled me gently to the children, I accepted coming and they accepted that I came.

I look at the burning village. It is no longer my village; like all the people, it is dead to me. I am no longer interested in coming to it. I turn from the village, but then turn back to wave goodbye. My hands are no longer clenched, they are open and relaxed.

The session is finished.

It takes time for scars and habits to change and to heal, but from that day, I began to have fewer and fewer flashbacks and less and less nightmares. However, I would still wake up screaming most nights, but my loving, caring, patient parents did not care. They knew, at last, why they never had any children of their own. Their karma was to wait for me, a very special child that would need very special parents. Things happen as they should.

The Power of Four

"Today," the Master said, looking up from his steaming cup of Po Cha, "is a four day."

"A for day? A day for something?"

"No, today is a day to honour the number four." He smiled at his young disciple.

"And how should we honour the number four? Drink four cups of tea and eat four Zanba cakes?"

"No, but the idea is certainly tempting. Come," he said, starting to stand, "it is time to begin."

"Are we to be going far today, Master?" Dhargey had become suspicious of daylong journeys without taking food or drink.

"No, today your body will not journey far from here."

"What does that mean?"

"That we will drink and eat our four cups of Po Cha and four Zanba cakes here, during the day and evening."

Dhargey, clearly relieved, quickly cleared the breakfast dishes and was soon ready to leave.

The Master walked for some minutes up the mountain path, turned towards a little hillock, and stopped atop its grassy knoll. Dhargey stood and waited, watching him, wondering what he would do next.

"Well, what are you waiting for?"

"For you, Master. Where are we going now?"

"In what sense do you mean, where are we going now?"

"In the sense of, where are we going now?"

"So much to learn, so much to learn. Come here, boy." He walked up to the old man. "Come, stand here, what do you feel?"

"I feel the ground under my feet."

"And?"

"My clothes?"

"And?"

"And? And what?"

"What else do you feel?"

"Confused, irritated?"

"Oh my gods, I've been sent a complete idiot. You are standing on a hill, on the top of a mountain. Is there not maybe something that you might feel because of that?"

"Well, it's still quite early. I'm feeling a little cold."

"And what makes you feel cold?"

"Not much sun?"

"Keep going."

"There's a bit of a cold breeze."

"Exactly, there is the air."

"Yes, there is air on the top of mountains." His tone might just have lacked a little respect, but the Master didn't seem to notice this slip.

"Yes, here we are perfectly in contact with the air, pure, flowing, life-giving air. Now, sit down here, as I have shown you." The trainee monk sighed heavily; he was having problems adapting his body to the lotus position.

"Do the best you can." He could see that Dhargey was in difficulty. "Today, the focus is on other things."

"What other things?"

"The four, of course."

"Of course, the four."

"Yes," he nodded, with a smile, "of course, the four. Now, listen very carefully to my voice, very carefully. At some point, your eyes will feel heavy and start to close. Allow them to, it is normal and will help you to concentrate on the other experiences. Allow your body to breathe naturally. Good, good. Now, concentrate on the feeling of the air as it touches the exposed parts of your body. As your body breathes, the body and the air become one. As the air brushes your skin, the skin and the air become one. As the air contacts the parts of you, you and the air become one. You and the air, you are the air. Lighter and lighter you become; like a feather, a petal, and a cloud. Floating, lifting, flying, falling. You are the wind, the breeze, the squall, the gust, the gale. Up, up, up you go, light as the air, strong as a hurricane. Off you go, experience the air in all its forces. Stay as long as you wish, and when you have experienced all you have to experience, I will be waiting for you here. Enjoy."

And with that, the Master found himself a sunny spot next to a rock and sat himself down. Leaning back on the rounded stone, he too closed his eyes and released his aged body.

He was light, he was fast, he was supple, he was free. He had power, he had grace, he had size, he had space. He was here, there, and everywhere. The experience was enormous, limitless, infinite.

And yet, being formless, without shape or size, brought fear to the experience. Without a clear physical form, without limits or boundaries, he had no protection. Unsubstantial, weightless, drawn up, down, and across the earth's surface, he was also powerless and helpless.

The excitement had passed; a heavy sadness pulled him back down towards his heavy, safe, limited body. It was time to return, to release the air and to resume his individual, human existence.

He was hungry, it must be lunchtime. He stretched, yawned, and opened his eyes.

"At last. I was thinking that you would never finish. What is an old Master to do to get some lunch round here?"

"Don't worry," he said, hurrying down the slope, "lunch will not be a long time coming."

"I should hope not." And he too started down towards their little homestead.

Lunch passed in silence, each one keeping to his own thoughts and experiences.

"Shall we continue?"

"Yes, Master, I am ready."

The walked together, still in silence. The disciple was in a very contemplative mood, still partly linked to the morning's experience, while also wondering what the afternoon might bring.

They stopped by a fast-flowing stream.

"Take off your clothes and lie in the waters."

"Yes, Master." There was no need for discussion or questioning.

"Good. How is the water?"

"It is cool and refreshing, Master."

"You will join with the waters; flowing, ebbing, seeking, swirling, buoying up, dragging down, bringing death yet being the source of all life. The cold black of the depths, the heaving waves of the storm, the wild rushing floods, the peaceful blue lagoon, the clear fresh mountain streams. You are one with the waters. Feel as she flows around and through you, as you become softer and smoother, longer and lighter, and finally liquid."

After a full lunch, a walk in the hot afternoon sun, and now lying in the refreshing, relaxing, gurgling stream, it didn't take much before he had released contact with his restrictive body and had become part of the gushing, rushing, pulsing waters—plummeting downstream, heading somehow towards the rivers, and somewhere, way, way down, was the ever-beckoning sea and home.

Being water was similar to being air; the feeling of body limits was removed. The connection with all the waters of the earth was there, but the link was not total. Yes, his part of the stream was directly linked to all the stream above and the rivers below, and, by stretching his consciousness, even to the seas and oceans, vast and profound. But not all the seas were joined, nor did all the rivers end in a sea; some just filtered down into the rocks, losing their sense of unity in the process. Or when the water evaporates, again it loses its connexion with the whole, becoming individual tiny droplets, later to fall as rain or condense as dewdrops.

Although there exists static water, in ponds and such, for the most part, the waters were all in constant movement; the streams and rivers seeking out the downward paths; the waves, lifted and stoked by the winds and then below the surface; the swirling, churning, sucking, thrusting currents.

It was, finally, the associating with the currents that pushed him out of the experience. The force was too great and the twisting too strong; he was starting to feel slightly nauseous.

He took a deep breath and shook himself back into this ordinary reality; the water was starting to feel cold. The sun had started to descend and the air was already becoming cooler.

"Come, let us make a fire so that you can dry off and we can make ourselves a nice hot cup of Po Cha. We have also promised ourselves some Zanba cakes to go with it, have we not?"

The fire and the tea and cakes were most welcome, but the day was far from over, so they then gathered up their blankets and returned up the mountain.

"Choose a rock."

"How big?"

"Big enough to lean on."

"Will this do?"

"How does it feel for you?"

"I suppose that it is okay."

"Then I feel that it is okay, too. Just sit down and lean on the rock. Good. Allow your body to move at any time so that you can contact it in different ways, with different parts of your body. For the moment, the rock seems hard, it resists your body. And yet, without any effort on your part, just by being here, just by sitting quietly, just by letting yourself relax, by letting yourself go. Yes, let your eyes close, that's good, that's very good. By letting your body relax into the rock, the rock will welcome you and you will become one with it. There is nothing to do, only to be—be here, be yourself, be open, be the rock."

The experience came very slowly, gently, and peacefully. At one point he was himself, and yet then he was one with the rock. It wasn't as if the rock had opened and he had dropped inside it. No, he just became a rock.

The first thing that he noticed was the speed, or rather the lack of it; the rhythm of the rocks was a hundred or maybe a thousand times slower than our rhythm. The idea, the concept of rushing, couldn't exist, just as the idea of patience, being such an integral part of the rocks, didn't exist either. The rocks are part of the earth, as are all the plants and trees, and of course, the earth itself. The rich, black, solid earth, like an ocean, is also a mother of all things; all things either are created through her or grow from within her.

He descended into her darkest depths; he touched the fiery, molten core; he tasted some of her many territories—the peaty bogs, the sandy deserts, the humid forests, the hard mountains, and the soft grassy plains. He felt the richness of gold, of diamonds, of copper, of iron, of salt, and of a thousand other minerals. All these, and yet nothing could compare with the infinite varieties of trees and flowers and grasses and plants growing from within the outermost extremity of his earthy skin.

Time had neither sense nor meaning, and it was only the sound of his Master's voice, gently calling him back, that forced him to return to the consciousness of a human being.

"It is time."

"Time for what, Master?"

"Why, to eat, of course. Why else did I bring you up the mountain with me? Not to spend the whole evening resting on a rock. Your job is to look after me. And now it's time for me to eat."

And so, slowly, as he had not yet accelerated back to human speed, he got up and drifted off to prepare the evening meal.

"Look into the fire." They had finished eating some time ago and were gently nursing a salty cup of Po Cha in their hands. "What do you see?"

"The flames dancing, wisps of blue escaping from the fresh wood, red and black embers."

"Build the fire high; she needs to dance even more."

"Is that high enough for you, Master?"

"Yes, yes, that is quite high enough. Come and sit again."

"Would you like another cup of tea, Master?"

"Maybe later. Come, come sit. No, come sit here on the floor, in front me. Yes, it is okay for you to lean on my legs. Good, yes, good. The fire is exciting, isn't it?"

"Yes, it is exciting."

"Look, look closely into it, and listen carefully to my voice. Feel the friendly warmth of the fire, feel the burning threat of the fire. Notice how it feeds us with its heat, notice how it feeds itself from the wood. Notice how you are feeling that you are being drawn in by her dance, her shadow play, her sizzling sparks, her sensual, languid flames. Go dance with her; give yourself to the heat of her passion—GO."

It was so very easy to just slide into the energy of the fire; to jump, to dance, to rage, to shriek, to cry. Everything and everywhere was movement and action. Again time was different, but this time it was accelerated; life was only the instant, the now. Being here meant living every single instant, every single second, as if it was the only and last moment of your total existence.

He was just a moth in a flame; it was the most wonderful, exciting, dangerous, and destructive experience of his life, and so much more so because it just couldn't last and was never to be repeated. He lived it fully, until she began to falter and die. There was nothing he could do for her. He couldn't leave to add more wood, because if he did, then he could never return. But by not leaving, he would have to stay and share in her death. And yet that was exactly what he had to do; the life of a fire is short and intense. He had drunk from and bathed in the fury of her appetites; now he was to witness her weakening towards cold and death. The final flames were ebbing into the smouldering embers; the fire was slowing and cooling. The time had come for final farewells, and so it was...

"Thank you, Master, for this four day."

"And thank you for your participation." They smiled and made their way to bed.

The Fire in the Ice

The months passed, life settled into its rhythms, summer passed and the winter blew in. This village was much higher up than mine; the winter brought cold and snows. I fell sick; not terribly, not awfully, but enough to bring down my already fragile mood. I almost stopped eating altogether; I lived almost entirely on warmed yak's milk.

Slowly, slowly, the winter and my sickness passed, but my mood did not improve. A shaft of barley can be bent, even walked on, and it can straighten and grow, but if you roll on it for a while you break its will to strive, and it just lies there until it rots with the weeds.

I had been rolled on too much by life and now there was no more spring in my soul to stretch up to the sun and reach for the skies. I was flat and listless, nothing interested me. My new parents were totally at a loss for what to do.

Kunchen had been sent away for some months, and was very concerned on his return to find me in this sorry state.

Some days later he sent a message for me to come to the monastery. As it was early March, I was to bring clothes warm enough to spend some time outdoors. My parents were concerned that, with my fragile health, this wasn't a good idea, but it was Kunchen who had brought me to them, and as he clearly had my best interests at heart, they sent me off as asked.

There was still much snow on the ground, and the path leading up to the monastery was often blocked by drifting snow, or icy, where the snow had been mostly blown away and the afternoon sun had melted what was left, only for it to freeze over during the night.

I thought several times about stopping and turning back to the safe warm house of my parents, but I loved and respected Kunchen, and I was also a little afraid to disobey a monk. So I trudged on, finding the force within necessary to overcome the white barriers and the transparent traps.

The chambers in the monastery were not cold; they had little ovens, covered in decorated tiles, that heated up slowly and even more slowly let the heat out in the room. When I arrived, after taking off my hat with four flaps, my fur jacket, and boots, he then sent me to the kitchen to fetch us both a bowl of hot milk.

"Come, Jangbu, sit here against this column. Good. Now drink, and notice the warm milk flowing down your throat and gently heating you from the inside."

I sat and meditated on the warm milk and its journey from my mouth, down into my throat, and then finding its path to my belly. He then began to tell me a story.

✳ ✳ ✳

Once, a long, long time ago, when people still believed in bears as tall as two men and elephants as big as temples, there lived a tribe of people. These people had lived in the same place for many generations, but year after year the winters became colder and harder and longer.

Eventually, the elders of the tribe decided that they would have to leave their caves and risk to travel south, in the hope of finding another land where they might settle and call their home.

The new winter was coming, so they hastened to prepare their limited belongings for the long journey, for they had seen how the winters had already pushed many animals south, and they realised that if they expected to find a new living space and not have to move again soon, they would have to journey many moons to escape the advancing cold.

The going would be difficult, especially for the older members of the tribe, and one in particular would have to pass on her important function because she was no longer able to walk and to fulfil her mission. This woman's job was the "keeper of the flame." For in that time, man did not know how to create fire, he only knew how to capture it and keep it alive so that the tribe could cook and keep safe and warm.

The fire was kept in a special box, fed constantly with animal fat, which kept it steadily burning.

There was a long discussion amongst the tribe elders. The keeper of the fire was traditionally a woman, but for this long and difficult journey, maybe it would be better to leave the job to one of the young men—fit, strong, and healthy.

They had all but made their decision as to which man to give this important task to, when an old man stepped into the firelit circle.

"Do you not wait for my presence or my words before making such decisions?"

"I am sorry, caster of bones, I thought that you were asleep. We did not want to disturb you."

"You did not want me to interfere, you mean." It was true, there was a certain conflict between the leader of the tribe and the old sage. The old man often questioned the younger man's choices, and this time the leader had wished to discuss the situation without the older member's input.

"So you wish to pass the task of keeper of the fire to a man, do you?"

"It would be more reasonable to give the job to a man."

"The gods are not reasonable, and if we upset them they can be even more unreasonable."

"What would you suggest?" It was another man that asked the question.

"I will ask, as any intelligent man would." Here he shot an ugly look at the leader. He then bent down and drew a circle in the dry earth, chose one of the bags hanging from his worn belt, thrust his hand in, and threw the small bones in the direction of the circle. He then bent down and counted the number of bones that had landed inside the dusty circle.

"Twelve. Find me all the children of twelve suns, and bring them here now." Two of the men separated themselves from the group and went off to find the children that had reached twelve years old.

Some minutes later they returned with three young people. There were two boys and a girl. One of the boys had trouble walking; he had gotten a thorn in his foot as a child, which had become poisoned, and though it eventually healed, he could never walk properly again. The other two were both quite healthy; the main difference was, while the boy was confident and courageous, the girl was quiet and nervous.

"Well," reflected the leader on sizing up the three possible candidates, "there seems to be little question as to which of the three will take over the role of keeper of the fire. Granted, he with the bad foot must be excused from the task, but the two others seem equally fit and therefore equally capable of assuming such a role."

The others waited patiently to see what would happen next. The leader made as if to speak, but then thought better of it and joined the other men to wait for the old man to continue.

"Here," he said, and brought out another sack of bones, "collect the small bones and put them in here." He gave the first sack to the girl. "Carefully empty this sack into the circle and spread out the bones," he said, giving the second sack to the boy.

Both did as they were told, and a few minutes later the small bones were rearranged in their sack and the larger bones were spread out in the circle.

"Now," he continued, "each of you is to choose one bone that you feel is right for you." The two children looked questioningly, first at the sage, then at the other men. "Just look at the bones and pick any one that feels right for you. It is not difficult. Better not to take too long to think about it. Here, turn towards the bones, pick one, bend down, and pick it up."

The boy, without further hesitation, hunched his shoulders, bent down, and picked up one of the largest bones. The girl hesitated for a moment more before choosing her bone, smaller and curved.

"You see," cried the old man, somewhat pleased with himself, "this is what I thought." Of course, everyone looked at him in a totally confused way. He then shook his head. "You really don't understand anything, do you? Look, here," he said, and took the bone from the boy, "this is a leg bone, good for running, towards or away from things. This is one who is good for hunting, for catching, for escaping; we have no need of that here. Now," he said, taking the bone from the girl, "do you know where this bone comes from?" He looked around the group for a second before continuing. "This bone comes from here." He placed his hand on his chest. "This is one of the bones that protects the heart. It does nothing else. That is the type of person we need to protect the heart of our people, one whose only function is to protect the fire, and who will do no more."

The men looked around and then to their chief. The leader took some moments before speaking.

"This is not my decision. I do not agree with it, and I will not agree to it, but I will not go against it. If the rest of you choose to accept this choice, then the choice is made." And with that, he got up and returned to his cave to get a good night's sleep. There were still many things to be done before starting the long and difficult journey, leading his people to an unknown but hopefully more hospitable world.

The other men had all left, leaving the young girl and the old man alone.

"But I cannot be the new keeper of the fire." She was almost in tears. "Please, please choose someone else."

"There is no one else to choose, the choice has been made."
"But I can't do it. I will fail, and then there will be no fire and then the tribe might die."

"You have been chosen, not be me but by yourself. You are the new keeper of the fire and you will bring fire to our new land." And with that, he slowly raised himself up and disappeared into the outer darkness, leaving the young woman staring hopelessly into the fire, of which she was now both mistress and servant.

She didn't sleep well, and worse still, the whole tribe awoke to hear an awful row between the chief and the old sage.

"We are not ready to leave yet. The meat is not dried, and there is fruit ready to be gathered. We will leave when the moon is full!"

"Listen to me, I have seen the omens; as the sun was rising, I saw a flock of birds already flying to the south. Then to be sure, I cast the bones; most fell in the same direction. It is clear as day, we must leave now. Maybe it is already too late, since even the winter berries have started to appear."

"But we are not prepared, if we are caught in the mountains with nothing to eat, then we will all die."

"If we do not get far enough south before the worst of winter hits us, then we shall surely all die before the spring."

"I will call another meeting of the elders tonight."

"We should leave today."

"If they agree with you, then we will leave tomorrow."

"Then you have one day to prepare."

"If they agree with you."

"Prepare to leave tomorrow, for I have read the signs. You, keeper of the fire, come here to me." He had noticed her, watching the row.

"Yes, what do you want?"

"Have you spoken to her, the one you will replace?"

"Not yet."

"Then hurry yourself. We will leave tomorrow and she must show you what you must do."

"I have already watched her; she is my aunty and would look after me when my mother would go off gathering."

"Do you know the sacred songs of the fire?"

"I am not supposed to know them." She lowered her eyes as she spoke.

"Good, it is important that you know them. Go to her now. I will come soon and hand over the fire to you. Practice the songs with her. It is important that the fire is called properly."

That night he appeared to the whole tribe, clad in his sacred bear skin; the small teeth bones made a collar for his neck, the large teeth, almost twice as big as the girl's hands, hung on the belt around his waist. He could no longer wear the upper part of the bear's head as a headdress; it was now much, much too heavy for his old neck. His young apprentice carried it respectfully behind.

"We of the bear tribe know about the winter. We know how the bear dies and is reborn each spring, so we know of death and rebirth. Our lives here, in this place where our fathers and their fathers and their fathers before them lived, will die and we will never live here again. So it is the way of all things; the moon grows and dies, the trees and bushes grow with each new sun, it is so. I have seen the omens, I have seen the signs, I have asked the questions of the spirits, and we must leave as quickly as possible. The long winter is coming and she is coming now! We must leave immediately. We should have left today; tomorrow we are already in danger."

He didn't wait for any discussion or disagreement; he just looked once at each and every member of the tribe, turned, and returned to his cave. The chief readied himself to start a discussion, but it was already too late; many of the tribe had started to leave. The old man's word was not law, but few would dare to ignore a direct message from the spirits.

The next day everybody collected what was most dear and important to them. The men had all their most sturdy hunting gear; the women carried sacks for gathering and utensils for cooking. The children carried what food they could, as did everyone that could carry more than they needed.

Only the keeper of the fire carried nothing more than the firebox; the animal fat to feed it with and dry mosses and fine sticks, so as to light another fire when needed. She kept mostly to herself, sometimes humming, sometimes singing quietly to the fire, sometimes just walking and climbing in silence. There was nothing that forced her to isolate herself from the others; some women would lead a very social life while watching the fire. It was her own personality and choice to keep her own company.

For the first few days, the walk, although long and difficult, was without incident. On the fourth day came the first accident, one of the women slipped climbing down a hill where the rocks were small and moving. She slipped and grazed her leg. It was not a disaster, but it was only the first of many of such events.

To begin with, it was the old man, although he himself had difficulty walking, who was constantly demanding that they walked faster, took fewer breaks, and slept only when the sun was not in the heavens.

Then they started to notice the heavy grey clouds appearing in the north, and the increasingly cold winds that started blowing from that very same direction. Now it was the chief, realising that he had erred to have ignored the sage's predictions, who starting pressuring the tribe to advance as quickly as possible.

It was this pressure from the chief and a heavy rainstorm which created the recipe for the disaster that followed. The storm had begun to threaten from early morning, and although they all knew that it was coming, there seemed to be little choice but to continue.

The firebox was built like a house, with a type of roof that sloped down all four sides, and four walls reaching almost up to the roof part, which overlapped the wall, leaving a small space, protected by the overhang, for the air to enter and the smoke to exit, all the while protecting the precious flame from wind and rain.

By high sun, the rain had started to fall; heavier and heavier it flooded down. Nobody dared to complain; the chief was giving no signs of stopping, and there weren't many places to stop, either.

It was already a water course, but with the rains it had become a foaming river. They crossed over, using the great boulders as huge stepping-stones; slipping and sliding over as best they could.

Falling off the boulders and into the frothy waters was painful and unpleasant, but without great consequence—for everyone, that is, who wasn't assigned the difficult task of keeping the fire safe and dry. Twice, she lost her balance, but caught herself in last moment. Once, she even fell into the river, and by a miracle kept the box high and dry, but, as nothing in life is eternal, luck has its limits, and when a vicious gust of wind pushed her off balance, just as her left foot slipped on a wet rock face, she fell backwards, totally into the rushing waters. The moss, the twigs, the box, and the fragile flames were all immediately submerged in the icy, wet, wet waters.

The rain streaked her face with tears, wretched, wretched girl. She had failed her sacred task and there was no more to be done or said.

If this wasn't bad enough, worse was to come. The white demons came in the night. As the tribesmen tried to find some warmth in their furry skinned covers, still wet from the rain and, for some, the icy river bath, the last thing they needed was the snow.

Flakes of cold and wet, creating their own blankets of frosted misery, shrouded the sad group. Without fire for heat or light, there was nothing they could do except shiver in their skins and wait for the feeble morning sun to light the path enough for them to continue.

The girl kept even more to herself than before, not daring or wishing to approach the others for fear of being scolded for having lost the precious fire.

There was nothing to do but continue. The only person that didn't seem to be too concerned, strangely enough, was the old man. Firstly, he was quietly satisfied that he had been proven right—they should have left immediately. If they had heeded his directive, they wouldn't have lost the fire and they might even have avoided the first snows. Secondly, there had been signs along the way that had portended good omens for the journey: one of the small horse creatures had run alongside them for a moment; a bird had landed on a rock face and had spoken to him in his mind; even the river, crashing and foaming, had given him hope, as only one that knew how to contact the elements would be able to understand.

That night he sought out the girl, sitting alone except for her misery and guilt.

"Don't trouble yourself too much, my daughter."

"But I have lost the fire. I have failed the task that you have given me, and maybe we all shall die because of my clumsiness."

"No, we will not die because you have lost the fire. The fire from our old home had to die; it was part of the death of leaving our old world. There is a new world out there, a world that we know little about, a world that is changing, and we need to release the old, so as to be able to receive the new."

"But the fire is part of our lives. We do need it to live."

"Our ancestors survived without fire, we know, because we are here. Look, now is the time of change, a time of miracles, a time of—look, look, look up there!" In amazement, they looked to the heavens to see a silver streak pass overhead, only to dive down, behind the mountain they had just descended.

"You see? A miracle! What I have been talking about, a miracle."

"But what is it, father?"

"I have heard that it must be a part of the sun that has been sent to earth as a warning to us not to forget that the sun must be honoured and respected."

"But what is the sun?"

"It is the God of Fire."

"Then that must also be made of fire."

"What are you doing? Where are you going?"

"I am going to catch some of the sun's fire."

"But it is not possible, and it is night. It is dangerous to go, even for a man, in the night, in the snow."

"It makes no difference. I cannot stay with the tribe after losing the fire. I cannot face anyone, I am too ashamed. I am dead already; nobody will look at me, either. I would sooner die trying to do something for the good than die from shame."

"Listen, I knew that the fire would die. It was not your fault. If we would have left when I said so, we would still have it. It is the fault of that idiot of a chief."

"Why did I get the task of keeper of the fire?"

"Because it was meant to be."

"Then maybe I am meant to go and seek the fire of the sun."

"Maybe, maybe, but it troubles me that you might never return."

"Then I will be an offering to the gods, and then they might offer us again the fire."

"Here, take a tooth of the giant bear, it will bring you luck and protection."

"Thank you. Goodbye." And with that, she took the firebox and her sack over her shoulder, stuffed the long bear's tooth, now hanging round her neck, roughly into her tunic, and faded into the heavy night.

The going was not easy; fortunately, the snow clouds had cleared and a weak moon shone a soft, diffused light to give some illumination to the climb, but the slope was covered with layers of snow and ice. More than once she caught herself in the last moment so as not to slip down between the rocks.

If there had been the least doubt in her mind as to the rightness of the choice and the impossibility of continuing with the tribe without finding a new fire, she would surely have stopped quite early on and turned back. As she felt that without the fire, her life had no more meaning, she gritted her teeth and fought on.

Time passed; she had no idea if it was long or short. She had left the ordinary world of existence. She sang to the fire, she prayed to the fire, she called to the fire and the fire called back. The path became obvious, her hands and feet occupied themselves with her physical movements; she had no need to concern herself about such things now.

> Oh fire, fire of life, fire of love, fire of heart.
> Fire from above, fire from below,
> Fire that comes with the rain
> And fire that comes from the dry
> Fire of the earth
> And fire of the sky
> Fire that warms

Fire that burns
Fire that lights
Fire that cooks
Fire that brings death
And fire that brings life
Come to me, oh fire
And I shall warm you with my life.

She felt neither cold nor warm; was there rain, was there wind, was there snow?

There was nothing, nothing of this world, her world was elsewhere.

She was now no longer climbing, she moving upwards, propelled by the energy that she had contacted by her song. Her soul had been joined with another, not human, not material, not of this time nor of this place, but a soul that resonated with her young, pure, innocent, girl-child's soul. And together, the two kindred spirits travelled up the slippery slope without a thought, without a pause, because the slope only exists in our world and in the world through which the two were connected; that obstacle wasn't existing.

Suddenly, she found herself arriving at the top of the incline, onto a wide, flat ledge. In front of her was a thick curtain of steam. The burning mass had buried itself into the ledge, and the thick carpet of snow all round was melting and boiling in the incredible heat.

She had had no thought as to what to do when she arrived close to this fragment of the burning sun, and now, here she was, still no clearer.

For the first moments she just stood and looked at the wondrous sight; the thick white curtain of clouds, hot and damp, reaching up, towards the very heavens, which, when you let your gaze drop, coloured more and more orange, just to the base where the orange merged with a deep red tinge.

She then carefully approached towards the heart of the system, worried that she might slip and fall on the melting snow and finish in the hidden, burning mass. As she passed the thick outer layers, she could feel the increasing heat, turning the mist into a thick, sweaty vapour through which it was more and more difficult to breathe. Added to this was an odd sweet smell that made the inside of her nose hurt, right at the top, in between her eyes, which, by the way, were watering heavily.

The ledge, although quite flat, was still slightly sloping, which meant that the snow on the side of the hole on which she was standing had flown down the incline on that side and now, just here, the area underfoot was quite hot and dry.

The clouds of steam were coming from the melting snow on the other side of the hole, flowing down from the mountainside just above and beyond.

For want of anything better to do, she sat herself down on the warm rocks, her still-damp clothes warming and drying from the contact. As she noticed the effect on her clothes, she quickly set about emptying the damp moss and small lighting sticks from out of their pouch and spreading them out on the heated surface.

Feeling her clothes warming, even before they really began to dry, was already agreeable, and for a moment she was feeling quite content with the world and with herself, until the question of how to dry the firebox and relight the flame within began to drag her spirits down once again.

It was then that a gust of wind blew the clouds away to her right; just for a second or two, a large bush, with long thin branches, was exposed from its steamy covers. She got up and walked towards it, keeping her eyes a little towards the ground, for fear of falling. It was then that she saw it, one of the large branches, only as thick as her finger but almost as tall as her, lying broken underfoot. It might have been broken off by the great rush of wind as the object passed, before burying itself into the ground just a few feet away. She picked up the branch and returned to the edge of the pit.

The end of the branch had been twisted off from the bush, leaving a hook-like curl to it. Very carefully, she hooked the loop of the top of the firebox onto the branch and edged it out until it was swinging freely above the searing mass.

Every few moments, she would pull it back to check if it had dried or not. It would only take one moment of inattention and the firebox would be just that, a firebox, blazing in an instant of glory, but then to be no more.

Good, it seemed quite dry; she could now unhook it and leave it beside her. The hot rock could only reinforce the drying process.

Now, how to get fire out of this ice hole and into the firebox? The answer came quickly enough; she would plunge the branch into the hole and the sun god would light it for her.

She began preparing herself, focusing her energy on the spirit of the fire, opening herself up to this force. She began to sing.

She sang of heat, of light, of life, of death, of the fire from the skies and the fire from the earth.

Now, she thought, now it is time. She took the long stick and stuck it out into the gap. She kept her hand just inside the protection of the rock, which, although very hot, was nothing compared to the direct heat coming from below. It took a lot of courage and willpower to keep herself so close to the burning mass, but she knew she had to do it, there was no choice.

Then, in an instant, the wood was aflame. She rolled back away from the opening and threw the burning branch away from her—and just in time, too. The whole length that had been exposed had ignited at once, and very quickly the rest had caught hold, too. The whole of the branch was a flaming wand; it was impossible to get close to it. She just had to wait until the flames subsided.

And all too quickly they did, but then there was nothing left. The intense heat had totally dried the inside of the thin wood and the flames had consumed everything.

And so there she sat; empty, lost, disappointed, and despondent. All alone; there was no one to turn to, no one to ask, no one to help her. She lay on the ground and started to cry, to weep, to sob. She rocked from side to side, she even wrapped her arms around herself to try and feel some comfort, and it was exactly then that she felt it.

Something hard and sharp was pressing against her chest. She had totally forgotten the old man's present, the giant bear's tooth. It had scratched against her. She was taking it out to throw it away in anger when, holding it tightly in her little hand, she felt something, strange.

The tooth was hard and smooth, but what she felt was as if it was moving and vibrating, and even, in some impossible way, communicating with her. Her first thought was of the old man. He was the caster of bones, the communicator with the spirits, with the elements, with the great bear. Could it be possible that she too could call on this powerful spirit? Could she ask for its help, for its support to relight the fire, to help save her tribe? Was it not also its tribe? Are we not the tribe of the great bear?

Breathing quickly and heavily, she squatted down, taking the tooth in both hands. She called to the spirit of this long-disappeared king, singing without words, seeing without looking, sensing without feeling.

She sang, and sang, and sang, until, exhausted, she fell into a deep, deep sleep. In a dream, he came to her; he spoke a language that she understood. "Do you wish for me to help you?"

"Yes, please do what you can, oh Great Spirit."

"Move yourself over and I will direct your body, and offer you my strength and my cunning."

She didn't understand, but she managed to do what was asked. The dream continued; she got up from the rock and walked heavily over to the bush. Taking the tooth, and with a strength not of her own, she starting to hack away at the branches. When she had broken off quite a pile of sticks, she took them towards the heat and stacked all but two of them to build a future fire. She then tied the two remaining branches together with the leather cord of her belt to create an even longer pole, and then waited to understand what to do next.

She saw the bear, herself, standing in a stream; there were fish-type creatures in the water. She, the bear, swooped down with her claw, catching a swimming fish and, in the same movement, batting it onto a pile of other fish already on the shore.

Somehow she would have to grab the fire, and in the same flowing movement, bring it back out and onto the woodpile on the rocks.

Holding on to one end of the two joined branches, she took a deep breath, walked over to the opening, and plunged the other end deeply into the seething mass. She did not wait to see if it had caught fire or not, she immediately pulled it out and threw it onto the waiting pile of branches. It was already well aflame. The branches smouldered for a moment or two before catching fire, but the fire was nowhere near as intense as before. She took some dry moss and placed it lovingly inside the dry firebox, onto which she cut some fat and turned to the fire.

Taking a lighting stick, she approached the now roaring fire, but then reared back in great fear. What was happening? She had never been afraid of fire before. Then she understood. The bear—the great, wonderful, powerful bear—he was afraid of the fire.

She turned away again from the flames and knelt down, bowing deeply.

"Thank you, Great Bear, spirit of our tribe, you have helped me and saved them. But now it is time for you to leave, for I have to link with the spirit of the fire, and fire is not your friend."

She let herself drop, and simultaneously felt as if all her breath had been pulled out through her back and there she was, empty. It took her some moments to gather herself back into herself. She felt a moment of great sadness to be separated from such a wonderful, powerful contact, but the fire would not wait too long, and now was the moment to relight the firebox.

A second time she turned to the fire, taking the lighting stick she placed into a flame. It lit and in a slow but flowing gesture the flame danced from the fire into the firebox. And so, once again the firebox was the home of a living, glowing fire and she had relighted the fire within.

＊ ＊ ＊

"So, Jangbu, what do you understand from that story?"

"That a child cannot succeed unless he has help."

"And if the child has help?" Kunchen continued patiently.

"Then he can relight the fire?" I replied hopefully.

"Exactly." I wasn't at all sure of what he was trying to get me to understand, but I was happy that he accepted my answer.

"Come, we need to relight your fire."

"Will I get the fire from inside the snow, or will I need to contact a great bear?"

"A little of both." Kunchen smiled down at me. "Come, get dressed, we are going outside."

"Where are we going?"

"To find what you need to relight your fire. Didn't we just agree to that?"

Confused, I put on my winter clothes and boots and left the warm building, hand in hand with my saviour and best friend. He led me round the back of the monastery, where the snow was even deeper than on the road, and there, there it was, my fire in the ice. It was big, black and white, very hairy, and when it barked, it could wake the whole village.

111

"A *do-khyi*! Is it for me?"

"It's to help bring back the fire into your heart, Jangbu."

And so it did, so it did, yes, yes, it did.

Sleep Is Habit-Forming —
Part One

The disciple was just finishing clearing away the dishes from the evening meal. The day had passed like many others over the last few weeks. They had walked up and around the mountain; the Master had instructed him on matters of ceremony and attitude; they had stopped and practiced meditation exercises, hand positions, body postures, breathing, and mindfulness.

"I'm a bit sleepy," yawned the disciple.

"Sleep is habit-forming," mused the teacher, in the form of a response.

"Pardon?"

"Sleep is habit-forming," he repeated, smiling and slowly nodding his head.

Dhargey didn't quite know why, but the way that the Master had smiled just then for some reason started to make him feel suspicious. Maybe things had been going too smoothly, too "easily" for too long, and the Master felt it was time to teach another of his unorthodox lessons, or maybe he was getting a little bored with normal daily teachings, or maybe he just wanted to shock Dhargey for the pleasure—but just the same, something was up and he didn't like it. Whatever it was that the old trickster was up to, he didn't want to know, he just wanted to go to bed.

"Sleep is habit-forming," he repeated for the third time.

"And a very good habit it is, too. So good that I am off to indulge in it, right now. Good night, sir."

"Just a minute, young man." This was just what Dhargey was fearing might happen, that he would be blocked from going straight to bed.

"Can we not discuss other matters tomorrow? Tonight I am tired; I would find it hard to concentrate on any new teachings."

"Exactly, you feel that you must go to sleep."

"Yes, Master. Good night, Master." He turned quickly and started towards the building. Not quite quickly enough.

"Make me another cup of Po Cha."

"But you've just had one, and I've put everything away and it's late—"

"And it's my request." The disciple had no choice; if the Master asked for something, that clearly and that directly, he had no choice but to carry out the task.

"And be sure to make yourself one, too."

The tea was soon made; the fire was re-enforced, and the young, tired man resigned himself to keeping company with the old sage, at least for the time it took to drink the freshly made tea.

"Do you understand what the purpose of sleep is?"

"To give the body time to rest."

"Not only; sleep is the time when the body refreshes and repairs itself, yes, but it is also the opportunity for the mind to organise and digest the events of the day."

"So it is a necessary and important habit."

"Yes, yes, it is."

"So then I should be going to bed." He yawned again, as if just the idea of going to bed made him yawn.

"Generally one would agree," he said, and held up his hand to signal for him to wait, "but sleep is not essential!"

"What do you mean? Of course sleep is essential."

"You have no real logic, only simple reasoning. Because the body and the mind need certain things, and because those things can be had during sleep, doesn't mean that one has to sleep for these functions to take place."

"But that is what sleep is for, that is why we sleep." He was sure of his argument.

"Exactly, that is why nature has created sleep, so that all of the animal kingdom would function."

"And as I need to function like any other animal, I need to go to sleep." The Master picked up a nearby stick and hit him roughly on the leg with it. "Aw!"

"You are not an animal! You are not even an ordinary human being, you are my disciple. The body does not need sleep

115

to refresh and repair itself; it just needs for the person to deeply relax, allowing the usual body functions to slow and for the energy to focus on other things. As for the mind; what is necessary is to release it from your control and the preoccupations of your petty thoughts and worries. By relaxing into a deep meditative state, one can replace all the functions of sleep without ever losing consciousness."

"So we are to continue with our exercises of meditation, then?"

"Not now, not now."

"But you said that we can replace sleep with meditation."

"Absolutely, but only when the body and mind need."

"My body and mind are surely ready for sleep now."

"Not your body, just your mind."

"I don't understand."

"Your mind is telling you that because it is night and that you have been up for a few hours already, then it must be time to go to sleep."

"But it is time to go to sleep."

"It is the time that we have the habit, the habit of going to sleep."

"But what's the difference?"

"Higher thinking is supposed to be what separates the humans from the rest of the animal world, and yet so few humans ever choose to benefit from this ability. Now is the time when you generally go to sleep. Time is only a convention; release the convention and you release the idea that it is time to go to sleep."

"But I'm tired."

"Another false idea."

"It's not any idea, it's a fact. I'm tired." Again he felt that he was about to be tricked and manipulated into something that he hadn't agreed to, and being, as he had just said, tired and ready to go to bed, this was starting to make him feel angry.

"Are you not listening to me at all this evening? I just said, your mind is telling you that it is time for bed, and hence you must be tired."

"It is NOT my mind, it is my BODY that is tired." His temper was starting to come up and he had no desire to control himself.

"How do you know that your body is tired?"

"Because it's my body and I can feel it."

"But how can you be sure that it is your body that is really tired, and not just your mind telling you that your body is tired?"

Why was he continuing like this? He knew that his body was tired. It was late; they had gotten up early, they he walked quite a lot, and now it was time to go to bed.

"But my mind is telling me that my body is tired BECAUSE my body IS tired."

"Is it? You seem to have quite enough energy to shout at me." "That's nothing to do with anything."

"Where has this energy come from?"

"It has come from you—you have made me angry."

"First of all, I do not have the power to make you angry, and even if I did, how does making you angry give you energy?" "Being angry makes energy."

"So, tell me, how does that work?"

"What?"

"You keep telling me that you are tired, that your body is tired and the only way to re-energise this tired body is to go to sleep. Now you are telling me that just my talking to you has given you energy so you do not need to sleep. I must be getting old, as I cannot keep up with your logic."

"You are trying to trick me."

"And you are trying to confuse me."

"I'm not trying to confuse you."

"Are you feeling tired at this exact moment?"

"No, not at this exact moment."

"Have you just been to sleep?"

"No, of course not, I've been with you all the time."

"And if we agree that if your body is tired, the only way for it to recuperate is to relax."

"Like, as if, going to sleep?"

"Yes."

"Yes?"

"Then, leaving aside the fantasy that I can send energy into your body by some magical force, the only real possibility is that your body was not really so tired, it was only your mind suggesting that it was because it is evening and it wants to go off and dream."

"And so?"

"And so, young man, you are not at all as tired as you think you are, and your body is much, much, much tougher than you ever thought it was."

"Which means?"

"Which means that I am ready to share with you a little more of my story."

The Lost Tribe – Part One

The night had been difficult; I had had painful dreams. I was lost; I was seeking, searching, screaming for them. They had gone; I was lost, lost and abandoned. Sometimes I thought that I could hear them or catch a glimpse of them, but it was hopeless. They were not to be found, I was not to be found.

Now, there was no clear representation of who "they" were, but the feeling of loss and abandonment was still as strong.

They, my fellow monks, said that I was screaming and crying in the night. It was not the first time that this had happened.

The old Master called for me that afternoon.

"Go to bed now."

"But Master, it is the afternoon, I have tasks that I must do."

"You are relieved of your tasks, I have seen to it."

"But I can do them, even when my sleep is disturbed; I can still fulfil my obligations."

"I do not doubt it, but I will need you to be able to stay awake late tonight and I don't want to have to beat you every five minutes to keep you awake."

I understood nothing of what the Master was talking about, but the order was clear, and I went to my cell and lay down on my bed mat. It was more than likely only a matter of seconds before I fell asleep, and it seemed to be only a few more seconds before I was roughly woken again. In fact, several hours had passed and it was already getting dark. I was to go and get something to eat, to wash, and then go to the Master's chambers.

The Master was waiting for me, but he wasn't alone; he had with him a man with skin darker than I had ever seen before in my life.

"Come, sit down here beside us." I was a little intimidated by the dark-skinned man; even though he wasn't any bigger than I was, he was so different from us. His hair was black, thick, curly wool; his nose was large and flat; but it was his hands that were the most impressive—hard, rough, and black on the outside; smooth, soft, and pink on the inner.

I sat down between the two men...and waited.

The Master smiled gently at the other man, but neither spoke. They seemed quite comfortable to just sit. I was not comfortable at all; the waiting, and not knowing why I was here, seemed eternal.

Suddenly, the Master looked up and exclaimed, "At last we can begin!" I was confused as to why all of a sudden something had changed, until I noticed a young monk, not much older than me, entering with a tray of tea and bowls.

He settled the tray and served each of us a drink. I was most honoured to be allowed to take tea with the Master and his guest, but I was much too nervous to say anything. I just took the bowl, bowed in gratitude, and placed by my side.

The stranger took his tea, sipped a little, and also set it down by his side. I noticed that he was using his left hand; maybe it was their custom. He then turned to me and started to speak.

"Young man," he began, his voice rich and low. He had a very strange accent and the way he spoke was somehow wrong. It was a little later that I realised that the strangeness was because our language was not his own. I had never before met a foreigner that had come from so far away that our language, not just the local dialect but the whole language itself, had be learnt from nothing.

"Your master has told me something of your story and has asked me to share with you something of my own. I come from a country many, many moons from here, a land of great heats and forests a little like those to the south of your country. We live together in tribes of a certain size, and most of the time the tribes live in harmony with each other. Sometimes, a king, who is the ruler of one or more tribes, will decide to wage war on the tribes of a neighbouring king."

✳ ✳ ✳

Once there was a child; a small, weak child that had been sick when very young. The child when just a baby had been very sick; the local healer had sung to the spirits, boiled plants, offered sacrifices, and the tribe had danced so that the sickness would leave the young body and would be sent elsewhere. The spirits were kind and accepted the offerings, but not totally; the child lived, but one arm and one leg remained weak as a reminder that the spirits must be properly respected.

The child grew, and as he would never be strong enough to become a warrior or a hunter, when his mother became sick and left to join the ancestors, he went to live with the old man and become the apprentice of the healer that had saved his life.

The child had mixed feelings towards his teacher; he often was made aware that the old man had succeeded in saving his young life, but he could not forget that it was also his fault that he would spend the whole of that life as a weak cripple.

And so the years passed and the child grew into a young man. His love and appreciation for his master, Sekou, also grew and flourished, but the deep anger and resentment, like a worm in an apple, ate away at his soul.

It was at that time that a pest arrived in the fields of a neighbouring tribe and most of their harvests were spoilt. Greed, jealousy, and hunger are three evil brothers that enter into the souls of men and turn their attention from their own lands to those of their oldest cousins. And so it was that the tribe to our south gathered the men together and attacked our village.

As the warriors started to arrive, the women and the children ran off into the jungle, as well as the old people. The fight did not last very long; quite a few of our men were killed, others ran off to escape, and the rest were captured. Our leaders were killed straightaway and in front of us, with the threat that if anyone would try to fight anymore that more would be killed. Some women were also captured and were sent away as slaves to the other tribe.

Sekou was brought out before the new leaders.

"What is your name?" Sekou would not answer; to give your name is to give the other power over you. They asked again, but he would not speak. Then they started to beat him; I watched as the bright red blood flowed over his wrinkled black face, but he still wouldn't answer. I do not know, nor likely will I ever know, but something forced me to step out of the shadows and speak. Up until then, it seems that they had not noticed my existence.

"What is this cripple?" they laughed.

"I am his apprentice. Please do not hurt him anymore, his name is Sekou." Sekou managed to raise his head to look at me. His expression was difficult to read; was it anger, relief, or just sadness? There was no time to tell, for the leader turned back to him, grabbed his hair, pulled his head up and back, and silently slit his throat.

"There, I will not hurt him anymore, boy." I could not speak nor move nor look away. The blood was flowing in spurts out of the open wound. Sekou wasn't dead yet, but no noise came out of him. The two men that were holding him seemed to be unconscious about the dying man between them. They just stood and waited patiently for him to die, and then they casually dropped him, like a bag of old fruit, there on the floor, in the meeting place between the huts.

It was almost silent but for the flies that started to buzz around him. I watched in total fascination as one fly came and sat on his ear. The other flies seemed to fly, then to settle, and then to fly again, totally excited by the hot, fresh blood, but not that one. It just sat there, perched on the just dead man's ear, waiting, waiting for something. *What are you waiting for, fly? Are you waiting for Sekou's spirit to softly steal away like the steam of a cooking pot, out of his ear? Are you waiting to catch on to it? Are you really only a fly, or are you a disguised demon, waiting to snatch his passing soul to keep for yourself?*

Suddenly, someone kicked me, quite hard, on my good leg.

"I'm talking to you, boy." The leader was shouting at me. I looked up at him.

"What is your name, boy?"

"Will you kill me, when I tell you?"

"I will kill you if you don't."

"My name is Talib."

"And what do you do, Talib? What do you seek?"

"I do nothing, I am a cripple. And what do I seek? I seek a meaning to my miserable existence." For some reason this made the leader laugh. I had not intended to try to make him laugh; I was too angry and too shocked to do any more than say what came into my head in the moment.

"Well then, little seeker, you must stay alive a little longer, so that you may continue your search." And with that, he turned from me, went into the head man's hut, and disappeared from my sight. The warriors started to look after their own dead and wounded. The few of us that were left soon realised that it was up to us to gather up and dispose of our dead family and friends.

Most of those that were left were the old people. Some older mothers returned, who felt that they would not be interesting to be taken as slaves, and anyway, they had no means to survive in the jungle, so they chose to take the risk to return.

We pulled the dead to the river and washed them. We then started to dig the graves. It was very hard to do, but it is important that it is done. It was late when we had finished digging and we then all went to bed.

Early the next day we all got up. We bury the dead in the early morning, because at that time of day the sorcerers are asleep; otherwise, they could use the corpses for evil purposes.

That night, when everyone was asleep, I took a chicken that had secretly been given to me, killed it, and used the blood to begin the ritual of helping the souls to pass from the earth into the place of the ancestors. If I didn't do this, their souls could become trapped on earth, wandering here and there, causing trouble to many of our people.

I sat cross-legged in my hut and softly began to beat my drum. Beating the drum is a very special job for my people, and I had beaten it many times for Sekou. He had instructed me on many things, and the communicating with the ancestors and spirits I had tried, but I had never led a dead soul away from the earth before. Now, I was alone, no Sekou, no one to beat the drum for me, and many souls to lead.

I had to clear my head, to focus my mind, to open a channel through which I could communicate with the souls, to leave my physical body, to enter into that special state...to go. I beat the drum and I beat it some more, and then more again. Every time I felt that I was succeeding, the idea that I was going to succeed was enough to distract me and I lost it again.

I was getting tired and thirsty. *I should get myself a drink of water.* It was then that the idea struck me. *I should drink something stronger*. Sekou had some strong beer in his hut. I had tasted beer a few times, but I found it bitter and too strong, so I never drank it if I could avoid it, and then, only in the smallest of quantities.

The beer is made from sorghum flour, which we use for many cooking purposes. Depending on how it is prepared it can be either light or very strong. Sekou had a pot of strong beer in his hut and I knew where it was hidden. It was a good thing that it was hidden, as the warriors had made a quick search of the village and had taken away all the beer they could find.

I could hear the sounds of singing and laughing where they had made their fires. There was also another sound; it was the sound of my girl cousins, the younger ones, who were screaming. The warriors were having their way with them, and some of them had never been with any man before.

I stole into the hut, found the pot and slipped out again. No one saw me doing this; nobody cared what the crippled young man was doing. Well, not really nobody; some of the village people knew that I was going to try and do the ritual. Many of them had no belief in me, some a little, but just the same, I was the only one that could try to do the ritual and it was very important that someone did it.

I took the pot back to my hut, sat down, opened it, and took a big drink. I wanted to spit it out; it nearly came back out by itself, but I forced myself to swallow it. I waited a moment; already I was feeling quite sick, but I knew that I needed help to leave my body. I started to bang the drum again; it seemed very loud, and I hoped that no one, none of the warriors, would come and find me.

I called for some friendly demons to come and help me; I focused on their faces. I called for my power bird to help me;

I focused on its body. I focused on the drum and my drumming. I tried not to focus on the sickness in my throat. I began to nod my head to the beat, my body then followed, my energy was going inwards! It should be going out! There was nothing I could do; I was too scared to stop. Either I would be sick and feel too bad to start again, or maybe I would just fall asleep and then all would be lost.

I kept on drumming, allowing myself to fall deeper and deeper into a black space inside me. I followed myself into myself, I followed my demons, and I flew with my black power bird. I felt the power start to build up inside me; we were flying, faster and faster, deeper and deeper, higher and higher—and we were OUT. Out of my body, out of my village, out of this world.

We were in the world between, a world where I was whole, a world of power and of great, great danger. Here, my only protections were my demons, my bird, and my own power as an initiate (which, to some degree, I was).

I was to seek the souls of the dead members of my tribe and direct them towards the home of the ancestors. I flew this way and that way, but I saw nothing. Then I realised that I must be too far away from my village and the souls would likely still be near their old bodies and the places that they knew.

I thought about the village, I imagined it as I could see it from above, clearer and clearer, closer and closer. And here I am, here we are, flying, floating above the village. I can see the fires, I could fly over where the warriors have their fires, but I remember the screams of the cousins, so I don't.

I start to think about the dead village members, how they looked, what they wore. Something starts to drift up towards me;

it takes on a form, it is a man. His face is not very clear, I cannot totally make it out, but I know who it is, it is a neighbour. I greet him, but I do not look into his eyes when I do, it is not our custom. "It is time for you to go," I say.

"But my family need me, it cannot be my time. I must stay."

"Listen, I am telling you, it is time. If you do not go soon, a sorcerer will steal your soul and you will never return to the ancestors."

"Is what you are telling me the truth?"

"Look at the demons, look at the bird. Are these of the world of man?"

"Can I just say goodbye to my wife?" His wife was taken as a slave, to the other tribe's village.

"Your wife is not here."

"Then my daughter?" His daughter is in the jungle with the warriors; she is one of those doing the screaming.

"Your daughter is not here."

"I do not believe you."

"Believe what you want, do what you what. If you stay here much longer, you will end up a slave until the end of the world. Is that what you want?"

"I want to say goodbye to my family."

"I will say goodbye in your place. Please come with me now. I am very tired, and I have others to find and to help find their way."

"I am ready." I took him by holding my mind on his form and allowing myself to be drawn upwards towards the passage. I cannot describe it more clearly; it is a space different from all the rest. If it is night, it might seem like a light, the light from the other side comes through. If it is during the day, then it seems like a dark patch, as in the jungle when the sun is blocked out by the top of a tree, the ground is a little darker—so is the passage, during the day.

"I am to enter here?" I did not answer, I didn't need to, his ancestors were there waiting, on the other side. They called to him; he did not wait, and did not look back at me. I did not see him enter into the passage, but I felt when he passed over to the other side. I could feel him no more; he was where he was supposed to be. So I left and returned to the village. It was not easy, this work to do, the people did not want to leave the family still alive. Many of the villagers had escaped into the jungle and some had been taken away by the warriors to their village. This made it easier for me; the people were not there so the spirits were more easily convinced to follow me to the passage. The hardest were the children. I did not see any children killed, but they were there just the same, crying and looking for their parents. It seems bad, but when one of the mothers of a child appeared, I was very glad that she was killed, too. Together, she and I found the dead children, we told them of the wonderful place on the other side of the passage. We told them that their grandparents and their parents were all waiting for them, and they would have a big party when they got there and would be very happy. The children, as children are, forgot about finding their families in the world and went up with us to the passage. As we got closer, some of them began to cry again and said that they were scared, but just in time, the ancestors started to call them home, and the children got excited and passed through the troubled space.

I returned once again to the village, seeking out another fresh soul to lead up to the other world, but I immediately knew that there were no more. All my dead friends and their families had passed to the world of the ancestors and my work for that night was done. I floated down, onto the roof of my hut, through the roof and down, once again to join my heavy body. And then I slept.

It must have been late morning when I awoke; the sun was high and it was already quite hot. As the shaman's apprentice my tasks were all to do with him: make his meals, clean his hut, get him water, and stay close to him so that if he should want or need something, I would be there to do or to get it for him.

The village was very quiet; nobody was talking, but people were doing like it was any other day. At first I found it very, very strange that the women were preparing food for the day. That the few people that were left had already gone into the fields; that the cows had been taken out. Then, I asked myself, "What else are people to do?" The warriors must have been up all night, drinking and making the young girls scream, so they were still asleep. The people must have woken up as usual, waited to be told what to do next, found no one to tell them, so they just did what they always did.

Not only that, but some of the women with children, who had run away into the jungle to escape, had found that they had no good food or shelter, so they had come to the edge of the jungle. One had run back home to see what was happening and found out that most of the warriors had left, and those that had stayed were not interested in the other women and had stopped killing people.

So quite a few women came back with their children, and the old people who had left came back with them, too. The village was missing many, many people, but it was still a village and people did what they had been doing since the time of the ancestors.

I was feeling not too good after the beer and the heavy work of the night. Some people stopped me; they didn't ask openly if I had done the work, most of them just looked at me, waiting for me to speak. I would look back at them, slowly nod my head yes, and then continue on my path. I went to bathe in the river, allowing the running waters to cleanse me from the contact with the dead, which everyone knows is like nectar is to bees for evil spirits.

On my return, I was surprised to find food and fresh water waiting for me outside my hut. At first I thought that it must have been some mistake, but then I realised, as the only person left in the village that knew how to call on the spirits, I had become someone important.

I sat down to enjoy the food and the newfound status, but as I was eating, I realised that I had only got this because I'd got my master killed. I stopped eating, I'd lost my appetite.

Sometime after noon the warriors woke. They were not in a very good mood; they had drunk too much and were irritable. Before anyone asked me, I mixed up a big bowl of banana, milk, honey, and crushed dates, and offered it to them. At first they thought I was trying to poison them, but all the children asked if they could have some. I gave the children some bowls to share; the warriors watched the children drinking and then they drank it themselves. After the children drank quite a lot, and since the warriors liked it so much, in the end I had to make three big bowls to have enough.

When I went to get some more bananas, one of the villagers stopped me roughly and asked why I was helping the warriors. I was being "a traitor to the village." I explained that the warriors, being in such a bad mood, could easily start killing people again, and it was better to help them feel better than to risk the danger of their anger.

Soon the warriors were starting to feel better. They stopped shouting at people and pushing them roughly, they just looked like normal people. It was hard now to think that only a few hours ago, these same men had rushed screaming into our village and had killed men, women, children, and elders. They just looked like normal men, most of them quite young, not much older than me.

They were now just sitting in the meeting place, doing nothing. After some time, an old woman, too old to worry if they should kill her or not, walked slowly up to them.

"Young men, what is it that you want of us?" They had turned to look at her as she approached and stopped their "nothing" to listen to her.

"We are here to take your food, the stocks in the village and the crops from the fields," one of the men answered. Maybe he was the leader.

"But if you take all our food, then we shall all die."

"You can die now if you want to," replied another man, taking out a big curved knife and smiling at it.

"You don't want to take all the food." I spoke before I realised I was about to speak.

"What is that you are saying, cripple?" It was the first man that asked. The second one added, "Who gave you the right to speak?"

"You don't want to take all the food," I repeated. "If you take all the food now, we won't have any strength to work in the fields and you'll only get what is ready now or already dried. If you let us have enough food to live on, then we can keep working and growing more food, and you will have more food all the time."

"I said, who gave you the right to speak?" He got up and lifted his blade.

"I give him the right to speak." He must have had some position of authority, as the other sat down again. He sat playing with his sharp knife, then he gave me a bad look. I was thinking, *He is not my friend.*

The leader spoke again. "Okay, little cripple, maybe you are speaking the truth, but don't you try and do clever stuff with me. I'm not stupid."

"Yes, yes, you are not stupid, that is why I'm speaking to you, that is why you are listening to me." I was becoming bold, but it was not confidence that was making me speak, it was fear. I had fear for the one with the knife; he would like to cut my throat. I had made him look stupid in front of the others, he did not like that. I had to find a way so that the other would protect me; as a weak cripple, I have always needed someone to protect me.

"You, you will be in charge of the food for the village. You will come to me each day and you will show me how much food the villagers will eat. If you bring too much, I will take the double of how much you do not need. If anyone eats any food that I have not agreed, I will kill them myself, and you know that I will."

"Can we pick fruit?"

"I'm only interested in the crops."

"Then I will see that what you want is done." I had done it. He had given me a job, the other could not interfere. I was working for the new head of our tribe; now I was protected by him.

The others in the tribe were not sure if I was to be treated as friend or enemy. I had spoken up so that all the food was not taken, but I had also agreed to show him all the grain that we would eat every day, knowing that if he thought I had taken too much, he would take back the double of what he thought was too much.

The next day was the first day that I was to present to him the sorghum flour that the women use as a base for most of our meals. I had gotten up very early so that I would have time to discuss with the women how much to put into the bowls to show to the warrior. There was much discussion; some older women wanted to put in a lot, saying that if we showed that we didn't need much, then that would be all we would get for the rest of our lives. Others argued that if we asked for too much, the man would take away a lot of it and we would starve today. After much arguing, one elder man pointed out that to go very hungry for one day or be a bit hungry for many years, it was worth taking the risk to add a bit more flour this first morning.

As I knew very little about the cooking, I just stood and waited until the discussions had finished, then took the bowls to the camp of the warriors. They had made a little camp about twenty yards away from our last hut and I could see the sleeping figures of the men. I stopped about five yards away and waited. Everyone was still asleep. What should I do? Should I wait here or should I go on and wake up the men? It didn't take me very long to make up my mind. These men could be dangerous; they had killed people for nothing. If they became angry with me, they could chop off my hands or maybe kill me, too. So I chose not to wake them up.

There I sat, for quite a long time. We Africans know how to sit and wait; it is something that one learns when very young. And so I waited, the sun continued his journey across the sky, but no one moved, they must have stayed up late again that night. It was mid-morning when they started to move; someone saw me and shouted to the others. One of the warriors began to run towards me, waving his knife in the air.

"What are you doing here?" he screamed. "I'll kill you!" He was the one that I had made look stupid the day before; I knew he would like to kill me. I stopped in terror, like a frightened animal; if I didn't move at all, maybe, somehow, I would survive.

"Wait!" screamed an order from the camp. "It is the cripple." The first man stopped running towards me but continued at a walking speed.

"What are you doing here, cripple?" he asked in a nasty way, slowly waving his knife in front of me. I was feeling very scared. Had I done something wrong to have waited here? Should I have returned to the village and waited for the men to come to me?

Anyway, he didn't care, he just wanted to cut me with his knife. He knew who I was before he started running towards me, that's why he ran, so he could kill me. Pretending that he didn't know who I was or what I was doing there was a lie. He wanted to kill me, quick, before the others had a chance to see who I was.

"I have come to show the man the flour that we need to cook, so that we can eat today." I shouted it loud so that all the others could hear and know who I was. The leader, who had stopped the other man with his order, was walking towards me. The first man was playing with his cruel knife, swinging it quite close to my face, but he also glanced behind from time to time, watching the leader approach.

The young lion had cornered the sick antelope and was ready to pounce, but the head of the pride had roared a no. The young lion's claws were out and ready, one quick strike and the prey would be down. It was rare to catch an antelope; he didn't want to let it go, didn't want to let it live. The head lion continued to advance and turned to the shivering prey.

"How do I know that that is how much you need for today?" I was surprised; he had no idea, either, of how much we needed. I had to think fast—if he didn't know, he could easily think that it was too much. I shook off once again the fear of imminent death and focused on the question.

"I can prove it," I replied.

"How can you prove it, little cripple?"

"Get one of your men to come and sit by the cooking pot. He can see that all the flour is being used to make the food and then he can watch us eat it. He will be able to see that we are not eating more than we need, but we are using all this flour for that." The leader stopped and thought for a moment. He then turned to the other man with the knife.

"You wanted to know what he was doing here, now you know. And since you are so interested in his business, you can go and watch the cooking and make sure that all this flour is used, and see that what is cooked is not too much."

"This is not a job for a warrior." He almost shouted at the leader.

"This is the job that I have given you."

"I will not do it!" The leader moved towards him, his own nasty knife flew towards the neck of the other. "You will do it, and you will keep doing it until I tell you to stop doing it!" The leader's eyes seemed to turn red; I could see the veins of his neck start to stick out. The other man was angry, but he was also scared of the leader, and could not say no. I think that other people had said no before but they were no longer alive to talk about it.

"Take me to the cooking place," he said, and pushed me with the end of his knife. It hurt a bit, I think he made me bleed a little, but I didn't say anything. I just continued back to the village, dragging the two big bowls of flour with some effort.

As I passed, shadowed by the man with the knife, the villagers stopped and looked. What were they thinking? That he was going to kill me? That he was protecting me? Surely not that he was going to sit and watch the women cook, this day and for many days to come.

We arrived at the cooking place. I set the bowls down in front of the women; they had been waiting to start preparing the food for some time now. They looked at me, as if to ask, "What had happened?" and if it was okay for them to start working.

The man sat down a few yards from the women, under the shade of a date palm. He already looked bored. I was not eager to see how he would be after some hours.

137

"He is here to watch that this is how much flour you need," I said as an explanation, as I set down the two big bowls heavily. I said no more; I just put the bowls down and went off to the river to wash off the dust and heat of the morning and the fear of death, which I had again carried.

If everything is eaten, it is difficult to say that one has cooked too much. Mashama, the man with the knife, had sat and watched them prepare and cook the flour and the fruit and vegetables all day.

When I came with my bowl for my food, I expected to find him looking even more angry and sullen than in the morning, but I did not. He had seemed to relax as the day passed. It was some days later, hearing the children chatter, that I came to understand why.

There was a young girl in the village, about my age. Her name was Chifundo. She was supposed to be quite pretty, only I found her to be very skinny. It seems that during that first day, Chifundo started doing a special woman thing—she started not to look at Mashama. This is something that I haven't understood yet, maybe since it has never happened to me. It seems that by not looking at a man, a girl shows the man that she is interested in him. The man then, so I understand, starts to look from time to time at the girl, but not too much. The girl then turns herself to the man and again doesn't look at him, or if she does, it is only for one second and then she turns away. It seems that they had been playing this game already on the first day, and by the evening, all the women in the village knew what they were doing.

By the next day, all the children knew, and by the second evening, everyone knew except me. Mashama was careful (so I found out later) not to say any of this to Oladele, the leader of the warriors. He just acted grumpy and remained silent. He was careful to keep quite far away from Oladele, not because he was particularly frightened of him, but because he didn't want to give him the opportunity to release him from the job of watching the cooking and then rob him of the chance to see Chifundo every day.

Often, in an African tribe, it seems that the men do little. One can see them sitting, talking, laughing, smoking, and drinking. The women cook and do most of the work in the fields.

True as that might be, the men have many important jobs: they hunt, collect honey, look after the animals, and forage for fruit and nuts. They also make, build, and repair everything.

And so, only a few days later, I found myself once again seeking out Oladele to talk to him. I waited until the evening, after he had eaten his evening meal, hoping to find him in a good mood. I walked over to the warrior camp.

"Hello," I called out, so as not to surprise them and risk having my throat cut for my trouble. "It's me, Talib, the cripple, and I wish to talk to Oladele, if it's okay."

Suddenly a figure appeared by my side. I felt more than saw the knife cut through the air in front of me. I stopped breathing. So I was to die now, in the dark of the night. I closed my eyes, waiting for the pain to come and release me from this life.

"If you close your eyes, you might fall over a branch and hurt your good leg." The man was laughing at me. "Oladele is waiting for you by the fire, come." I started breathing again and made my way towards the fire. I was surprised to see how many of the girls of the village were there, but I was even more surprised when

139

I realised that they seemed quite comfortable and relaxed, sitting next to the same men that had made them scream so much on that awful first night.

"Well, cripple, what do you want of me now?"

"Oladele, it was a good choice to have left you in charge of our village. You are both strong and smart."

"Don't try and buy me with sweet words, cripple. You want something. Speak clearly or I'll cut your tongue out." I did not take that as an idle threat.

"We need the men back," I blurted out. "Things are getting broken and used, they need to be repaired or replaced. We are running out of fruit and nuts, bark and roots. We cannot look after the animals and work in the fields, and we have no means to hunt meat or fish. So we need for the men to come back."

One of the men spoke up from the back. "You know where they are hiding, cripple?"

"There are some places in the forest where they might be hiding out."

"Then you will lead us to them."

"It would do you no good. They know this part of the forest much better than you do. They will have lookouts and will have set traps. If you try to find and attack them, they will kill you all."

"Why would you warn us of this?" Of course, it was Oladele who asked the question.

"Even though you and your warriors have killed the people of my village, I would not rejoice to see you killed. All life is sacred. And killing leaves a scar on the soul. I do not want the men of my village to have such scars on their souls."

"And so you would protect us from the vengeance of your own people?"

"All I ask is that you promise that if I bring the men back to the village, you and your warriors will promise not to harm them."

"And if promised, what would stop me from waiting until they came back and then killing them all? It would make a great feast, we could eat their souls."

"Two things: first, you have been fair to us since the first day; you promised that we would have enough to eat and no one has been hurt. And second, you know that we need the men back so that the village can continue to work to grow the food that your village needs. If bringing the men back will mean that your family and tribe can eat well this winter, then it is very much in your own interest to do this."

"But how do we know that after letting the men back into the village they won't attack us? They have good reason to want our blood," another of the men asked.

"Well, snake tongue, what do you say to that?" I was starting to feel that somehow Oladele was beginning to like me, if only a little. *Please, please continue to protect me, leader of the warriors.*

"The men of the village know that your warriors, those here and those that have returned to your village, are many and are well trained in fighting other tribes. Our men are hunters, not warriors. Maybe they could kill some of you if they waited and planned it, but some of you would fight back and kill some of them. And then your village would send all the warriors to destroy our village. Then, even if we survived, we would have nothing. Listen, our men would have little to gain even if they killed you and got some revenge."

"And you would convince them to return and not try to kill us?"

"I have no interest in doing anything else."

"Oladele, can you trust him?"

"I am convinced by his arguments, and are we incapable of protecting ourselves, even during the night?"

"It won't be necessary."

"I really hope not, because if just one man threatens any of my men, I will kill him, but slowly and painfully. And if, and hear me well, your men try and kill any of my men, I will destroy your village and kill everyone—man, woman, and child—and then that will be that."

"You can trust me on this."

"I hope so, for your sake and the sake of your whole tribe."

"So I can go and get the men?"

"Go and get your men. I promise that we won't kill them, unless we have to." This made all the warriors laugh. I didn't laugh, but after I had my back to them, I did allow myself a little smile of satisfaction—the men were coming home.

The next morning I got up quite early. The ritual of taking Oladele the two big bowls of cereal had already stopped; he said that as long as Mashama was watching the cooking and eating, that was good enough for him. It seemed that for Oladele, Mashama had found himself a fixed job.

Things like that seem to happen often in life; you do something a few times, and without anyone really thinking about it, it becomes a life job. One of the elders of the village used to take one or two cows out every day. He had done that since he was a boy; it started one day when the boy who was supposed to take the cow out got sick, his father was that boy's uncle, so he told his son to take the place of the other boy. After that, the other boy died of the sickness and so the job became his. Generation after generation of cows came and went; the boy grew into a young man, who married, became a father, became a widower, became a grandfather, and still, day after day his task was to look after the cows, all because his cousin became sick one day.

Of course, Mashama didn't mind; in fact, he had made it his business to keep that job so that he could stay close to Chifundo. He had also changed his habits; instead of just half sleeping, half watching the women cook, he would often offer to help lift or carry the heavier pots. He made himself responsible for the fire, making it, feeding it, and finding the wood.

As I no longer had to bother to take the bowls to Oladele, I had some breakfast, took some sorghum cakes, bananas, and dates in a pouch, some fresh water in a small gourd, and set off before the sun had properly risen.

It is not easy trekking through the forest for most people, but for me, with one leg and one arm both short and weak, it is much, much harder. Of course, I knew where the men were and it wasn't really that far away. There is a place where the land rises quite high and there are a number of little caves that enter into the hillside. If these caves were natural or made by our ancient ancestors, who had lived in them when the world was young and the spirits lived amongst us, we will never know, but the caves are there just the same.

As children, almost everybody had, sometime or other, come and played in these caves; even parents would bring their children to picnic, play, and even sleep. Often an elder would sit near the fire and tell stories of mischievous spirits that would come and do bad things to little children who didn't do as their parents and elders told them to.

What no one of the tribe knew was that this is also the home of a powerful demon, a demon that Sekou had a special contact with. Some nights we would come out to this place, make a fire, set out some offerings, and Sekou would call to his demon. I would not sit close to this ceremony. At first, it was because Sekou wouldn't let me, but as I grew more in his confidence, it was my own choice to keep away—this demon scared me. In truth, all contact with spirits and demons scare me. I now know some friendly demons and I have my power bird, but I'm scared every time I have to call on them. Maybe they will stop being friendly towards me, maybe I might not give them what it is they want for helping me, or maybe, worse still, other demons or spirits will follow my call and come to me and attack me. No, I do not like working with demons and spirits, but for some reason, like the man who spent his life taking the cows out, this job has fallen on my weak, narrow shoulders.

And so I came to be making my slow way through the forest to the place of the caves early in the morning, before the sun got too high and the jungle would feel as though someone had left a cooking pot of water, heated by a big fire, under the floor itself. The jungle can really steam like that pot of boiling water. The water, which isn't your own sweat, pours off every part of the body—down the back, between the legs, and, what I hate the worst, into the eyes. I get blinded by this steamy air, which cools on my body, my head, my forehead, and flows down into my eyes.

My eyes are very important to me; when you have a small, weak, twisted body, it is very important to know what is going on all around you. That way, if something bad should happen, you are prepared, and if possible, somewhere else. Not to be able to see properly is bad. Firstly, there is the constantly changing light in the jungle; every tree creates its own special shadow due to its position, grouping with the other trees, and its branches that can be yards and yards high above. That, with the wind moving the tree and the branches, and the movements caused by the animals moving through the trees, the light is always changing, often making it difficult to see. And then to have these tears filling the eyes, that's really bad and I don't like it at all. That was one of the main reasons I wanted to leave so early.

The second reason was to be as sure as possible that none of the warriors would follow me. They didn't know that I would leave the next day after getting the agreement from Oladele, but knowing that they liked to sleep until after the sun rose, leaving now would make it even less likely that some untrustworthy man would follow me.

The going is always slow; I move slowly, night or day, good light or bad light, I move slowly. My leg tires easily and I often half fall because I've tripped on a hidden root or there is a little hole under my foot that I notice only when I put my full weight on it. The day becomes hotter and my body becomes more and more damp. The little rivers of water start to flow down my head and body. I rub the water out of my eyes. I need to be careful not to rub too much, as the skin on the sides of the eyes is very fragile, and if I'm not careful it can quickly become very red and sore.

I am arriving at the place; I walk slowly and listen carefully. The men are likely to be quite scared, like hunted animals. It would only take them thinking that I was one of the warrior men for them to react like a sprung animal trap. Most animals, when they fear to be hunted, will just run away until they find a place far enough away from the hunter to feel safe. If for some reason they cannot run away, almost any animal can become very dangerous; they will be fighting for their lives. The men of the tribe have nowhere else to run. If they think I am the enemy, they could attack me very hard, and before they realise who I am, it would be too late for me.

I feel more than see that I am seen.

"Hello, it's Talib," I call out at the top of my voice. There is much movement in the trees, birds call and monkeys shriek. I don't move; I feel in danger. Like most animals, we can feel when danger is close. For many it is a lost reaction, but for a cripple that can get pushed about by the bigger boys, whenever they might feel bored or angry with someone or something, it is a sense that reawakens and reinforces itself throughout one's life.

The time passes slowly. I am sure that I am not mistaken, but doubt is a nimble thief; he steals into your mind through the back door of distraction, pillages your confidence, and strolls out through the open door of your fears without so much as a backwards glance. I was starting to get a little nervous and to sweat, and this time there was also my sweat, the sweat was pouring off my head and flowing into my eyes. I had to keep rubbing them, I needed to see what was happening, but the sides of my eyes were getting more and more sore.

"What do you want here?" I hadn't seen or heard him approach. I jumped, and as if my throat was full of my stomach. The stress and shock was too much for me; I felt dizzy, I felt sick. I half fell to one side and grabbed a branch to steady myself. Then it happened, I couldn't stop it—it must have been a reaction to the stress and the fear. I was sick. I threw up the little breakfast that I had had. I gagged, I retched, I just held on to the branch until my body had stopped emptying itself.

Maybe, waiting there, in fear and in stress, my natural defences were so down that an evil spirit had succeeded in entering me. And by a miracle, the shock of his coming had also surprised the spirit, and my body was able to take the opportunity to throw it out.

The man started to laugh. "Yes, yes indeed, it is Talib, as weak and incapable as always. It's okay, let us pass." And with that, he poked me, not so gently, with the end of his spear, in the direction of the caves.

The men were there; as a place that we all knew well and had often visited and camped, it wasn't so surprising that the place looked quite homely. The men had built some shelters to protect themselves from the sun; there were fires burning, piles of fruit sitting in date palms, cooked meats hanging on racks made of small branches. The place looked quite nice.

The men didn't look so good; their eyes, too wide, red-rimmed, heavy with lack of sleep yet restless and staring, like the hunted animals they felt to be. Their movements were also odd, slow and heavy, but then sharp and violent, like some animals when near death, life draining out of them but still their survival instinct makes them even more dangerous, one last slash or bite before they go.

"Why are you here, traitor?" I didn't see who asked, but I felt the question could have come from any one of them. Their looks towards me were all menacing, each as threatening as the other.

"I'm not a traitor."

"You sided with the killers, you betrayed Sekou and they killed him."

"I hoped that they would stop beating him."

"That they did, I saw them slit his throat." He spat on the ground as he finished saying the words.

"I did not want them to do that."

"I don't think that he thought they would kill him." It was a woman who spoke; I had not seen any women as I had entered the clearing in front of the caves. Maybe they had hidden themselves until they were sure it would be safe.

"What makes you think that, Ameena?" The voice was calm and sure of itself, so was the man with the scarred face, whose voice it was. Zuberi was the leader of our tribe, old enough to have seen much and to have acquired wisdom, but still young enough to fight off any opposition for his place as leader.

"Talib is a coward. He is weak, but he is not stupid. He knows that if he betrays us the bad spirits will come at night and steal his soul."

"Maybe he has made a deal with some strong demons and will be protected against the spirits." It was the man who spat that spoke.

"I have made no deal with no bad spirits!" I cried out. "I have nothing to do with those demons, either." And then I added, more to myself than the others, "I am scared of those demons. I have no power to control them."

"You see," laughed Zuberi, "he is still a scared cripple. So what are you doing here, Talib?"

"It is time for you to come home, back to the village."

"The warriors have left?" It was one of the youngest women, all excited, that called out. They all turned to look at me again, but it was Zuberi who replied.

"I would not believe that the warriors have already left our village. We do not even know why they came in the first place."

"They came because their harvest has failed and they have no sorghum to make flour with. That is why they made war with us."

"But if they are still in our village, it is not safe for us to return." For the leader, this was of course obvious.

"I have convinced them that, to continue to supply them with sorghum, we need for the men to return to the village."

"You want us to return to be their slaves, to work, to grow food for them?" It was again the spitting man that reacted, but almost all the men and some of the women were clearly agreeing with him, for they started to advance towards me in a very threatening way.

"What a good idea, let's beat up Talib. Just like when you were a boy, Mvula, that was then the solution to your problems. I'm sure that will help us all now." Mvula turned to Zuberi.

"And what have you succeeded in doing that was so great? Got us to run away like scared warthogs, backing into an aardvark hole in a termite mound?"

"They would have killed us all. Zuberi saved all our lives."

"I can speak for myself, Ameena. I did what I had to."

"You are a coward. We should have stayed and fought for our village. And even if we would have all died, we could go and meet our ancestors with pride."

"If you would have made the warriors angrier, they would have killed everyone, after they had made them scream."

"What happened after we left, Talib?" She looked worried.

"They killed some more people, your father and your father"— Zuberi and Ameena caught their breath—"quite quickly, and they died fast, with no pain," I added, hoping that would help a little. "Then many ran into the jungle to find you men. Those of us that were left chose to sit quietly and wait for them to return. There was nowhere for us to go, so we just sat and waited to see what would happen."

"And what did happen?"

"He betrayed Sekou. I know, I saw it, I was hiding in a tree."

"Some hero you are, Mvula," remarked Zuberi dryly.

"He did, I saw him."

"I didn't mean for him to die." The stress was becoming too much. Remembering all that horror and my part in the death of Sekou was just too much. I started to cry. I was not proud of crying in front of all these tribesmen and women, my village neighbours, but I just couldn't stop myself.

"I'm sorry, I'm so sorry for what happened to Sekou. I really, really didn't think that they would, that they could do that. They just cut his throat, like that, and I was just here and, and, and then they just left him...and then the flies came. And I thought that maybe they would do it to me. And I could feel the blade on my neck and I wished it to be over, like a nightmare, and then maybe I could wake up, and, and, and then it would be over, it would be finished."

I don't remember much that happened for a while after that. I just closed my eyes and allowed myself to fall. Gentle hands caught me and helped me softly down. I was lying on something very soft and warm. I opened my eyes to find myself with my head on the lap of Ameena. She smiled gently down at me.

"It's okay," she whispered in a soothing voice, "just go to sleep." And like a baby, in the safety of his mother's protective arms, in the middle of all those people, in the middle of the day, in the middle of that discussion, I just turned my head to one side, rested on my good arm and good leg, and gently, gently allowed myself to drift into the first peaceful sleep since the warriors arrived.

It was some hours later that I woke up; the sun had moved in the heavens and the shadows had run away to other places. I was no longer with my head on Ameena's lap; they must have moved me, as I was now on some soft leaves under a new shelter, attached to the outside of one of the caves.

I slowly sat up. I must have been left on or had turned onto my bad side, as my little arm and leg were aching. It is something that often happens when I sleep on my bad side.

One of the women saw that I was awake and brought me a bowl of water. I didn't want to look at her; I was feeling so ashamed of what I had done, how I had behaved.

It was only a few minutes before they all knew that I was awake. Quite quickly there was again a crowd around me.

"Bring him to the fire." There was no doubt that it was Zuberi who gave the order. I was then lifted, not unkindly, onto my feet, and more or less gently pushed towards the main fire pit. The crowd parted to let me pass and so I found myself at the fire pit, surrounded by all my tribesmen and women. I was not at all at ease, I didn't want to be there, I just wanted to run away, for a demon to take me in its mouth and fly away with me, for the ground to open and swallow me up, anything just not to be there, in front of all those people.

I bowed my head before Zuberi. "I am sorry for my crying. It is not okay."

Ameena stepped forward. "For me it was okay. You have lived some hard things these last few days, Talib. We all need to cry sometimes. It is okay." Ameena was soft and kind. I looked to Zuberi.

"We have things to discuss," was how he dealt with the subject of my crying. "We were talking about your idea that we should return to the village."

"It is stupid, it is suicide!"

"Mvula, I have not asked for your opinion."

"Well, you will get it anyway. Your father might have been our leader, you are not."

"Until we have time to discuss that issue, I am acting as leader, and the others are okay with that."

"You seem very sure of yourself, but I doubt that everyone is likely to be as stupid as you and go back into the village to have their throats cut."

"They won't have their throats cut, not as long as they don't try and fight with the warriors."

"So, my little Talib," he said, advancing towards me, like so many times in the past. As Zuberi had said, when he was not happy with something, he would look for me and empty his anger or sadness on my little crippled body. "You would like me to leave my knife in the sack and be a woman for these killers?"

Zuberi moved softly but quickly to shield me from my own childhood demon. He spoke quietly. "Mvula, go and sit down, we need to understand why Talib had come for us." Mvula gave me a bad look. This time someone had come to stop him. Having neither father nor cousins in the village, there had been no one I could turn to for help.

"I have said, we need the men back in the village because the women, the old men, and the children cannot do our own tasks and yours. There is no meat, or fish, or fruit, or nuts. Things need to be repaired and new things made, heavy things need to be carried. We cannot do it all."

"But why should we want to go back?"

"Because it is our village, and your mothers and fathers and wives and sons and daughters want you and need you."

"To be slaves? Is that how they need us? We should ready ourselves and then rush in and give those warriors a taste of our knives. We can also slice throats."

"Mvula, you are not wrong, it is one of the possibilities."

"No, he is wrong." He turned back to look at me again. Maybe Zuberi wouldn't protect me a second time, but I had to speak, I had no choice. "If you attack the warriors in the village, even if you kill them all, you will not be strong enough to protect us from that other tribe. They have many warriors and they know how to fight. You know how to hunt, how to wait, how to trap. Their warriors know how to look you in the eyes and stick a knife straight into your belly. You do not know how to do that."

"Yes, I can!" roared Mvula. "I am not a coward!" This time he turned towards Zuberi. "Some of us are not cowards, Zuberi. We are men, and we are ready to fight and die like men."

"Would you like to fight and die like a warthog, and for nothing, or would you have brains enough to wait and maybe rescue our village?" They all looked at me; they could not believe that this was little Talib, standing there, screaming at Mvula like he was a silly child, caught sticking a branch in a scorpion's nest. To be true, I must have been the most surprised of all, but he was being just so, so stupid.

Mvula stopped and looked at me; he was too shocked to be angry. The anger would come later, and I had better find some good protection or be a long way away before then.

It was Ameena who spoke then. "Do you have some sort of a plan, Talib?"

"The warriors will not leave the village because their tribe needs food. I believe that the sorghum has not grown because it was not planted properly, not with the proper offerings to the spirits."

"What do you plan to do, Talib?" she asked softly.

"I will go in the planting season and I will ask the spirits to give them a good crop."

"Are you MAD?"

"No, Mvula, I am not mad. These are people like you and me, with friends and families; they have done what they have done because they were hungry. If they have food they will not want to fight, and they will not care if the warriors stay or leave our village. Then, if the warriors will not go, you can kill them, the rest of their tribe will not bother to revenge them."

"I will not ask if they wish to go, I will kill them all, that is all."

"When it is time," added Zuberi, "when it is time." Mvula seemed happier. Yes, Zuberi said that he would be able to kill all the warriors; yes, if necessary he could wait. Strangely enough, Mvula was quite good at waiting. He was one of those types of people who liked to plot. Only one thing that he was not happy with—me.

"You—you never, ever talk to me like that again. Do you hear me?"

"I hope the warriors in the village can't hear you, Mvula." One of the men laughed. "Leave him alone, what he said was right."

"Is this how you convince the warriors that we should come back?" Zuberi smiled at me. I could feel the tension start draining out of me, and I sat down heavily on the floor.

"Talib, would you be able to call the spirits to bless the new crops?"

"Yes, Ameena, I think that I can."

"And when you return to the village, could you help send my father to our ancestors? I hope that it is not too late and his spirit has not been already taken by a bad sorcerer or demon." Her voice began to shake a little; she must have only now thought about her father being dead and what that would mean for his spirit.

"Do not worry, Ameena, his spirit is with your ancestors." She looked at me in a confused way.

"I should know, I took him to the passage myself. He was looking for you, but you were not near the village. He wanted to stay and see that you were okay. It took some time to convince him that he had to go or he would be trapped here in a bad way. He asked me to tell you that he loves you greatly and will take your love back to your mother, who must miss you." I wasn't looking at her as I was speaking, but when I had finished, I looked up and there were tears in her eyes. She came over to me and hugged me, not like before, when I was like a child and she my mother. This time, it was she who was the child and I the parent. I was holding Ameena like she was my own child, could this day show any more wonders?

"I still think it might be a trap." Mvula was not convinced.

"Then keep some men with you, hide in the trees, and if the others are killed or captured, then revenge them with the blood of the warriors." They were looking at me again in an odd way. "But then you must take everyone away, for the other members of the tribe will kill everyone they find after that."

"Well, Mvula, does that sound like a good plan to you?" the young leader asked gently.

"And you, Zuberi, you would trust Talib and return with him to the village?"

Ameena, straightened up from my lap, said, "I, for one, will go." Zuberi got up.

"It is simple. Everyone that wants to return to the village will come now. Those that do not will stay with Mvula and watch from a safe place. If we are welcomed and stay safe, then the rest of you will return tomorrow." And with that, it was decided. Most of my tribesmen started to collect their belongings, and soon we headed back to the village.

We arrived at the village before nightfall. Oladele must have had lookouts watching for us, as when we arrived at the meeting place, he was already there waiting for us with the warriors. They were standing; some had their knives out, the rest were ready with their hands on the knives' handles. I could feel that even Zuberi was a little scared; we all were. Zuberi walked slowly up to Oladele. It was clear that he was the leader. Zuberi looked straight into Oladele's face. Everyone became very tense. One only looks into the eyes of a lover or an enemy that one is going to fight. Zuberi put his hand on his knife and started to pull it out. Was he mad? Then he looked down, down to Oladele's feet. He continued to take out his knife. Nobody moved. The knife was now out. Nobody moved, nobody spoke; the world had stopped to catch its breath.

The knife hit the ground. Zuberi turned silently to the others. They all took out their knives and dropped them to the ground. That done, he walked silently to the cooking pots and served himself a small portion of food, took a spoon, found his spot by one of the huts, sat down, and started to eat. One by one, all the others followed his example, even the warriors. Except for one, he stayed long enough to collect the knives. Oladele was not so trusting as to leave all those chances for revenge just lying around waiting for someone to think to use them.

And that was how the men returned to the village.

Sleep Is Habit-Forming —
Part Two

"Wake up!"

He was so tired; he had allowed his eyes to close, just for the shortest second. "I am sorry, Master, I'm just so tired. I cannot stay awake any longer."

"Yes, it is difficult to stay awake so long, just sitting and listening to an old man's stories."

"Yes, it is. No, no, not the story, even if it is a bit long. But it is difficult to stay awake."

"Good, off you go, then."

"I can go?" He got up, wrapping the blanket around himself as he walked to the simple dwelling and his waiting bed.

"Do you know what it is that you are going for?"

"Yes, I'm going to bed."

"Bed? Who said anything about going to bed?"

"But—"

"No buts. I agree that just sitting is giving the body the message that it should relax, even sleep. That is why we shall take a pause from the story and activate your body, therefore giving it the message that it is not the moment to sleep."

"So I can't go to bed now?" He had already imagined himself curled up, under his cover, drifting off into the world of soft dreams.

"Not now." His voice was gentler than usual. "This is an exercise for you to realise just how strong your body really is, even if your mind remains weak."

"Why do you say that my mind is weak?"

"Because you allow it to convince you that you cannot continue."

"But I'm falling asleep."

"You were falling asleep. Now you are not falling asleep, you are going inside to get my Damaru for me."

"Oh?" And, almost as if in a trance, he went inside to get the Master's Damaru. Some minutes later he returned with the little two-headed drum with the two little balls attached to either side.

"And now you will dance."

"Dance? I can't dance, I don't know how to."

"Again the little mind is blocking you. Maybe you think that you don't know how to dance, but your body knows how to move to a rhythm. Listen to the drum and follow its rhythm, listen to my voice and flow with the melody." The old man twisted his right hand; first to left, then to the right. The little balls swung in parallel arcs, hitting the two drum heads, almost as one, then curving backwards only to beat on the other drum head. As so the rhythm began.

At the same time, the Master began to chant, but the sound he emitted was not a single sound but a complex combination of throat and tongue and mouth and lip sounds.

Dhargey looked on, for a moment totally lost for what to do. He hesitated a little, but as it seemed that there was nothing else for it, he started to move his body. Maybe it was his tiredness, maybe the chanting of the Master, maybe something from deep within himself, but soon it wasn't that he was moving his body; he became aware that his body was moving itself and he—his mind, at least—had become an independent spectator.

The drum beat, the Master chanted, and the disciple's body danced.

The rhythm started to increase, then faster and faster; his body spun and swept and circled and leaped.

Time and space had lost all importance; there was only the music and the dance. However, the mind was not totally absent; it soon began to realise that the body, which, only a little time before, was falling into the black abyss of exhausted sleep was now full of golden, shining energy. It could not understand, it would not understand, but just the same it could not deny its own reality.

Gradually the music slowed down; the drumbeat stopped and the chanting faded into air.

"Come, it is now time to relax your body a moment." He pointed to a nearby spot next to a large rock. "Here, sit, lean your back against the rock. Good. Allow your eyes to close for a few moments and carry on the dance."

160

He sat down as directed, pulling his blanket tightly around him to ward off the very early morning chill, and closed his eyes. He returned to the dance; again he could feel his body, floating and falling like a kite in a mad wind. Further and further, he entered into the movement and the endless flow of energy, but somewhere in all that he must have fallen asleep.

"Come, it is time to continue." The Master woke him up gently, a fresh bowl of hot tea in his hand.

They returned to the fire.

"Now, where was I? Oh, yes, the tribesmen had just returned to the village..."

The Lost Tribe – Part Two

The next day, things were a little difficult to begin with, but quite soon the men and the women that had come back with them returned to their normal everyday tasks. There was a little problem when some of the men had to go to Oladele to get their knives back—one cannot work without a knife—but he seemed not too worried to return their knives. He must have thought, as I had, that if anything should happen to him and his men, the men from their village would come and kill everyone in our village.

Mvula must have been close by, watching, because quite soon after the men got their knives back, he arrived with the rest of the men and women, and so most of the village had returned home.

It was some days later when I heard one of the men complaining about something. He was saying to another man that it was all right for him to live in this way, that even if he was a slave to the warriors and their tribe, his life was almost the same as before.

You see, the second man was living with his wife, but the wife of the first man had been taken away to the other village.

I spoke to Zuberi about this and then asked to see Oladele. I explained the problem to him, but he said that it was not his business, nor was it my business, and that I should not get involved in things that didn't concern me.

I was about to leave, when I found an unexpected ally.

"Why not let him go and see if he can convince the others to release her?" My ally was none other than Mashama. "It would do no harm to get back those women; they could help in the fields. And if the men are happy they are less of a threat."

Oladele was surprised to hear Mashama speak like this and it had a strong effect on him.

"Do you wish to take Talib?" How long had he known my name? "To the village and support him to try and bring back the women?"

"I think it is a good thing to do."

"Okay, tomorrow you go to bring back the women if you can."

"Thank you, Oladele, thank you, Mashama," I said, and ran back to the village centre as fast as my unequal legs could carry me, to share the news with the others.

It was there and then that the explanation for Mashama's attitude became clear. One of the women that had been carried off was the sister of Chifundo, and Mashama was in love with Chifundo.

The village of the warriors was almost a day's walk to the south. It was not a very difficult path because it was mostly downhill, but going down meant that it got hotter and drier. As long as the path is fairly smooth and even, my short leg doesn't bother me walking.

Now I could see in front of me the dry fields. They must have had too little water to grow their crops.

I wondered if they had a shaman to call on the ancestors and the spirits to bless the crops and to pray for rain, and if he knew the best things to give as offerings and the best songs to sing and dances to dance.

We arrived towards the evening. The village was very big; there were many cooking places and many, many people, more than I had ever seen in all my life.

Mashama took me to his family, where I was welcomed and offered food and drink. It was most strange; even though the two tribes lived only a day's journey away, we had never had any contact before, and even the food tasted different.

I agreed with Mashama not to try and start looking for the girls tonight. I unrolled my sleeping mat, turned onto my good side, and gratefully slipped off to sleep.

The next day Mashama began to ask around to find out who had taken the girls. After that, it was just a matter of finding them and trying to convince the men—and sometimes also the girls— to allow them to return with us.

To be honest, we were not very successful at all. One man was forced by one of his wives to send back the girl; another found his girl to be lazy and unpleasant, and couldn't be bothered to beat her enough to change; a third was a very soft man who let the tears of the young girl soften his heart, so he let her go.

Anyway, the next day, we said goodbye to Mashama's family and, taking the three girls, we set off, back to our village.

It was harder for me on the return trip, as it was almost all uphill, and not having two strong legs it isn't easy to climb.

We arrived back just before the evening meal and were welcomed with excitement tinged with regret. Many of the parents, brothers, sisters, husbands, and boyfriends had built up hopes and expectations of seeing the women return with us. Most, of course, were disappointed.

Mashama had taken his meal and, as was now his custom, went and ate with the warriors. He would then wait a while and return to our part of the village to spend a few moments alone with Chifundo.

What was not the custom was that after having eaten, he returned with other members of the warrior group, one of them being Oladele.

We became a little nervous. I could see the women backing away into dark corners. The men started to stroke the handles of their knives. The warriors came close to the fire and squatted down as we men do. There was plenty of space, as the women had all run away. We waited, looking at Oladele, wondering what he was going to say, hoping that he had no reason to be angry and to punish us. We continued to look towards him, but he wasn't the first to speak.

"We have been talking about the women from your village," Mashama began quietly, "and we think that it is not right that your women should be the slaves of our tribesmen." It was surely not by chance that he was looking towards Chifundo when he said this.

Zuberi moved to speak, but Ameena touched him gently on the shoulder. He stopped and looked at her as she took the turn to speak.

"Oladele, what is it that your warriors think to do?"

"We feel that our tribe has forgotten us here. They do not care what happens to us as long as we send enough sorghum for them to keep eating." Oladele was also speaking quietly, but we could all hear him well enough. "You people have not made trouble for us, you have even promised to help us please the spirits when we plant our seeds next year." Some people of the village did not understand what he was talking about. I had not told them of my offer to perform the rituals before next year's planting, so the other tribe would have a good harvest and then leave us in peace.

Zuberi turned his head slightly towards Mvula. "As you treat us right, there is no need to fight."

Oladele nodded and continued, "These women are your daughters, sisters, girlfriends, and wives. We warriors have talked about the situation and have decided to help you."

"And how would you help us?" Mvula was not so easy to convince.

Mashama jumped to his feet, quite excited, and said, "We will steal back your women."

It seemed to me that several weeks of having very little to do, especially after all the excitement of attacking our village, had ended up with them being some very bored warriors. Bored and a little angry with their own tribal leaders for having left them away from their family and friends with nothing much to do.

"Some of the women said that they didn't want to come back." They didn't much appreciate my bit of information, but I felt that I had to warn them of that.

166

"Mashama has already told me of this." Oladele seemed very confident. "The women were forced to go to our village. We will steal them away, if they want to or not."

"You won't hurt them, will you?" Ameena was always thinking of things like that.

"They are offering to do a good thing for us. I'm sure they will do their best not to hurt them."

"Your shaman is right, we are offering to do a good thing for you. We will not hurt your women." I was amazed, not that Oladele was offering to do a good deed; he and his warriors had enough reasons to do what they had offered. No, what amazed me was that he had called me a shaman.

"Then we will come with you." Mvula was still not happy with the idea.

"Zuberi, can you explain to Mvula why that might not really be a good idea?"

"Just because someone chooses to call you a shaman doesn't mean that you have some sort of position here." Mvula didn't like my reaction to his suggestion, but Zuberi had understood my worry.

"If any of us are found sneaking around their village, they will think that we are attacking them and will kill us straightaway. Then they could even decide to come here and kill more of us, to warn us not to try again."

"It would be good if someone from the village would go. The girls would be less scared if there was someone they knew."

"Ameena is right, but it might not be safe to send a woman." Zuberi was thinking out loud.

There is a thing that happens, sometimes, so I've been told, when different people or animals, in different places but at the same time, all think of the same thing at once. And it seems that was what happened here. As if they had all practiced a special dance, to the beat of an invisible drum, everyone turned and looked towards me.

"Yes, let the shaman go. He's not a girl, but he's not really a man, either." Mvula had to say something, but it didn't matter either way; it was decided by general agreement.

I left to go to my hut quite soon afterwards. Although I was sure that everyone thought it was a good idea, I was still worried. Anything could go wrong, and I needed someone to talk to, to help me decide what to do. My hut is by itself, quite a long way away from the other huts. That way, I do not keep the others awake if I beat my drum or shake my gourd rattle.

I closed the curtain of my hut, pulled out my rattle, sat down on my mat with my back against the wall, closed my eyes, and started shaking my rattle. Shaking a rattle can help you clear your mind and open yourself up to see and hear the spirits, but only singing can call them to you.

I shook my rattle for some time. It helped me to settle, to relax, to reconnect to that part of myself that is linked to the unchanging flow of life; that knows who I am, but also who I was, and maybe even who I will be. After some time with the rattle, when my mind was ready to focus on the question and who I wished to ask it to, I started to sing. The song of a shaman is not a song that anyone can know. It is either passed down to him by another shaman or it is taught to him by the spirits.

I sang and I shook my rattle, and sang and shook, and sang and shook, until I was no longer in my hut. My earthly body was inside, propped up against the back wall, but I was no longer there. I was somewhere else, and I was no longer alone.

"What is it that you have come to ask?"

"Should I go with the warriors to bring back the women?"

"Why do you ask this question?"

"I am scared that it will end badly, that I might be caught, that they will cut my throat like they did to Sekou, and the flies will drink my blood."

"Why do you fear this, Talib?"

"I am scared."

"What are you scared of?"

"That they will kill me."

"Are you scared of death, Talib?"

"No, death is not a problem. I will go through the passage and meet the elders and my ancestors."

"Then what are you afraid of?"

"That it will hurt; I am scared of the pain."

"Did Sekou suffer?"

"Sekou died quickly."

"What are you scared of, Talib?"

"That I will act like a coward and cry like a child for them not to kill me."

"Will you cry like a child for them not to kill you?"

"No, no, I will not."

"What are you afraid of?"

"I'm afraid that I might die before I become a man."

"Is not dying with honour and courage not being a man?"

"I could die with honour and courage."

"So, what are you afraid of?"

"He called me *shaman*."

"Yes?"

"It is a great responsibility."

"It is."

"I am very young. I caused the death of Sekou. I am not worthy of this title."

"Who else can take on this work?"

"There is no one."

"Will you take on this role for power and pride?"

"Maybe."

"Is that what you are afraid of?"

"I am only little more than a boy and a cripple."

"When does a boy become a man?"

"When he takes on a man's tasks."

"How much physical strength does it take to be a shaman?"

"Physical strength has no value in the worlds of spirit."

"So?"

"I am neither a boy nor a cripple in this world."

"What are you scared of?"

"There are those that have abused me in the past."

"And you are scared that you will abuse your powers to take revenge?"

"It would feel good."

"When would it feel good?"

"When they realise that I have power."

"And you need to abuse them for them to see that you have power?"

"When I have power, then they will know it."

"Will hurting them prove that you have power?"

"No, I know that I have power, they are starting to see and to feel it."

"How does that feel?"

"It feels good, but I'm not used to it."

"Will you get used to it?"

"I am getting used to it."

"What are you afraid of?"

"That if I don't get some sleep tonight, I will not be awake for the raid."

"So what will you do about that?"

"I will thank you and then I will sleep." And so I did.

The next morning the warriors and I started to repeat the walk that I had made the day before. As Mashama was again with his friends, I walked alone and in silence. I found the path even easier than the first time, as this was now the third time I'd gone on it in two days and I was learning which bits were more steep or slippery than the others.

Suddenly (for me, that is, maybe the others were already aware), Oladele called out for us to stop. He led us off the path and into a little group of trees to rest and hide until the night would come. I was very thankful for this, as I had slept less than I would have hoped the night before and was feeling quite tired. We ate and drank; I think that some of the warriors were to keep watch, but I didn't care too much about that. I was already turning onto my good side to make myself comfortable, and was gently falling asleep.

It seemed that I had just found the good position to sleep in, when someone gently kicked me on my bad leg. I forced myself awake and was just about to ask him why I wasn't supposed to go to sleep, when I noticed that it had gone dark. I must have slept for the whole afternoon without being aware of it.

The men were all standing or sitting together; some were eating sorghum cakes or chewing on dried meat, but they seemed also to be waiting for something or someone. Then I heard a noise coming from the path. Everyone tensed up, but nobody moved. I squinted into the darkness. I saw something moving towards us, then I noticed the eyes; these are often the first thing you notice when a black man comes towards you at night. It was Mashama, who must have gone back into the village to check where all the women were so that the warriors could get to them quickly, without wasting too much time looking for them.

Altogether there were eleven women from my tribe in the village. Most of them were either sleeping alone or with other women; that would not be much of a problem. Three of them were sleeping with a man; one of them wanted to come home, but the other two had said to us, when we asked them yesterday, that they were happy here and wanted to stay.

It was decided, then, to leave those two that wanted to stay because it was too dangerous to try and kidnap them, against their will, with a man next to them. To take all the women not sleeping with a man, whether they wanted to come or not, and after they had all been brought here, to go back and try and rescue the last one, even though she was in the man's bed, because this was Chifundo's sister, and Mashama couldn't go back without trying his best to rescue her.

My job, as explained to me by Oladele, was to go with Mashama. He would take me to the women who had asked to return to our village but were not allowed to by the men who had taken them. I was to gently waken them, so they would not make any noise, make sure they knew who I was, and then lead them out of the village, where one of the warriors would bring them back here.

I followed Mashama down the path towards the village. The moon was hidden by a blanket of clouds, and as it was dark and I did not know the path well, it was a little difficult. The spirits were looking after me, and soon the clouds parted enough for me to see better. I said a short prayer of thanks.

We entered the village by a different way than before, so as to be closer to my first woman. She was not sleeping in a hut, but in a tent with some other women and young children. I was worried about going inside because I was very afraid that I would wake up one of the other women or a child. I remembered a magic phrase to become invisible—not that I had ever tried to use it before. I started to chant the spell, over and over again. I do not know if it made me invisible or not, but at least it stopped me worrying about the other women and the children.

I walked softly into the tent. There was not a lot of space to walk between the sleeping people. I managed to get to the girl, knelt down, and softly whispered her name. It is well-known that even in the deepest sleep, if someone whispers your name, then you will hear it and wake up. I hoped that there were no other women with the same name.

I just kept repeating her name, and after what seemed like quite a long time, she started to turn and wake up.

"Don't make any noise," I whispered urgently, "don't say anything. It's me, Talib. We've come to take you home." She looked lost and confused, but after a moment of squinting at me in the darkness, she finally recognised me. Her reaction seemed a little strange; she saw me, looked again to be sure, then she shook her head as if to say, "It is not possible." But then she shrugged her shoulders, silently got up, grabbed some clothes, and slipped out of the tent.

We made our way back to the edge of the village and were met by one of the warriors. She took one look at him and made as if to run away. It was only by chance that Mashama appeared at that moment. She accepted that we really were there to take her home, and not just to catch her and abuse her with someone else.

We then agreed that Mashama would wait for me outside the huts and he would pass them over to the other warriors at the edge of the village.

There were three more women for me to get.

The first was quite easy; she was sleeping alone in a small hut. I had a bit of a problem to wake her, but as she was alone, I could make quite a lot of noise without worrying too much about waking anyone else.

The second was sleeping with two other women, and one of them turned or moved every time I made any noise. I tried to whisper the woman's name, softly in her ear, but either it was too quiet or the other woman would threaten to wake up. I was not made to do this kind of thing. Every moment that passed, I would get more and more stressed, more and more frightened. Eventually I placed my hand over her mouth, to make sure she didn't scream, and quite roughly shook her awake. She woke very suddenly and tried to pull my hand off, but I was too scared to let her. With my other hand, I pulled her head towards me so that our noses were almost touching. I mouthed the words, "It's me, Talib, it's me, Talib," several times. After some time, she stopped struggling and I released her mouth. I pointed towards the door and she nodded her head to show that she understood. From then it took only a few seconds for us to be out and into the cool night air.

The third woman was sleeping with one other woman, who had a small baby. As soon as I walked into the hut, the baby moved. It turned its head towards me and started to agitate its little body. I could feel the panic start to rise in my body; it would only need to start to cry and we would all be lost. I crept softly into the hut; the baby followed my every movement with its eyes. I crept over to the third woman, bent down, and called her name. She woke quite easily, saw that it was me, and quietly sat up. I pointed out to her that the baby was awake and she nodded her head to say that she understood. We slowly got up and went to leave. This somehow disturbed the baby, and it balled its little hands in tight fists and started to cry. I just wanted to run away as quickly as possible, but the girl pushed me towards the back of the hut and ran to the baby. At that very moment, the mother, hearing her baby cry, even in her sleep, sat up. The girl already had the baby in her arms. She turned to the mother and said, "Here, I think he must be hungry."

The mother, still half asleep, took the infant, opened her loose top, attached the baby to one of her ample breasts, turned over, and went back to sleep. The baby was now happily sucking; it hardly reacted as we quietly slunk out of the hut and into the protective, black invisibility of the African night.

We quickly found our way to the edge of the village, where we were met by Mashama. From there to the meeting point was only a matter of minutes. Everyone was already ready to go; they didn't want to be too close when the villagers realised that the women had been stolen away. Many of the warriors were carrying women that were tied up and had sacks over their heads. I imagine that they must have struggled to begin with, but now they seemed to have exhausted themselves and lay quietly on the shoulders of the warrior carrying them.

The other women, those that had wanted to return, seemed happy and excited but also scared and nervous, all at the same time. They were not allowed to talk, even if they had wanted to. They grouped themselves together as if that way they would be safer. Every time there was the slightest sound, they turned as one; a herd of frightened antelopes, their huge eyes staring into the dark, ready to run for their lives at any given moment.

Mashama led the group and Oladele and another warrior stayed back to block any villagers that might try to follow. I overheard Mashama saying to someone that if the people came after us, he would wait until they were quite close and then run away in a noisy way in another direction.

The return was quite difficult and slow going; there had been a little rain and tiny rivers had sprung up everywhere, creating small ponds and slippery, muddy tracks which I had much trouble to walk up.

I was exhausted from the walking and the nervous tension of getting the women out, and we were going back up in the dark. The women walking were scared and nervous, and not used to walking on a path they didn't know and in the dark. The warriors were taking turns to carry the tied-up women, but there were more women than warriors so no one got a long break before he had carry again.

We were getting slower and slower; it seemed that we would never get back. Then there was a sudden movement in front of us. My first thought was, how had they managed to move so fast so as to get in front of us? Everyone stopped moving, everyone stopped breathing, everyone stopped trusting that they would ever get back to the village.

Suddenly, the girl that had carried the baby screamed out, "Ameena!" The two sisters rushed into each other's arms. It was Ameena and the men from the village; they had been waiting for us. The warriors were relieved of their burdens, and the women we half helped, half carried back. I was the only one that no one thought to help.

"Feeling a little tired, oh great shaman?" It was Mvula, come once again to mock me. "Here." I knew that I was tired, but I didn't think I had fallen asleep, and what I was seeing was surely a dream. Mvula was offering me his arm as a support and was smiling at me.

Surprised but appreciating the help, I made my way back to the village. It was only when we got there and I watched Ameena's sister jump into Mvula's arms that I finally understood why he had suddenly become so friendly towards me.

That night we had a big feast and everyone, including the warriors, joined in. Then I could also see that most of the girls that, to begin with, were forced to be with the warriors were now acting as their girlfriends. So it was not such a big surprise that they had been so open to support bringing back the friends and sisters of their new mates.

The village had become alive again. Even though we still had to send food to the tribe, the people were happy and contented. I was worried for a while that the men would come looking for the women we had stolen, but Oladele was sure that the elders would not support them, as they would not wish for a fight between the warriors that had helped us and the other tribesmen. After a few days, I became sure that he was right.

The only thing that still was not perfect was that some of the warriors did not want to live with us. They themselves had families and girlfriends of their own.

Sometimes they returned to their village, but they had been instructed to stay with us to make sure that the food would keep coming.

The time passed and it soon came to be the season for the planting of the seeds. I took my drum and my rattle and set off once more for the other village. I was not alone; Oladele, Mashama, and several other warriors came with me.

This time when I arrived at the village, there were people to welcome me. I was not used to this, I felt uncomfortable and embarrassed.

"You are a shaman?" an elder challenged me.

"He is a shaman for us," answered Oladele for me.

"You are very young for a shaman," he continued, without responding to Oladele.

"The spirits do not question the age of those that summon them." I was starting to feel irritated. I was quite scared during the walk to the village, but my fear was quickly being transformed into a growing anger because of the old man's questioning.

"We have no shaman in the village, and since he passed into the world of the ancestors, our crops have not grown. Talib has the confidence of his village. I feel that we are fortunate that he has offered to ask the spirits to bless this planting." Oladele spoke in quite a formal way. I think he was a little frightened of the village elder. But I had succeeded in convincing him that without the support of the spirits, it was very likely that this crop would also fail.

"And why would you want to help us?" The elder continued to challenge me.

"When two elephants fight, it is the grass that suffers." This was a proverb known to him and he stopped for a moment to think.

An old woman walked into the circle where we were standing. She had no right to join into a discussion between men, but she did not look as if she cared about this custom. I think that she must have been listening from somewhere close but hidden, since she carried on the conversation.

"Two people can bring an elephant into a house," she added. The old man looked at her in a less than friendly way.

"Women should not interfere with men's talk."

"When men gibber like monkeys, they should stay swinging in the trees." I had not heard that saying before. The old man turned again to her and spoke in an irritated way.

"What do you want here?"

"The boy has come to request the spirits to bless our crops. I have heard that it was his own idea. He is not stupid; if our crops grow, our warriors will leave his village and all their crops will be again for them. If we have poor crops next year, then they will have to share their harvest again with us. A good crop for us means more for his village; his idea is good for all of us. So, stop asking him useless questions and offer him a drink of hospitality." And with that, she turned on her heel and walked off.

The men didn't speak for a moment, but then the elder took a deep breath and turned back to me. "Welcome, shaman, we are honoured by your presence. Please accept our humble offerings." And with that, he ran off, as fast as his old legs would carry him, to order the women to prepare a welcome drink and dinner for me.

I had never been treated like this before and I wasn't very comfortable with it, but I also knew that for the spirits to see the village honouring me like this would make them more willing to do as I asked.

After the meal was over I walked to the fields. I had my drum in my hand. The others had left me at the edge of the fields and then returned to the village. I sat down in the middle of a field and started to beat the drum. I had brought a blanket with me, as I knew that it would be a long, cold night.

First, I needed to know if the spirits would accept to bless these fields for the crops to be planted; otherwise, there would be no sense planting anything, it just wouldn't grow. Then I had to ask when they could plant the seeds, which seeds to plant, and if there was any special thing they should do so that the spirits would make the crop grow big and healthy.

I slid my bottom around on the ground to find the most comfortable position and changed my breathing. There are many ways to breathe; most people do not know this. Most of the time we breathe without thinking; this is the everyday breathing. It is not deep, it is quite quick. Then there is the breathing of fear; it is quicker and shorter. It connects us to the animal world, to the antelope so we can run to escape, to the chameleon so we can stop and hide, or to the lion so we can roar and fight. There is the sleep breath, which takes us slowly to the world of air and sleep and dreams. There is the breath after running or fear, which is deep but short, and which joins us back to the earth. And there is the breath of fire, which is very long and very deep. This is the breath that connects us to the power of the soul; that opens up the body to allow our energy to leave and to fly, and to talk to the spirits and the ancestors and the demons and the dead.

And so I beat the drum and began my breathing. Sometimes I would sing, that would also help to call the spirits, but mostly I just beat the drum and let my body breathe the fire.

It became colder and darker, time passed, nothing happened. It is like that; there is the drumming, the breathing, and nothing happens, and nothing happens, and nothing happens, and then I'm out. Out of my heavy earth body, out of this dimension and into the worlds of spirit. Looking into and through the darkness, I seem to see shapes; moving, floating, swaying, swooping, sailing on the winds. These are the spirits of these fields. There are other spirits that I must talk to that can bless the fields and help the harvest, but first I must ask the spirits of these fields if they will agree for the crops to be planted here this year.

My hand touches the hard earth (even when I am in contact with the spirits in the lighter worlds, I am still in contact with my own heavy body). I understand there is a problem: there is not always enough water, the ground becomes too dry and the plants die. I ask what there is to do. While I am waiting, I notice that I myself am thirsty. I get my gourd and take a drink of water, but in this state I am very clumsy, and I spill the water on myself. Some of the water is caught in the folds of the blanket. I take the blanket to let the water drain out and then I understand. I remember the pools of water when climbing back to my village after the rain. They need to make something to collect the water in when it flows down from the hill after the rains. Then they can feed that water to the fields when it becomes dry, and the plants will not die, and the spirits of the fields will be happy.

I stop for a moment; I get up and walk around for a while. My body is aching, especially my bad side. I walk and I stretch, I breathe to reconnect to the earth. I need to ground myself again before my next journey.

I take maybe five or ten minutes; after that, I begin to feel bored. I hunt inside my sack and pull out some sweet sorghum cakes, which I leave on the ground behind me. I plunge my hand once again into the sack; this time I pull out a bag full of grains. These are some of the grains that I have brought from our village, healthy grains from our rich fields. The sacks had been brought some days ago and one member of each family of this village had taken a handful of seeds from a sack. From these seeds, they had each given me one, and it was these token seeds that I lay out in front of me now.

I then sit once again on the hard earth, shift my bottom to find a relatively comfortable position, and this time I start to sing. The song starts off slowly and quietly and gently, the spirits need to be attracted like little scared animals, like bees to a flower, like a warrior into the arms of a maiden. I wish them no harm, it is I who is scared of them, but still I must call to them with a song of honey and sweet sorghum cakes.

I feel their presence; they are here all around me. I offer them my song and beg them to bless this ground and the seeds that the villagers had chosen, and to bring the rains for the plants to drink so that they can grow.

I sing for quite a long time, until I feel that the spirits are satisfied and accept to bless the seeds and the fields. I then get up; I do not look behind to see if the spirits have taken the cakes that I have offered. Tomorrow, someone will come and then they will tell us all if the offerings have been accepted. I have done all that I can for this night, so I make my way back to the village.

As I leave the field, I hear a small movement. Fear starts to enter my body and I begin to breathe in my animals.

"I have been waiting."

"Mother, it is late and it is cold."

"I will take you to your hut and then I will bring you some warm Zebu milk." The old woman was still looking after me.

Even though she was old, it was she that helped me to the hut they had set aside for me. All the sitting on the hard earth had been difficult for my bad leg, and her help was not useless.

My mother is with the ancestors and my father is unknown to me. The tenderness of this old woman touched me deeply, and when at last I was comfortable in my hut and she had left to fetch the milk, I found myself softly crying.

I didn't look at her when she brought the hot drink, but just thanked her quietly and then she left. I took the milk, drank it, thankful for the warm, comforting feeling as the hot liquid slipped down my throat and into my cold belly. Then I curled up on my mat and drifted off into sleep.

The next morning, I shared my experiences of the previous night with my friends and the village elders. I could see that there was again hope in their eyes when I told them that the spirits seemed to accept my request that they bless the fields and look after the crop. They were even happier when a small boy ran back shouting that the spirits had accepted our sacrifice and had eaten all the cakes I had left for them.

All that was left to do now was to purify the fields and the village.

That evening, after the meal was eaten and everything was put away, I took out my mask. This was the first time I had ever put it on to lead anything, so I was a little nervous. What was good was that the moment I put it on, something within me changed. I was no more Talib; I was now my power animal, the golden eagle, strong and powerful, beautiful and dangerous. The tribe looked to me as a leader and helper; the months and months of seeking and collecting its feathers now became all worthwhile.

The villagers themselves were covered in a huge pile of raffia, each carry a carving of Chi Wara, the antelope god, sitting in a basket, attached to their heads. I start the dance; the men leap up and down, often scratching the earth with a long stick that they are holding. For each man, there is a woman following him, dancing behind, fanning him, spreading his powers in all directions.

The drums beat, the men leap and scratch, the women dance and fan and lead them on, through every corner of the village and then round and into the fields. The tempo increases; faster and faster they drum, and they jump and they scratch, and they dance and they fan, and I leap and I shout and I sing to the spirits: "Bless us, bless this village, bless this field, bless these crops."

And suddenly, it is all over. I must have fallen down at some point, I must have lost contact with my heavy physical body, I must have fainted or fallen asleep. For now, here I am, on my mat, in my little hut, waking up, and through the gaps in the roof and walls I can see the sun already high in the heavens.

I crawl, painfully, off my mat and pull open the curtain to force myself into the day. The light is too bright, it hurts my eyes and my head, but after a few moments of breathing in the day, I become used to it. I then notice that the floor outside the hut is carpeted with presents and offerings: food and drink, fans, carvings, knives, and beads. So this is what it means to be a shaman in a big village.

But that was not all. My new adoptive mother was sitting some ways off, waiting for me to awaken, and as soon as I did, she sent for some cold sweet water and some hot spicy soup. My life was at last complete.

I was very happy to stay in that village for the next few days—maybe I could stay there forever—but no. No, my place was in my own village, and some days later I was ready to say goodbye to them and to her, promising to return whenever they should need me again, or maybe just for a visit.

It was much easier to leave than I had thought. You see, it seemed that all I was lacking, that had been stolen away or never given, was there, in that village. What I realised by leaving was that these things had entered my soul; it had found or recovered that which it was missing. And as they were rightly mine, as I left, these parts of me, they came, too.

The time passed; the villagers of the other tribe planted their crops on the next new moon, which is the best time to plant crops like sorghum. They built water traps to collect the rainwater flowing down the hillside during the rainy times and used it when the rain would not come. So, it was not much of a surprise that the crops started growing well.

And as the months passed, the sorghum grew and grew, until it was time to begin the harvest, and at last the village was again able to feed itself.

This was the moment that my tribe was waiting for, or at least that is what I thought. I had expected that as soon as the sorghum was ready for harvest, my village would throw out the warriors, or they would seize the opportunity to leave and return to their own village. This was true for some of them, but many others had become so integrated into the village that they didn't want to leave. So in the end, we had succeeded to get back, to recover, almost all the people in our village that had left or been stolen away, and we had also extracted most of the people that were not of our village.

In the end, with the warriors replacing the men that had been killed, the village ended up with more or less the same workforce as before the troubles began.

And the lonely, insulted, crippled boy had become the new, respected, trusted, and confident shaman.

✳ ✳ ✳

The black man stretched his body in all directions; we had been sitting quite a long time. It was only then that I noticed the thinner and shorter arm and leg. He made to get up, and almost out of nowhere a young black man appeared to help him to his feet.

Understanding this as a signal that the lesson was over, I too got up, bowed to him and then to my master, and turned to leave.

"You will return after you have cleansed yourself." I had not thought to go and cleanse anything; I had thought to go to bed. However, as I had now been instructed, I did as I was told. I left the chamber, cleansed myself, and returned.

When re-entering the chamber, I was surprised to see that there were two mats spread on the floor in the centre of the room. Smoke was curling up to the ceiling, snaking out of a decorated clay pot placed near one of the mats.

"Come," the old master said, and directed me towards a mat, "you will sit and listen and do as you are asked, but nothing else or nothing more." Having already the habit of doing what was asked of me, I didn't see the need to repeat that I should do as I was told, but just the same I walked silently to the mat and sat down.

The black man walked over to the pot, picked it up, and walked round the room consecrating the space with the purifying smoke. This I guessed without any help from the men around me. After the room was prepared, he passed and blew the smoke at and around me, then his helper did the same for him. After all was cleansed, he placed the pot in a space at the end of the two mats, between them. He then sat down on the other mat facing me; I was facing the master at the end of the room, and he gestured for me to turn and face him.

"The story that I told before is a true story. The tribe was separated, bits were lost or stolen, other bits that had nothing to do with it."

"The warriors?"

"Yes, the warriors, they shouldn't have been there. Our souls are like a tribe; when danger comes, bits of our souls can run and hide, some bits can be stolen, and even some bad bits of the souls of others can become joined with our souls." I nodded my head, I could understand this.

"I am a shaman, and as a shaman, I know how to journey to the dimensions of the souls. I can seek out the parts that have run away to protect themselves, that have been lost, that have been stolen away. I can move through this dangerous dimension, find those parts of yourself, and bring them back to you. I can also send my healing animals to eat out those parts of others that have attached themselves to you, to rid you of their evil influence."

"What do I have to do?"

"You open yourself up to me, you let down your barriers, and you let me and my power animals have access to your deepest parts." "But how do I do that?"

"Lie down, listen to the drum when it starts to be beaten, and let yourself be carried where the energy takes you. Resist nothing. Whatever you see, feel, hear, sense, be open to it and flow with your experience. We will do the rest."

I lay down on my mat as requested and waited for the drumming to start. My heart was beating quite fast; I didn't know what to expect. I had experienced so much fear and horror in the past and was scared that any, if not all, of this might flood back into my mind and body.

The drumming started; it was much faster than I had thought it would be. Beyond any desire or control of my own, my body tensed, my breathing and heart speeded up. I could feel my hands clenching into two tight fists, ready to fight, to hit, to defend myself against the awful memories of my childhood years.

And then, nothing happened. There were no flashbacks of the killing of my parents, no memories of my walking, lost for hours or days. The moving finger had really succeeded in emptying those wounds of their pain and left me in peace from that repeated torture.

Slowly, slowly, I and my body began to relax; my heart rate and breathing began to quieten, and my mind to release itself to float where it wished.

At first, I was still clearly in the chamber; I was listening to the drum, beating its quick rhythm. I was aware of all that was happening around me.

Sometime later, I had the idea that I was going down the mountainside. I was slipping, I was falling, I was not able to stop myself. Fear came and sat on my chest, it stopped me breathing. I wanted to push it off and away. But then, I realised that even though I was falling, I was no longer afraid. Maybe it was due to the time; after continuing to fall for quite a time, I was neither hurt nor did I land. I continued to fall. *How can I still be falling?* Then, unexpectedly, I landed, but really quite softly. I was confused. To have fallen so far and for so long, I must surely have gained speed and should have hurt myself quite considerably, but I didn't.

I got up and looked around me. *Where am I?* I wasn't in a cave, nor was I next to the side of the mountain. I had fallen for quite some time, but I found myself in the open air, high up, near the edge of a cliff face, over a huge expanse of water. As I have never seen a sea, I marvelled at the view, vast and limitless. I was scared to go too close to the edge; the ground might not be totally solid, it might crumble under my weight and I might find myself plunging to my doom to the rocks below. I was sure there would be rocks at the bottom of the cliff.

Just then came a massive gust of wind, blowing me towards the edge. There was nothing to hold on to. I tried to push myself, with all my weight against it, but it was no good. It was carrying me towards the edge and I couldn't fight it. So I didn't; I released my resistance and let myself be carried off by the wind—and so I was, carried off by the wind, into the very air.

I have seen people flying kites; light constructions of wood and cloth, thrown this way and that way by the playful wind.

Bobbing, like old bits of wood in a fast-flowing spring river. This is how I felt, but only for the shortest moment. One second I was a toy in the hands of the child wind; the next, I was a soaring eagle, swooping from warm upwind to warm upwind.

I had no physical awareness that I was flying, I was not flapping my arms or anything, but flying I was. I flew over the vast waters, came to jungles, passed over deserts, and then back up to and over snow-capped mountains.

And the rhythm changed and I was called back to my body, back to the chamber, back to my normal existence.

It took me a moment after the drumming had stopped to want to open my eyes and re-join the people there.

"Sit and I will tell you what you need to hear. I went to a dimension of the soul; it is a dangerous place, only experienced shamans dare to go to such places. I looked into your heart and felt your pain. I opened myself to your soul and I could sense the lacks. I reached out with all my senses to feel the threads which would lead me to the lost parts of your soul.

"I followed one and then another, it wasn't difficult for me. I found a child, an innocent, he was playing with a stick. I told him that it was time to go home. He asked me if he could take his stick with him. I said that he could and so he agreed.

"Another time and another child; this one had lost something, something important. He said that he couldn't go home without it. I assured him that it wasn't a problem and he could look for it another day, but it was now time to return, and so he came back.

"A third child was holding a piece of cloth. It belonged to someone, and he was looking for her, but she was not to be found.

I told him that it was time to go home, but he insisted that he could not return until he had found her. This time I was forced to capture the child in a magical trap and then bring him home. He is now safe and will not leave again.

"Then I went off again. There is much fear and violence in this story. I had to fight to get to the next child, but when I got there I could not get him back. He is a prisoner of your weakness. It is not for me to return him to you, that is your journey. You must learn to accept loss and receive love, to become strong and conquer your fear. You must vanquish the foe that still lives inside you. Only then, when he is beaten, can you extract him from your soul and open the path for the other parts of yourself to return."

He then turned his back to me, signalled for his helper to help him up, bowed to my master, and left the chamber. He didn't turn again to me, and I never saw his face ever again in my life.

Sleep Is Habit-Forming —
Part Three

The sun had already come up, and Dhargey was surprised that he had not fallen asleep yet. The Master had allowed him to doze off for little more than fifteen minutes, but that was all the sleep he had all night and now they were about to restart the day.

"Breakfast time," declared the Master, and off went the disciple to do his bidding.

They ate in silence, each one seeming to focus all his attention on the food, as if, by not sleeping, their taste buds had become much more sensitive.

"Come, let us walk."

"Should I bring food and drink?"

"No, we will return for lunch and, as in the past, we might allow ourselves a short nap."

This plan seemed good enough for the younger man. And so, after clearing away the breakfast dishes, they set off up the mountain.

"The body has a very simple form of intelligence, like that of an animal."

"How so?"

"The body has only a few, simple needs: to eat, to sleep, to move, to urinate, and to defecate."

"To do what?"

"To go to the toilet."

"Oh, right."

"If those needs are met, then the body is happy and will gladly serve the mind to do whatever we might wish to do at that moment."

"But we can force it, or not give it what it needs."

"Of course. As with many domesticated animals, the master can mistreat the animal and, to a certain degree, it will accept this mistreatment and continue to do as asked."

"But surely the mind controls everything."

"The mind likes to think that it controls everything. If you consider the four dimensions of a human being: the mind, the emotions, the unconscious, and the body. The emotions, the unconscious, and the body form a type of mass, like a big elephant. The mind is a little man, sitting on the back of this elephant. Most of the time, the elephant is happy to be directed by the little man on its back. It doesn't have to worry itself about what to do or where to go. However, if the elephant is a bit thirsty, it will want to go to the river to drink. The little man can let it go or force it to work. Being a good-natured beast, and being only a little thirsty, it will accept this restriction without much resistance."

"Exactly, the mind is in control."

"If, however, the elephant becomes very thirsty, the little man will have to use an increasing amount of violence to keep the elephant from the river." The disciple smiled and nodded his head. "Sooner or later, the elephant will either ignore the little man, if the violence is not too extreme, or it will go on a rampage and destroy everything in its path. The little man will be lucky if he survives at all! So much for your mind being in control."

"But the body never goes on a rampage."

"No, that is more the domain of the emotions. The reactions of the body are much more fundamental. If you don't eat, you faint; if you try and stay awake too long, you will fall asleep; if you don't move enough, you become weak and fat; and lastly, if you don't choose to stop and go to the toilet, then either you have pain or you just lose control and go anyway."

"But how do you really know what your body needs? I thought that I had to go to bed to sleep, but I'm still up with only a few minutes of sleep."

"Like with everything else, you need to learn to communicate with it. Not to be an abuser or a victim to something, you need to open an appropriate channel of communication with it. That way, you can understand its wants, needs, and desires, and it can understand yours."

"What do you mean, abuser or victim?"

"Abusing your body or any animal is when you choose what suits you without any care or consideration for the other. Being a victim means that, through fear, you are not able to fully live out your life as you would wish."

"And how does one learn to communicate in those circumstances?"

"Listen and I will tell you. My own story continues..."

Ride n Wild Horse

One morning my master called for me to go to him in his chambers. I dutifully changed my clothes, washed, and came to his door.

"Come, Jangbu, come and sit," he said, and so I did as I was bid. "Are you still having your dreams?" he inquired gently.

"No, Master, I have no more dreams. No more do I see the horrors of the attack, nor do I seek what I have lost but cannot find."

"But I hear that you still scream in your sleep, that you wake up soaked with sweat, that often you wander the corridors until late in the night."

"I am sorry, Master, I know that it is not correct and I will stay in my chamber."

"No, you will not stay in your chamber. You have to leave."

"Master, I am sorry, I am truly sorry. If it was such an error, why has nobody spoken before? It isn't fair, it isn't just. You cannot throw me out after all these years just because I couldn't sleep and I walked in the corridors. It just isn't fair."

"Calm yourself, child!" His voice was commanding. "You are not being thrown out."

"But you said—"

"I said that you have to leave. I did not say that you were being thrown out."

"I do not understand."

"Understanding comes with wisdom, wisdom comes from knowledge, knowledge comes from information, information comes from listening, listening comes from silence."

I breathed in, preparing myself to ask another question, but his look reinforced his demand for silence. After a moment, the idea came to me that maybe to stop and meditate might not be a bad idea. I changed my position to the Padmasana, positioning my hands in the Vajra mudrā gesture, and I closed my eyes and waited for some form of enlightenment.

It did not take many minutes to arrive.

"Good, it seems that you have learnt something from the years that you have spent here. Look at me, Jangbu." I opened my eyes to find him gently smiling at me. "I found you; lost, frightened, alone. I brought you to your new parents, I brought you here to this monastery, I brought you into my heart." I couldn't be totally sure, but I thought I could see tears forming in his eyes. "You have managed to grow and to learn in spite of the deep suffering that you carry inside you. For that, you can be very proud, but there is little more that I can do for you to help you deal with your wounds. You are still suffering, and I cannot allow my desire to keep you by my side block me from doing what must be done."

Here, I dared to ask the question. "And what would that be, Master?"

"You must learn to listen. I have already told you." He shook his head in mock despair. "You need to leave this place, so that you might find the means to heal yourself."

"But I don't want to leave. I have nowhere to go."

"Life is a path, whether there are signposts or not, you must walk it."

"But where am I to go?"

"For the moment, I will be your signpost. Do not worry. I will direct you to your next port of call. But first you will need to learn to use your means of transport."

"I do not understand, Master."

"To go where you need to go, first you must learn to ride." As he pronounced the words, it was as if a cloud of freezing rain had burst above my head and I was drenched with the icy liquid. I shook, I gasped, I stared, I froze.

Then I screamed out. "No! No, I cannot do that. Please, please do not ask me to go near a horse. You know how I am with horses." It was no good, just the idea of a horse was too much for me. It was the other thing that still awoke the images, the story, the screams, the blood, the line of red and black.

I was breathing fast, too fast. My heart was beginning to race. I could see them, hear them, feel the fear, smell the smoke. I could see the axe as it shone in the sun, swinging down, swooping down like a beautiful silver bird, diving to catch its prey, grabbing the smooth neck of my mother, ripping it open with its shiny claws, cutting me forever from her as her head flew and rolled away from the useless floppy mass which, moments before, had been her young, alive body.

The horses—the massive, scary horses—had reared and jumped, snorted and whinnied, then galloped away, carrying their masters of death on their smooth, muscled backs. Except one; the one that carried the executioner of both my parents. It seemed to be looking at me, he then urged it forward. They were now coming for me, to kill me, too. I crouched down in the long grass, trying to make myself as small as possible. They came galloping towards me, I screamed a silent, dreadful scream, the horse jumped over the small object, and then they were gone. Gone, but never, ever to be forgotten.

No, no, no, I could not, not ever, go near a horse. Never in my life could I imagine to touch such a beast, let alone ride one. The idea was too crazy. Why would my master even think to speak of such a thing?

He was bringing me a bowl of something. I thought it was water, so I just drank it like that. I was wrong; it was a bowl of *raksi*, a strong rice *raksi*. I coughed and spluttered, but it shocked me out of my nightmare memories. I felt empty and wretched, as I always did after revisiting that awful world of my past.

"Can I have a drink of water?" I asked weakly.

"No, get up and go to the kitchens and get yourself some sweet cakes. I fear that you have missed your breakfast, and until you leave this place, you will fulfil your duties like every other monk."

I slowly got up, bowed, and hurried off to the kitchens to see what there was left of breakfast that I could gulp down before I was due to start my daily tasks.

Some days later, I was instructed to pack some clothes and cleansing materials, to collect a bag of food prepared for me from the kitchen, and to make my way to the gates.

My master was waiting for me.

"You will go to tame your fears and learn to ride a horse. Your chamber will still be here for when you return. You have now started on the path that will only end when you can release all the pain of your past."

"Can I then return here?"

"I hope to see the day when you can take my place." I was shocked and humbled by this remark.

"But there are many others much, much further along the path than I could ever be."

"Jangbu, you have suffered terribly, you still suffer. To grow beyond all that you have lived through will take great courage and faith. If you can grow beyond your weaknesses, fears, anger, pain, and loss—and how long it will take you—is not something we can know. But if and when you do, then you will be the one that I would choose as my successor." He then bowed and walked away.

I picked up my belongings and passed through the gates. Waiting outside was an old man, sitting on a little cart drawn by yak. I went up to the beast to caress it.

"I have never stroked a yak before," I remarked carelessly.

201

"And you still haven't," remarked the old man, smiling at me. The inside of his mouth was like a forest after a fire, only a few blackened stumps remained. "That isn't a yak, it's a *nak*, a *dri*."

I must have looked a little confused.

"It's a female, it's clear enough to see, just look at the horns." I looked. "They're much smaller." I smiled back at him; it was clear enough to see that I was a monk and not a field worker. "You monks, you cannot tell the difference between a male and a female?" He shook his head, happy with his own little joke.

We rode for quite some hours, mostly towards the north and mostly in silence. My driver, after informing me of the important differences between male and female yaks, seemed to have little to say, so we carried on pretty much in silence. I tried once or twice to ask questions: as to our destination, how long would the journey take, if we would be arriving sooner or later. The responses were all monosyllabic and not at all informative. Eventually, I gave up trying to converse and satisfied myself to marvel at the changing scenery, as only someone who has never travelled for more than a day's walk, there and back, can marvel.

Night was going to fall soon as we topped a small hill, and I noticed smoke snaking up from somewhere in front of us. As we came closer, I remarked that it was coming from a big, round, grey tent. Coming closer, I also noticed that there was a big enclosure, built out of branches, in which one might expect to see horses or cattle penned up. The enclosure was empty, and what was even odder was that when we approached, I could see two horses roaming freely outside it.

The horses were not alone; there was a man next to them, with his back to us. The horses must have been quite big, because the man's head reached only to the height of the horses' backs. I had hoped that my image of horses being huge and dangerous was due in part to my trauma and the fact that I was very small and lying down. Now, looking at the relative size of the man and the horses, I could estimate that they would indeed be big.

However, as we got closer and closer, both the size of the man and of the horses seemed to shrink down. Was this due to some weird function of my brain, something to do with fear and my inner representation of the scene? Before I had time to reflect more on the subject, we had arrived. In fact, being so close up, I could now see for certain that the horses were not so big, it was the man that was particularly short!

He was dressed in a usual fashion for a northerner: leather boots, leather trousers, sheepskin jerkin, and a Xamo Gyaise, a golden thread hat. His long, curly black hair reached halfway down his back. He turned as the waggon approached, but I had the feeling that he had been aware of our coming for quite some time; he just chose to finish what he was doing before occupying himself with us.

He must have been very young, I thought, for his face was totally smooth, not even the slightest sign of a beard. It was only when he spoke to my driver that I realised my mistake. This wasn't a man, this was a woman. Maybe the driver was right after all, about monks having difficulty differentiating between men and women!

She thanked him warmly and some money changed hands. I had very little experience of money, as I had lived in the monastery all my life. I had no experience of women, either. This was to be quite a learning experience for me.

She then turned to me. "Come, you will need to wash, then we will eat. We will begin the work in the morning." We left my stuff on the floor outside the tent. I found my washing pack and followed her as quickly as I could. She was not a slow walker.

About five minutes' walk from the tent we came to a stream with a natural pool created by a number of large stones. She left me to strip, wash, and relieve myself after the long ride.

I returned some minutes later. The two free horses fortunately had little interest in me, so we kept a respectful distance from each other. She was not to be seen, so I called inside the tent.

"Hello, hello, are you there?"

"My name is Ainura." She almost jumped out of the tent. "And just where else would I likely be?"

"I'm sorry, I didn't know if it would be all right for me just to go into the tent."

"My name is Ainura, and these tents are called *boz üy*. From now on, this is also your home." She opened the flap and made a traditional sign of welcome. "You are my honoured guest, come in and take the best honourable seat."

I bowed in return and entered the *boz üy*. It was really very big for a tent; there was a cooking area with a lit fire, a sitting and eating area, and another space where she had her sleeping mat. I looked around to see if there was another part separated off, but I couldn't see one.

"Where should I sleep?"

"Either on the ground or standing up, inside or outside, whatever are your desires and your customs."

"But there is nowhere separated," I tried to explain.

"We sleep together, that is our way. There is no other space. As I have said, you can either sleep in here or you can sleep outside." So I looked around, found a spot some distance away from her sleeping mat, and arranged my affairs there.

On a low, round table she was putting a white tablecloth. She noticed me looking at her.

"It is called a *dastorkon*. Is there anything else you need to know?"

"Not for the moment." She turned her back to me to carry on preparing the meal. First, she offered me a bowl of green tea and some flat breads. Then, she served up a bowl of noodle soup with potatoes and meat.

"This is very good, what is it called?"

"We call it Kesme."

"Did you make it yourself?"

"Yes, yes, of course I did. I always pass three or four hours a day cooking. The horses, they help as well, they roll on the dough to help make the noodles." I just looked at her, surprised by her violence. "They say that you are frightened of horses."

"Yes, yes, I am."

"How I've let them saddle me with a coward and a fool, I really don't know. Do you at least know how to wash dishes?"

"Yes, I can do that."

"Then make yourself useful while I see to the horses. Then we will go to bed, to sleep. There is much to do in the morning." And with that, off she went, leaving me to tidy the plates, pots, and pans, take them down to the river and wash them.

It was quite dark when I got back, and the tent was also dark, except for the glowing embers of the dying fire. I could feel that my energy was dying, too, so I was thankful to be able to sink onto my mat. I remembered to give a small prayer of thanks for the day, before falling heavily into a very deep but disturbed sleep.

It was dark all around me, yet I could see totally clearly. I was in a forest; the trees were all round me and I could feel their presences like normal people. They were whispering, talking to each other, but I could not make out what it was that they were talking about. Their branches became more and more agitated, their leaves were shaking in all directions; danger was coming. I didn't need to understand the words to catch the meaning. The trees were frightened, danger was coming, danger was coming, closer and closer, I could feel the tension mounting. Then suddenly, there it was, an enormous black horse galloping towards me, its nostrils flaring, and then it opened its great mouth and spurted an awful river of fire. The trees were drenched in flames, they shivered and screamed their agony, bark and branches blazing. They screamed and screamed and screamed.

"What is wrong with you?" She was standing over me, her hands balled into fists, her hair a wild mass of black tangled cords, her eyes wide with anger and fear.

"What's happening?" I sat up and shook myself awake.

"What do you mean, what's happening? It's you that's screaming like someone's sticking a knife in your belly and twisting it."

"Oh," I said, "sorry, but that happens sometimes."

"What do you mean, that happens sometimes?"

"That I scream in the night. I used to have nightmares often. Now it's more that I just scream, but I don't have as many nightmares."

"And I suppose that's better, is it?"

"Yes, I'm much better now than I ever was."

"Well, it's not that good for me, or for anyone else who happens to be sleeping close to you."

"I am really sorry. It's not anything that I can control."

"Does this screaming happen all through the night, or just once and then it's done?"

"What do you mean?"

"I mean, is it safe for me to go back to sleep, or am I likely to be awakened again?"

"They tell me that it usually happens only once a night."

"Will that be once every night?"

"No, some nights I sleep without screaming."

"Great. Not only am I lumbered with an idiot and a coward, but one that cannot sleep at night without screaming like someone is slaughtering a pig." Then she turned as quickly as that and disappeared to her side of the tent, and I suppose returned to her mat to go back to sleep.

If I was to deal with a wild horse, I hoped it wouldn't be wilder than this one.

I woke up the next morning to find the table already set with hot tea and heated round, flat breads. There were also several bowls, which I soon discovered contained jams and a type of soured milk called *ayran*.

We ate our breakfast in silence. I thought it much safer not to try and start any conversation. Her reactions seemed difficult to understand, and I decided that it would be best to try and begin the day without being screamed at.

"Come, we have wasted enough time stuffing our faces. It is time to start." And with that, she got up and made for the doorway. I grabbed my unfinished bread roll, thought better of taking the time to finish my tea, and ran off after her.

"Wait here," she instructed me, pushing me back towards the tent. *First she forces me to leave my half-finished breakfast, then she tells me to wait while she goes and does something else.* I was feeling quite irritated, then I realised that I was still holding the remains of my bread roll in my hand. I squatted down, leaning against the tent, taking the time to enjoy the last crumbs of my breakfast, watching her do whatever she might choose to do.

She was walking up to the horses; she had picked up a short cord from somewhere in passing. When she got to the horses, which hardly moved as she approached, she placed the cord gently around the neck of one of them, mainly black with a lightning streak of white on its forehead, and led it towards the paddock.

The paddock was made up of a number of upright posts, big straight branches to be exact, which were then connected by several smaller branches, tied horizontally with cords. At one point, facing the tent, the cords holding the horizontal branches were made loose enough for the branches to be slid out, therefore making an entrance and exit point.

She led the horse through this opening, released it from the cord, and turned to close the gap. She bent down to pick up one of the branches, but before picking it up, she stopped and looked hard at me.

"If madam has had time to finish her breakfast, perhaps she might care to give me a hand." This was not without a fine edge of sarcasm, but I didn't give myself the time to reflect on that, or the surprise that while getting and bringing the horse she had had the awareness that I had something more to eat—which I had long finished before she had looked towards me.

I quickly got up and started to run towards her.

"Stop!" she screamed. "What the hell are you thinking? Are you trying to traumatise my horse?"

I stopped dead, as if her voice and energy were a huge wind which suddenly blew in from somewhere, blocking any possibility to advance. I stood there, shocked and surprised, and once more feeling very angry with this crazy woman. *First she calls for me to come to help her, but before I can get to her, she screams like a lunatic to stop and that I am about to traumatise her horse!* How could I possibly traumatise a horse—a big, dumb, dangerous beast like that? After all, it was me that had been traumatised by a horse, not the other way round.

"What's wrong now? Can't I do anything right?"

"Obviously not! Now, without running or screaming or doing anything weird and scary, could you please pretend to be a reasonably normal human being and come and help me close this barrier?"

I was shaking with anger, like I've never experienced in my life. I walked slowly and carefully towards her. In fact, I was walking—intentionally—very, very slowly, somehow hoping to incite another criticism so I could respond that I was only doing that which she asked of me—but she didn't.

I got to the paddock, where she was, surprisingly, patiently waiting for me. I bent down and together we replaced the branches to close the gap.

"Okay, let's start, then."

"Not with you in that state." What was wrong with her now?

"What do you mean, 'not in that state'?"

"Come, I'll show you." She took the cord and went to the other horse, then she looped the cord around its neck. "Come here, gently and slowly."

I did exactly as she asked. I still felt very scared of the horse, but with everything that had already happened, I was too lost in the moment to worry about that. I just wanted to prove to her that she was wrong. I breathed deeply but quite quickly, once or twice, then, slowly and carefully, I walked towards the horse.

Nothing seemed to be happening, at least not that I could see, but when I got to about fifteen yards away, she put up her hand to stop me.

"What's wrong now?" I complained.

"Can you see her ears?" Yes, I could see the ears, but there was nothing to show that it was a she.

"Yes, what about them?"

"Can you see that they are lying back, almost flat?"

"Yes, and?"

"That is not a good sign. When a horse is upset, the ears go back like that."

"And then what?"

"Come a little closer and then you will see."

So I started walking again. The horse started to pull on the cord, more and more as I continued to approach. Ainura began to have difficulty just holding her.

"What's wrong with her?"

"She's scared."

"Scared of what?"

"Scared of you, scared of your anger."

"I don't feel that I'm that angry." I was starting to question my own awareness of myself.

"Horses are mirrors, they are very sensitive and very expressive."

"And you can tell that by looking at their ears?"

"Amongst other things. Their eyes, like our eyes, also express a lot, but there is also their breathing, and the tensing of muscles as well, much the same as we humans."

"It seems that you know a lot about people."

Here, she stopped for a moment. "No, I know a lot about horses. Humans still remain a bit of a mystery to me. Come, you must relax before your first lesson."

She let go of the horse, which immediately ran off several paces away from me, then stopped and turned and, looking at me, waited.

"Come." Ainura turned, took me roughly by the shoulders, and led me off towards a small group of trees some distance away. When we got to the trees, she pushed me down to the ground next to a large tree.

"Do you know anything about meditating or relaxing?" she asked impatiently.

"I'm a monk," I said, "I know about meditating and relaxing."

"Good, so meditate or relax any way you want, and when you start to feel a bit calm, then I'll be waiting for you in the *boz üy*." And with that, she turned and, without giving me a second glance, went off to the tent.

She is so... And that is when I realised that I was really very, very angry. The anger had been growing since my first contact with her. She had been difficult and disrespectful towards me. After all, I was a monk and she was just a trainer of horses, and yet almost every word or look was degrading or denigrating. Of course I was angry with her, who wouldn't be?

But what was I to do? I couldn't leave, I had nowhere to go. To go back to the monastery without the yak and cart was impossible, and yet that was the only place I could think to go. On the other hand, if I stayed here I would have to cope with this awful woman person. I would also have to deal with the horses, of course, and to do that I would have to release my anger.

She seems to think that I can do nothing right, but I do know how to meditate and relax. I can calm myself down, I can release my anger. That's what I will do. I will show her how I am capable of doing this thing. Maybe she is hoping that I will not succeed, and then she can criticise me again for something else, but she will see.

I move into the Padmasana, positioning my hands in the Ksepana mudrā gesture, then focus my attention on my breathing. To begin with, it is the in-breath that is important. I breathe in slowly and fully, I hold my breath for fifteen beats, and then I release. At the same time, my eyes focus on the tips of my fingers pointing downwards towards the earth. After a while, the focus starts to move by itself. My body continues the breathing cycle, but now, instead of the negative energy leaving with the air from my mouth as I exhale, slower and slower, I experience the stresses and the tensions flowing from my lungs and back, through my shoulders, arms, elbows, forearms, wrists, and hands, and finally out through my fingertips down to the cool, pure earth.

My body breathes in and my fingers breathe out; there is a circular energetic motion. In flows the pure, clear air, out flows all the stress and the tension. I know not how long I have been sitting here, neither do I much care. I am feeling more and more contented; the morning is gentle, there is a slight breeze that caresses my cheek, I am floating on a cloud of meditation.

Somewhere, something is calling me back. It has no body, of course, no face, not even a recognisable voice; however, it has the feel of my master. I feel the Zen stick, and I feel his voice, and I feel the meaning of his words, "Wake up, wake up, now is not a time to sleep." I am shaken back into this hard world; the ground is hard beneath my unprotected bottom, my legs have gone to sleep, and I have let my back fall forward, so the fact that my back aches is all my own fault and I deserve the Zen stick.

I slowly unwind my body and gently get to my feet. It takes a minute or two to be again fully the present in this world. I slowly and carefully made my way back to the tent.

"Hello," I called out, into the tent.

"Oh, it's you, is it?"

"Yes, it is," I replied calmly. She came out of the tent, looking attentively at me.

"How are you feeling now?" she asked.

"I feel calm," I replied evenly.

"Yes, yes, you are much calmer now. It seems that you do know how to meditate and relax." She too seemed to relax, and even smiled a little smile. "Come, let us try again, shall we?" And with that, she roughly but gently took my arm and led me to the corral.

Her horse was patiently waiting for us. She climbed the barrier and entered the wooden pen. Not knowing what else to do, I just stood and waited outside.

"Come here." I reluctantly went to the wooden barrier and placed my foot on the lowest branch. The horse turned towards me and snorted. Panicked, I arched my body backwards, released my grip, and fell heavily to the ground. Fortunately, it was my shoulders and then my arms that first came in contact with the ground, but my head soon followed and I painfully bumped the back of my head on the earth.

"What the...?" I heard her running, then a short breath (I think she must have jumped the fence), and then, there she was. I was in quite some pain, a little from the upper back but mostly a deep, dull pain coming from somewhere inside my skull. *At least*, I thought, *I'll get some sympathy now*.

"What is wrong with you? Do you want to traumatise my horse at any price?"

"I don't what to traumatise your horse," I growled, slowly sitting up. "In truth, I don't want anything to do with your horse. I hate horses. They scare me and make me see horrible things."

"What do you mean, horrible things?"

"Nothing that I would ever share with you." And with that, I turned to go back into the tent.

"And exactly where do you think that you might be going?" "Back into the tent, to lie down."

"So it's not true, then?"

214

"What's not true?"

"That monks have some sort of hidden strength. An inner determination, built from years of prayers and meditation. So they really are just wimps that cannot make it in the real world."

"I don't know about this deep inner strength thing, but monks are not just wimps that cannot make it the real world."

"Is that why you are going into the *boz üy*, to lie down, to show me that you are not a wimp?"

Of course, I knew what she was doing, but that didn't stop it having the desired effect. I turned back towards the corral.

"If you can keep your horse from further traumatising me, then I'll do what I can not to traumatise it."

"It, by the way, is a he. Okay, it's time to get you to work." I climbed over the gate just after her, using her body as a protection between me and the horse. He seemed to understand this manoeuvre, as he allowed me to stay safe behind my human shield without his moving to approach me from the side.

She walked right across to the other fence, where she bent down to pick up a thin branch that she must have left there on purpose. It was about two feet long and there was a bunch of long grass attached to the end. She turned to me and shoved it into my left hand.

"Here, this is to help you make the horse move, when, where, and as you want."

I looked a little lost for a moment. "Am I supposed to hit it with the grass bit?"

"If you hit my horse, I'll hit you!"

"Then what am I supposed to do?"

"First, maybe you should try and listen." *Why does everybody keep saying the same thing?* I wondered.

"Now, if you want the horse to move in a certain direction, first you have to show it clearly the direction you want it to go in. So you take your arm"—she took my right arm—"and you point it like this." She placed my arm horizontally, pointing towards the tent. "Then, if you want the horse to move from the back, you need to be standing close to the back of the horse." She moved me towards the horse's back leg. "Now, if you want it to move, you have to give it some energy." And with that, she took my left arm and violently brought it down towards the ground, where the grass made a loud *shhh* sound. The horse, a little surprised, made a small jump sideways, advanced several steps towards the tent, and then stopped. "Good."

"But he just moved two steps and then stopped."

"First of all, you got him to move, secondly, it was in the right direction, and thirdly, it was not one but two steps. You now have started."

I was too caught up in the moment to have noticed my fear of the horse, but the fact that it was me that got him to move, and not the other way round, made a small effect on my fear. *If I can just do it again.* I advanced towards the horse, moving in the direction of the tent. I stuck my right arm out and waved the stick. Nothing happened, so I stuck it out some more, and then I started beating it on the ground.

"It's not a drumstick, you know. The idea is to get the horse to walk or trot, not to dance." I felt a little vexed, so I advanced towards the horse, shaking the stick. He did not like this much, and after a moment he started to walk away. Only this time he turned his front legs away from me, away from the tent, and not in the direction that I was indicating.

"Stupid horse!"

"More like, stupid monk."

"Oh yes, so what did I do wrong?"

"The first time, when he went where you wanted him to go, did you put pressure at the front or at the back?"

"You said to go towards the back."

"And just now, were you more at the front or at the back?" *Stupid monk*, I cursed at myself, and went to position myself at the back of the beast.

"You are not trying to scare the horse. You need to push him with your energy and will." Moving energy was a concept that I had worked on with my master, so I could understand the idea of projecting a non-physical force, a force of spiritual energy, towards an object.

"Yes, I understand what you are talking about."

"Well, if you do, then it should be very easy for you. You push the horse from behind, and at the same time, you open up an energy path for it to run along in."

I could do this! I understood exactly what she was talking about. The stick was a type of energy pump; as I thrust it up and down, I was pumping a line of energy from me towards the rear of the horse. The pressure would build behind him until his resistance was overpowered by my energy push, and then I would lead him around the ring with the energy flowing out of my right arm.

I stopped seeing him as a horse, the symbol of the worst moment of my life. He transformed into a resistant energy object that I was to move.

I am nine years old, I am in the Master's chambers; there are a number of small smooth spheres resting on a little slope. "Try and push them down the slope without touching them. It is a little game for us to play." It took me months to get the spheres to roll down the slope, but I finally found out how to project my energy in a very fine line, towards the back of a sphere, and get it to move.

A horse was going to be easy. *Yes, yes, yes. Come on now, boy, a little bit faster, faster, faster...*

"That's okay, it's enough, it's enough. You don't have to get him to gallop like that. Stop!"

I was really somewhere else; I was no longer with her or the horse or even in this world. I was in a parallel place, a world of colours and energies, and in that world I was just flowing energy out, towards the chosen object, watching with interest and amusement as it was carried by my energy to where and at what speed I wished.

Coming back into the world of people and solid things, I realised that she was asking me to stop, so I did. She was looking at me in a rather strange way.

"Where did you learn to do that?"

"In the monastery. It is linked to Ku work."

"Ku work?" The question seemed to be more to herself than to me. She then turned, walked over to the gate, and started to remove the branches. I stopped, confused for a moment, but quickly gathered my thoughts and ran to help her, before she might have an excuse to criticise me again.

After the horse was again liberated, she led me back to the tent where a light meal of dried meat, breads, and water awaited us. She did not seem eager to talk, and I was a little afraid to start a conversation with her, so we ate in silence. Once or twice, or so it seemed to me, I noticed her looking at me in a strange way, as if she wasn't quite sure what sort of animal she was dealing with.

After lunch I washed up the plates and mugs and we returned to the corral. This time she brought both horses, and I started to move them at the same time. This was very similar to the exercise of the morning; I just needed to place myself and my energy behind the back horse, but also on the second horse, and then "push" them off. Often they would move together. If only the back horse moved, then I would simply focus on the rump of the second horse until it also moved.

The second exercise was more interesting, as I was to focus on only one horse and not at all on the second. Which was to say, one horse to move and the other to stay still. It took a little time to train myself to focus only on the back of the horse I wanted to move. It was also interesting to notice that before, when I believed I was succeeding at focusing all my energy towards the horse's rear, in truth, there was much of my energy that was directed elsewhere.

Although I was very focused on this work, a part of me was thinking of how this exercise could be of much interest and use for our training in the monastery. Learning to focus our energies with the immediate feedback of the horses would be much more useful than spending months and months of frustration trying to move small balls down a ramp.

After I had mastered the technique of moving the horses, one at a time, I was to learn how to split them so that they would leave in opposite directions. Again, the trick was quite simple; I had to place myself between the two horses and create a bolt of force that ran between them. I visualised a stream of energy leaving the end of the grass-stick, hitting the ground behind and between the horses, exploding outwards in both directions.

All this time Ainura sat silently on one of the posts, watching; watching me, watching the horses, maybe watching the clouds, for all I knew. Neither did she comment nor did she interfere in any way. From time to time, out of the corner of my eye, I got the impression that she gave a slight nod, as if she was satisfied with something, but I wasn't at all sure.

After I had succeeded in splitting the horses a few times, she jumped off the post and came towards me.

"The horses are getting tired. It's time to stop for the day." I too was tired; the exercise seemed not so much, but the effort and energy that it cost must have been considerable for me. I turned to go to the gate to start removing the branches.

"What are you doing?" Could I never get anything right? "You said that the horses were tired. I'm going to open the gate."

"We have not yet finished, master of the energies." Was she making fun of me again? Was she being sarcastic? I didn't have time to worry about that now. I had something else to do.

"What do you want me to do?" I was starting to really feel tired and easily irritated, not an emotion that I had experienced much before meeting her!

"Come here." She held out her arm and smiled at me. It was not a huge smile, but it was a smile; a weak, solitary ray of sunshine escaped the cloudy skies of her moods. "Come here."

I walked back to the centre of the ring. She took my right hand in her left and turned us to face the horses. What had been comfortable during the day had been the fact that I had somehow "forgotten" that I had been dealing with horses. I had been coexisting in a different dimension; they had simply become energy forms that I was playing with, to see if and how I could move them as I chose.

In a horrible moment, now, here, close and in front of me, they had resumed their original forms and I was again confronted with my nightmare nemesis—horses!

My first reaction was to back off, to distance myself, if possible to run away. All the body fear reactions simultaneously triggered; muscles tensed, heart rate increased, breathing short and fast. I went to pull away, but Ainura was too fast for me. She gripped my hand with an iron grip, much too strong for any girl. And when I tried to pull away, she managed to root herself to the spot. It was like trying to pull down a great tree with your bare hands. In short, I was trapped—and again, that little smile. Now I knew why she had smiled at me. She was about to trap me and now she had. Here, in front of two of these terrible beasts; here, unable to escape, hardly able to move; here I was, and here she kept me.

My fear was quickly turning into panic. I was pulling more and more in a desperate attempt to escape. She reached over and took the stick from my other hand.

"Quiet, you'll frighten the horses. If you don't stop pulling, I'll hit you with this!" Even in my excess of emotion, this threat, this very real threat, got through to me. I turned and looked at her face. Her mouth was as tight as a drum and her eyes were burning embers. I suddenly became more frightened of her than of the horses.

Then, in a voice totally and completely calm, she said, "You are now going to do your breathing exercises, and you will relax and calm down." I felt, in that moment, that I had absolutely no will of my own. I took her instruction and started to focus on my breathing; focus on my point of calm and of clarity. I de-focused once again from this world of people and of things and returned to one of the other, more abstract worlds. I focused on a point between and above my physical eyes, just below my forehead, just above the bridge of my nose. The point of clear sight, clear vision, clear understanding; I directed all my energy to that point.

I had never done this exercise standing before, and once or twice I almost lost my balance. Fortunately, it was impossible to fall down, being that I was attached to this solid rock of a woman. Clear sight could be imagined to be something only positive, to see things as they really are, without our own filters and prejudices distorting our perceptions, but the truth is only agreeable to those that can assume it, and most of us are far from ready for or capable of that.

My first awareness was that my fear of the horses, here, today, was a mixture of many things: my relationship with my trauma and the loss of my parents, my general fear of things I didn't know or couldn't control, my fear of restarting my nightmares, and my desire to be in contact with Ainura. I also became aware of Ainura's complex emotional state, which somehow included mixed emotions concerning me. And, of course, the horses themselves, which had total confidence in her, but saw me as too difficult to understand; hence, better to stay vigilant, as I might be capable of doing anything and everything.

I opened my eyes, only to find that she was staring into mine.

"Are you ready?" she asked gently. Not at all knowing what she was talking about, I nodded my head and waited to find out exactly what I had agreed to.

"Take your hand and offer it to the horse in friendship." She must have dropped the stick at some time, for she stretched out her open free hand, palm upwards, towards one of the horses.

I could easily see what she was doing; it was the exact opposite of the exercises of the day that I had been doing. I would just need to return to the other dimension, inverse the polarities of my energy. Instead of using the force to push away the object, I would attract it to me. Easy.

But no, that wasn't at all the purpose of this moment. The purpose of this moment was for me, Jangbu, to confront myself with a real, living, big horse.

I put out my hand as she was doing and together we approached the horses. Hers, as soon as we moved forwards, turned her ears round and towards us, lowered her head, and came to Ainura. My horse shook its head a little from side to side, lowered its ears towards the back, and started to back off.

"It doesn't like me."

"It doesn't trust you. You have to approach it with love. He has to feel that you love him, or else he cannot feel safe. And if he doesn't feel safe, he can only protect himself by moving away."

"How can I approach it with love? I'm still scared myself." I had no problem being totally honest with Ainura. For reasons that I hadn't had time to understand, I felt totally safe with her.

"What's your name, monk?"

"My name is Jangbu."

"Jangbu, listen to me, listen carefully. Has any man ever done anything to harm you?"

"He killed my family!" It came out just like that. I wasn't expecting the question, so I had no time to think about the answer. Even if my response shocked and surprised me, it must have shocked and surprised her even more, for she totally stopped moving and talking for some moments.

"Okay." She breathed heavily once or twice. "Good. You have had a"—here she spoke very slowly and clearly—"very bad experience with one man." I nodded my head in agreement. "As a monk, I suppose that you have an older monk that is responsible for you, like some sort of teacher."

"I have my master. It was he who found me and has taken care of my well-being all my life."

"And your master is also a man?" I nodded my head, a little confused by her reflections. "So there exists in this world a very horrible man who killed your parents, and yet also your Master who has looked after you for most of your life?"

"Yes, yes, that is so."

"Do you love your master?" That was a question I normally would never allow myself even to think about, much less answer aloud.

"Yes, yes, of course I love my Master." I could feel the emotions welling up through my body. This was not the place; I should not be becoming aware of these emotions, not here, not now. Not with this wonderful, crazy woman; not in this makeshift horse pen; certainly not here, in front of these great beasts that have haunted my dreams and my unconscious all these years.

I needed to turn, to run away, to hide, to protect these deep, scary, wild emotions. No one should see the tears that were blurring my vision. She should not see me like this.

"So you can still love a man so much, even if another man has done you so much harm?"

I had totally forgotten the other in this moment of revelation.

"Yes, yes, I can!" I had no idea what she was talking about, but she was not going to get me to say that I did not love my Master!

"Then there is nothing that should stop you loving this horse, even if another horse has caused you grief." Now I could see her reasoning. I could see her truth and her logic.

"Yes, yes, it is true, I can love this horse. It is not the same horse."

"This horse will look after you and protect you. Horses are made this way. If they feel that you will look after them, then they will look after you. You must learn to ride this horse, so you must also enter into a relationship of care and trust. For these next weeks, this horse will be your Master. It will care and look after you like your own Master. Show it the love you have for him and

225

it will return that love with the same attention that your Master gives you."

Somehow I knew there were things in what she was saying that were not exactly true or logical, but I was also convinced that she was right, so I did as she asked me. I focused my love and trust for my Master and projected it out towards the horse. The first reaction was not that of the horse but of myself; I felt my body relaxing, my breathing became easy and flowing, I felt all the tension in my face flow away. I wanted to smile, but more than that, what I wanted more than anything else was to touch him, to stroke him, to caress him, to make him understand that I loved him. The effect on the horse was startling; he seemed to look twice at me, as if he wasn't really sure of what he was seeing. At the same time, his ears started to move in all directions, but mainly towards me, and also towards Ainura. Eventually, the ears settled almost exclusively on me. He started walking slowly towards me, still slightly tense and nervous, or so it seemed to me. Closer and closer we came. Ainura had been stroking her horse already for quite some time. He sniffed my hand and she released my other.

Even though I still felt a little intimidated by his size, it seemed natural to move around to his side and start to stroke him. After some minutes of that, without at all knowing why, I placed my arms around his neck, pressed the side of my face against his warm, furry coat, and dissolved into tears. The tears flowed; sometimes soft and silent, sometimes loud and violent. Somehow I was well aware of where I was and what the circumstances were, but neither could I nor would I choose to do anything to control or to stop myself.

Time passed. I didn't have any awareness of time, but at some point I noticed that it was becoming dark. And as the sun was completing his daily task and preparing to abandon us, I was also starting to notice that I was feeling cold.

"Come, it is time to eat." She gently separated me from my horse, which had stood patiently all this time, silently supporting me in this deep moment of liberation. The gate was already open; I hadn't noticed when she had opened it. That meant that my horse had stayed, immobile, all this time, when he could simply have left and gone to graze with his mate.

She threw a blanket over my shoulders and directed me to the tent. There, she helped me to sit and served me some hot stew. We ate in silence; not a cold, distant silence, but a silence of deep sharing. We had shared a moment of the deepest of experiences that I have ever had, and she had opened to that moment and watched over me until the moment had drawn itself to its own conclusion.

Now, in respect for that profound connection, as at the end of a long prayer festival, there was no place for words; words would only dilute and diminish the experience. There was nothing they might add. You would not want to listen to the grunting of a yak after meditating on the music of a waterfall.

And so we ate in silence. After the meal she led me to my mat, helped me get down on it, even if really there was no need, and left me to go and wash up after the meal. I suppose that I must have fallen asleep before she returned, for I have no memory of her coming back.

It must have been late in the night that I felt a soft kick in my side, and then another. I turned and opened my eyes. She was standing above me.

227

"Can we finish with the screaming for tonight? I have a strange habit of sleeping at night." She didn't wait for an answer or a remark. I thought to get up and follow her, to excuse myself, but then to what benefit? We both knew that I couldn't help it. And, thinking back, she didn't really seem angry at all; if anything, she seemed slightly amused. It was too late and I was too tired to worry about it then, so I just went back to sleep.

The next morning, I was keen to see my reaction to "my" horse and to discover what exercises were planned for me today.

I had no idea what time she must have gotten up, but when I emerged from the tent to wash myself and the dishes, I noticed that she had constructed some sort of circuit out of more tree branches.

"Put the pots in the *boz üy* and pick up a cord as you come out." I did what was asked and returned with the cord.

"Now, don't forget to approach him gently." I walked slowly towards the horse. Although I was feeling a little stressed, it was really nothing compared to the day before. "Now, take this end of the cord and gently pass it over and round his neck. Okay. Now, you see that this end is tied in a series of loops? Good. Now you pass this loop over the muzzle, the nose. Not like that!" The cord ended in a complicated mess of tangled knots. I was expected to somehow pass the nose and then the ears, and then somehow tie all that around the neck of the horse. Of course, it was impossible.

"You are impossible. Have you not learnt anything in that monastery of yours?"

"Tying knots is not a usual part of a monk's training."

"No one is asking you to tie any knots yet, just to succeed in placing a few simple loops over a horse's head."

"If these are simple loops, I'd hate to be asked to deal with hard ones."

"Here, I'll do it for you this time because I'm getting bored, and I don't like getting bored."

"Then maybe you should do some work on learning a little patience."

"When I'm dealing with intelligent and willing creatures, then I have all the patience I need."

"And would these intelligent and willing creatures include human beings?"

"No, I've rarely met a human being that I would call an intelligent or willing creature."

"Neither intelligent nor willing?"

"Neither intelligent nor willing." Saying that, she roughly grabbed the cord from my fumbling fingers and deftly looped the loops around the nose, ears, and neck, tied it in a twist, and handed the long cord to me.

"Follow me," she instructed. She walked me around the circuit; along one branch, in between two others, into a square construction where I was supposed to get the horse to turn a full circle, over a little barrier built with four branches on top of each other (supported by two posts at each end), then there was a corridor that started straight and turned at an angle to the left and then back to the right. After that, we had to weave in and out of ten trees that edged onto a forest area some ways off. The horse followed at some distance; he was not obliged to do any of the exercises yet, other than follow us in and out of the trees, for which he had little choice.

"I'm going down to the village to get some more food. I want to see you doing this perfectly by the time I get back." And with that, she jumped onto the back of her horse and rode off.

So there I stood, my hand holding the cord, the cord attached to a horse, the horse looking at me, waiting for something to happen.

"Come on, let's do this." I turned and walked towards the first exercise, walking alongside a branch. I walked, the cord tightened then stretched, then stretched some more. I turned to see why the cord had tightened so much and, not at all to my surprise, the horse hadn't moved.

I pulled some more but it had no effect. I shouted for him to come on—again, nothing. This lasted for another ten to fifteen minutes before I started to become quite irritated. This was really a moment in my life where I was to experience large doses of frustration and irritation. I stopped and thought of what to do. What he needed was a good whack on the backside. I looked around and, as if by a miracle, there it was, the grass-stick. I dropped the cord and went to pick up the stick. When I got back, the horse was quietly grazing. It was if I didn't even exist. I picked up the cord, walked round to the back of the horse, and prepared myself to give it a hefty whack. However, something then stopped me. Was it the fear that if I told Ainura that I had hit the horse, she would be angry with me? Was it the awareness that I wanted to hit him to relieve my own anger of his ignoring me? Or was it that I was beginning to like this horse, and hitting him with a stick was not only an act of violence against him, but also an enormous act of violence against all my teachings as a monk?

The outcome was that I was not capable of hitting him; however, I had spent the whole of the preceding day learning to get the horses moving, using that very same stick and without any violence. I focused my energy on the stick and then on the behind of the horse. "Move!" I called out, shaking the stick and sending my will for him to advance. "Move," I repeated. "Move," for the third time. His head came up, his ears pivoted, he shook his head and he started to move forward. I quickly ran in front of him and we started to follow the circuit. Keeping him on line and in between the branches was not easy; sometimes I really had to fight with the cord. Getting him into and doing a circle in the little square seemed impossible, so I soon gave that up. To begin with, he would often just stop and I had to use the stick to get him going again, but by the end of the morning, other than the impossible square, we were able to do the whole thing without any problem.

After a time we both got a little bored. I took quite a while to manage to undo the cord from the horse's neck, but eventually I succeeded in taking it off, without undoing all the loops.

The horse was grazing and I was meditating when Ainura returned.

"Working hard, are we?"

"We have been working hard, but now we are resting." I was feeling quite sure of myself for once. I neither moved nor opened my eyes.

"You have succeeded at doing everything?"

"Everything except that square thing."

"Forwards and backwards?" I opened my eyes and looked straight at her.

"You never said anything about forwards and backwards."

"I must have forgotten." She smiled at me as she dismounted. "It'll keep you occupied for the afternoon." And with that, she untied the sacks from the horse, carried them to the tent, and disappeared from sight. Several moments later she reappeared. "And the cord? You know how to put it on now?"

"No," I smiled back, "that will give you something interesting to do this afternoon." And with that, I closed my eyes and returned to my meditation.

The meal passed again pretty much in silence. Ainura asked me one or two questions about my experiences of the morning and how I managed. She seemed quite satisfied with my responses, as she made little comment and passed on to other things before we again settled into a comfortable silence. Having lived in a monastery, I had much experience of silence, so it was quite normal for me to pass large amounts of time without conversation.

The afternoon began with her demonstrating again how to loop the cord around the horse's nose, ears, and neck. It took me a little time to succeed in getting it right, and Ainura mocked me for my stupidity and my clumsiness, but it was light and goodhearted. She seemed to be less irritated and frustrated with me than yesterday. It seemed that it wasn't only my path that led to the lessons on these subjects at this time.

We then continued the exercises of leading the horse through the obstacles. We were all quite pleased to see that the morning's practice had not been forgotten with the small break for lunch. When we got

232

to the square, Ainura took over. She walked into the square with the horse following her, stopped, and waited for the horse to stop totally within the square. She left him standing still in the square for some moments, then she gently but firmly moved his head round. The body, being attached, obviously followed. It certainly seemed easy enough, until she passed me the cord and left me to repeat the exercise. First I tried and nothing happened, then I used more strength and got the horse to move, not only round but also forwards. I then had to walk him totally out of box and back in again. After several attempts at that, I realised that my mistake was that I was pulling him forwards while also pulling to the side. I must have then overcorrected that, for the horse turned and reversed out of the box.

Ainura seemed to be taking this in a very relaxed way. She was sitting a little off, leaning back against a tree, sipping (so I found out later) a drink made of fermented mares' milk that she called Kumys.

Eventually, I managed to gauge the pulling forwards, sideways, and pushing backwards correctly, and then managed to turn the horse round without it putting one hoof outside until I wanted it to.

By the time that I had managed to do all the circuit forwards, it was already late afternoon. She called me over to the tree and offered me a drink of her milk. It had a slightly sour flavour with a bit of a bite, which I guessed must be due to the slight alcoholic content. This she informed me of only after I had drunk a large bowl of the stuff.

We sat for a while, drinking and watching the horses graze and clouds drift overhead. It was a unique, peaceful moment that we both appreciated and neither wanted to end.

"I suppose that I'll have to show you how to make the horse go backwards and how to make it turn its hindquarters."

"I suppose that you will have to." She yawned and stretched her small, tight body, then sprang up with a little bound.

"Come on, you lazy monk, there's still much work to do." And with that, she turned and walked towards the horse. I scrabbled to my feet and ran after her. Unfortunately, I had had no prior experience of drinking Kumys, and even if it was as lightly alcoholic as she had promised, the three large bowls that I had, quite quickly, drunk had more effect on me than I would have wished for.

It didn't take her long to notice that I was more than a little drunk.

Making the horse go back implied standing in front of him, waving my arms as if pushing him backwards, while at the same time adding an energetic pressure against the whole of the front end of the beast.

To begin with, after all my efforts, I managed to get him to move not an inch.

It seemed that what was lacking was my own presence; I was not enough there. I had learnt how to focus and project my energy, what I was yet to learn was how to incarnate it.

"It's no good. The horse is just not seeing you. It's as if you're not here."

"So what should I do?" I moaned. "I'm a monk, not a magician. I cannot not be here, then be here, it's just not possible." Irritated, this time more with myself than anyone else, I turned and walked off, back to the trees where we had sat, so peacefully, just short while ago. I let myself drop and leaned heavily against a tree.

Ainura followed some moments later. She was not angry with me, it was clear that it wasn't my fault, but it was her job to find a solution to the problem.

"Get up," she ordered me, so I got up. She placed her right foot behind the other, turned it to a ninety-degree angle, and sank down a few inches, as if she was sitting on a high stool. "Now put your hands here, just in front of my shoulders." I put my hands just in front of her. "Put your hands on my shoulders, here. Have you never touched anyone before?"

"I've never touched a woman before."

"Monks! Here, that's it. Now, slowly and gently start to push me backwards." I had my hands on the front and tops of her shoulders and I started to push very, very gently. "Harder!" I pushed a little more. "Harder." I increased the pressure. I was a little scared of pushing her over, but for the moment she hadn't moved at all.

I kept increasing the pressure but she didn't move. Then she bent her legs a little more and raised both her arms, coming up and between mine. Her movement broke my hold on her. Then she placed her hands on my chest and pushed with her arms while her legs straightened, driving her body up and forward. The outcome of all this was that I found myself hurled heavily against the tree behind me.

In a moment of unconscious rage, I closed my eyes, blocked my right foot against the tree trunk, pushed hard to get the most force, and launched myself into her. I caught her around the waist and knocked her to the ground.

Suddenly I realised what I had done. I opened my eyes; I was sitting on her, I had her arms pinned down, my hands grasping her wrists. I threw down her wrists and sat up, wondering how to get off her, wondering how I could ever explain my actions, wondering if she could ever forgive me.

"Not bad, for a monk." I hadn't dared to look at her face, but now I did, and to my total surprise, she was smiling at me.

"I'm, I'm, I'm so sorry." I leaned back and put my weight on my right hand, then lifted myself back, then up. "I don't know what happened. I must have just lost control."

"I think it might be something like that." And she smiled again, not just with her mouth but also with her eyes.

"It was just like I was trying to move a tree, as if you were planted into the ground and you just, just pushed me like I was nothing."

"If you take a horse that has never been tamed and you need to show it that it cannot pull you where it wants to, then you learn how to fix yourself to the ground. Before you learn how to do that, you learn that being dragged across the hard ground by a galloping stallion is not the most fun of experiences."

"I'm really, really sorry."

"Well, I'm not. At least I can see that, hidden somewhere behind that priest's training, there lives a man." Suddenly she stopped. "What were you saying about my being like a tree?"

"I said that it was like trying to move a tree." I must still have been a little drunk because I was not understanding at all the interest in this.

"Go rest and sleep off the alcohol. I'll be back soon." And without another word, she saddled her horse and was gone.

As the afternoon was still quite pleasant, I collected a blanket and settled myself to sleep under the tree.

I slipped into sleep and dreaming; the dreams flowed one into the other until I found myself in a forest that I remembered from somewhere. The trees were tall, majestic, wonderful, with long, strong branches, resplendent with green and golden leaves. The trees were communicating with other; something important was happening, I could feel the tension of the event to come. Then I heard, felt, sensed its coming; a huge, magnificent, jet-black horse. The trees gibbered then shivered in anticipation. Here he was. The trees froze into silence, nothing moved, not a gust of breeze, not a branch or a leaf so much as twitched.

The horse stopped, its ears turning in all directions. It sat back on its hind legs. I held my breath. Then they arrived, our two horses. They were miniature next to this huge beast, their heads reaching only as high as its shoulders. By lowering their heads, they galloped easily under the body of the dark giant. Surprised by their arrival, he stood equally on all four legs, and followed the movements of the two small copies as best he could.

As I watched in amazement as something started to change between the three horses; the two were no longer able to pass under the body of the third. Were they getting bigger or was he shrinking? I dragged my eyes away from the spectacle and focused on the surrounding trees. By comparing the horses to the size of the trees, I could better gauge just how they were changing. By this method, it quickly became obvious that the black horse was shrinking, not that the other two were growing.

The moment that the three arrived at the same height, my horse turned and led them away. Off they galloped, *de-dum*, *de-dum*, *de-dum*, *de-dum*. The sound became louder and louder, deeper and deeper, more and more hollow...

Somewhere there was a drum beating, closer and closer, closer and closer.

"Keep your eyes closed," the man's voice whispered in my ear. "Keep the sleep in your heart." I went to sit up; I wasn't at all clear what was happening, but I had heard the instruction. I kept my eyes closed.

The drum continued to sound out its lively rhythm.

"Stand up slowly." It was the voice of Ainura this time. I slowly stood up; I could feel her sure hands and arms helping me up. "Now walk where I lead you." I slowly and carefully allowed myself to be led by her. After a few moments of walking, we stopped.

"Take your time to find your balance." I already had quite a lot of experience of standing up with my eyes closed, so it wasn't hard to find my balance. I shifted my weight slightly left, then right, until I found my inner balance.

"Good, very good. Now, we are standing here, we have entered the forest, the trees are here all around us. Take your time to breathe in the energy of the trees, of the forest, of the earth. The trees are straight and strong and tall." His voice seemed to resonate with the constant beating of the drum.

"They can only grow so straight and so tall because they have strong and powerful roots. Feel your feet, solid on the ground, rooted to the earth, growing into the soil. Your toes are becoming roots, feeling their way, deep, deeper, and deeper into the soft, rich, black, fertile Mother Earth. Allow them to seek out the nourishment and security that can only be found in the very depths of her generous being."

I found myself seeing, feeling, sensing the truth of his words. My critical mind was totally silenced by the hypnotic, rhythmic drumbeat. Deeper and deeper I was burrowing into the soft, sweet, rich matter below.

"And now, now that you are deeply and firmly anchored in the very depths of life's bounty, now is the time to focus on the outer. The tree grows thicker and taller from its roots. Now your roots are in place, now you can become more and more solid. Feel your body, your trunk begin to expand, to broaden, to widen, to form that firm, unyielding, sturdy mass. Stable and sure, rough yet sensitive, living, breathing, growing strength. And from that base of strength and stability can grow the branches and leaves, higher and wider, generous and rich. Take the time to breathe your tree. Absorb from below, inspire from above, feel the power and the presence of your existence, here, here in this forest, here, here in this country, here in this life. Take the time to know who you are, here, solid, planted in the ground. Nothing and no one can move you. You are one with the very earth, as solid as a rock and as unmovable as a mountain."

And so I stood, tall and strong, solid as a rock and as unmovable as a mountain. There is no question, no reflection, no need or space to reflect; I am and that is all.

The drum beat on and on and on.

I stood and stood and stood.

There was no time, or thought, or tiredness.

And then it was over. The drum stopped, I wasn't sure exactly when; if it slowed down or if the beat softened; if he said something or if he just stopped like that. All I knew was that suddenly it was all over and I was feeling totally and completely exhausted.

For a few seconds I didn't move at all, as if I was waiting for something, a signal from someone, or something from within me? Then, for want of anything better to do, I opened my eyes. It was quite dark; how long I had slept and for how long I was in the tree experience, I could in no way ascertain. It did not matter either way; here I was, dreadfully tired and lost in the woods.

"Are we to stand here all night?" I was so glad to hear her voice. I turned to see her smiling at me.

"Can you show me back to the tent?"

"The *boz üy* is this way." She just turned and started to walk off through the trees. I hurried to keep up with her; I didn't want to lose her and find myself lost in the woods.

We were not at all deep in the woods. Thinking about it, we couldn't have been, she had guided me only for a few moments before he had begun the experience. He? Who was he? Where was he? I had heard the voice and the drumbeat, but I had never seen him at all. It was almost as if he was just a strong character in my dream. Of course he wasn't, but then...

A few minutes later we were safe and warm in the welcoming tent. It didn't take long for Ainura to heat up some stew, which we ate in a warm silence.

I didn't wash the pots that night, she didn't ask me to and I didn't volunteer. I just put down my empty bowl, said good night, and dragged myself to bed.

The next morning she was very impatient to begin, so we started very early and just took some round breads to chew on while working. She showed me two other techniques to get the horse to go backwards. Both involved the cord attached to the harness. The first was to whip the last foot or so of the end of the cord left and right, in line with the front of the horse's face from about three feet away, and increase the speed and the energy in the movement until the horse chose to move.

As the horse chose not to react straightaway, by increasing the arc and speed of the movement, I ended up whipping myself on my arms and even on my back—much to the amusement of Ainura.

The second new technique was to take the part of the cord between the horse and myself and again agitate it left and right. This created a ripple effect in the cord. Again, if the horse didn't react, I was to increase the intensity until it did.

To begin with, I had very little success. I was very focused on getting the techniques right, but somehow that turned out to be counterproductive. It was only when I "forgot" the techniques and focused on being centred in myself, with my physical body rooted to the ground, and then pushing the horse back with the pressure of my energy body, that I started having results.

We were quite pleased with ourselves as we stopped to have a late breakfast or early lunch and to give the horse time to relax and graze a bit. We heated the round breads over the fire and stuffed them with some cold meat, and as the day was quite cold, she heated some water to make bowls of *tongba*.

When the water was hot, she poured it over the fermented mash and there we sat for a while, drinking through our wooden straws, sipping the liquid and avoiding the bits of millet. She didn't make much, knowing my limited capacity to cope with even small quantities of alcohol; it was just to warm ourselves up before returning to the horses.

The second part of the morning was spent learning how to make the horse turn on its front legs. By moving to one side, focusing my energy on the flank that I wished for it to move, and circling the cord vertically, as if I would hit down onto that point, he would, with good sense, move his bottom away from me.

After I had mastered this turning technique, we returned to the square structure that Ainura had constructed and I quickly succeeded in getting my horse to turn inside the confines of the box. After that, just for the pleasure, I took him over the whole course once or twice, walking and then trotting.

This was starting to feel like fun. However, that was just the morning; the afternoon would have surprises in store for me.

When I returned from washing the pots, she had already saddled the horse. From what I could make out, the saddle had a big pommel and was covered in soft sheepskin. Although the idea of sitting on a soft sheepskin seat was not unpleasant, having a big, hard, horned object between my legs, when the horse was going to be moving...that, I must admit, concerned me quite a bit.

Although I was less than comfortable with idea of actually getting on the horse's back, I seemed to have totally forgotten my fear of horses in general.

"I suppose that I have to," I remarked.

"No, you can leave now and walk home." I gave her a half smile in response and walked up to my horse.

"You put your foot in the stirrup, grab the mane here with your right hand, the side of the saddle with your left, bounce on your left foot, and up you go." I did as I was instructed, and in a second I was four feet off the ground, looking at the world as if from a tree.

She showed me how to hold and move the reins, and where to place my heels for riding and for turning the horse. It seems that although the horse is alive and intelligent, the rider needs to give it quite specific instructions or it doesn't know what to do.

My first reaction was to think that the horse was much dumber than I had given it credit for, and it was only much later that I realised that expecting clear, precise instructions was based on its capacity to notice, understand, and react to incredibly subtle messages.

First, she just led me with the cord around the field, then, in and out of the trees, and then she completed the circuit with me on the horse's back. The riding motion was a little scary at first, but as nothing bad happened, I soon got used to it and was quite enjoying myself after all.

The only problem was after coming down off the horse I found it very difficult to walk. I hadn't realised that my thighs would have been so called upon in these first riding moments.

Supper was much more animated than usual and I was a little surprised that no alcoholic drink was proposed. The reason became clear after I had returned from again washing the pots— my horse had been saddled for the second time that day.

"It'll be getting dark quite soon. Wouldn't it be better just to leave it till tomorrow?"

"You are here to learn to ride. I do the thinking." Although the words were a bit tough, there was laughter in her voice.

I followed the instructions from the afternoon and then I was ready to continue my lessons.

"Here, put this on," she said, handing me a small bandana.

"What am I supposed to do with this?"

"Tie it around your head. It is to cover your eyes."

"You are serious?"

"Sometimes."

"Like now?"

"Like now." It seemed that she really was serious, so I did as I was told and tied the cloth over my eyes.

"Could you pass me the reins? I seem to be having a problem finding them."

"I have not attached them. You won't need them tonight." I was getting more and more confused, but she seemed very clear about what we were to do, so I just waited to be told what would follow.

"I am going to lead your horse with mine, and I will start to shake a bell necklace. You will listen to the sound of the bells, you will feel the movement of the horse, and at some time you will connect to the *rlung rta,* the wind horse, he that comes out of the river and flies off into the air."

The sun was setting; I could feel more than see the difference in the light. The air was getting cooler, and I was thankful that I had thought to put on my sheepskin jerkin. As I had my hands free, I could even close up the buttons, since we hadn't started moving yet.

From a little ways off, I heard the tinkling of bells. It came nearer and nearer, passed very close to me, and stopped for a moment. I could feel my horse moving slightly.

There was a tension and then we were off. *She must be riding very slowly.* I could feel the strange movement of my horse walking. A walking horse, so she had told me, moves in a rhythm of eight. I wasn't sure what that meant, but I was very aware of how he was shifting his weight with every step.

The bells were gently ringing, also in rhythm with the steady, sedate horse steps. After several minutes the rhythm began to increase. At first, I was very scared that she would do something crazy, like get the horses to gallop, but the pace settled at a fast walking speed and no more.

I have spent many, many hours meditating throughout my life, allowing my conscious mind to quieten and to settle. Even when meditating on an object—a candle flame, a mantra, OM TA RE TU TA RE TU RE MA MA A YUR JNA NA PUN YE PUSH TING KU RU SOHA, or a symbol, the Triratana—there are moments when the attention moves and the object disappears for some time. When riding on a horse, it is impossible to forget what you are doing; otherwise, you might well just slip off!

So here I am, blindfolded, in the night, on a moving horse, listening to the gentle tinkling of a bell necklace. A gentle breeze is blowing, it is agitating the horse's mane. The hair is moving in my hands; I can feel it on my shirt, I can feel it on my face.

I know that the horse is not accelerating, but I feel that it is. The combined effect of being blindfolded, the increasing breeze, the *cling-cling* of the bells, and the fast-paced walk of the horses confuse my senses and I experience my steed—strong, steady, and powerful—taking me faster and faster, faster and faster, until at last the inevitable happens and we lift off, up, up there and into the air.

And as we join the sky, I find that I can see, see like I've never seen before. Here, high above the world, I soar, but not alone.

Huge, black, monolithic eagles fly alongside us, leading us up and on, far from my normal, ordinary world into this new, rich, fabulous, extraordinary world. I can see them and yet, somehow, I can see all that is there, all that is happening in that pedestrian, regular, unremarkable daily world. Love and hate, pride and humility, generosity and greed, healthiness and broken souls. And stretched out, like a simple dirt road, the whole of my life and lives, reaching back, back to the very dawn of time, and forwards, forwards towards infinity. This moment, this hour, this day, even this year, from this vantage point, is but the size of my nail compared to the whole of my body. What does it matter if it rains today, or tomorrow, or yesterday?

This life is but a small chapter in a big book, in an infinite series of books. My pain and my childhood suffering is like a major forest fire, all is burnt and charred and destroyed; there is nothing left, all has been burnt to cinders and the land is awfully scarred. And yet, in years to come, new shoots will sprout, young saplings will have taken root, the space cleared by the heat will again offer life and opportunity, and the forest will grow again.

So here I am, flying on my winged wind horse, flanked by a legion of massive night eagles, masters of the sky, masters of the universe.

I feel the energy dropping. The bells, which I have not been aware of for quite a while, are slowing down their chiming rhythm, and my horse is also slowing down. I am again myself, we are but two and two. I cry out a final farewell to my protective predators.

We stop. I untie my blindfold and slowly and carefully dismount the horse. My legs are even worse than in the afternoon;

they seem to have lost all their strength. I feel that I can hardly walk. It seems such nonsense; I don't seem to have used them at all this night, and yet my thighs ache like I've run a marathon.

Ainura is looking after the horses. I feel quite guilty. I know that I should be helping her, but it's no good, I can hardly stand. I stagger over to my sleeping mat and pretty much fall onto it. I don't hear Ainura coming back into the tent. The next thing that I'm aware of is that I need to get up to go to the toilet. I stagger off my mat, crawl out of the tent, find a spot some ways away, do what I need to do, and find my way back to my mat. Or maybe that bit was just a dream...

The next days follow some sort of rhythm. In the morning Ainura gets me to ride round and round the field, correcting my position—the placing of my feet, my thighs (my poor agonising thighs), my hands and arms—it seems that I'll never get it all right. As soon as I understand and more or less get something right, she focuses on something else that is wrong. The worst being, of course, that the new thing I'm doing wrong is something I was doing right only half an hour before.

Ainura is now almost always in a good humour and shows a lot of patience with me and my inability to learn.

Then we have a morning break before working on my directing the horse. Going forwards is, of course, only the very first step; directing from one side to the other is already more complicated. The reins have to be pulled, in parallel in this direction, this hand directed towards my shoulder, and at the same time to touch the horse's flank, just exactly here, and with just exactly this amount of pressure with the heel.

After dinner I get to show off what I have (or have not) learnt during the morning, before we leave for a long ride, walking the horses up and down hills, across streams, over sand, rocks, grasses (dry or wet, we ride the same), and sliding pebbles.

Everything is advancing quite well; I am even learning how to get the horse to turn a full circle, pivoting on either the front legs or the back legs. From this advance, I can now walk him into the square construction and get him to turn a three-hundred-and-sixty-degree turn while staying inside the branches, which are the sides of the box.

I can get him to walk forwards, backwards, and even a little sideways (I still need to work much more on that), but where it all stops is when she wants me to get him to gallop—I panic. We have tried trotting, but my fear of hurting myself on the pommel proved too true. I have great difficulty keeping the up and down in time with the movement of the horse, and I hurt myself quite often. After she had managed to stop laughing, Ainura was quite supportive, but being a woman, she had no way to really under-stand my problem in terms of finding a solution. As for the men of her tribe, all had started riding before they had learned to walk; for them, it was so totally natural that no one ever had any problems there.

We soon dropped any idea of trotting; trotting wasn't impor-tant to learn, anyway. For her, one either walked or galloped, there was no need for anything in between.

However, that still didn't solve in any way my fear of galloping. Of course, Ainura found a solution. One morning I returned from washing the dishes to find her saddling my horse, but what she was using was not at all a usual saddle. It was a very thick type of saddle blanket (which usually goes between the horse and the saddle), with a girth to attach around the horse and onto which were somehow also attached a pair of stirrups.

"Come, monk, let's go for a ride." I placed the pots inside the tent and walked towards my horse. Her horse, unsaddled, was quietly grazing some ways off.

"Who's going to ride the horse?"

"We are. Wait, while I get round here." She ran round to the other side of the horse and grabbed hold of the blanket to stop it slipping as I pulled myself up. "Here, now you help me up." She held out her arm, which I gripped with my hand. She also gripped my arm with her hand. "After three, you pull me up, okay?" I nodded. "One, two, three." Up she swung on my arm. She seemed to flow from the ground, into the air and onto the blanket behind me. "Now give me the reins, I'm in charge here." I held the reins so that she could take them off me. She pressed herself lightly against my back, clicked her tongue to signal to the horse to advance, and off we went.

To begin with, she spent some time just moving the horse—forwards, backwards, left, and right—so as to give me time to get used to the experience. Although it was not a proper saddle, having the stirrups made me feel much safer and balanced. Not having the reins to hold, I grabbed the horse's mane; it felt odd but okay. I thought that I wouldn't be falling off, as long as she wasn't thinking of getting him to gallop, of course!

We then left the fields and entered the forest. We walked for quite a while and I was starting, if anything, to feel a little bored.

I had absolutely nothing to do; I was just sitting and watching the scenery, hardly even noticing the movement of the horse. We arrived before a long, level patch of ground and I could feel Ainura's arms start to tense, to press against the sides of my rib cage.

"Relax," was all she said, before making an odd sucking sound and starting the horse on a soft, steady gallop. The sensation was different, but not unpleasant; my body was sliding forwards and backwards with the movement of the horse. "Use your hips and your belly. Try not to slide. It will help when we go faster," she said into my ear.

For a moment I was feeling quite good. The horse, although galloping, was not going very fast at all. I was in fact quite surprised that it could gallop slowly. I thought that galloping could only be fast.

Slowly, slowly, she got the horse to increase the speed. Faster and faster it went. I could start to feel myself bouncing a little on his back. She slowed him down again. "Hips and belly," she reminded me. We speeded up again. Things were okay for a moment, but again I started to bounce. Again we slowed down and speeded up, and slowed down and speeded up. And then I had it: my body started to flow. I was a wave, my middle was a wave, my back bent inwards and my belly flew out, and then back and then out and then back.

Faster and faster we galloped. My breath came fast and short; I could feel the excitement gripping my very soul. And Ainura, tight behind me; I could feel her breath on my neck, hot and damp. The little hairs reacted, sensitive, excited. As the horse speeded up, the force of the movement pushed us closer and closer together. I could feel all the contours of her little, lithe body. I could feel the pressure of her small, hard breasts, pressing themselves deep into my vulnerable, open back. The movement also pushed me towards the front of the blanket and the mount of the horse's long neck. The big, hard, horned object between my legs also threatened to be a problem.

And on and on we galloped, free, free, free to scream with joy and pleasure and delight.

We returned to the tent, tired and spent. Ainura threw off the reins and the blanket and we just let ourselves drop, there, in a heap on the soft, warm grass, to sleep.

The transition from non-galloping rider to galloping rider had been made, and it didn't take me long to feel capable of galloping at full speed, as long as the path was flat and straight.

The days and nights passed peacefully; my riding continued to improve and we spoke of many things. One night Ainura was talking about some of the habits and customs of her people, which had many links to their nomadic heritage and a long association with horses.

"So tell me more about this race between the men and the women," I stopped her, asking for more details.

"It's not men and women, it's a man and a woman," she corrected me. "It is called Kyz Kuumai, and a man chases a girl in order to win a kiss from her, while she gallops away. If he is not successful, she may in turn chase him and attempt to beat him with her *kamchi*."

"What's that?"

"This!" And she whacked the carpet on the floor with her horsewhip. The dust created a thick cloud that took some moments to dissipate. "Would you like to try?" She was laughing at me.

"Maybe on a straight, level track, I might have a chance."

"You like to be whipped, monk?" She smiled at me mischievously.

"Do you like to be kissed, horsewoman?"

"That depends on who's doing the kissing." And before I had time to reply, she thrust the pots into my hands and pushed me out of the tent.

The next morning was as usual. It seemed as if the discussion of the previous evening was all but forgotten. However, that afternoon, riding in the forest, she turned to me with a wicked smile.

"So, do you want to try for your kiss?" So saying, she took out her whip and whacked my horse's rump with it. He was startled and began to gallop. Ainura appeared from behind, her horse already galloping to pass mine.

"My whip will be waiting for you."

Everything in the world reduced to a single focus—the backside of her horse. Somehow, I couldn't see her, I couldn't think of her. I knew that I had to catch that horse. It was if my whole life depended on it. I found myself leaning slightly forward, crouching in the stirrups, my backside lifted just inches off the saddle. I called for help, who knows why I should think to do such a thing. I called for the night eagles to come and carry us, I called to the wind horse, I called to the gods.

The ground flowed beneath us. I took no notice of the terrain, that was not my concern. The horse was the expert in that. My job was to find the energy to drag us forward, to pull us towards them, to hook on to their energy, to catch them.

Suddenly, her horse seemed to stumble. It slowed, just for a moment or two, but that was all I needed. She couldn't accelerate quick enough to escape me and so I had her. We passed them just as she was gaining back her speed. In an instant she was again in front, but nothing counted now—I had won, we had won, she had been caught and I had won my kiss.

She didn't stop straightaway, and it took a moment to catch her up again. The horses were panting heavily. We had left the forest and arrived in a grassy field.

"I won, I won."

"So I won't have to whip you after all. Shame."

"So when do I claim my kiss?"

"Not so fast, my impetuous monk, a woman still has some rights, you know."

"I don't know all the details, but it must surely be soon after winning the race."

"I won't make you wait for too long, don't you worry yourself about that." And she just slid down off her saddle to go lie on the grass while the horses took a well-earned rest, to relax and graze. Nothing more was said of the race, and part of me was a little irritated that the whole thing had just been a trick to get me to gallop at full speed.

We returned walking and galloping in turn; the gallops were quite fast, if nothing to compare with the speed on the outward leg. Ainura was particularly silent from the moment she had descended from her horse. Knowing how difficult and moody she could be, I decided not to risk upsetting her by talking. Maybe she was angry to have lost the race, maybe she really didn't want to kiss me. Well, I certainly had no desire to insist if she really didn't want to.

The silence continued throughout supper, and I was starting to worry that our relationship had been wrecked because of a silly race. The meal ended and, as usual, I took the pots to the river to wash up.

When I got back, it was already beginning to get dark, and I was surprised to see that there was no light coming from the tent. Usually Ainura would light the hanging candles that were attached to the roof at various points, which gave out quite a lot of light.

I opened the tent flap and was buffeted by a wave of heat; she had built up the fire to a great height, much too high for the night, as we would soon be going to bed.

I entered the tent, squinted to see in the semi-darkness, and carefully made my way over to the kitchen area to relieve myself of the clean pots.

"I'm ready for my kiss now." I turned back towards the fire; I had been so attentive not to fall down in the darkened tent that I had not noticed the still form lying close to the roaring fire.

"Here," said the voice, "drink," and she passed me a tiny clay cup. I sat down next to the form that was covered in furs. Her arm, I noticed, was naked. I took the cup and tasted the liquid; it was rich and smooth. Velvet fire slid down my throat, warming my chest in its passing. My body shivered in pleasure and in reaction to the strong alcohol content.

"It's very hot in here."

"You're just wearing too many clothes. Come, take some of them off." I don't know if it was the heat, the rice *raksi*, or the fact that she was lying next to me, wearing very little if anything at all, or that she was inviting me to take my clothes off, but my pulse began to beat at double its usual speed.

"Would you prefer that I beat you with my whip, monk?"

"I won the race, so I get the right to a kiss."

"Quite right; so why don't you just come and get it?" She opened up the skin covers and invited me to come to her. She was naked, warm, soft, open. She smelt a little of the *raksi* that she must already have sampled, and of something else—yes, a slight odour of horse, and something else. It was her own smell; she had sweated under the covers, a heady, musky, smoky smell.

I was already a little drunk from the wine, but here, so close, touching her silky skin, her strong arms and legs entwining me into her web of passion, her mouth, so close to mine, closer, closer, and then— the kiss. I was falling, falling, falling down, down, down. Spinning, dragged into a whirlpool of sensations; every inch of my body alive and active; every single micro contact between us noted and experienced. The touch of her lips on mine, the texture, the taste, temperature, tension; the movement of the jaw, the activity of our tongues. How our arms, encircling the other, holding, drawing, protecting yet seeking, searching, probing, experimenting with pressure, place, and position. I found her breasts; small, delicate, perfect miniature moons, firm and ripe, her nipples; hard and protruding, excited for me. And elsewhere, I too was ready, hard and protruding, my first time, yes, but the body knows how it is to function.

I was hard and she was ready; she helped me to focus, to direct, to enter. For a long moment my body stopped breathing; it was a type of enormous shock, too strong, too powerful to easily cope with. My body was thrusting, pushing, delving, but also vibrating, as if every atom in my being was being shaken, like a leaf in a storm. Faster and faster, harder and harder, deeper and deeper, my body was galloping but I wasn't keeping up. I felt like I was being shaken apart, the energy was too much for me, to throw me off or rip me totally open. And then I had it, my body started to flow. I was a wave, my middle was a wave, my back bent inwards and my belly flew out, and then back and then out and then back. Yes, I was the wave, and we were together, a single shared soul, flying high and free in the crazy, spectacular universe, linked by a single silken thread to this world, or else never to return.

We spun, we dove, we wheeled, we soared, faster and faster into the kaleidoscope of colours and sensations, faster and deeper, higher and freer, exploding into the excellent night skies.

The fire was drowsy, the lazy embers radiating the last remnants of heat and light from last night's blazing passion. She was still there; slumbering in my arms, her soft body, limp and languid, warm and welcoming, her short legs draped over mine like a soft, rolled sleeping cover. Gently I slid myself out from under her, she moaned softly, turned, huddled into the sheepskin, and carried on sleeping.

Don't women ever need to go to the toilet? I slipped out of the tent and went to relieve myself. I was also desperately in need of a drink of water. The alcohol and the hot, dry atmosphere in the tent had left me particularly dry.

"Good morning, my innocent monk." She had at last woken up. "How are you feeling after your kiss?"

"I think I could get used to it."

"Not with me, I'm sorry to say."

"Why not? What did I do wrong? If I've done something, please tell me."

"Oh no, there was nothing wrong, nothing wrong at all. The reason why we will not be able to repeat last night is because you are leaving today."

"What?"

"Last night was my present to both of us, for a job well done."

"A present?"

"Was it not a good present?"

"It was, it was, it was wonderful."

"Yes, it was a good present, but now we have to prepare for you to leave."

"When will the driver arrive?"

"What driver?"

"The man with the yak, to take me back to the monastery."

"There will be no man with a cart, and you are not to return to the monastery at this time."

"I don't understand. I don't understand anything."

"So I was right all along, ugly and stupid," she said, but this time she was smiling. Yes, she was smiling, but I think that maybe I could also see tears forming in her eyes.

"First, we need to have a naming ceremony."

"What are we going to name?"

"Your horse, of course."

"What do you mean, my horse?"

"This is now your horse. He was paid for by your master, in the hope that you would succeed in learning how to ride him. Now, as he has not been named yet, it is your right to choose his name."

I looked in my bags and found some incense. I had never heard of a naming ceremony for a horse, but lighting some incense and chanting prayers was something I knew how to do well.

I went into the tent and prepared the space for the ritual, then we brought the horse into the tent, where I sang and chanted, praying for health and strength for my horse, which I then named Dorjee.

We then celebrated and drank a toast of rice *raksi* out of the tiny clay cups in which it is served.

"Now that your horse has a name, you will need a saddle and a bridle."

I remembered something that I had heard somewhere, more than likely from Ainura during one of our evening talks.

"Didn't you tell me that your people would lend a friend your horse but never your saddle?"

"A good saddle is worth much more than a horse."

"So how come you are offering me a saddle?"

"The saddle was my father's, and when he died, as I was his only child, it came to me. I have been carrying it round ever since, waiting to find someone worthy to give it to."

"And you want to give it to me?"

"Anything to get rid of you and have a decent night's sleep." She turned away from me. I knew that she was crying, I also knew that I must not mention it.

"And where am I to go?"

"You are to go to another place, in the south. There is a monk, his name is Honest Pride, he will be waiting for you in the inn of the village at the bottom of the mountain. He will tell you where to go."

"And will I ever see you again?"

"Where will the wind blow the leaves in the

winter?" "Our paths will meet again."

"If they do, I will not regret it."

I did not go to her; I just bowed, took my belongings, loaded them on Dorjee, mounted as she had taught me, waved, and left.

Satisfied that, in a few short weeks, I had learned how to ride a wild horse.

Letting Go

They were just finishing breakfast. Dhargey seemed particularly quiet that morning. The Master had noticed this and had
chosen to respect the young disciple's silence.

"Are you finished, Master? Should I clear away the breakfast
dishes?"

"No, make some more tea. You are not ready to start the day."

"Master?"

"You have been particularly silent and reserved this morning,
there is something on your mind. It is not my business to pry, but
until you can move whatever it is to the side of your consciousness,
there is nothing I can teach you today."

Following the demand of his elder, he got up to heat more
water to make some more Po Cha.

"Master, can I tell you what is troubling me?"

"It is not my right to insist that you tell me, but it is my right
to assist you on your path." Although not totally understanding

260

the response, Dhargey took it as a signal that it was okay to talk about his problem.

"Today is the anniversary of the death of my brother."

"Whom you never met."

"Yes, but every year on this day, they take out some of his clothes and place them around the house. Nobody talks, but they are both very sad. My mother cries for most of the day."

"They should ask for help to work through their grief. Grieving for so long means that they have not faced the loss, they have not released your brother. His soul is not free to advance on its own path. This is not a good thing."

"But maybe they don't want to let him go. Maybe it is their way to keep some sort of contact with him."

"When something is gone, it is gone. Here, look into your cup, what do you see?"

Confused, he looked into his cup. He looked at it from several directions, turning it first this way and that. Finally he looked back to his Master. "I see nothing," he admitted.

"Exactly."

"I don't understand."

"There is nothing left in your cup. You have drunk all the tea."

"Yes, I drank the tea."

"It is gone."

"It is gone," repeated Dhargey, quite lost.

"Did you enjoy the tea?"

"Yes, yes, it was good. Yes, I enjoyed the tea."

"Will you miss it?"

"Will I miss the tea?"

"Yes, will you miss the tea?"

"Maybe if I couldn't have it again."

"You will never have it again."

"Never again?"

"Never."

"I have to give up drinking Po Cha?" He sounded a little dismayed.

"No, you idiot, the cup of tea you have just drunk—you can never drink that one again."

"No, I've just finished it."

"Exactly."

"Good, I'm glad that is sorted out. Shall I clear away the breakfast things now?"

"You have understood nothing, and I was starting to think that maybe you could succeed at becoming a monk."

"But I do understand, of course I do. I drank the tea and now it is gone."

"And?"

"And if you want I could make some more."

"And what has that got to do with your brother?"

"I, I don't know. He died quite young. I don't think that he ever made tea." The old man sighed deeply, closed his eyes, and withdrew into silence. Dhargey waited a few moments; he didn't dare to speak and disturb his Master's meditation, but he didn't know what else to do. Finally, he took the only action left open to him—he made some more tea.

"Master?" He brought the tea to the old man. Slowly, he opened his eyes and looked at the young disciple.

"Yes, Dhargey."

"The cup is the body, the hard, empty shell. The tea is the spirit that fills the body. When the tea is gone, that is death. The cup is empty, the body is empty, nothing is left."

"Not quite nothing, there is always the memory. As long as we remember, nothing ever truly dies. Our sacred texts were written by the Masters before us, their wisdom lives on in the words they left behind. Songs, dances, chants, prayers, instruments, sacred and non-sacred objects; all of these bear witness to the passage of certain incarnations of important souls."

"And my brother's clothes?"

"Of course. Your brother came into this world for the time that he was meant to be here. The quality of anything is not measured by its size but by the value it carries within it. A wise man speaks little, a fool is rarely silent. But it is the wise man's words that are remembered. A common blackbird is small and weak, especially when compared to a mighty yak, but which would you prefer to wake up to? A yak grunting, or a blackbird singing?"

"And the value of a life is not based on how long someone lives, but...but on what? I'm sorry, I haven't quite got it."

"The value of a life is not based on how long one lives, only on the achieving of the soul's purpose for this incarnation."

"But how can we know what the purpose of an incarnation is?"

"We don't. We can only trust that whatever your brother's soul was meant to experience, it did."

"And then?"

"And then, just as his soul released its human body, so should your parents release your brother's soul."

"It's not easy. You can't understand. For my parents, they only had him for a short time. It isn't possible to release something special that you had for only a short time."

"Come sit, bring your tea, and I will tell you another little story from my life."

The Monkey's Tail

The journey towards the southeast was not unpleasant. The Old Master had sent a young Monk, Honest Pride, to come with me, as his sister had married a nomad that had settled towards the south and he had not seen her for some years.

As we were still in spring, the days were cool yet long. We kept to quiet roads, as I had a great fear that we might cross a band of marauding raiders— worse still, the Wave of Red and Black!

Honest Pride found his sister in good health, surprised but very pleased to see him. They invited me stay and visit with them for a few days, but I was impatient to discover what the Old Master had intended for me, in the jungles of the south.

The days started to get hotter and hotter. It wasn't due to the coming summer; the change was too quick for that. No, I was moving into a different climatic region, it was also getting more and more humid. For someone like myself, having grown up in the north, it was much too early for the rainy season to have started, and anyway, it wasn't raining, it was just more and more humid. Soon after, I noticed the vegetation changing, and I quickly entered through the deep green curtain which announced my arrival into this new, unnatural world, the jungle.

To say that it was worse than my worst nightmares would not honestly be the truth; my nightmares, although now reduced to night terrors, were still very much with me. Not a week would slip by without my waking in ice-cold sweats, winter and summer alike, but just the same, the entry into the jungle, for the first time, was still quite, quite horrible.

The heat and the humidity were totally oppressive, but the thing most awful was the noise.

Never before in my life had I ever experienced a noise quite like it. It was everywhere. My poor horse, also never confronted with such a phenomenon, tensed into a state of pure panic. His ears spun this way and then that, like prayer flags in the winter wind, forwards, back, one side and the other. He stopped dead still, expecting to be attacked from any and every side. His head was now also starting to twist, trying to rip the reins from my hands, or just a sign of his growing panic. I half jumped off his back; better off on the ground by my own choice than be thrown off by a panicked horse.

As soon as I was off his back and he was released from my controlling presence, his own basic instincts imposed, and he turned and bolted out of this hell of noise and shadows.

I, for myself, was of two minds—whether to follow him or not—but my master, the Old Master, had sent me here, to the jungle, for an experience that he hoped could help me to deal with some of the scares of the loss which still haunted me so much that some nights they woke me with my own screaming terror.

However, I had another major question that continued to trouble my tortured mind. "Why would my master send me to a Hindu temple?" For it was to a temple of Hanuman that I was to direct myself, and this path, through this hell of a leafed cavern, was supposed to take me to this unlikely objective.

My horse, being so far from home, would hopefully wait a while outside the jungle area, long enough for me to send someone to find him and keep him safe until my return to the north.

I stumbled on, deeper and deeper into the forest. At every step, the noise seemed to increase, but worse than that was the growing feeling that I was being watched, and from every side.

Suddenly a branch would move, swaying left to right, up and down, one way, then another. There would be a movement; a creature, now here, now gone. I'd see but a glimpse of its fur, but before I could recognise it for what it was, it was just a blur and an uncomfortable memory.

There was another effect of the movement, though; as I followed the trail with my eyes, my legs also continued along the same axis. Without any conscious awareness, I was gently but clearly being led deeper and deeper into the thickening forest.

And then, turning, for almost no good reason, here I was, in front of an old, old Hindu temple, paint peeling from every wall. The face of the huge gold monkey statue was now almost totally black. The once black roof, now grey, was white from the monkey droppings. Dozens of these furry animals surely lived here on a more or less permanent basis.

"Now you have arrived." I spun round. The little old man was standing behind me. Had he walked past me without my seeing him, or had he been walking silently behind me, or had he suddenly materialised out of thin air? In the moment, all these possibilities seemed equally plausible.

"Now you have arrived," he repeated, patiently but with insistence. I blushed; I was so surprised with this apparition that I had totally forgotten my manners.

"Sir, it is." I dug out the *jáldar* and presented the scarf to him. Smiling quietly to himself, he twisted it into a ball and threw it up into the air. The branches of a nearby tree shook, my eyes sought the reason, a blur passed and the scarf was gone. The monkeys on the roof danced and shrieked with delight.

"Your gift has been accepted. You are welcome, young man." I remembered my horse. "Master, my horse took fear on entering the jungle and bolted. Would it be possible—"

"It has been taken care of." I must have shown some reaction of surprise. "There is little in this part of the jungle that I am not aware of."

"Thank you, Master."

"You may call me Swapan."

"Master Swapan."

"No, Swapan; that will do."

"Swapan, as you wish." I hesitated for moment. "Swapan, where should I leave my affairs?"

"You would like me to show you your room?"

"If that would be possible. I would also like to wash before eating or drinking."

"So you want to see your room, the washing area, and then prepare food and drink?" He then started to laugh, the monkey chorus echoing his old, shrill voice. "Here, here, here is your chamber." He opened his arms wide. "There, there is the river," he said, pointing to a spot behind the temple. "Your washing and drinking area. And food? Food is here, wherever and whenever you choose to pick it." And with that, he turned his back on me and disappeared into the jungle.

For the whole of the next few days I was left alone, if one could call it that, in this mad world teeming with life and noise and activity, day and night.

Quite soon, my surprise and bemusement at my short welcome and abrupt abandonment turned to irritation, then to anger, but finally, as the day began to fade, to pure fear.

The jungle is a dangerous place, even during the day, even for those that know and understand its traps and perils. I had never entered this world before, and even if I had, I still would not have the knowledge or experience to know how to survive it. But yet, here I was, alone and vulnerable in this huge, forbidding nightmare land.

A small child in a very hostile world.

The monkeys started to jump and call. I looked up; were they calling to me? Were they trying to tell me something? They seemed to be looking towards me then looking towards the roof they were sitting on. They seemed now to be getting irritated; they would look at me, point at me, then look to the roof, jump up and down, hitting the rooftop, and scream and scream and scream.

Then it hit me; literally, something hit me. From somewhere in the trees, someone—some ape, I suppose—threw a nut at me. I turned in anger; another hit me, and another. I turned away from the onslaught and ran towards the temple. The monkeys on the roof shrieked with laughter, but somehow (who knows how?) I sensed something like satisfaction.

It was then that I finally realised what was happening—they were trying to communicate with me. The little lost child wasn't all alone and helpless against this horrible, scary, threatening existence. No, he had friends that were there to help and support him. He only needed to learn to see and to hear them, to trust that their presence was to support and to protect, to open, to understand their message and advice, and to have the confidence to follow their good counsel.

So what were these snub-nosed midgets attempting to communicate to me? The roof, of course, the roof; I should climb on the roof. Where else would I find safety and security for the night where most predators would be unable to reach?

Climbing onto the roof was not a simple affair for me. Climbing is not something that I had much done in my life, and the muscle groups for climbing are not those that one tends to often use in daily life.

I was at a loss to find a way up until a baby monkey dropped down in front of me and led me to a dark corner round the back of the temple where some vines had chosen to climb up one of the ancient pillars.

With much effort and several failed attempts, I finally managed to scrabble my way onto the roof, to much acclaim from my newfound friends.

It was now quite dark; the incessant jungle orchestra played on and on. Deep down in my psyche I knew that I should feel fear; fear of the dark, of the unknown, of snakes, of the ever-present, ever-haunting shadows, shadows from the past. But now, here and now, with no weapon other than my hand knife, with neither roof nor wall, surrounded by a small group of weak, dumb apes, for the first time in my whole life I felt that my soul was safe.

With that wondrous yet incredible realisation, I allowed myself to drift into the most peaceful of sleeps. A sleep so deep, so absolute, that it was only the jumping of another (or the same) baby monkey on my back that woke me up.

They took me in, this group, a (relatively) big, furless, tailless human being. They tried to feed me a variety of delicacies—grass, lichens, and buds—but in the end, I just settled for fruit.

And so I was left, just me and the monkeys, and it was, if anything, a little weird when Swapan eventually returned to the temple area.

"*Nyado delek.*"

"And good morning to you, my little monkey," he laughed back at me. The monkeys joined in with his little joke. Could they really understand him? It almost seemed as if they could. "You are not to eat today."

"Nothing?" I had just woken up and was already looking forward to my breakfast.

"You may drink water until the sun touches those treetops." He pointed towards the trees on the western side of the temple clearing. "You would do well to bathe in the river and to rest in the afternoon. Tonight you will need your senses." And with that, he

271

turned and left, leaving me irritated with frustrated hunger, both for food and for information.

The thought that the monkeys could understand him was further reinforced by the fact that they offered me no food this day. They knew that I was to fast. Neither did they bring food onto the roof, so as not to tempt or frustrate me further.

The night came soon enough. Although I was very keen to find out what the old man had planned for me, I also admit to being rather apprehensive. The tension began to mount as the sun dipped down past the western trees.

The forest was becoming quieter and quieter. Of course, there was no reason for it. Maybe it was always like this just before sunset, a sort of changing of the guard, when the daytime animals prepare for sleep and the nocturnal ones have not yet woken up. Maybe I'd just not noticed it before; maybe I was more than a little nervous...

"Come down," he said, directing me in front of the temple doorway, "sit." I sat down in the lotus position. "You have not eaten?" I nodded my head. "Good, drink." He handed me a small container. I smelt the liquid, something hit the top of the inside of my nose. It couldn't have been physical pain because nothing had touched me, but it hurt just the same. At the same time, the back of my throat closed up. Once, I had been poisoned by bad water and I'd been sick for some days. Without eating or drinking anything but water all day, just a quick smell and I was ready to be deeply sick.

"Drink." He smiled at me.

"But I will surely just bring it all back up."

"Not all, you will get used to it. Watch." He took a mouthful to show me that it wasn't the pure poison my body was screaming that I should avoid if I hoped to ever see the sun again.

"Drink." There was no refusing him. I took the small object, closed my eyes (as if that could help in any way), opened my mouth, and allowed the bitter, bitter liquid to flow down my throat and into my defenceless system.

To begin with, there was not much reaction. I started to feel a little giddy, as when I drink strong barley wine, but the sensation didn't last too long. First it felt like falling, then falling and twisting. Once, I had fallen in a fast-flowing river; it grabbed me with all its watery force, pulling me first one way and then another, but always down, faster and faster, until I didn't know which way was up or down, and I was drowning and sliding and falling and flying. It was wonderful, exhilarating. My body no longer existed, I had neither will nor power. The river god had me in her grip and my life was in her hands. Fear had given way to acceptance, and I had broken free of the limits of my human body and human mind.

Again I was being taken and pulled and twisted and ripped from my frail human, limited existence, but this time I felt nauseous, terribly, terribly nauseous. He had poisoned me, I was going to die, it was clear, I could tell. My body was trying to vomit out the poison, but it must be much too late, I could already feel my links to this existence weakening. I was seeing colours and shapes where I knew, from the little live human part, that nothing existed.

It was no good, I couldn't hold it. Why should I? It's poison. I turned and vomited up the vile substance, and crawled away from the evil-smelling slime.

I was having trouble breathing. *So this is death, is it?* The colours, yes, yes, they were quite, quite beautiful. Now it was the trees, the trees were looking at me. *I will die a crazy man. What happens to the soul of those who die in insanity? Can it be damaged?*

"Welcome," said a tree.

"I have no scarf to offer you," I replied in my deliria.

"It is of no importance, I have my vines."

"I am dying."

"No," smiled the tree, "you are being born."

"Young Master." The old man was calling me by my human name. "Listen closely to my voice."

"I'll try, at least while I still live."

"You are not dying to your world, you are opening up to a new one."

"I'm not dying?"

"If you do not shut up and listen to me, then I might kill you, but that should not be necessary." I felt reassured by his rough humour.

"I am listening, Swapan."

"You have been welcomed into my little family of monkeys. Now it is for you to enter into their family."

"Yes, yes, I would be happy to."

"You will now take on the form of a monkey. Deep, deep, deep within the furthest, deepest memories of your body is the form of the monkey—the head with its small snub nose, the round shoulders and back, the long arms and legs, the black and golden fur, the long prehensile feet and toes, and most important of all, you now have a beautiful, articulated, wonderful tail."

As he spoke, even with the minute portion of my usual consciousness screaming, *Nonsense, nonsense, nonsense!* it was true. I was a monkey: small, bent over, with those long feet and toes, even a tail. However, I still walked almost like a man, albeit bent almost double, touching the ground with my long arms from time to time. And yes, the tail, which I really did have, but hanging limp and dead like an extra three metres of waistband, badly attached, trailing behind me.

"Walk, monkey, walk. Feel how your body moves, how your arms and legs swing in harmony, how your hips move. What you see, what you hear, what you feel, what you sense..."

And for a time, a time without beginning or end, here I was; a living, walking, seeing, smelling monkey. Aware of many, many things that had never before existed for me.

And then it was over.

My sleep was confused and disturbed; dreams came and went, monkey thoughts and images appeared, but these were dream experiences, not the same as those I had experienced early on in the night.

I woke up feeling awful but exhilarated. I wanted to ask questions. What had happened? What had he given me? Would we do it again? When? When? When? We must do it again.

My relationships with the monkeys grew stronger from that day on. I got to know each one individually. I gave them names; we learnt more and more to communicate with each other.

Three days after my first experience with the "poison," Swapan came again. "Tonight" was all he said, but it was enough for me.

It tasted just as foul, the nausea was more or less as bad, I vomited after some little time, but none of that worried me. I was ready and willing to allow all these minor inconveniences for the chance to re-experience something of that first time.

And here I am, back in the body of a little monkey.

"Tonight we shall start to learn to use our feet and toes. Come, let us walk down to the river. Now put your feet into the soft mud. Feel the contact with all the parts of the sole of each foot. Move each foot, one at a time, slowly into and out of the mud. First entering with the toes; feel as the mud slides under each part of the foot. SLOWLY, slowly, take your time, take your time, feel each millimetre of the foot, each little patch of skin, feel the movement, feel the contact. And now, again the same, but turn the foot from side to side, bend and flex, feel the muscles that you've never felt before, and again. Now enter the foot flat, straight down into the mud, always slowly, carefully, consciously. Feel the contact, move the toes. Try and move each toe, one at a time. Not easy, is it? Good, good, enough. Wash your feet in the river and let them dry off in the sun. Now, we will try another little exercise. Take each toe in turn— take your time, take your time. Take a toe between your thumb and index finger, now bend and straighten it. Keep bending and straightening it until you feel that you can make your toe bend and straighten by itself."

And so I did. The work took a long moment. Strangely enough, it was the second and third toes that were the most difficult to train, but by the end of the session I was able to bend and straighten each and every toe individually at will.

The next days were very frustrating; even my monkey friends could not distract me from my impatience to continue the work of fully inhabiting my monkey body. The only thing I could think to do was to continue the feet and toe exercises in the mud and using my fingers, which did seem to have some effect on my own ability to manipulate my feet and toes, but was mostly frustrating, as the human foot and toes have nothing like the potential of that of our monkey cousins.

My next lesson in my monkey skin was becoming aware of my tail, a work that proved to be much less difficult than one might have imagined. First, I just stroked it for a while, touching its whole length, becoming aware of every slight twist and turn, fascinated by the unevenness of it. When I had gotten to know my new appendage, I then began to move it. First, I had to move it to the limits of the reach of my long arms before I could even begin to feel the reaction on my lower back. Then I began to succeed to create a slight resistance in the tail, pulling it gently against my hands, first this way and then that way. The resistance began to increase, and slowly, slowly, I began to feel the small articulations along its length.

I move my back just so. Well, I would have called it my back, only now my back is so much longer than before. I move it like that and my tail moves—left, right, up, or down. I have a tail, it is part of me, I use it, I move it as I wish.

My time is up—the session ends.

The next session is climbing and jumping. Using my hands and feet together for climbing is fairly easy; jumping is another story altogether. Jumping uses not only the hands and feet, but also the balance of the tail. With my limited experience of using my tail, finding the exact angle and holding it there is not obvious. The other monkeys appear to help me. They show me how they leap, the curl of the tail, the balance, the grip. They seem to have infinite patience with me. Again and again I try but fail, and yet their good humour keeps me going. Eventually I get it; I jump, I swing, I do not fall, I am exultant. I can run up and down trees, swing from branch to branch, even hang from my own tail.

I awake. The morning is bright and I feel great. Only a day or so to wait, and again I will feel the power and freedom of running and swinging through the trees.

Swapan arrives.

"Good morning, Master, am I to continue again tonight? I did not eat yesterday, but I would be willing to forgo food again today to continue my training."

"But your training is now complete."

"What do you mean, 'complete'?"

"You have completed your training. It is time to return to the north."

I couldn't believe what I was hearing. I'd only just mastered my monkey form; the feet, the toes, the tail.

"But, no, not yet, I've only just learnt how to use my tail properly. You can't really mean it. Please, please, you cannot mean it."

"You have completed your training. It is time to leave."

My tail, my tail; it was as if he had amputated a real part of me. How could I pass the rest of my life never feeling the swish and flick of my tail again? "Please, please, just one more time, just to feel it part of me once more."

"When it is gone, it is gone, that is how life is. But then again, you know that already. This is not the first time that you have had important parts of yourself cut away."

He must have said that intentionally, he must have surely known of my history. Now he had dug deeply into the very depths of my pain. Here I was, already a man, but flooding through the whole of my being was a lost seven-year-old, cut off from everyone and everything that I'd ever known.

Again, the non-understanding, the confusion, the pain, red and stabbing, then the fear, the black, black fear. The awful wave was washing over me once again.

"You see, to have something cut off is always painful, and yet something always remains."

"I don't understand."

"Climb the tree."

"But I'm me, I'm not a monkey now."

"Climb the tree." I kick off my shoes, grab the trunk with my arms and legs, and start to climb. I am feeling angry, angry and hurt. *No, no, no, he cannot mean it, he cannot cut me off from my tail.*

"Stop climbing the tree." I stop, I look down. I've climbed high up into the tree. "Now jump to the next branch." A certain mental exhaustion limited my immediate, normal reaction of, *No, I can't do that*, so I do. I jump, and I must have calculated right, as I manage without accident to land, unscathed, on the branch. The monkeys scream with laughter and with joy.

"Now tell me that nothing remains of your monkey self." I slowly but easily climb down the tree.

"But what of my family, my parents, my village?"

"What about them? Does nothing remain of any of those things? Is not the man also the fruit of the child?"

279

I stop to think, to feel, to dig deeply into that small, fragile part of myself that I had spent so many years running away from. Yes, it is true, the man that I am is also a product of the boy that I was. There were so many good and rich moments in my childhood, and my relationship with my adoptive parents and with the Old Master is just a continuation of my relationships from before. Even now, to accept and to be accepted by my new family of snub-nosed monkeys is the same as with my friends in the village.

"Yes, Master, you are indeed correct. Nothing is truly totally lost. We always carry the good of what we have experienced within ourselves. We just have to give ourselves permission to connect to it."

"Today you may call me Master, for today I too can call you Master. Your horse awaits you at the edge of the tree line. Now it is time to make your goodbyes to another family that I doubt you will ever meet again." I follow his eyes up to the temple roof, where my long-tailed family are watching me closely. I turn again to bid him thanks and farewell, but he has already disappeared, as softly and gently as waking from a dream. Without thinking, I grab the vine and effortlessly swing up to join, for one last meal, my furry jungle relatives, and then, with strangely few regrets, I leave the temple, the monkeys, the jungle, the south, my night terrors, and my losses.

I Have a Body — Part One

The day had been going well; they had walked quite far that morning, and the Master was in a particularly good mood. He had revealed certain anecdotes of his early years in the monastery, where it seemed he had gotten up to his fair share of mischief.

They were enjoying the walk so much that they chose not to stop for lunch until it was quite late, which was why they had happened to have walked so far.

Lunch had been good; the Master continued to entertain his disciple with stories of innocent misdeeds and not-so-innocent gossip. He then remembered a dance that he had made up when he should have been practicing meditation.

"I wonder if I can still remember it. I think it was something like this." And that was when the badness happened.

"One to the—ohhhh!" His foot somehow had twisted out from under him and he fell heavily down.

"Master, Master, are you all right?"

"Unfortunately, I don't think so. I seem to have twisted my ankle. Here, help me get up. I'll see if I can...oh, no, it's no good, I can't put too much weight on it."

"What shall we do?"

"First of all, tidy up the food, and then we shall see."

It didn't take long for the pots and plates to be rinsed, and then they and the remains of the food were put away.

"Here, help me up again." The old man leaned heavily on the younger and they started back along the path that they had taken some hours earlier, but instead of the light spirits and easy walking, this time the spirit was much heavier, and the pace painfully slow.

"It is no good, Dhargey, I cannot continue. You must return to the monastery and get help. I will wait here for you to return. Just leave me the food that is left from lunch and I will be fine."

"But I cannot get to the monastery before nightfall, and even if I could, it would be tomorrow afternoon at the soonest before we could get back."

"Well, do you have another solution?"

It took him about a minute before he came up with an idea. "Maybe I could carry you."

"You, the fragile boy that couldn't even walk up the mountain? What makes you think that you could manage to carry me?"

"I did manage to walk up the mountain, and that was weeks ago. I'm much, much stronger and fitter than I was then."

"We could always try, but if you don't succeed, then you would have wasted time that would better have been used going for help."

"At least let me try and see if I can manage to carry you at all. After all, you are not very big or heavy."

"I might be heavier than you imagine."

"Well, we will see." And with that, he turned his back on the Master and beckoned him to climb onto it. It was true that the Master, now quite old and a little frail, did not weigh that much, and that weeks of walking in the mountains, carrying food and cooking utensils, had toughened him quite considerably.

He was pleased to find that he could walk quite comfortably with the old man on his back, and was feeling happy and proud of himself.

"Would you like me to continue to recount my story while you are carrying me? It might distract you from the effort."

"Yes, Master, I would enjoy for you to continue your story. I remember that you were just about to leave the jungle."

"Quite right."

Fi_ghtin_g Shadows – Part One

I left the jungle, suddenly worrying about what might have happened to my horse, Dorjee, which had run out into the open, as soon as I had released him, on the first day of my arrival.

Swapan had said that Dorjee had been attended to, but no more details than that.

With all the strange experiences that I had had, I had completely lost track of time. I did not know if I had passed days or weeks in the jungle, learning to be a monkey.

So, when it was time to leave, I started to really worry. It is a poor horseman that abandons his horse in a foreign place without even thinking to check that all is well with it.

I came out of the jungle, following the path back to where I entered, hoping that for some reason my horse would have chosen to stay close to that area. Also, Swapan had reassured me that my horse was "taken care of." What could that possibly mean?

"Hello, Jangbu." I had only just left the wall of trees that began the jungle. I was in no way expecting someone to be there, to know me, to call my name. But even more than that, I would never, could never in my life have imagined that it would be her.

"Ainura, what are you doing here?"

"Waiting for you, looking after your horse."

"But why you?"

"Because I am the best person to look after Dorjee."

"I don't understand. If you had already decided to come all the way down here to look after Dorjee, why didn't you ride with me here?"

"I had other things to do."

"What things?"

"That is not your business, my young monk," she answered with a smile. "Come, your horse is waiting for you, and we must leave soon or we will miss half the day."

Still full of questions, I allowed her to lead me to where the two horses were tied, saddled and ready to be ridden. Dorjee seemed quite excited to see me; he turned his head towards me, his ears twisted round and down in my direction, his muscular body dancing from side to side.

"Where are we going? Back to my monastery?"

"No, your master believes that the anger you hold against the man that killed your parents still blocks you from your inner path."

"So what must I do?"

"You must learn to fight."

"Who? Me? Have you looked at my body?"

"Not for some days now. Has something important changed since then? Have you grown a tail? It could be interesting to be with someone that had a tail."

"As a matter of fact, I did have a tail and I know how to use it, but now it's gone, so you'll just have to fantasise of how it could be." Somewhere, deep in the back of my mind, I was marvelling at the comfort and ease that I could joke about such things, and with this attractive woman, of all people.

"Another time, then. Come, let's give the horses some real exercise. They've been hanging around waiting for you for too long." And without another word or a backward glance, she kicked her horse into a gallop and we were off. Dorjee, as with most horses, was clearly aware of the tiny signals that Ainura had given off before giving her horse the explicit message to gallop, so, only a split second after her, we were off to a triple gallop.

Riding back with Ainura was wonderful, if frustrating at times. We would laugh and joke and spar, comfortable in all aspects of our contact together, but there were many areas of her life, and even some of mine, that she chose not to share with me, no matter how much or in what way I tried to coax her.

"But you must know something about this place. You seem to know so many things about so many subjects."

"Maybe I do and maybe I don't. What I do know is that when you get there, you'll surely find all the answers that you need to find out."

"But I'm not strong. I'm small and quite weak. How will I possibly be able to keep up with the other monks, who must surely be much bigger and stronger than me?"

"First, try and keep up with me." And off we'd go again, almost flying across the grassy mountain passes.

My journey with Ainura finished all too quickly. Up ahead I saw a walled edifice, atop a steep mountain path.

"Could you not come with me for just a while longer?"

"Not brave enough to go all that way alone?"

"We seem to have had so little time together."

"Don't get attached to people or to things, it makes losing them much more painful."

"Do I have to lose you?"

"You never had me, you idiot." And with that, she leaned over, gave me a quick kiss on the mouth, turned the horse, and was riding out of my life, maybe this time forever.

I directed my horse towards the upwards path, not knowing how I would be welcomed; surely the masters must have agreed to my entering their monastery, but how the other monks would react to me, that concerned me more than just a little.

I must have been quite lost in my reflections, as I hadn't noticed the others arrive. Dorjee had started to react, but not seeing anything in front and not expecting anything from behind, I just tightened my grip on the reins slightly and carried on.

"And what would you expect to be doing here?"

I jumped a little in surprise before turning to find several horsemen coming up from behind me. The speaker was mounted, I somehow noticed, on a great black horse with white socks.

"I am on my way to the monastery."

"If you have a message, you can give it to me and save yourself the rest of the climb." He seemed only a few years older than me, but where I was small, he was tall, where I was weak, he was strong, where I was nervous, he oozed confidence.

"No, I don't have a message. I have been sent here to learn how to fight."

"This is not a joke."

"If it is, it is not of my making."

"Our order is not for the weak. You would do well to think again before choosing to enter."

"I have not chosen to enter, I have been sent by my master to come here to learn how to fight. I know nothing more than that."

"Then there has been a mistake."

"My master does not make mistakes. Please lead me to the gate." I had not intended to be disrespectful, but he had begun to irritate me, and I would not allow any disrespect towards my master.

"We shall see. You will not be allowed to start any training unless you succeed in passing certain tests."

"Then if I manage to pass these tests, that means I am capable of being able to be trained."

"But if you fail the tests."

"Then I won't have to see you anymore. I have a win-win situation." Maybe it had been my last few days of riding with Ainura, or maybe something had changed in me after passing so much time with the monkeys, but I felt much more confident to respond to this arrogant monk than ever before.

"I will lead you to the gate, then we shall see just how long you manage to stay." And with that, he advanced his horse, at least a head taller than my own, in front of me and led us to the great gates, behind which I was to be tested; but exactly in what, I was, gratefully, for the moment, ignorant.

True to his word, the young monk led me to the great gates, then turned his horse and carried on in the same direction. I later found out that the stable entrance was a little further on along the monastery wall.

The gates were open, so I lightly dismounted and, leading Dorjee by the reins, I entered. In front of the gates was a great open space, beyond which, surrounded on three sides by buildings, was a paved square, three feet higher than the open space, accessible by a flight of stairs, running the full length of the square.

Although from my entrance point it was hard to see either the square or the stairs. My vision was blocked by a great number of monks, standing, it seemed, motionless, their V-shaped backs presented to me, as they were all, of course, facing the other way.

After some moments of just standing, watching, and wondering what to do, I realised that they were not at all motionless. They were all moving, very, very slowly. Their whole bodies—arms, legs, shoulders, trunks, and heads—were in motion, slow motion. I stood there watching, fascinated.

Time seemed to stop. Dorjee must have been taken, too, as he didn't move, either. What were these strange two legs, moving so slowly, silently, smoothly?

There must have been some sort of a signal, one that I neither saw nor heard, for all of a sudden, everybody stopped, just for an instant, then they quickly returned to a position with their feet slightly apart, knees slightly bent, their hands hanging loosely by their sides, elbows also slightly bent.

Another signal must have been given, for then they all burst into movement. It was exactly the same series of moves that they had been practicing in slow motion, but this time it was lightning fast. Again and again they repeated the series, even faster and smoother with each repetition.

And then it was finished. They returned to the neutral position, bowed to the unseen master, and started to leave in all directions. Bunching up in little groups of friends, punching, laughing, and chatting, as young men do. Soon I was left all alone wondering what to do next.

"New here?" He was a big man, although not likely to be much older than me. He was more than a head taller than I was, with everything else in proportion. Actually, he was more like a little giant than a big man. He was also unusual in that his hair was copper-coloured and his round face had a slightly reddish/pinkish tinge to it. He looked at me with a disdainful air and said, "I hear that you want to train here with the monks."

"That is why I'm here."

"They don't accept just anyone, you know."

"Did they accept you?"

"Not yet, but I'm both strong and fast. I'll have no problem passing any tests."

"And you think that I might?"

"You're small and weak-looking. I don't think they'll want your sort in this temple."

"Why have you not been tested yet? Do they only test every few days or weeks?"

"You were expected, it seems, so they've made me wait. That way, they can test us both together, I suppose."

"Then we shall be initiated together. My name's Jangbu." I made a respectful sign of greeting.

"I doubt that we shall be initiated together." There was a slight mocking in his repeating of my phrase. He hesitated for a moment, and then said, "I am Dharmapala." He looked at me in quite an arrogant way, repeating my sign of greeting, but lacking some of respectful grace of mine.

"Do you know where I can take my horse to look after its needs?"

"Come on, I'll show you."

And that was my first meeting with the imposing Dharmapala.

He showed me where I could brush down, feed, and stable Dorjee, and hung idly round while I cared for my steed. He then took me to the sanitary unit where I washed off some of the dirt from my travels, and then to a monk that assigned me a cell. "Not that he will need it for long," mumbled Dharmapala as he trailed after me, surely for want of anything better to do.

"Would it acceptable for me to rest here for a while?" I asked the monk who had accompanied me.

"You will be called shortly for testing, but until then your time is your own."

I thanked him, closing the door, happy to be on my own and away from the heavy energy of Dharmapala. The monk's room was not so unlike the one that I had lived in for some years in my monastery. A cupboard for clothes and personal belongings, a small cot, and a simple table and chair for study. I took my outer clothes off and sat on the bed. Some call it the lotus position, but whatever it might be called, it is one of the most basic meditation postures, and just folding my legs into themselves already started to help calm my nerves.

"If it is for me to be allowed to enter this order, then it is meant to be. If not, then it is not meant to be. My Master wishes for me to do this, so I will do my best to fulfil his desire. I can do no more than my best, and if my best is not good enough, then so be it."

By allowing the thought process to flow unhindered, so did the tension and the stress. I would do my best, I could do no more, there was nothing more to worry about.

Time passed in silent focused meditation, until the gentle knocking on my door brought me back into the room, but only long enough to take my boots before returning to the outside. It was the moment for the testing.

The great open space was again filled with monks facing the paved square, where four men, dressed as masters, were patiently waiting for me to arrive. I noticed that Dharmapala had already joined them. He seemed somewhat pleased that I was the one that everybody had to wait for.

I started to feel uncomfortable, even a little guilty, until I reminded myself that I had been waiting in my room to be called, and as soon as I was summoned, I came immediately. If for some reason I was in any way late, it could in no way be considered my fault.

"Welcome, Jangbu," one of the elders welcomed me.

"Master," I replied, placing my palms together in front of my heart and bowing slightly, "I am sorry, I have no *jáldar* with me to offer you. I was not informed in advance as to my coming here."

"Of that, we are of course well aware. There is no dishonour or disrespect for your lack of traditional manners. As you have said, you had no time to prepare your arriving here." He smiled fleetingly at me and turned round to the massed monks.

"We have two new young hopefuls who wish to join us on our journey towards enlightenment through the disciplines of the mind and body. They will, like you all before them, be asked to pass certain tests to confirm that they are apt to join our order and follow our trainings."

He then turned towards the two of us. "Are you both ready?" In response, we bowed slightly and waited for him to conclude. "Then we shall begin. The first test will be the 'mirror.'"

"I will lead Jangbu." It was the arrogant rider that had stopped me when I first arrived.

"As you desire, Zigsa. Zopa, you will lead Dharmapala." Another monk stepped forward and bowed, first to the masters and then to Dharmapala.

The master turned back to us. "In this test of speed, perception, and precision, you are to watch the movements of the person facing you and copy each and every movement. Do you understand?" We both nodded our heads that we understood and then turned to face our leaders.

I could see a slight smile playing on the lips of Zigsa, but his eyes were not friendly. He had not volunteered so as to help me to succeed, but to fail.

Before starting, I pressed my palms together, fingers pointing upwards to perform the Anjali mudra, thumbs pressing on my sternum. He was a little surprised and taken aback that I should "honour and celebrate" him. I then raised my hands to my Ajna centre, at the top of the bridge of the nose, this time for myself; to honour myself, for linking my left and right sides, to increase my focus, and to relax into a meditative state.

"Begin!"

Zigsa wasted no time. His right hand started to form small waving motions, which increased and increased in amplitude. Then to waving left and right, then he added his left hand to the dance.

Out of the corner of my eye, with the smallest grain of attention I had to spare, I noticed that Zopa was slowly moving just his right hand, horizontally across his body. Zigsa had chosen to make mirroring much more interesting.

I followed with my eyes and body, but my mind and breath were focused towards the inner. There were no more thoughts, not even the effort to try and project what he would think to do next. The conscious mind is much too slow; only the animal, survival, instinctual, reactive part could possibly read his subtle signals.

I am Dorjee, a horse, a prey. My survival is dependent on my ability to perceive what the predator, Zigsa, is going to do next. He is focused on me, he is thinking to change. His eyes de-focus, seeking something high, up to his right—he is remembering. His breathing changes rhythm; he has found what he is looking for. He glances, fleetingly, towards the ground. The muscles in his right thigh twitch slightly. His weight subtly shifts onto his left leg. We raise our right legs in unison. I see the shock and surprise register on his face and in his eyes.

He speeds up his movements and the changes. We are now at the level of both hands and arms and a leg raising or lowering, or twisting the body at once. He is about to try a new trick, maybe to spin right round, so that we end back to back, when...

"Enough! The first test has been passed satisfactorily. You may sit, drink, and refresh yourselves." We took the water offered. As it was nearing midday and the sky was blue and clear of clouds, the water and the rest were most appreciated.

"Are we rested?"

"Thank you, Master." Dharmapala was back on his feet even before he had finished speaking.

"Yes, Master, thank you." I too was now on my feet and ready to continue.

"Since you are two, you can pass the next test, one against the other." I could feel Dharmapala tense slightly. Here, he could prove his superiority over me and reinforce his chances to be chosen to enter this place.

"You two," he said, pointing to Zigsa and Zopa, "demonstrate 'push hands' for our two new friends."

They bowed to the Master, turned to each other and bowed again. They raised their right arms and advanced them towards the other. The two wrists came in contact. First, Zopa pushed his wrist, arm, and body towards Zigsa, then Zigsa twisted his wrist in some way. Zopa's wrist turned as well, and then it was the turn of Zigsa to push Zopa backwards. The movement started quite slowly and gently, but quickly it turned into a blur of movement, until without any clear way to see what happened, Zigsa had moved one more step forward, hooked his right leg behind that of Zopa, and Zopa was down on the floor.

"Good, good. Now you will take these two and show them how to perform this movement."

The two again bowed to the master, then turned to us and bowed again. I must admit that I was a little apprehensive to have Zigsa teaching me this move, considering that it could help me to be accepted, which did not seem to be his highest priority. However, he showed me well enough how to move the arm, the wrist, and the body to achieve the fluid movement that I had witnessed some moments before. Anyway, I reasoned to myself, he would not dare to teach me incorrectly, being directly under the eyes of the masters and all the students.

"Come, now show us how well you have learnt your lessons."

Dharmapala and I faced each other, bowed, and advanced. I could feel the tension in his arm and body from the very first contact. I had to fight to remain relaxed; again focusing on my breath, but also on my hips, legs, and feet. The moving contact between me and the ground was almost more important than the twisting, turning, pushing, absorbing of the wrists, arms, and upper body.

He stumbled; first from a backward step, then, some moves later, while advancing. His face began to become redder and redder; his breathing increased in its rhythm and he began to increase more and more the pressure on my wrist. I knew that I couldn't continue like this for long. The sun was high in the sky, I was getting hotter and hotter, more and more exhausted, and he was putting more and more force into each exchange.

I could take it no longer; I would give up, but how? I could not just stop like that, it would be too humiliating.

I had an idea. As I retreated, I stopped to change the direction. As usual, he stopped as well. However, instead of starting to advance on him, I took another step back. Our wrists, although connected by nothing more than the pressure of our arms, stayed in contact. Dharmapala had no choice but to take another step forward, bringing him totally off balance. I then advanced towards his right side, pressing his wrist towards his left, and stepped around his side.

I know that I shouldn't have done it, but I was angry with him, so I let myself act without care or respect. As he was still well off balance, weight almost totally on his left foot and his body twisted towards the left. It only took the slightest push to topple him down to the ground.

And so the second test was over.

"I am sorry, Master. I did not have the stamina to continue, but that is no excuse for what I did." I bowed low, waiting for the Master's reproach.

"Get up, both of you, the second test is over. You may rest while we prepare the third and final test."

Not quite understanding why he had not commented on the last exercise, we both got up and took some water. Sitting some way away from the other, we wondered as to our fates.

The monks had separated themselves into two groups, creating a passage between them from the paved square to the entrance gate. They then sat down, all but two lines of monks; these remained standing, forming two lines, one on each side of the passage.

Each monk had with him a heavy, highly polished, fighting long staff, which he held lightly in his hands.

"You will have to pass the length of that avenue without touching or being touched by any of the poles. Do you understand?" We nodded to show that we had understood. "Who wishes to try his luck first?"

"Master, please allow me to show how it can be done." I don't know if it was arrogance or fear that had made him speak so, but he had, and he was to be first.

"Watch the rhythm of the poles, now!" The monks, who clearly had been trained for this, began to wave their staves in the air, then bring them down vertically as if to smash the head of any unfortunate opponent in their path.

I stood next to him at the entrance of the tunnel of crashing poles. The Master inclined his head and Dharmapala rushed forward. He quickly found that running as fast as he could would not work, and after a few seconds he stopped to contemplate just how to proceed. He was of the impression to be safe, between two sets of poles. What he wasn't aware of was that the monk behind him was preparing to attack with a horizontal thrust.

In the space of a fraction of a second, I went from a feeling of satisfaction that this superior young man should find his comeup-pance to being taken by the flash of the polished wood, reflecting the sun off its non-existent axe blade.

"Nooo!" I screamed. I could not let it happen again, not another head to be served up like a pork roast for a village feast. I sprang forward with all my years of guilt and frustration to have not had the means to protect my innocent mother. Before the pole could land on the back of his head, I landed on his back, knocking him to the floor in a heavy mass of dust and dirt.

"What the...? What are you doing? Are you crazy or what?"

"I'm sorry, I'm so, so sorry. It just came over me. It was like with the axe, but I know that it wasn't an axe, only a long staff." I was babbling, I must have sounded crazy, I must have looked crazy; actually, what I did was crazy. I turned and ran to the Master and prostrated myself at his feet.

"Master, please, Master, please, please forgive me. I apologise for my crazy actions. I will collect my belongings and leave as quickly as possible." I waited some seconds for his response, but none came. "Master, please give me your permission to remove myself from your presence, that I might return to my own master."

"Not quite yet." I couldn't help myself; I leaned back on my heels and looked him in the face.

"Master?"

"You may return to your own Master when you have finished that which you are destined to do here. That is what has been agreed and that is what is going to happen."

"But I do not understand."

"If we were to understand everything, then where would be the motivation and the wonder of learning?"

"But I am to stay?"

"That much it is important that you understand." He turned towards Dharmapala and said, "Come here."

Dharmapala, brushing the dust off his clothes, shoulders slumped, head bowed, approached the old man.

"You have proven yourself very courageous this day. You have nothing to be ashamed of." His head straightened and his shoulders pulled themselves back. "I am happy to welcome you both to this order." We turned to go. "One more thing." He looked gently at Dharmapala. "Jangbu risked everything to protect you this afternoon. He did not compete with you for his place here. He saved you from a very nasty lesson that would have hurt both your body and your pride. Think on that while you pass your training together."

And that is how I entered the order and found my most loyal of protectors.

j Have a Body – Part Two

"You are starting to tire."

"But we haven't gotten that far yet."

"We have walked a long way this morning. There is no benefit in using all your forces now, and surely not making it to the end. Put me down now. Please do as I say. Now, relax a little. What you have done so far is no little task. Maybe you should just leave me here. There is a little cave here in the rock. I could stay safely for the night."

"No, Master, I still have energy, I can carry you further."

"As you think, but now, just rest a few moments and get your energy back. Yes, it is okay to rest your eyes. Let them close. Feel the weight of your body, feel the weight of your tiredness. As you relax into your breathing, breathe in energy, breathe out tiredness. The weight of the tiredness will slowly lift. Your body will start to feel lighter, stronger, more and more energised."

He allowed his disciple to slip into a deep, deep sleep. For well over an hour, he patiently watched over his charge before gently tapping him with a piece of stick.

"It isn't the night, you know, we still have a long way to go."

"Master, why did you allow me to sleep for so long?"

"I am investing in your energy. To allow you to use it all up in the first stage would mean that you would be exhausted in an hour or two. From that point of exhaustion, it would take you many hours of sleep or relaxation for your body to become functional again. By letting you sleep now, your body was able to recover most of its energy. And anyway, isn't it much more pleasant to sleep when it is hot in the afternoon, than walk in the heat and then sleep in the cold?"

"I don't understand all that you are sharing, but I do feel refreshed and I am keen to continue."

"Then bend down so that I can mount my trusty steed. Good. Now, where was I with my story? Oh, yes, I remember..."

Fighting Shadows – Part Two

The daily schedule in the temple was generally the same throughout the year: 5:00 a.m. – up and wash; 5:30 – morning meditation; 6:00 – breakfast; 6:30 – morning exercise; 7:30 – work in fields or other chores; 11:30 – lunch; 12:00 – free hour; 13:00 – fight training; 16:30 – evening meal; 17:00 – free hour (those of us with horses would use this hour to take them out for a run); 18:00 – chanting, dance, creative expression; 20:30 – evening meditation and teaching/stories; 22:00 – bed.

From time to time there would be a celebration at the monastery. They would drink millet *chang*, sing, and dance around a great bonfire built in the centre of the space in front of the paved square. I had acquired a bit of a taste for the whitish, thin beer drink with the refreshing sweet-sour taste.

And so the months passed, until one morning, we were called together.

"It now the moment to start to prepare for the annual competition. Not all are obliged to compete, but I expect the most advanced to lead the teams and the most recent members of our community to participate."

Of course, Dharmapala was amongst the first to enter into a team; however, I was just a little bit surprised to find out that I had also been inscribed.

"Come on, he said that you were expected to compete, so I put us both down together."

"But who is leading the team?"

"Don't worry, I wouldn't put us in Zigsa's team, would I?" "So, who?"

"Zopa."

"Okay, that's okay, Zopa's all right." I quite liked Zopa; he was a bit quiet and serious, but not at all rigid.

The competition was little more than a series of exercises or tests:

- Tests of strength and endurance, like long hikes and short runs carrying heavy backpacks
- Tests of balance; walking and jumping on and between thick bamboo poles
- Defensive moves; passing through the tunnel of poles, only this time the other monks would attempt, intentionally, to strike you; you would have your own staff to defend yourself with
- The floating steps

The floating steps is a very particular type of exercise. In a passageway between two buildings there is a rectangular pool the same width as the passage and about twelve feet in length. Leading up to the pool there are a series of gaps in the floor, making it almost impossible to run up to it, if one should wish to jump over the pool. At each of the four edges there is an eight-foot bamboo pole to mark the edge of the pathway. In the pool are a large number of blocks of wood, each one about a foot long, floating in horizontal and vertical lines, attached together by a series of chains.

A monk that has mastered lightness and speed is able to run across the wooden blocks without falling into the water. I have rarely seen anyone succeed at this. In the competition, points are given for the number of blocks that have been passed before the monk falls into the water. One is allowed to pass any way that one wishes to. One is even allowed to try and jump the gap completely. That I have never seen done. If one tries to jump but fails, he scores no points.

We started as eight teams, each member scoring points individually. The score for each team was simply the totals of all the members added together. There were three rounds to the competition, each becoming more difficult, and with each round half the teams were eliminated. By the third and final round, the teams left were ours, led by Zopa, and the favourite, led, not surprisingly, by Zigsa.

For this final round there was one little change in the rules: all the members of the team had to be attached by a cord.

How this was done was that the first and last of the team had a cord tied around their waists, and all the others wore a type of belt with a large loop on it, through which the long cord was threaded. The rope was quite long, about twenty feet in all. This gave us quite a lot of room to manoeuvre. The choice of who should be at the ends of the cord was open to the leader of the group, and could be changed before the beginning of any of the challenges.

I felt that we did quite well in all the tests, and so we should have. After all, we were one of the finalists. Unfortunately, Zigsa's group was a little better, so we arrived at the floating steps well behind. Their group had already passed, and although their results were not so wonderful, it would be almost impossible for our group to catch up to theirs.

"We cannot win, but we can at least lose honourably, so everyone, no matter what, do the best you can."

"Zopa?"

"Yes?"

"Since we have more or less already lost, I'd like to try something." It was an idea that had come to me in the moment. Desperation often can do that, if only we allow ourselves to stay open to unexpected solutions.

I explained my idea and we asked the master who was supervising this trial to change the end person. The other monks, who were watching us through the windows of the buildings, were a little surprised to see me taking over the end of the cord, but they would likely be much more surprised to see what I had in mind for the rest.

Having the cord so long was also to allow one monk at a time to cross the steps without being impeded by the others. Zopa ran across as best he could, and he didn't do that badly at all; he easily crossed three-quarters of the blocks before he hesitated and fell. A loud applause came from our supporters at the windows, then silence fell.

I kicked off my slippers, grabbed a pole in each hand and, using both my hands and my feet, I pulled myself up the parallel poles. The window monks watched me in silence, wondering exactly what I was up to. When at the top, I blocked my hands and feet between the two poles and waited for the other members of my team to hoist up the second monk of our group onto the shoulders of one of the others.

"Ready?" Zopa pulled his end of the cord taut, as I did mine. The monk wrapped his legs around the rope, held on tight to the loop, and let himself slide down from my position eight feet up in the air to Zopa at the other end. Zopa had some difficulty keeping the rope high enough for the monk to reach the other bank completely. He landed on a block some feet away from the end.

"No points," declared the judge.

We tried again, this time with two people holding the other end. There was no problem and he scored maximum points.

"Foul!" screamed Zigsa, appearing from somewhere in the crowd behind. "This is not allowed. Their team is cheating."

The master turned quietly towards Zigsa; with infinite slowness, he bowed and saluted him. "Good day, young Master Zigsa, I regret that I was not informed that you had taken over the surveying of this test."

"But Master, this is not how this test is supposed to be done."

"Ah, so you are now the expert on this thing?" He smiled softly at the angry monk facing him.

"So you are going to let them carry on like that and give them full points for cheating?"

"No, I am not going to give them full points for cheating, I am going to give full points if a monk succeeds in crossing the steps without placing a foot in the water. If a monk chooses to jump and manages to reach the other side, without placing a foot in the water, then he is awarded full points."

"But they are using the rope to slide down."

"There is no mention of any restriction of using a rope." The soft-voiced Master bowed again, slowly and politely to Zigsa, and turned back towards us. "You may continue."

And so we did. From there on, we took maximum points from each pass. Dharmapala had placed himself last, but being the biggest and strongest, he was the most suited to carry the others on his shoulders, so they could "take off" from as high as possible.

He knew that he could not manage to climb up to me, nor was I strong enough to pull him up. He also knew that running across the steps was almost impossible for him, so he just jumped straight into the water. All our team cheered him on as he waded from my side to the other side.

"No points," declared the Master. Dharmapala saluted him politely and carried on to the other side. When he got there and the crowd fell into silence, all heads turned to me. What was I planning to do?

My group backed away from the edge. I climbed to the very top of the poles. Standing with my feet on the tops, I crouched down, judging the distance to the other shore. I allowed my breathing to slow, searching deep, deep down into the body memory. I moved left and then right, smelt the air, felt the wind, its direction and its force. I could feel my body start to tense, to flex, to angle. My tail was high and it was ready. I threw myself with all my strength and all my force towards the poles on the opposite side, trusting that my eight feet of altitude would compensate for my lack of strength and the distance between them.

Fly, monkey, fly. I spread out my arms and legs, grabbing the air as a support and a cushion, watching myself and the poles as they approached nearer and nearer. No, no, I was not going to make it; it was just a little too far. I was going to land in the water. Then I felt an enormous tug and my body was wrenched forwards. The cord was being pulled, up and forwards. I looked towards them; it was Dharmapala, his huge frame in front, his face red with effort, pulling me through the air and onto the other side.

My foot landed on the very edge of the first paving stone. I felt that I was going to lose my balance and fall backwards into the water, but there was absolutely no chance of that. I was grabbed on all sides, hoisted into the air, and carried off to celebrate our well-earned victory.

I Have a Body – Part Three

"It is again time to rest."

"But we still have far to go."

"It is exactly because we still have far to go that you must rest now." The disciple stopped and lowered the Master to the ground.

"I am sorry I cannot make you tea, but by chance I have brought a small gourd of barley wine and we have some Zanba cakes to go with it."

"Barley wine and Zanba cakes, those will make a good break." So they sat down and shared the treat.

"Dhargey, name me the three bodies."

"The physical body, the emotional body, and the mental body."

"And where is the soul located?"

"In the mental body?"

"No."

"The emotional body?"

"No."

"Surely not in the physical body?"

"Surely not." As he was already tired and a little woozy from the barley wine, he couldn't understand why he couldn't find the right response. He might have gotten angry, but he was already too tired.

"I don't understand, Master."

"Think, Dhargey. When you die, what happens to the three bodies?"

"They die, they stop working."

"And the soul, does it die, too?"

"Of course not, it carries on its journey."

"So where is it located?" A sudden thought entered the young man's head, and he smiled.

"Not in any of the three bodies."

"Yes," the Master smiled back, "not in any of the three lower bodies. And if I was to ask you, what is Dhargey?"

"Don't you mean, 'Who is Dhargey'?"

"If I would have wanted to ask, 'Who is Dhargey,' do you not think that I would not have asked, 'What is Dhargey'?"

"What am I?" He stopped for a moment to think. "You asked me where my soul is located, so it has to be something to do with the...I know, I am my soul."

"Why?"

"Because all the other bodies die and that which carries on is my soul. So that means, I am my soul."

"And what of the other heavy bodies?"

"Well, I have a physical body."

"Good."

"But I am not my body."

"Very good. Now try repeating it like a mantra, 'I have a body, but I'm not my body.'"

"I have a body, but I'm not my body."

"Good. Now bend down and pick me up again, if you think that you still have the strength."

"Yes, I think that I can carry you a little further." So saying, he bent down and picked up the old man a third time.

"Now we shall create a tune for your mantra."

"How do I do that?"

"Just repeat the words and let the music of your soul infuse them with a melody. Go on, try it."

"I have a body, but I'm not my body."

"Again."

"I have a body, but I'm not my body."

"Play with the sounds as you pronounce the words." And so he did; singing and chanting, they continued further and further down the mountainside.

The disciple, half drugged with wine, tiredness, and chanting, seemed unaware of the time passing, until he almost fell due to a half-concealed rock that he hadn't noticed in the now-dwindling light.

"Oof! Sorry." The near-accident had shocked him out of his stupor. "Wow, I'm nearly falling down. We need to stop."

"No, we have little distance left to go. If you stop now, you will not be able to find the energy to continue and we will have to pass the night here, with neither food nor shelter."

"But Master, I cannot go on. I am much too tired."

"Not at all. Again, your weak mind is telling you that you cannot do more, but your spirit is much stronger than that."

"But it is my body that is tired. It is nothing to do with my spirit."

"Idiot! It is your spirit, acting through your emotions, that gives you the force to continue. Your body is much, much stronger than you can imagine. What is blocking you now is not that your body is too tired, but that your mind thinks you are too tired because your emotions have communicated that. Why have your emotions communicated that? Because you are not correctly in contact with your spirit body."

"I'm not understanding you. I'm too tired to think."

"One good thing at least. Trust me, your physical body can go on. Come, sing with me: 'I have a body, but I'm not my body. I have a mind, but I'm not my mind. I have emotions, but I'm not my emotions.'"

"I don't understand."

"You don't have to understand. All you have to do is walk and to sing. Now sing!" There is a state of tiredness which we can arrive to that is similar to entering into a light hypnotic trance. This was the state in which the disciple now found himself. The command of the Master acted like a hypnotic injunction; the young monk immediately started walking, chanting the three phrases, a short, repetitive litany.

From time to time, if the chanting started to slow down or become slightly inaudible, the Master would join in and re-energise his faithful steed. By this technique, he succeeded in keeping the disciple focused on the sounds and the words, which in turn kept the pace of the walking steady and constant.

Time passed in a dreamlike state, but the progress was real enough, and before very long they found themselves arriving at the little cabin that they called home.

Without one more word, they both crawled their way inside to finally lie down and rest.

The disciple woke up to hear the Master singing loudly outside the house. He forced himself to his feet—which were, not so surprisingly, quite sore, as was his back—and hobbled out into the mid-morning sunshine.

"Oh, I see that you are finally up."

"But you are walking!" And indeed he was, walking straight and strong.

"There you go. You see what a good night's sleep can do for a sprained ankle." He smiled broadly at his apprentice. "I've even succeeded at making us both some tea."

Dhargey wasn't at all sure that he believed the Master, but what would be the point of lying to him and making him carry the old man all the way back here?

"Come sit, today you can rest and I'll continue with my own story."

Fighting Shadows – Part Three

My time in the order passed reasonably well, except for one thing: my control over my violence and anger. Most of the time I would fight in a quiet, disciplined, controlled way; the Masters, to begin with, were very pleased, as most of the other novices would often be overtaken by anger or violence and show great difficulty containing these forces. However, after the initial period of training, accessing these energies in a focused, directed manner is most important to move more energy, to access another level of speed and of force. In that, I was utterly incapable, but, if I was pushed and prodded enough, as some of the masters found to their stupefaction, I would explode like a fire bomb, and for quite some minutes, I was totally and utterly out of control.

There was no criticism of me from the Masters; they had all been informed of my history and of why I was training with them.

315

After they had gotten over the shock and had realised that there was nothing they could do, they just concentrated on teaching me their techniques and ceased to worry of how I would manage to use them if ever I was in a real situation of danger.

One evening I was called to go and visit one of the Masters in his receiving room.

"Come, Jangbu, come sit with me." I did as requested and sat down facing the venerable old man. "You have proven yourself to be a young man of courage, creativity, and a good comrade to your friends." I felt that he was enjoying himself with his word-play. Words were more than likely most of what he had left that he could really control.

"But you still present that knotty problem of your contact with your own anger." I nodded my head in agreement. "What do you remember from before you were found, before your parents were murdered?"

"Nothing. Everything before was washed out of my head. It was only the work of the Masters that has made it possible to put clear images of the death of my parents and the destruction of the village back into my mind."

"You know there must have been good memories of what happened before."

"I have no more memories, good or bad, of what happened before." I spoke in a matter-of-fact way. It was rare that I had emotions that came with my words, and they were, for the most part, negative feelings.

"Yes, sadly, that is way it often happens. When we block ourselves from sad experiences from the past, the good ones become blocked, too. Here, take a drink of this."

He offered me a bowl of golden liquid. I took it from him, thanked him, and put it to my lips to drink. It was like nothing I have ever tasted before; it was very bitter and very sweet at the same time, it almost burned my throat as I drank it down. It was so strong that I started coughing so much that I almost spilt the rest of the liquid in the bowl.

"Drink. It is good to drink it quite quickly. It will help you to relax." I trusted that the drink was strongly alcoholic, but not only that, I also trusted that this old man was not troubling himself for nothing so late in the evening. So I did as I was bid, opened my mouth, and emptied the bowl.

"Come here, look up." I lay down and looked up as he directed. Part of the ceiling was made out of large sheets of glass. The room being brighter than the outside, all I could see was the reflection of myself, lying there on the floor.

"What do you see?"

"I see myself, here, now, here on your floor." He started walking round the room extinguishing the candles, one after the other. "I am starting to see the night sky. The stars are beginning to become visible."

"Did you know that it takes many, many years for the light of the stars to reach us? What we see is only a past image of what they were, many, many moons ago. As you look at these past images, think that some of what you see now is how these were when you were just a child." He continued to put out the lights. The image of myself, here and now, become paler and more transparent, while the sky and stars became clearer and more and more real. I could feel myself connecting to them, to

317

these images of the past, to these pictures of what had been, to the visions of when.

"Allow yourself to relax. You must be quite tired; it is late in the day. Your body and mind must need to relax. Relax your mind, relax your body, relax your tensions. Go, go to the stars, go to the heavens, become one with the stories and pictures of the past." He put out the last of the candles. My reflection disappeared totally, I no longer existed, there were only the stars in the night sky.

"As you go up, into the skies, into the star lanes, into the past, notice how you can feel yourself falling backwards, back, back, back to yesterday, to the day before, and before, and before, and before. Spinning faster and faster, further and further, back to back to back."

I could notice my mind following his words. My body felt this slipping back. My thoughts were jumbled and confused; they wanted to argue, to criticise, to block his words, but they couldn't, lulled into pacification by his seductive tone, the rhythm of the words, the timbre of his voice. Yes, yes, yes, I was drifting—no, floating—no, I was flying backwards, yet all the time I was spinning up, up, up, up to very centre of the universe.

Time had become a moving, twisting, unsubstantial, slippery, curving, enveloping womb. She drew me in—lost, confused, scared but determined. I had decided, deep, deep, deep within the most hidden parts of myself, that I wanted to return—return to my life, return to my memories, return to myself.

It took the longest time, or so it seemed; I was here, there, floating out, above myself, in the skies, somewhere, some when.

And then it happened, like a simple door opening, and I was there, back there, back here, just back, back home, back to everything that I was, that I had, that I loved.

I could smell and taste and feel and hear and see and know that moment of my past. But it was the songs; my mother singing to me to go to sleep, my father singing as he worked in the fields, and the village singing for marriages, birthdays, deaths, and feasts. So many songs; songs for every season, songs for every occasion, songs for my mother, songs for my father, songs for me.

And so I started singing, and I sang, and I sang, and I sang, but the stars were fading out and I was returning to my mind. What had happened? Where had I been? What had he given me to drink? Many, many questions invaded my head, blocking out more and more of the past that I had only just connected to.

The sun was coming up. "Master," I said, turning to the old man as I got up, "it is late. It is already morning and I have tasks to perform."

"Boy, before it is too late in your life, the most important task to perform is to connect to yourself."

"But I cannot just take a holiday like that."

"What a good idea, let's us have a holiday." I had no idea what he was talking about. He called out to his helper, who must have been sleeping somewhere not too far away because he appeared sleepy and dishevelled quite soon after.

"Go and announce that today has been declared a holiday and all non-essential tasks are to be dropped. We will need a bonfire for tonight and instruments all day. Off you go, go tell the Masters. They will organise for the rest of the order to be informed. Go!"

319

The helper must really have still been half asleep because the Master had to tell him all of three times before he was sure that he had heard right and went off to deliver his message.

"Master, if today is to be a holiday and tonight we will have a fire, will you permit me to retire to my cell and sleep for a few hours? I am in great need of some sleep."

"Sleep, you go to sleep? Why, of course not, what a ridiculous question to ask. This day of holiday is for you."

"For me? Why for me?"

"To give you time and support to sing and to remember. You will sing, and everyone will sing and play and dance with you. That way, your memories will become anchored in the here and now. That will hold the door to your past open, and the blocked feelings and emotions can begin to flow as they should. Go wash, change your clothes, eat, and then meet me in the square."

By the time I had done all things that he had asked me to do, I found the square and the space in front full of people and activity. Some monks had already started to bring in wood to start to build the bonfire, others were bringing out tables and benches, and a number of others had musical instruments of different sorts. All were laughing and chatting, happy but surprised to find themselves relieved of all non-essential tasks without any warning at all.

"Come, I need some singers and musicians." Some monks came up to the square, some with instruments, some without. "Jangbu has remembered bits from some of the songs from his childhood. You and other singers and players of instruments are to accompany him throughout the day. He is not to sleep. It is your responsibility to keep him awake. Make him dance, make him sing, make him fight if you have to, just do not let him fall asleep." And with that, he turned and left me in the musical hands of my fighting comrades. More than likely, he himself was off to his warm, comfortable bed to get some well-earned sleep.

As was my habit, if a Master instructed me to do something, then I would do all that I could to fulfil his request. So, for the next twelve hours, I sang and I danced to the music and songs of my childhood. The monks would change "guard" every hour or so, but each one played his part to the full and they kept awake, in spite of the momentary lapses when I almost fell down into sleep.

The fire was lit and we danced round it, singing and drinking. The Masters had given the instruction that it was to be a night when alcohol would be permitted, and the casks of millet beer were rolled out and the night became a full celebration.

I know that I was getting drunk; drunk with tiredness, the beer, and with the crazy energy of my brother monks.

Suddenly, through the great gates rode a number of horsemen. They were clothed in garments of red and black!

The leader, riding a huge black horse with white socks, called out in a voice of menace and authority, "Where is he? Where is the boy coward that hid from me? Where is he that watched his mother and father die by my hand but crawled away like a worm, scared of the smallest of birds? I have been looking for you, boy. Are you here? Will you show yourself? Or are you to live a coward the rest of your life?"

"Here I am. I am Jangbu. I am not afraid of you anymore. Get off your big horse and fight me man-to-man." I was so very angry.

Here I was, in the middle of this wonderful celebration, and now he comes, looking for me, to harangue and insult me in the presence of my friends and brother monks. I walked over to find a long staff, but while my back was turned, he had jumped off his horse, taken out his own stick, and hit me across the back with it.

I went down quite heavily; hands came down to help me up, another placed the wooden weapon in my hand. I could hear him approaching again; this time I was ready. He was trying to crack my skull with a descending blow to the head. I raised the staff over and then behind my head, blocking the blow, then I spun round. His stick still pressed against mine, forcing his arms to remain up in the air, his body was totally defenceless. I twisted my stick and swung the left side downwards and into his unprotected body. He tried to drop the right side of his staff to block or deflect the blow, but he had no chance. The wood crashed into his rib cage and he went heavily down. *You are getting slow, old man.* He dug his pole into the ground to lever himself up. I kicked it away from under him and he fell once again into the dirt.

"You are old and you are useless. I will not waste any more time with you." I was feeling so very tired, I was finding it hard enough just to keep on my feet. I had no more energy to fight him, no matter what he had done in the past. He was just a broken old man, no match for me now. "Go home and tend to your women, you have nothing more to do with the world of men."

I turned from him. Using the stick as a support to help me climb the steps up to the square, I slowly and painfully made my way back to my room, threw the stick and my clothes onto the ground, and fell heavily onto my bed. I don't remember anything more, only waking up the next morning feeling disoriented and nauseous, but also victorious. I had faced and beaten my life's nemesis, the leader of the men in red and black.

Since that night, two things happened:

Firstly, I had much more and easier contact with that energy of anger and violence that I had been frightened to contact. In our fighting classes, I could feel that power and force, inflaming my belly and then mounting up through the whole of my body and finally filling my arms and legs with fire and will. Unfortunately, it was still very difficult to control. Once the demon was out of the bag, it was almost impossible to put him back in. I would feel real hatred for my opponent, I would want to hurt and damage him. I would, of course, hold myself back, but that made me short-tempered and irritable, a state that often could last many hours after the lesson, until the molten lava in my brain and veins would cool, and the red fire in my heart quieten, and the psychological scars recover themselves. Only then would I return to my normal, balanced state. The Masters were again at a loss of what to do. They had succeeded in giving me access to the wild beast within, but nobody, it seemed, knew how to tame it.

The second event that followed that night was that Zigsa had been sent away to do something for one of the Masters, but nobody knew exactly what. Even some days later when he returned, and not in total health, either, his whereabouts for those days remained a mystery.

"Jangbu, we have been discussing your situation between us for many days now." I was again in the great chamber with the old monk. "It seems that we have well succeeded to have helped you connect to your hidden anger and hatred for the murderer of your parents. Unfortunately, it seems that that energy has nowhere to go and so cannot be released into the universe."

"So what am I to do?"

"You must confront the man that killed your family."

"But I..." It suddenly all became clear to me. "That man, it wasn't...?" Of course not, it couldn't have been. "Zigsa?"

The old sage smiled slightly and inclined his head, just the merest fraction of an inch. "It is time to confront your destiny."

"When will I leave?"

"When you will be ready."

"When will I be ready?"

"When you know how to use this." He turned to a table and took a large object, wrapped in a beautiful prayer shawl, which he then slowly and carefully unwrapped. "Do you know what this is, Jangbu?"

"It is a curved Khadga Fire Sword, Master. It is made of brass, copper, and iron."

"And what is its purpose?"

"It is a symbol of enlightenment and is used to destroy ignorance."

"The sword of wisdom destroys the darkness of ignorance by the fiery rays emanating from the end of the sword."

"The red destroys the black."

"What is that?"

"Nothing, Master, I was just thinking out loud."

"You will learn to wield the sword of wisdom, and when you can also master your own inner wisdom, then it will be time for you to leave us and complete your own destiny."

The Khadga, being a ceremonial object topped with a copper end in the form of flickering flames, is only useful for cutting or for slashing. To be able to use her appropriately, one must learn how to cut exactly where and exactly how deep one needs to.

My first lessons were the usual ones for those learning to fight with a sword. We were given blunt wooden replicas and allowed to practice on each other, without fear of doing too much harm.

Soon after starting this training, I was also given a real sharpened sword to work with. My task was simple; I had to learn to plant the sword a long ways along the line of the blade, into a thin wooden plank, on a drawn line—horizontal, vertical, or angled—at a certain depth.

Managing to enter the wood along the higher vertical lines was not so difficult. Certain angled lines were also reasonably easy, but most of the horizontal ones were very difficult, as were the lower verticals and many of the oblique angles. More than that; to judge just how much force to use to get the blade to protrude—one, two, three, or four finger-widths through the other side—was almost an impossible task.

"I'm never going to manage to do this."

"I'm sure that you will, you seem to be able to manage most things." Dharmapala had become one of my most fervent supporters and we made quite a good team; he with his power of body and of will, and I with my softer, more reflective approach. One of the Masters had nicknamed us Yin and Yang, it suited us well enough.

And so I continued, day after day, hacking at the boards; across, down, to one side, to the other side, deeper cuts, shallow cuts, almost no cuts at all. Soon I lost interest in counting how many days I had stood facing, yet again, another board crisscrossed with intricate patterns of lines of different thicknesses and directions. It just became another form of meditation technique. I had long ceased to argue with the Master about whether the chunk of protruding blade was two fingers or three fingers deep. I just considered this to be another of my life phases—not too bad really, even if a bit boring.

I still had my one-hour ride each day, and I had become accepted by all the monks—well, maybe not all of them. Zigsa still kept himself a little aloof, but then again, most of the other, more advanced students didn't mix with us, either, so maybe it was just my own prejudice.

Of course, the moment that one totally accepts an unacceptable situation, that is moment when it comes to an end, or so it seems to me. I was quietly practicing on a new board when the old monk descended the steps of the square and made his way over to me.

"I hear that you have been advancing in your skill."

"I am working at the task that you have set me, Master."

"Come, it is time to test your efforts." He turned and walked back towards the square. I started to have the feeling that this test was not going to be a private affair. From all directions, monks started to spill out onto the practice yard. I climbed the few steps onto the paved area. Waiting for me was Dharmapala. He was holding a very large bow by the wooden arc; the string was facing me.

"Come here." The Master gestured to me. "Look at the bow carefully, what do you see?"

"It is a very big bow." Dharmapala was doing his best to attract my attention to something, looking hard at me from his side, nodding his reddening face towards me, but I could not catch what he was trying to communicate.

"Look closely at the string." At first glance there was nothing special about the string, but that was because I was facing it directly. By moving closer to it and moving my head to one side, I was then able to see that there were in fact two strings, one tied just behind the other.

"What am I to do, Master?"

"It is quite simple: you are to cut the first string with one blow of the Sword of Wisdom."

"And the second string?" I had to ask, even though I already knew the answer.

"The second string is to remain intact." The two strings were not even a finger-width apart.

"How am I to succeed at this?"

"Use the wisdom that you have and you will succeed. Here, take your blade. Be careful, she is very, very sharp, sharper than the tongue of a wife married for thirty years." He smiled at his own joke as he handed me the package containing the sacred sword.

I slowly unwrapped it, all the time thinking of how I could manage to cut the first string and yet avoid damaging the second, not even a finger-width away.

I held the Sword of Wisdom in my hand. The two strings were less than a finger-width apart, but only if measured from a point perpendicular to the string. The more the angle became acute, the further the distance between them.

"Dharmapala, turn the bow so that the strings are horizontal, parallel to the ground." The crowd stirred and then fell into an expectant silence.

I picked up the sword in both hands, swung it first to the left, then to the right. Finally, I slid the blade across the string almost as if playing a musical instrument. The blade bit more and more into the string as it slid across its length, until, just after the halfway point, it was weakened enough to snap from the torque of the bow itself. Not daring to try and stop the swing, I angled the blade away from the second cord and allowed it to continue until it passed the left end of the bow and I could end the movement, safely away from the first string's fragile twin.

The short seconds of the cut had seemed much, much longer, and the crowd had fallen into some kind hypnotic trance, until Dharmapala hoisted the bow into the air and whooped, "He's done it! Jangbu has succeeded in cutting the one string. He has beaten the challenge."

I was still a little under the shock of the experience, but the response of the monks, if anything, shook me even more. In total and complete silence, each monk walked up to the square's steps, saluted me, then turned and left.

It seemed to take forever; it was the strangest dream that I had ever experienced. The silence was almost total. Except for the sounds of moving towards the steps and then away again, there was nothing at all.

Even the advanced students took their turns, Zigsa included. And then, even for this dream, I cried like crazy, for after the advanced students came the Masters. One after another they stood before me, bowed before me, and revered me.

"Now, it is time for you to leave." I turned towards the oldest of the Masters; he bowed towards me and left.

"Do I put the bow down before I bow or do I bow holding it?" "Dharmapala, don't be such an idiot. You don't have to bow to me."

"But everyone else did."

"Yes, well, maybe they did, but you don't have to, okay?" "Well, if it's okay with you, I'll just go and put this bow away." "Please. Maybe then we can go and find something to eat. All this bowing has made me ravenous."

"Just give me a few moments and I'll be back."

Five minutes later we were in the kitchens begging for food. We didn't have to beg very hard.

It was not easy to leave the monastery. I had made good friends in the time that I had passed there. Most difficult was Dharmapala. We had become almost inseparable; eating together, fighting together, laughing, and, when the occasion arose, drinking together.

Even so, there was now a fire burning in my heart and belly to end this story, once and for all. So, only two days after the test with the sword and the bow, I was ready to ride, ready to seek out the man who had killed my parents and had scarred my life.

Dorjee was saddled with all my usual belongings, and the fire sword strapped around my back. Almost everyone had stopped what they were doing to come and wish me well. I didn't want to hang around too long; I wasn't so good at goodbyes.

I kicked Dorjee and we were off. It seemed a lifetime away, the moment I had first entered through these great gates, but that time I was led and surrounded by Zigsa and his riders...

329

"Going somewhere?" So that's why he wasn't there to see me off. He was waiting at the bottom of the climb, waiting to bid "good riddance to bad rubbish." At last he would be rid of me. "Don't worry, you won't have to cope with me anymore." "And what makes you think that?"

"Hadn't you heard? I'm leaving today."

"Of course we have." I looked at him blankly. "And knowing you, you're likely to get yourself into an awful lot of trouble if there's no one to keep an eye on you."

"What do you mean?"

"Someone will need to accompany you, to make sure that you don't get into too much mischief."

"Did one of the Masters send you?"

"They wouldn't ask such a thing."

"Then you volunteered to come with me?"

"Not just me"—he stopped and looked round at his fellow riders—"we're all coming."

"But why? Why would you want to do such a thing?"

"As the old monks would say, 'If you don't already know, there's no point in me telling you.' My sources inform me that we are to travel to the east." And with that, he turned his horse and we were off.

Confused, my head full of unanswered questions, I could not help but smile to myself as I pulled my horse round to follow my comrades towards the closing chapter of my childhood trauma.

A good Day to Die

The summer was already coming to an end. It seemed such a short but also incredibly long time since the frail teenager had started to follow the Master up the mountain.

Soon, he estimated, it would be time to return down the mountain. The barley crop would be ready, and after the harvest would be a time of feasting. Little did he realise that that sickly, fragile boy would never return again.

It was still dark when the Master woke him.

"What is wrong, Master?"

"Why should anything be wrong?"

"Because it is still dark, it is still night."

"No, it is not still night; it is just quite early in the day."

"But why have you woken me now?"

"For the one and simple reason, that if you don't hurry and get up, there will be no time for breakfast before we leave."

Trying to understand why this answer could not be satisfactory, yet still seem totally reasonable and logical, Dhargey forced himself to get up and prepare himself for the day.

Breakfast was quickly made, and they were soon closely huddled around the cooking fire, drinking tea and eating *tsampa*. He tried several times to ask the Master why they needed to be up so early, but the old man refused to enlighten him. Soon enough the meal was over and the utensils tidied away.

"Come, we have much to do today, there is no time to lose."

"But where are we going? How long is it? Do I need to pack food?" The disciple had already suffered the Master's choice not to bring along food or drinks.

"Your pack is already prepared. Some of us are capable of getting up early when necessary." The barb seemed particularly unfair, as he had not been warned at all of this early start, and he had, just the same, forced himself out of bed almost immediately after he had been awakened.

They walked all morning in silence; it seemed that the Master was choosing to keep the purpose of this day's endeavours as a secret to himself. They stopped for a moment by a thin silver thread, which was all that remained of a once-flowing mountain stream.

"Even the waters die in due course."

"It's just drying up because it's the end of the summer and the rains haven't passed this way this year."

"Death is just a term, a manner of speaking."

"But is it correct to say that a river is dying, just because it hasn't rained for a while?" He now dared to question the Master so, all the more due to his frustration of being ignored all morning.

"When all energy has left, then there can be no life, so we speak of death."

"But when it rains again, then the river will live again."

"Exactly. The energy that we know as water is not lost or destroyed; it has just left the stream. Eventually, it will continue in its cycle and return to the stream, and then we would say that the stream lives again."

"And is it the same for all living things?"

"It is the same for all creation, only for conscious beings there is a unique identity."

"But our bodies die. They do not get resurrected."

"That is how we progress. Knowing how to die correctly is very important."

"What do you mean, 'knowing how to die correctly'?"

"I will explain shortly, but first you must fill this pouch with the water from this source."

"Can I also drink some?"

"Yes, but not from the skin." The disciple drank some of the fresh water and then filled up the leather water kettle.

"Why did we have to leave so early this morning?"

"Because there is much to do and to experience before the day is reborn."

"Master, I am not understanding you."

"My child, when you can understand everything that I am saying, then you will have passed by all that I might teach you, and you will be sharing this teaching with your own disciples."

He was struck, both by the tone of kindness in the address, "my child," and by the idea that one day, already in the foreseeable future, he too would be a Master and have has very own disciples. His reaction to all this was an unusual but comfortable silence.

The Master seemed also happy to pass another moment in silence. And so, quite quickly, the leather water skin was filled, both enjoyed a long, refreshing drink from the dwindling stream, and again they were off.

They stopped for lunch not long after that, but did not dawdle over the cold food that the Master had prepared at who knows exactly what point the night before.

"Here would be a good spot."

"For what, Master?"

"To collect some of the earth and a plant." He pointed to a rock, where a honeysuckle had managed to lodge and grow in a handful of earth, which had accumulated in a small hollow in the rock.

"What do I do with it?"

"Here," he said, passing him a square of hide and a long leather cord, "dig it out and put it in here."

"Are we to take it home with us?"

"All will be explained shortly." What was clear enough for the moment was that the disciple was not going to find any answers in the next minutes. As there was nothing else to say or to do, he did as instructed and started to dig out the plant.

"Don't forget, we need the soil as well."

"But we don't need so much soil. When we replant it, we can use the soil that's there."

"When I wish for you to think, I will inform you. When I wish for you to follow my instructions, then you do as I ask, and trust that I haven't yet lost all my mind."

Muttering under his breath that when old people start to lose their minds, they are rarely the first to notice, he, just the same, did as directed, and placed the plant and all the soil in the makeshift bag.

"Come, we now need to find some wood."

At least we will soon be stopping for a hot cup of Po Cha," thought Dhargey, smiling to himself. At this height, only pine trees could survive, but their fallen branches made fine firewood, easy burning and pleasantly scented.

Remembering the criticism surrounding the plant and soil, Dhargey thought to ask, "How much wood should I collect, Master?"

"Quite a lot. Pile it here, near this ledge." The Master had found a spot, several metres long and wide, that was unusually flat but opened onto a sheer drop of several hundred metres towards the base of the mountain.

"We shall need to be careful not to walk too close to the edge," he remarked, carrying a pile of branches towards the sage.

"Unless it is time to die," replied the teacher coolly.

"Well, it's not time to die yet. Is this okay for the wood?" "Yes, you may place the wood there, and yes, it is not yet the time to die."

Why did he keep talking about death? Yes, he was quite old; yes, it was important to prepare oneself for death, but why keep talking about it today?

"Why are you talking so much about death today, Master?" Yes, he had dared to ask the question.

"Because, Dhargey, today is a fine day to die."

"But you are not going to die today, Master?" He was suddenly concerned. Could this rather odd old man be thinking to just walk off this ledge to his death?

"Do not worry; everything is not always the way it seems."

"So you are not going to die today?"

"I certainly hope not. I have already made some appointments for after I get back." Feeling relieved, yet still vaguely troubled, the disciple continued to pile the logs on top of each other, waiting for the Master to declare himself satisfied. Then he could make them a nice strong cup of hot tea, and hopefully, from somewhere in his many secret pockets, just maybe, the Master might produce, almost magically, a few Zanba cakes, to add to the pleasures of the evening.

"Shall I start preparing the fire now, Master?" He could almost taste the tea and cakes in his greedy mouth.

"Whatever for? It is still daytime; the fire is for much later."

"Much later?" What could the Master be thinking? It was already quite late, even if it didn't go dark until after eight, and he had been up well before the sun, which meant sometime before seven.

"Come, you have one more pouch to fill." He straightened himself up and walked over to the old man. "Here," the Master said, and handed him another pouch.

"What am I to do with it, Master?"

"You are to fill it with air."

"And how do I do that?" Maybe it was the tiredness, or that his mind was still taken by the disappointment of not having tea, but for the moment, he could not succeed in imagining just how to fill the sack with air.

"Easy." The Master did not seem at all put out by this lack of thinking. "First of all, you fill up a sack that you know how to fill, then you transfer the air from that sack into this one."

"But there is only one sack."

"The other sack we usually refer to as *lungs*. You do have a pair of lungs, do you not?"

"Yes, yes, of course I do."

"Then breathe in deeply, even a little deeper than that. Good. Now you blow the air out from the lungs, here, here, into the sack."

Hence, in several moments, the disciple had blown up the pouch with air. The Master produced a cap and the air was finally trapped inside the inflated skin.

The disciple was beginning to feel more and more abused by the situation. Not only was he not about to enjoy the tea and cakes that he had fantasised to be enjoying just about now, but he was having to carry all the equipment and food, plus the bags of water, earth, and air.

"Master, can I put the bags down now?" he asked in a slightly irritated tone of voice.

"What? Yes, no. You can release yourself of that," he replied, pointing to the bag of food and equipment, "but the other three you must carry until your death." He said it in such a matter-of-fact fashion that for several seconds, while he was extricating himself from the provisions' bag, he didn't integrate the full sense of the Master's words.

"Wait a minute, what was it that you said?"

"I said that you might put that bag down on the ground, which you have done. Good."

"But what about my having to carry these bags until I die?"

"I did not say that."

"That's a relief."

"What I said was, the other three you must carry until your death."

"What is the difference?" Again, feelings of increasing irritation were starting to manifest themselves.

"Today is a good day to die. It is important, as you know, that we befriend death. That way, we can understand and link to it without fear or anguish. To do this we need to experience death. Today, tonight, you will experience death, but maybe you will not die. That we will see."

"Master, again I do not understand what you are telling me, but I really do not like the sound of it."

"It is an initiation; it is an important step that you pass through. It is the last lesson that I will teach you this summer."

"If I die, it'll be the last lesson you teach me ever," he muttered under his breath, turning towards the pile of firewood. "Before I die, can I least get a little warm and have something to eat and to drink?"

"We will have no need for food or drink for the moment, but we will have need of a fire. But that can also wait a little while."

"But it is almost night."

"Yes. We should both venture into the darkness of the night, and a fire might light our way for a moment, but not just yet. Find yourself a comfortable place to sit, but do not sit down yet. Take the bag with the earth in it, gently take out the plant and place it in front of you, link yourself with it. Now, very slowly and consciously, allow the soil to empty out of it. No, no, slowly, slowly. Yes. Be one with the sack; as the soil flows out, so part of you is also emptying out. Allow yourself to feel the energy also flowing out of your body; it becomes thinner and thinner. Yes, now is the moment to allow your body to contact the earth. Your limbs become loose and smaller, your body is sinking into the earth, it becomes weak and powerless. Your sight is becoming unclear, things appear darker; maybe you will see images. Now your body feels its strength flowing out. That is okay, it is just the first phase of the death experience. Stay with your experiences. I will light a fire."

Some short time later, the fire was lit, burning brightly and fiercely. Dhargey had been attracted by the warmth and light and was now sitting up.

"Master?"

"No, don't talk now. Your time for talking can be after. Now is a time for silence. Talking comes from the mind, experience is of the body. Now is the time of the body. Sit for a moment near the fire and contemplate your experience of just now. I will tell you when it is time to continue."

"But when do we eat?"

"For these experiences, food and drink are not necessary. In fact, eating and drinking are exactly what one shouldn't be doing."

"But why am I doing this?"

"Death is the greatest of all human experiences. It happens to all of us, and knowing how to meet it and accept it shows us how short our lives are, so we will make it more meaningful. Also, dying with serenity and without fear is the only way to ensure a good rebirth."

"And you will teach me this thing?"

"If you will stop troubling me with pointless questions, then we might well find the time to continue these exercises."

"What need I do, Master?"

"Take the water kettle, in the same way that you allowed the earth to flow out of its sack. Now tip the neck of the kettle until the water starts to pour out. Again, not too fast. This time you are to concentrate on the liquids of your body. Now they too will begin to dissolve or evaporate; your saliva, sweat, urine, blood, and fluids will become greatly reduced. Yes, lie down. Good. Your mind will no longer be able to contact your emotions. Notice this difference, and for the time being you will also find that your hearing, both of outside sounds and of your own inner dialogues, will become less clear."

The disciple felt as if something was sucking out all the moisture from his body. It might have been due to the suggestion of the Master, but he was experiencing it just the same. There was something that seemed to link the liquid with emotions. It was as if the dissolving of the water element also affected the ability to feel. His awareness was there, present but cool and distant. He was aware that in some ways his body was truly dying, but it was no more than an objective fact. He had no emotional reaction; there was no reaction to have.

"Come, it is time." Maybe he had fallen asleep; time seemed to have less and less meaning for him.

"Master?"

"It is time to watch the fire."

"But it is starting to die. Should I put some more branches on it?"

"No, it is the time for the fire to die. It is time for the fire element to dissolve."

"What do I do, Master?"

"Come sit here, watch the fire, watch it die, watch for the sparks within the smoke. The faces, names, and memories of your family and your friends will fade with the flames and disappear with the dying embers. Your sense of smell will also diminish, as your breath becomes more focused on exhaling than inhaling. As the firelight becomes smaller and smaller, so your eyes will become smaller and smaller, until they close altogether; you will fall gently back and you will experience another level of release."

His attention turned to the fire, which in turn became his whole life. As the last of the fire consumed itself, so, it seemed, did major portions of his memory. There was no yesterday, no past, not even really a present; he just was, as was the fire. Slowly, slowly, the fire began to fade into nothingness and, as instructed, so did he. His eyes gently closed, and he half slid, half fell backwards onto the soft moss, and experienced being himself.

"Gently, it is time to release the last of the elements and the last cycle for this time. It is time to release the demons of this life. It is time for your conscious and unconscious minds and memories to liberate themselves from the limiting experiences of this incarnation. It is time to die."

He half woke up, still partly lost in the experience of self.

"Come, carefully, the edge is just here."

"I cannot see anything, Master."

"I know, I have covered your eyes. No, do not touch or remove the blindfold."

"Where are you taking me?"

"I told you, we are going over to the ledge."

"But I might fall."

"No, not that you might fall, you will fall."

"Master?" Suddenly he was starting to feel panic rising through his body.

"Do not be afraid, death and rebirth are only different states of consciousness. You will be experiencing both in the next few hours."

"I don't understand." He was starting to tremble, his breath was becoming shorter and shorter and his heart was pounding fast.

"Re-contact the state of emptiness, of indifference, of simple contact with the essence of yourself." The disciple stopped thinking and worrying and allowed the link to the three states of being that he had just experienced to return.

As his mind released its bond to his physical body and to his emotions and then to his past, a deep feeling of peacefulness wrapped itself around his being. The breathing slowed and deepened, and his heart responded by returning to its usual rhythm and intensity.

"What am I to do, Master?"

"You will squeeze the air out of the bladder, which will harmonise with your own breath. As that air is released, so will the air in your body dissolve. You will become incapable of physical acts, and your last links to this physical world will also fade away. At that moment you will fall backwards, which will drop you over the ledge. The fall will destroy your human body and you will experience the destruction of this vehicle. How you will experience this, in what symbolic fashion, that you will only find out in the moment. What is sure is that you will suffer the dismemberment and the destruction of this human body, both from within the shell and from the position of any observer. This process might be repeated several times. Some of us believe that this is due to having lived many lives before and it is a form of memory, but that is of no importance to you now. After some time, your body will be reconstituted and it will return to its usual physical form. Do you understand all this?"

"Yes, Master."

"Here, take hold of the bladder. I have untied the cord, you only have apply the pressure to assist the air to escape."

And so the disciple began the fourth process of dissolution. Slowly and gently he pressed on the soft material, squeezing it between his folded arms and against his bony chest. The trapped air made a soft noise as it joined with the cold, early morning mountain air.

He felt the last of his life energy seeping away as the bladder was finally emptied out. He knew that now was his time to die and it felt totally, peacefully, blissfully fine. He let go of the bladder, opened wide his arms, and allowed himself to fall backwards and over the gaping cliff edge.

The falling seemed to last an eternity, and yet it was over in a second. A pair of arms caught his fall and gently lowered him onto the grassy bank.

A small part of his consciousness noted the deception, but it quickly floated off to observe the unfolding of the rest of the experience.

He was at the bottom the cliff. His bones were not only broken, but some of them had been smashed apart by the force of the fall. He could see and yet also feel his fragmented corpse, the wrecked bones and flesh of what had, just moments ago, been his functional body. He felt linked, yet totally dissociated from this object, and he watched in fascination and in wonder as a troop of ants appeared and quickly cleaned off all the flesh and soft innards from his cooling remains.

The sun grew hotter and the bones started to melt and to crack. Before long he was just a series of small masses of stuff littering the foot of the mountain. Then came the rain, and he became diluted in her flow and yet reunited with the separated parts of himself. The rain carried him some distance away before starting to be absorbed by the earth. Going into and joining with the earth was an impossible paradox; he could feel himself submerged and totally merged with the very ground, as if every microscopic cell had become fused to individual particles of earth. And yet, notwithstanding that, he could feel the essence of his body still having its own coherent form.

And the force of that form was now hovering over the soil, calling for its material elements to return. The cells started moving; he could feel these parts of himself start to flow up through the earth, towards the energetic envelope. He could also see this energy body and feel its force and its form. His particles were emerging from the soil and began to re-join together. The bones reconstituted first—he could already feel their weight and solid-ity—then the organs regained their places. His heart had restarted, he could feel his heart beating, then it was the lungs and he again could breathe. The flesh, nails, and hair were the last to reform, but as for his brain, he had no awareness when it had disappeared or reappeared.

And then he was alive again. He could hear the birds singing, could feel the morning sun on his face, and could smell the salty aroma of the bowl of hot Po Cha that someone had just placed not far from his young head.

He opened his eyes, stretched, sat up, yawned, and reached over for the steaming bowl.

Yes, today is a good day to be alive.

The Rivers of Red and Black

The ride itself was not unpleasant. The twelve monks had not had the freedom or the opportunity to ride for more than a few hours per day, and that was only from time to time.

To be free from all monastic duties, from their routine, daily chores and from the watchful eyes of the masters, made it seem like they were on some sort of stolen holiday.

Of course, the purpose of their mission was more than serious: they were to help me to locate the leader of the group that had destroyed my village and who had personally killed both my parents. To help me get close enough to this demon of a man, close enough to confront him with what he had done, and if necessary, close enough to kill him.

However, riding through the wild plains—the open sky above, sun on their shoulders, wind in their hair, sure-footed steeds under them, walking or galloping as the mood took them—this was a moment in their young lives to appreciate to the fullest.

I had been surprised—even shocked, one could say—with their offer to accompany me on my quest. I had never thought that these men held any special affection for me. Now again, seeing the benefits of this choice, I began to question their real motives and to wonder if, in case of difficulty or danger, I could really count on their support.

In any case, it was much more agreeable to ride in a group than all alone, and as some of them came from this region, they would easily fall into conversation with the local people, and thanks to them, we eventually found the information that we were looking for.

The leader of the "riders in black and red," as they were known in those parts, was a man called Wangdue, who came from the northeast but had not been seen for some years now, so nobody could say whether he was still alive or not.

Speaking the man's name brought me back into contact with the deeply buried thoughts, memories, and feelings of my destroyed childhood. My right hand sought out the leather strap to which the bundle containing the sacred sword was attached. If he was still alive, it might not be for much longer.

We directed our troop in the indicated direction and continued. Dead or alive, I would have to confront my past. I would need to stand on his bones, whether his soul still inhabited them or not.

As the days passed, like walking through the mountain mist, the information became slowly clearer and more precise. Wangdue was still alive and camped in a high meadow, the exact placement being known to our informants.

Suddenly, we were surrounded!

It was like that; one moment we seemed all alone, quietly riding through a pass, large boulders all around us. Then, from all directions they appeared, lances and bows at the ready. We had no chance and no choice—we just stopped and waited.

"Why do seek Wangdue?" He was directly in front of us, standing proudly on a big smooth boulder, obviously the leader of this group.

"What makes you think that we seek Wangdue?" Zigsa, being the eldest and most advanced, was the natural leader of our group. I was more than thankful that he was here with me.

The other looked at him for a moment and then spat contemptuously in his direction. "We are the riders in black and red." It seemed that that was all the explanation he deemed necessary to give us.

"I have a gift for him."

He then turned his gaze towards me. "What gift?"

"It is a holy sword. It is a Prajnakhadga, a sword of wisdom."

"I know what a Prajnakhadga is," he replied, irritated. "Give it me."

"I have been instructed to give it only to Wangdue. It is only for him. I have given my oath."

"What do I care for your oaths? I am a rider. I answer only to Wangdue and to no other."

"It is a sacred sword, a sacred gift," Zigsa remarked. "If you force us to give it to you, you will have desecrated a holy relic."

The other warriors following the conversation now looked to their chief to hear his response. Taking advantage of their moment of distraction, I gently nudged the reins. My horse, having the opportunity to stop and nothing to do, had half fallen asleep. The slight tension in its mouth brought his attention back to me. I was about to ask something of him. His ears twisted back towards me, his muscular body tensed. I kicked hard on the barrel, at the same time thrusting my hips forward on the saddle.

We jumped into a fast gallop; with three of his four feet in the air, it must have seemed as if we had suddenly started to fly. The warriors jumped back in shock and surprise. It took only the shortest second for the other horses to follow suit, as they had all noticed the few seconds of preparation and were ready to follow our lead.

With the horses suddenly galloping in all directions it was impossible for the warriors to know what to do, and in less than no time, we were all too far away for them to do much of anything to stop us. All of us, that is, except for Zigsa; for some reason he hadn't followed us. He must have sensed his horse tensing up to leave, but had chosen to block the movement.

Not knowing what we were likely to find if we advanced towards the encampment, I had chosen not to take any more risks for our safety, and had led the group back the way that we had come.

I turned back towards Zigsa; he rose up from his saddle and twisted his body in our direction. We could easily see each other from this distance. He gave me and wave and a salute, and then turned back towards the leader of the riders.

Feeling not at all safe, we decided that the surest course of action was to return to the last village that we had passed and then try and decide what to do next.

And so we did; we camped in a field adjoining the village and organised an all-night watch so as to assure ourselves that the riders would not surprise us during the night.

The next morning, we sat around the fire drinking Po Cha and eating *tsampa*. Some of younger monks suggested that we should use our trainings to infiltrate the camp of Wangdue, attack the guards holding Zigsa, and then I could assassinate Wangdue. Others, the older ones, were more for sending one of us, alone, to try and negotiate the freeing of Zigsa, and to give up on my need to settle my account with Wangdue. The others were undecided and suggested that we just wait here and see what developed.

The answer to our deliberations came from the most unexpected of sources; Zigsa arrived, unscathed and unharmed.

"What happened?" asked one of our group.

"As you saw, I decided to stay. If we were to gain access to their camp, we would have to prove to them that we are not a threat, nor are we to be forced to do what we didn't wish to do. By staying, they had no choice but to take me to their camp and to inform Wangdue of what had happened. He, of course, sent for me to question me on what we were doing looking for him. I explained that I had come from a region that he spared from his 'activities' and the master of our monastery had wished to ask him, as a powerful warrior, if he would be willing to accept the sword as a gift and a charge. That if he should accept to take it, then he would be responsible for its safety and safekeeping, and if the monastery should need it again that he, as the sacred protector, or his successors, would be asked to bring the sword back for such an important ceremony."

"And how did he respond?" continued the questioner.

"First of all, he became irritated when he understood that the gift was not really a gift but more a guardianship. But he then realised that he would have in his possession a real fire sword, and whether or not, in name, it was his or not, it would be in his hands. So here I am, with a guarantee of safe escort, and an invitation for all of us to dine with him tonight."

As he said that, he pointed towards a spot just outside our camp site and we then realised that he had not returned alone. The chief of the riders that we had encountered the day before and four of his men were there to escort us to their camp.

It takes a little while to break down a camp, even one as simple as ours, but quite soon we were on our horses heading back in the direction of Wangdue's encampment.

We arrived in the mid-afternoon; we unpacked our tents and saw to the needs of the horses. We had plenty of time to make ourselves a bowl of butter tea while we were waiting for the eve-ning's feast to be prepared. As one might well imagine, we were not offered a tour of the encampment. Quite the opposite; we were watched, if quite discreetly, from the moment we had arrived, and every move, even to go to the toilet, was supervised.

We were pretty much left alone without incident, except for one particularly difficult moment. The chief, as we called him, who it seems had inherited us as his particular charges, came to inform us that we would be closely searched for any weapons that we might be hiding before being allowed to enter into the main tent.

Zigsa replied that that would not be a problem; however, our staves were also ceremonial objects and we would need to bring them with us. The chief's first reaction was a clear and adamant no, but Zigsa protested. He asked if Wangdue had bodyguards with him; the chief affirmed that. Then he asked if the bodyguards were armed with swords; again, yes. Then he asked if there would be other warriors like himself present; yes. And would they too be armed with swords? Again a yes.

"So," concluded Zigsa, "your trained and armed bodyguards, with support from you and your men, also fully armed, are scared that thirteen monks carrying only sticks could present a danger that you would be incapable to contain?"

And so ended the discussion. We were to be allowed to enter into the enormous *ger* with our staves; however, we were thoroughly searched for any other weapons before entering. There was some discussion due to the fact that I was bringing in a sword with me, but since it was the gift for which the whole occasion was taking place, there was little they could do other than shake their heads at each other.

Zigsa had explained that I had been honoured due to all the trainings I had undertaken and succeeded to be the bearer of the sword, and hence it was an additional honour for Wangdue that it would be me that would hand it over to him.

I was a little uncomfortable with the ease Zigsa had in fabricating lies. As one that had always been brought up to be totally honest about everything and to everyone, his creative storytelling (as he put it) did not sit well with me. However, I would never have gotten to here without his efforts, and what I was doing felt totally right, so I just had to appreciate him for that.

I also had the time to realise that not even one of the monks had questioned coming into the riders' encampment, knowing that there was a real chance that they might well end up getting killed. It was then that I had to berate myself for having questioned their motives for coming. I looked at each one with love and appreciation, and before entering into the splendid, vast tent, I stopped and thanked and praised each of my spiritual brothers.

The felt walls were exceptionally thick, and even though it was still quite light outside, there needed to be many lights inside so as to be able to see. There were already quite a number of people inside the tent; men, women, and children. It was hard for me to imagine that this awful man, this butcher, this thief of humanity could be the leader of a tribe in which women and children could live and grow normally.

The people allowed us passage to walk towards the far end of the tent. I was looking for him, but all that I could see was a great fire facing me. It was only when I arrived near it that I perceived that, close to but behind the dancing flames, there were five men. Two men on each side, standing with their swords out but posed between their legs. Sitting in the centre on a great chair was Wangdue, but was this person, this Wangdue, the one that had destroyed my village and killed my parents before my very eyes?

Yes, he also had a moustache, even if it was now grey, as was his mane of hair. But that one had had pale skin; like everyone else, this one's skin was dark, like the African. No, no, but wait. On looking closer, I realised that it was not that his skin was of a different shade than mine, it was just that sitting so close to fire, and maybe not washing as much as one might, his face was covered with a layer of soot and ash. Every time the material that served as a door would be opened to let someone in or out, a gust of wind would travel the length of the tent and a thin cloud of dust and ash would float into the air. Being exactly in the path of that dark cloud, it would pass over him and the fine particles would attach themselves to the sweat of his face.

Yes, yes, now I could see, I could sense, I could feel, by the change in my breath, the tension in my muscles, the fear in my gut. This was he, this was the one, this was the person that had destroyed my early years and had hounded the shadows and my nightmares. Yes, it was he. My heart was racing. I had stopped moving; the others pushed me forward. I had to keep walking. I must not show him what is happening to me. I have to slow my breathing. My hand made a mudra; I linked myself to an image of myself in meditation.

Slowly, slowly, I left the tent. Part of my consciousness continued to move my body, to take the honoured seat facing Wangdue, to bow and to sit. I became a watcher, he who lets his awareness take the seat of power within the being. All the time, soothing and calming the frenetic emotional body in the safe, silent cell of the monastery, keeping the infantile, lower mind split between the two realities; hence, stopping it from the comfort it needs to create stories and possibly inappropriate actions.

Fortunately, again, Zigsa was there, my very own, personal, private guardian angel. Intelligent, strong, wily—again he had taken the initiative to speak for all of us. All of us? The others were now sitting down, taking the rest of the places around the crackling fire. My group, my protectors, just exactly how they would be able to give me the time and the space to confront Wangdue, I couldn't think, and even if they did, would any of us live to see tomorrow? The thoughts entered softly into my head, but then again, here I am in my quiet cell, alone, silent, meditating, the worries and concerns in the tent seem far, far away.

"Be calm, my son. Relax, follow your breathing, breath means life. The slower and longer the breath, the richer and longer the life."

Zigsa has finished speaking, he bows towards Wangdue. Wangdue motions for him to sit by his right side. The bodyguards take a step backwards but are still slightly between him and Wangdue. On the left side, Dorje is sitting in front of the other two guards. All the monks seem happy and relaxed. No, we cannot drink any alcohol, Zigsa excuses us from a customary toast, it is part of our discipline. Part of me smiles. Zigsa should release his vows and become a teller of stories; he is made of that fabric.

I am calm, my breath has slowed down and my heart has found its usual rhythm. There is no unnecessary tension in my body. It is time to return to full conscience.

I feel myself return fully into my body; I become much more aware of all the sights and sounds happening around me. The colours of the clothes and of the tent, the heavy mix of sweet and sweaty smells, the masses of people, coming and going, the serving girls, the food, which I can now experience and appreciate, with its rich complexity of tastes and aromas, the noise of talking and joking and eating.

The feast comes to its end and the plates are collected and cleared away.

Now we are coming to the moment of truth, to the climax, to the point of conclusion, of ending, of termination.

Somehow the message passes, and the room falls gently into silence.

I reach for the wrapped package that I have placed by my right side during the feast. I raise myself on one knee and slowly, aware that all eyes are upon me, without any stress or haste, I untie the bonds that hold the cover closed. One by one, with careful precision, I untie each cord; then, with the utmost patience and care, I unfold the cloths and uncover the beautiful curved sword.

I take the sacred object in my hands, turning towards Wangdue. I get up, straightening both my legs. I also bend my back and I bow towards the murderer of my parents.

"Wangdue, I have come many miles and wandered many paths to arrive here before you today. You have been an important factor in my life for many, many years. You have been the inspiration for many of my initiations and trainings. This day might be the most important day of my whole life."

"I don't understand. What am I to you? What have I done that I have been so important in your life?"

I turned to Zigsa and, speaking in a soft, relaxed tone, I said, "I think that it is time."

Zigsa slowly stood up from his place and looked smilingly around at everybody. "Would everybody please stand, it is time." He then looked to Wangdue, as if to ask his approval. Wangdue half shrugged his shoulders and nodded his head in agreement.

Slowly, without any haste or stress, the people got to their feet. The monks sighed, as if already bored with what was about to happen. The people of the tribe, slightly irritated with having to move so soon after eating and drinking, most of them more or less half asleep.

"Will the monks please step forward." Zigsa was master of ceremonies.

He looked round once again, smiling, gently this time, specifically at the monks. He took a slow, deep breath, as they all did, exhaled, nodded slightly, and in the softest of voices said, "Now."

As the last of the breath flowed out of their lungs, their bodies flowed into a fluid motion. I watched the dance in slow motion. Zigsa and Dorje turned towards the two bodyguards on each side of Wangdue. Sliding their staves into a horizontal line they hit the guards at the bottom of the neck, on the Adam's apple. Having their swords pointing towards the floor, it was not possible for them to react quick enough to block the attack. The shock and pain of the blows stimulated a reflex to bend the head forward; the two monks then stepped in closer, they violently crashed the poles on the now vulnerable back of the neck, just below the point where the neck and the head meet. They fell heavily to the floor, their swords dropping uselessly to the side.

At the same time, the other monks, creating a semi-circle around me and the fire, turned towards the tribesmen, their staves at the ready. Any man that moved to draw his sword was whacked smartly on the right shoulder, causing considerable pain and numbing the arm for some minutes.

In all, it took no more than thirty seconds for the monks to have taken charge of the tent.

"So, now you have the control, but you still have not answered to my question." His voice was still even and sure. Authority is something that cannot be taken by force. Our actions might have removed his power but not his personal status. "What have I done to you that I have become so central to your life?"

"Fourteen years ago, a group of riders dressed in red and black rode into my village. I was seven years old. I was playing in the fields. My parents ran into the field, to try to find me, to try to protect me. A rider followed them. He killed my father with a spear through the back, and my mother was beheaded with a swipe of his axe. The rider had a black moustache. That rider was you."

I looked straight into his eyes as I spoke. I did not know what to expect as a reaction; maybe nothing at all, total indifference, no effect, no emotion. What I did not expect to see was the fear that overtook his whole face; the eyes widened, the mouth opened slightly, and all the other muscles tensed.

"So now you know," I finished in a matter-of-fact tone.

"I have killed many, many people over the years. I was young and wild. I was often drunk; drunk with alcohol, drunk with excitement, drunk with power. I did not know what I was doing. No, I did know what I was doing, but I didn't know what I was doing meant."

Something strange was happening here, something very, very unusual, something that had never happened before. Wangdue was talking; he was talking about himself, about his feelings. He was showing the man who lived behind. The people started to sit down. When they had all regained their places, the monks too sat down; sticks at the ready but placed on their laps.

The bodyguards started to stir.

"Get up, you incompetents," Wangdue said, and moved enough to kick one on the thigh, "go and sit down back there with the women and children." They got slowly up, looked longingly at their swords, wondering if there was any way to recover them. Realising the impossibility of that, they painfully made their way to the back of the tent.

He then turned back to look at me.

"I cannot bring back your parents. I wish that I might, as I wish that I could un-kill every one of my victims." He sounded sad and genuine in his discourse. Was he trying some cunning ruse to get me to spare his life? This was a man that had killed or had had killed hundreds of people, women and children included. How could he suddenly have discovered a conscience, morality, human values?

"What has changed you?" I asked gently.

"The souls, they haunt me. They come to me in any moment. I see the face of a serving girl and suddenly I see the face of one of my victims, and then, there she is, here she is. And then with her come the others, the others of that time, of that raid or of another time, another raid.

"A guard pushes accidentally against me, I turn to tell him off, I see the look of fear in his eyes. I see the fear in the eyes of a child that we have chained up, that will be sold, and I see all the children and women that I have captured, that have been chained, that are chained to me, to my mind, to my body, to my soul.

"They come to me; they show me their pain, their hurt, their loss, their suffering. They come to me in the morning, they come to me in the afternoon, in the evening, but mostly in the night. The nights are so long. I have tried alcohol, I have tried women, but nothing helps. The moment that I close my eyes to try to sleep, there they are. My life is a nightmare, even when I am awake."

I looked closer at his face; in his eyes, I could see the red line of sleep deprivation above the black bags of fatigue. I could see the truth of his suffering etched deeply in the blackened lines of his face.

"My eyes burn with tiredness, they itch and they burn, but no tears can come to calm or cool their crime, the crime to have seen my evil and to have closed themselves to the reality of my acts."

The room was silent but for his speaking. No one moved, no one hardly breathed.

"Many a time I had thought to end it all, but I know that if I do then my soul too will haunt the earth, and I wish not to suffer for eternity."

"And now, I am here and you are defenceless to stop me."

"Please, it would be an act of mercy for you to revenge the death of your parents and the hundreds of others that I have killed." He knelt before me with his head bent back, exposing his neck, offering it to the blade created for the destruction of evil forces.

"Wait," he said, and got up. He had had second thoughts; death might not be so attractive when it suddenly becomes a hard reality. "Before I die, I will give one last command. Hear me and take notice of my words. This monk and each and every one of his brother monks are to be treated as my special guests until they choose to leave. They are to be escorted, safely, to wherever they might wish to go and left in good health and with all their belongings. These are my final words."

Again I was mistaken. I must learn to make fewer judgements. Again he was kneeling in front of me, his eyes closed, his breathing calm.

Again his head was bent back.

Again his throat was offered for my sacrifice.

The silence was now total except for the sharp crackling of the dying fire.

I took my time.

I slowed my breathing and focused my energy.

All eyes were on me, but I was no longer with them.

Wangdue and I had been transported to another, parallel dimension.

Time and space were no longer the same.

We were in the dream time.

I swam slowly towards him.

I placed myself directly in front of this being.

There would be just one cut.

It would be clean and pure.

It would be an act of charity, more than he deserved.

It would be the act that would release me from him, now and forever.

My body breathed quietly.

My eyes traced the line of the future trajectory.

My arm began its fateful arc.

Across to the left.

Then the quick, clean surgical slice to the right.

The sacred blade bit into his exposed flesh.

The skin peeled back following the metal's path.

The deep red blood line filled the opened fissure.

His eyes opened in reaction to the blow, to the pain, to the shock, to the surprise of still being alive.

He looked up towards me.

The blood and sweat trickled down from his brow and into his eyes.

The particles of ash and something other awakened the tear ducts.

The tears started to roll down his cheeks, mixing with the soot that covered his face.

The blood poured out and down from the open wound.

The rivers of red and black flowed across the old man's face.

The rivers of red and black covered and cleansed him.

The rivers of red and black released his hurt and pain and suffering.

The rivers of red and black released my hurt and pain and suffering.

He crawled to my feet and kissed them, one after the other.

And then he just waited there.

The only movement being the gentle heaving of his sobbing breath.

No one else moved or spoke.

There was, of course, nothing else to do.

I bent down and pulled the old, broken man to his feet.

And then we held each and cried for the losses that we had both suffered.

The Field Worker

The summer was drawing to a close. The summer rains had come and gone, but also a fair share of sunshine. The barley was tall and ripe, swaying in the gentle breeze. Each head bending over, whispering today's secrets into the ears of its neighbours. And so the gossip rippled, out from the fields, up into the village, along the streets and into the ears of all the neighbours.

A young man had appeared this morning, offering his services for the harvesting of the barley crop. A handsome, quite muscular young man, so tanned that it was not clear if he was from these parts or some traveller from the lands of the south. He had curly black hair, a stubby nose, and a ready smile. Some said that he reminded them of another young man, although much, much younger, but he had died many, many years before, leaving only a younger brother. The younger brother was but the ghost of a shadow of his lost older brother; timid, grey, and sickly looking.

As for the colour of his hair, that was quite a mystery, as no one had ever seen him without his hat on, in all seasons and with all four flaps down.

As the day came to its end, the excitement grew in the village. There was rarely anything different or of interest that happened here, so the arrival of the stranger had created quite a buzz around the community. The younger boys came running up to announce the arrival of the new celebrity. "He's coming, he's coming." The whole town turned out to see the stranger come.

The parents of a young man who disappeared some months ago, following a monk up the mountains, joined the crowd, as eager as any to see this handsome new field worker. And it was with a jolt of surprise that they recognised their own offspring as the centre of all this attention. They pushed their way forward and threw their arms around him.

"What has happened, what has happened? Has the Master refused you after all this time? Oh we were so worried for you. Has he treated you well? Why are you not wearing your hat? You have been too much in the sun, it is so dangerous, the sun. Come, we must rub your skin and try and take out some of the burn."

The young man stopped and allowed his parents to pour their questions and concerns over him, like an icy rain of anguish and tension. He waited patiently for them to run out of steam, like a pot of soup when taken off the fire, sooner or later it ceases to bubble.

"Mother, Father, look at me. Do I seem to be in poor health? Do I seem to be suffering?"

"But to have to work in the fields! What about the Master, becoming a monk, living in the monastery?" his mother bawled.

He stopped her with a small wave of his hand. "I have been accepted by the Young Master as his personal disciple."

"Then why have you offered yourself to work in the fields?" demanded his father.

"Why not? I am young and strong and I enjoy exercising my body, so I asked my Master if he would release me for a few weeks to help our friends and neighbours bring in the crop."

The parents just stopped and looked at him in amazement and confusion. Somewhere, they had known that they would never, ever see that sickly, fragile boy ever again. Of that, they were totally right.

Gentle reader, thank you for downloading this book and I very much hope that you have enjoyed it.

If so, please help others to make the choice to read this by sharing your views with your friends and writing a review on Amazon.

http://www.amazon.com/Adventures-With-Master-Edward-Gedall-ebook/dp/B00GY53XL8/ref=cm_cr_pr_product_top?ie=UTF8

Thank you,

Kindest regards

Gary

Other Titles

By

Gary Edward Gedall

Island of Serenity Book 1
The Island of Survival

Pierre-Alain James 'Faron' Ferguson is about to commit suicide. In his suicide note he attempts to understand how he has come to have wrecked not only his own life, but also all of those around him.

Pierre-Alain James 'Faron' Ferguson finds himself in a type of 'no-mans-land', between here and there, he must accept to visit the 7 islands before he will be allowed to continue on to his next steps. The islands are named; Survival, Pleasure, Esteem, Love, Expression, Insight and lastly, the Island of Serenity

In this first of a multi volume series, we follow Pierre-Alain through his early years, meeting his parents, brother, nurse and eventually the love of his life.

He also experiences the prehistoric island of Survival, where he must relink with the most basic of human traits.

Join us on a journey that will span all of human consciousness, time and the planet.

Island of Serenity Book 2
Sun & Rain

This is the second chapter of Faron's life history, in which he falls in love, becomes a real cowboy, starts boarding school and finds his two best friends.

He also comes face to face, for the first time of many of the dilemmas and choices of young adult life.

His conflicts and torments start him on the road towards isolation and betrayal.

How would you react, if you were caught on the same lonely road?

Island of Serenity Book 3
The Island of Pleasure vol 1

In this, the first two sections of the 4 part volume 'Pleasure'; Faron first finds himself in a past version of Venice, as the owner of an old but grand hotel that doubles as the meeting place for the wealthy men of the City and the high class escort girls that live in the establishment.

Faron can do anything that he likes without limitation or cost. Not only can he avail himself of the girls, but can eat and drink, without limit, but never suffer from a hangover, nor gain a gram.

In the 2nd section, Faron is transformed into an adolescent tom boy. In this more modern version of Venice, 'he' has just 7 days to be made into a high class escort girl.

What does this experience and the intrigues of the other persons within his sphere, mean for him, on his continuing quest to understand, and to experience, Pleasure?

Island of Serenity Book 3
The Island of Pleasure vol 2

Faron finds himself in the mystery of a long ago China.

Who is this sad, young man that he must help to find back his pleasure in life?

And how does he end up in the middle of a war that it is impossible for him to participate in?

How will helping others to find pleasure, aid Faron in his own quest towards integrating pleasure into his own life?

Faron then arrives in India; frequently projected into past moments of a young native Indian's life.

While also profoundly experiencing the realities of the present, Faron finally integrates the concept of pleasure into his tortured soul.

Tasty Bites

(Series – published or in preproduction)

Face to Face	A young teacher asks to befriend an older colleague on Face Book, "I have a very delicate situation, for which I would appreciate your advice"
Free 2 Luv	The e-mail exchanges between; RichBitch, SecretLover, the mother, the bestie, and the lawyer, expose a complicated and surprising story
Heresy	An e-mail from a future controlled by the major pharmaceutical companies, "please do what you can to change this situation, now, before it happens …

Love you to death   A toy town parable, populated by your favourite playthings, about the dangerous game of dependency and co-dependency

Master of all Masters   In an ancient land, the disciples argue about who is the Master of all Masters. The solution is to create a competition

Pandora's Box   If you had a magic box, into which you could bury all your negative thoughts and feelings, wouldn't that be wonderful?

Shame of a family   Being born different can be a heavy burden to bear. Especially for the family

The Noble Princess   If you were just a humble Saxon, would you be good enough to marry a noble Norman Princess?

The Ugly Barren Fruit Tree   A weird foreign tree that bears no fruit, in an apple orchard. What value can it possibly have?

The Woman of my Dreams   What would you do, if the woman that you fell in love with in your dream, suddenly appears in real life?

REMEMBER

Stories and poems for self-help and self-development based on techniques of
Ericksonian and auto-hypnosis

*Dusk falls, the world shrinks little by little into a smaller and smaller circle
as the light continues to diminish.*
*The centre of this world is illuminated by a small, crackling sun; the flames
dance, and the rough faces of the people gathered there are lit by the fire of
their expectations.*
*The old man will begin to speak, he will explain to them how the world is,
how it was, how it was created. He will help them understand how things
have a sense, an order, a way that they need to be.*
*He will clarify the sources of un-wellness and unhappiness, what is sickness,
where it comes from, how to notice it and... how to heal it.*
*To heal the sick, he will call forth the forces of the invisible realms, maybe
he will sing, certainly he will talk, and talk, and talk.*

Since the beginning of time we have gathered round those who can bring
us the answers to our questions and the means to alleviate our sufferings.
This practice has not fundamentally changed since the earliest times; in
every era, continent and culture we have found and continue to find these
experiences.

In this, amongst the oldest of the healing traditions, Gary Edward Gedall has
succeeded to meld modern therapy theories and techniques with stories and
poems of the highest quality.

With much humanity, clinical vignettes, common sense and lots of humour,
the reader is gently carried from situation to situation. Whether the problems
described concern you directly, indirectly or not at all, you will surely find
interest and benefits from the wealth of insights and advices contained within
and the conscious or unconscious positive changes through reading the stories
and poems.